PEOPLE OF THE THUNDER

W. MICHAEL GEAR

KATHLEEN O'NEAL GEAR

WOLFPACK PUBLISHING

— EST 2013 —

PRAISE FOR W. MICHAEL GEAR AND KATHLEEN O'NEAL GEAR

"Set in the 1300s, largely in what is now Alabama and Mississippi, this complex novel tracks three wanderers' quest to create peace in violent times. Blended with the carefully drawn suspense of court intrigues, colorful characters, and sharp plot twists, this is a terrific tale."

—*PUBLISHERS WEEKLY* ON *PEOPLE OF THE THUNDER*

"The knowledgeable Gears have firmly interwoven history, geology, and archaeology into a compelling narrative that reanimates and breathes new life into a neglected era of Native American history. This is historical fiction at its best, well researched and well thought out."

—*BOOKLIST* ON *PEOPLE OF THE WEEPING EYE*

"Drawing on their backgrounds in archaeology, the Gears vividly re-create Paleolithic America in this enchanting and instructive novel."

—*PUBLISHERS WEEKLY* ON *PEOPLE OF THE NIGHTLAND*

"[A] fascinating and imaginative narrative."

—*MILITARY.COM* ON *PEOPLE OF THE NIGHTLAND*

"*People of the Raven*...is a good read for those of us intrigued by the earliest Americans."

—TONY HILLERMAN, *NEW YORK TIMES* BESTSELLING AUTHOR

"People of the Raven draws you into a magnificent, sweeping world. It tells a bighearted story of war and peace, love and violence, with a cast of richly drawn characters. This is a novel that will stay with you for years."

—DOUGLAS PRESTON, *NEW YORK TIMES* BESTSELLING AUTHOR

People of the Thunder
Paperback Edition
Copyright © 2022 (As Revised) W. Michael Gear and Kathleen O'Neal Gear

Wolfpack Publishing
9850 S. Maryland Parkway, Suite A-5 #323
Las Vegas, Nevada 89183

wolfpackpublishing.com

Paperback ISBN 978-1-63977-833-1
eBook ISBN 978-1-63977-834-8

BY W. MICHAEL GEAR AND KATHLEEN O'NEAL GEAR

THE FIRST NORTH AMERICANS SERIES
People of the Wolf
People of the Fire
People of the Earth
People of the River
People of the Sea
People of the Lakes
People of the Lightning
People of the Silence
People of the Mist
People of the Masks
People of the Owl
People of the Raven
People of the Moon
People of the Nightland
People of the Weeping Eye
People of the Thunder

THE ANASAZI MYSTERY SERIES
The Visitant
The Summoning God
Bone Walker

BY KATHLEEN O'NEAL GEAR
Thin Moon and Cold Mist
Sand in the Wind
This Widowed Land
It Sleeps in Me
It Wakes in Me
It Dreams in Me

BY W. MICHAEL GEAR
Long Ride Home
Big Horn Legacy

To
John Lindsay,
who believes in books,
great stories,
and fine writing

AUTHORS' NOTE

People of the Weeping Eye and *People of the Thunder* are an anomaly in the "People" series. When the original manuscript for *People of the Weeping Eye* grew large, our publisher requested that we break the story into two. *People of the Thunder* continues the story of Old White, Trader, Morning Dew, and Two Petals. We have done our best to keep the tales independent, but recommend that the novels be read in sequence.

PEOPLE OF THE THUNDER

PEOPLE OF THE THUNDER

ONE

THE CONTRARY—THE woman once known as Two Petals— walked through the quiet night. Her moccasin-clad feet scuffed the plaza's trampled surface, the sound of leather on clay like the whisper of distant ghosts. Her straight body moved purposefully, rounded hips swaying. Black flowing hair swung even with her buttocks, and she clutched a beaverhide blanket closely about her shoulders. With each exhalation, she watched her breath fog and rise toward the black, star-encrusted sky. Overhead, the constellations seemed to shimmer and wink against the winter night.

Around her, the great Yuchi capital known as Rainbow City slumbered. Even now the size of the city, with its tall, building-topped mounds, thousands of homes, temples, society houses, and granaries, amazed her. The city's sleeping soul surrounded her like the low hum of insect wings. She could feel the immensity of it: all those thousands of souls breathing, mired in Dreams, their passions muted by sleep.

This was the western capital of the Yuchi—called the Tsoyaha in their own language. The city had been built on a high bluff over-looking the Tenasee River. The location had been chosen not only because it was well above the worst of the great river's periodic floods, but it was strategically placed just below the river's bend. Sheer heights on the east and north provided a natural defense, while the western and southern approaches were protected by a tall palisade bolstered by archers' platforms every twenty paces. Rainbow City controlled passage up and down the Tenasee—the trade route carrying goods between the southeastern and northern river systems.

Though Two Petals had walked in the ghostly ruins of Cahokia and climbed its great mound, Rainbow City left her feeling humbled. Cahokia was a place of dried bones; Rainbow City flexed warm nerve and healthy muscle. It lived, thrived, and bristled with energy.

High temples, palaces, and society houses perched atop square earthen mounds capped by colored clays sacred to the Yuchi. The buildings reminded Two Petals of brooding guardians overlooking the empty plaza. The image was strengthened by steeply pitched thatch roofs that jutted arrogantly toward the heavens. Beyond them lay a packed maze of circular houses, their thickly plastered walls and roofs a uniquely Yuchi architectural form. The dark dwellings hunched in the night, as though weighted by the countless sleeping souls they sheltered.

The Contrary needed but close her eyes in order to sense the occupants. She experienced their Dreams the way an anchored rock knew the river's current. The weight of their loves, hatreds, lusts, hungers, triumphs, and fears flowed around her. Were she to surrender her control, all of those demanding souls would filter past her skin, slip through her ears, nostrils, and mouth. Like permeable soil her body and souls would absorb them. Then, in the manner of a saturated earthen dam, she would slowly give way, carried off in bits, pieces, and streamers by the flood.

"But I am not earth." *No, I am a great stone. I stand resolute, lapped only by the waves of their Dreams. Feel them, washing up against me, seeking a grasp, only to drain away before the next.* Two Petals clasped her arms around her chest, hugging herself for reassurance.

She had come from a small Oneota village in the north, rescued from a charge of witchcraft by Old White. He was the legendary Seeker: the man who had traveled to the four corners of the world. Old White had chosen her to accompany him on this quest to the south. She'd heard of the great cities—places like Red Wing Town— and even seen the abandoned sprawl that had been Cahokia. Nothing had prepared her for this concentration of humanity. On the night of her arrival, the mass of Rainbow City's humanity had overwhelmed her. The impact had left her comatose, deafened, and paralyzed. Now, by dint of will alone, she barely kept panic at bay.

"You must learn to deal with what you have become," Two Petals told herself. "Trouble is coming."

She sighed, sensing the perpetual isolation of a person touched by Power. Forget the Dreams of others; her own were frightening enough. Not so many moons past, while in Cahokia, she had been carried away on Sister Datura's arms—borne off to the Spirit World. The visions she had had of the future remained just behind her eyes, as clear as when she'd first seen them. Were she to beckon, they would come flowing forward. She would again see the terrible black-souled chief, his hand trembling as it reached out to caress her naked skin. Or know the guilt-stricken eyes of a woman whose bloody hands dripped red spatters onto hard ground while she trembled beneath the twists of fate. In other scenes an angry war chief led a thousand warriors through a deadly and silent forest. And finally, swirling water washed over a great scaled hide that shimmered with all the colors of the rainbow.

She fixed on that final image, staring into the serpent's great crystalline eye, as though looking through time and worlds into another reality. As she did, a faint Song began to fill her souls with a tremolo that echoed from her very bones. The melody rose and fell, lifting her spirits like a leaf on the breeze. Two Petals could feel herself rising, spinning, carried aloft on the vibrant notes. She began to Dance across the hard-packed plaza, arms undulating to the beat, souls swaying in time to her skipping feet. The Song played within her.

"Soon," she promised, her body spinning in time to the melody.

As quickly as it had come, the Song faded, leaving her to stand alone and motionless in Rainbow City's great plaza—but one more of the many shadows that mingled in the night. In that instant she felt utterly destitute.

"You are never truly alone," a familiar voice remarked. Over the years, she had grown used to the voices that spoke in her head. Sometimes they told convincingly of things she knew were untrue. Other times, they offered a startling insight into the confused reality around her.

This voice, though, she knew. Two Petals turned, seeing the eerie outline of Deer Man. He stood off to the side, watching her through large liquid-brown eyes. In the beginning, it had bothered her that only she could see him. That Deer Man could be so apparent to her, but not to Trader or Old White, had perplexed her. In the end, she simply accepted Deer Man's presence as a manifestation of her Contrary Power. Half-man, half-deer, he had a human face; deer antlers and ears sprouted from his head, and the sleek hair that covered his body could have graced a buck's winter hide.

Frowning, she studied him, wondering how he managed to balance on those slender deer legs that ended in delicately hoofed feet, or why he never left tracks in the soft dust or silty mud. Why the oddity of it continued to puzzle her was elusive. He was after all a Spirit Being. She often had seen him standing on water, waves washing through his feet, and other times with his nether legions passing through some object like a pestle and mortar, cane wall, or fallen log. As with so many of the voices that spoke to her, or the Spirits, ghosts, and other oddities she saw, she had wondered if Deer Man were real.

"*Real?*" Deer Man asked, hearing her thoughts. "*Are any of them real? Old White? Trader? The Kala Hi'ki?*" He paused. "*Are you real, Contrary?*"

She tightened her arms around her, feeling the warm beaverhide cape, aware of the soft swell of her breasts, of the skin, muscle, and ribs beneath. The rise and fall of her chest with each breath she took reassured her.

"I am. At least for this moment." She frowned. "Can't say for sure about tomorrow…or yesterday. Sometimes the world slips and shifts around me. It just up and moves, and I lose track of what's what. Who's whom. Things become muddled and rushed. Then, when it all stops, I'm not sure where I am, or how I got there."

"*Come. Let me show you something.*" Deer Man turned, walking off toward the south.

Two Petals followed, head cocked as she watched his hoofed feet. Though Deer Man took long steps, his hooves never seemed to make actual contact with the earth; and though he moved at her speed, his feet seemed to be making faster progress than he was.

"How do you do that?"

"*The same way every other creature does,*" he answered. "*It is no different than the way you move backward in time.*"

Two Petals didn't answer. So many things were riddles. That the world ran backward around her was just one more.

"*Still bothers you, doesn't it?*"

"What?"

"That you're Contrary. That you can never be normal like Trader, Old White, or anyone else."

She nodded. A part of me, way deep down inside, still wants to be like normal people. But it is growing smaller and smaller. Soon, as we get closer to the end, it will shrink away completely. All that will be left is the Contrary. Two Petals will have been like a raindrop in the sunlight."

"The Kala Hi'ki has helped. I can see it in you: a strength that you didn't know you possessed."

She remembered the night when she, Trader, and Old White had first landed at Rainbow City. She had been frightened, overwhelmed by the images of a future that soon would be her past. The flood of souls around her had washed over and through her, drowning and suffocating. She wasn't sure exactly what had happened, but Trader had told her later that she'd cried out and fallen over. He said that she'd turned as stiff as wood, her muscles and joints locked and immovable. He'd carried her to the Kala Hi'ki's temple like some sort of oddly shaped log. All she remembered was a thick blackness until she'd awakened in the Kala Hi'ki's room. The terror of it was still too close.

Power had brought her here. Well, Power and the Kala Hi'ki's not-too-friendly and well-armed warriors. During her long trip southward from her native Oneota lands, she'd caught glimpses of the Kala Hi'ki. Even as far away as Cahokia, she had seen him in her visions: a terrible man covered with burn scars, his nose slashed away to leave two gaping nostrils. He wore a cloth wrapped over the empty sockets of his eyes, and his maimed hand had reached out for her.

"He brought you here to destroy you," Deer Man reminded.

"Instead he Healed me."

"You were a mystery to him. Trader was merely a temptation. And Old White? Ah, in the end he would have been the Kala Hi'ki's destruction. Mystery, temptation. destruction. Such a curious combination Power weaves."

"Old White is dangerous?"

"The Seeker is the most dangerous man alive. Not even the Kala Hi'ki fully understands the Seeker's obsession…or the dark secret he carries hidden between his souls."

"Where are you taking me?" Two Petals asked as they passed the base of the Warrior Moiety's large temple. The structure had been built atop a square mound, the high building having a commanding view of the plaza. Protruding from the thatch roofs peak were carvings of Falcon, Ivory-billed Woodpecker, and Snapping Turtle, their dark eyes glaring down at her as though the very Spirit beasts themselves watched her.

"We're going there" Deer Man pointed past several houses to a large, square-sided structure that rose above a low mound. The walls beneath the overhanging thatch roof had been plastered black at the bottom with a red band just below the eaves. The Spirit poles standing outside the west-facing doorway had been carved into the shape of vultures.

At that moment a shift in the night breeze carried the pungent odor of decay. "It's a charnel house."

"Oh, yes." Deer Man inclined his antlered head, the pointed tines gleaming in the night. *"Come, let me show you something."*

Two Petals glanced warily around at the darkened houses, corn cribs, and ramadas as she followed Deer Man to the entrance. Nothing stirred, the silence oddly discomforting.

Deer Man ducked into the low doorway, his wide antlers passing through the thick-plastered wall as if it were smoke.

Two Petals placed her hand on the unforgiving plaster, feeling its dense resistance. She shook her head, ducked past the door hanging, and emerged into a large room. Benches lined each wall, and raised platforms had been placed in rows throughout the center of the room. Most of these supported corpses in varying states of decomposition. The intense odor hung at the back of her nose and cloyed in her throat. She couldn't help but make a face.

"Why do you wince?" Deer Man asked. *"You are a Contrary. The smell of death is just the odor of life turned backward."*

"I...I'm just not used to it." She stepped forward, staring down at the closest of the bodies. This one had been a young man. His flesh sagged loosely on the bones, dry eyes recessed into the orbits of his skull. White teeth were bared behind hardened lips frozen in a rictus. Each of the man's ribs pressed out through the skin. His belly was a hollow, and the bones of the young man's hips seemed to jut up uncomfortably. His penis looked like a dried tuber, testicles like stones in the stretched scrotum. Flesh sagged on his thin thighs, the knees like knotted roots.

"He was young," Deer Man told her. *"They called him 'Chigger.' Said he*

was a bit of a nuisance. He didn't pay attention to the curious black mold that was growing on old acorns. Anyone with sense would have thrown them out."

Two Petals stared down at the wasted corpse. "Where are his souls?" She looked around, curious now as she cataloged the various bodies supine on the pole racks. Some were swollen with gas, others barely more than skeletons.

"That's what I brought you here to see. The souls are all around you, waiting. If you clear yourself of the noise made by the living, you will be able to recognize them."

She gestured to the bodies. "What will the Yuchi do with them?"

"When the time is right, the High Priest will slice what little flesh remains from the bones. He will pick away the loose tendons, strip off the scalp and any clinging tissue. Once the bones are cleaned, they will be Blessed, tied together, and given to the family for final burial in one of their mounds. Or maybe laid to rest in a place where the souls of the dead will remain close by and can help protect the living from the dangers in the Spirit world."

She tried to quiet her revulsion. As she did, she could make out the faintest yellow-orange objects, like dim lights glowing along the walls. Others hovered near the ceiling.

"Yes, you begin to see. Those are the souls of the dead."

"Why did you bring me here? I am not of these people. Why would my souls wish to lurk about watching my body rot? Who would I want to protect?"

"Exactly." Deer Man smiled. *"I wanted you to see how your body would end up should you fail to fulfill your Visions."*

"You mean if I don't find my husband?"

Deer Man smiled. *"He will find you when the time is right. It is, however, your decision whether to go to him, or not. People fear him for a reason, and it will take an extraordinary woman to go willingly into his lair. I wanted you to understand what would happen if you gave in to fear, temptation, or desire. You dare not love, Contrary. You can only surrender yourself to the future."*

She reached down, placing a finger on the sunken flesh inside the bowl of Chigger's hip. It gave, soft but leathery. When she withdrew her finger, the depression remained. She wondered what his souls thought of her poking him like that. Looking up, she saw two of the glowing lights drop, as though in concern. "Oh, I understand just fine, Deer Man."

"Are you sure?"

"I just have to take the most terrible man alive into my bed. And keep him from discovering what is happening right beneath his nose."

And if I fail, we will all die, and end up in a charnel house just like this one.

———

From Rainbow City, one could paddle up the Tenasee until it made its great eastern bend. By ascending one of the several tributaries that drained from the south, travelers could canoe their way up to the headwaters, then portage across the densely forested hills to the Origins of the Black Warrior River. Tumbling through the hills, the Black Warrior flowed south until it reached the fall line. There, after the last rapids, the river settled into a broad floodplain. The broken, forested uplands gave way to rolling country. The current grew lazy as the Black Warrior pursued its sinuous path toward the gulf. Back swamps, thick with bald cypress and tupelo, were clotted with cane-brakes; and yellow lotus, cattails, and duckweed thrived. Hanging moss draped from low-branches. Higher ground—on the terraces below the hills—with sandy, better-drained soils had long been home to the Albaamaha People.

It was said that the Albaamaha had come from deep in the earth, following the roots of the great World Tree to reach the earth's surface. There, half the people emerged from one side of the root to become the Albaamaha, the other half—separated from their brethren—called themselves the Koasati.

From the time of the emergence, the Albaamaha had farmed the Black Warrior terraces. In the dark forests of the surrounding uplands they hunted deer, wild turkey, and other forest game. The woodlands—rich in hickory, oak, and persimmons—had provided bountiful nut harvests from which the Albaamaha rendered food and oil. From the swamps they had taken roots, cane, waterfowl, and other game. The river provided fish, freshwater mussels, and clams. Up and down the river, the Albaamaha had built their bent-pole houses, thatched them with shocks of local grasses, and warred and squabbled among them-selves for generations.

Then the Sky Hand had come—a Mos'kogean People from the great Father Water to the west. The Sky Hand had made their way down the Black Warrior River, following an advance of warriors. At a high bluff that dominated a bend in the river, they made their new home. Immediately they began the construction of Split Sky City. Many Albaamaha welcomed the Sky Hand, brokering alliances with the newcomers as a means of settling age-old vendettas against surrounding villages. Cunning, and skilled in political manipulations, the Sky Hand pitted one Albaamaha village against another. Too late, the Albaamaha realized that their new benefactors had come not to share the land, but to rule it. Some Albaamaha resisted. The poorly organized farmers and hunters were no match for trained and disciplined Sky Hand warriors. Within a generation, any Albaamaha resistance had been crushed, and the Sky Hand moved quickly to take advantage of Albaamaha labor in the construction of their great new city overlooking the Black Warrior River. Within twenty years land had been cleared, surveyed, earthworks erected, and the first palaces and temples built.

Nor did they stop there, but expanded up and down the river, building new settlements and installing chiefs to oversee the Albaamaha lands. The Albaamaha had nowhere to go. To the west lay the intimidating Chahta, another invading Mos'kogee nation. To the south, the Pensacola brooked no intrusion into their territory. Though cousins, the Koasati resisted the temptation to accept refugees, worried enough about Holding their own lands. In the east, the Ockmulgee and Talapoosie peoples were just as dangerous as the Sky Hand. Going north into the Yuchi lands was unthinkable. The Yuchi had raided the Albaamaha for generations, taking spoils, scalps, and slaves.

Resigned but resentful, the Albaamaha had no choice but to accept their new overlords. The Sky Hand, for their part, provided protection from raids, enforced peace between the Albaamaha villages, and ensured order and security. In return the Albaamaha were required to expand their farms—the majority of the produce to be delivered as tribute to the high minko, or supreme ruler, of the Sky Hand. AH the backbreaking work—building, logging, carrying, and earth moving—was done by Albaamaha labor.

The greatest accomplishment of Albaamaha sweat and tears was the construction of Split Sky City, a complex of high palaces, Council Houses, and Temples built atop large earthen mounds and laid out according to moiety and clan, each in its place. Hickory Moiety and its clans lay to the east, Old Camp Moiety to the west. A great central plaza was dominated by the tchkofa, or Council House. The entire city was surrounded on three sides by a defensive wall of pitch-pine logs, four times the height of a man. On the north, where Split Sky City overlooked the river, the slopes below the bluff were cut sheer to prohibit any kind of organized assault. Gangs of Albaamaha had logged the surrounding countryside, clearing forests for fields and delivering wood, cane, and thatch to teams who constructed Split Sky City's edifices.

Once built, a city consumes like a voracious beast. A steady stream of Albaamaha bore food, water, firewood, clay, stone, thatch, and wood into the city. Each fall, at harvest, lines of Albaamaha carried basket after basket of corn, beans, squash, sunflower seeds, lotus root, goosefoot, and forest nuts to the elevated granaries. So, too, came fish, clams, wildfowl, and meat. Any surplus such as tanned hides, matting, cordage, shells, feathers, or other things the Sky Hand might fancy were brought to Sky Hand City to be traded for brightly dyed fabrics, ceremonial ceramics, talismans, or special services such as Healing or divination that the Sky Hand had mastered.

The Sky Hand specialized in higher pursuits such as sculpting, ceramics, the arts of religion and Healing, politics, games, and most of all, war. Among all the peoples in the Southeast, Sky Hand warriors were the most highly trained, disciplined, and deadly. Neighboring peoples, even the irascible Yuchi, quickly came to the conclusion that maintaining peaceful relations with the Sky Hand tended to be the sanest course of action. At least most of the time. Power, after all, had to be kept in balance. Insults of any kind required immediate and violent response. Failure to do so affected the Spiritual health of the people. Any sign of weakness invited exploitation by the chaotic forces of the red Power.

The notion of Power preoccupied the Mos'kogee peoples. While Creation was separated into the Sky World, Earth, and Underworld, the Power that flowed through it consisted of the white Power of order, peace, serenity, contemplation, happiness, and security. Its equal and opposite was red: the Power of chaos, war, creativity, procreation, lust, ambition, and desire. While the great Priests—called *Hopaye* by the Sky Hand—taught that all Power had to be kept in balance, many utilized a specific Power for their own ends.

One such man was the Sky Hand war chief. His full name was Smoke Shield Mankiller, of the Chief Clan of the Hickory Moiety. As the high minko's nephew, War Chief Smoke Shield was next in line to assume the high minko's position. Smoke Shield needed two things: The first was for his uncle, High Minko Flying Hawk, to die, or step aside. That it would happen was but a matter of time. Second, but of even greater importance, Smoke Shield needed confirmation by the Sky Hand Council. That was key. The high minko might rule, but only with the assent of the Council. This was made up of the clan chiefs from both the Hickory and Old Camp moieties.

Nothing a man did was accomplished without the Blessing of Power, let alone being confirmed as high minko. Smoke Shield had long ago made his bargain with the red Power. In return for his devotion, it had granted him each and every one of his desires.

Smoke Shield had little use for the prattling teachings of the *Hopaye*. The current one was a Panther Clan man called Pale Cat. Dedicated to tranquility, order, and reason, Pale Cat served the white Power. He and Smoke Shield had despised each other since they were boys. Things had grown worse in the years since Smoke Shield had married Heron Wing, Pale Cat's sister. Smoke Shield had used red Power to win the woman. Lies and manipulation had allowed him to prevail over his long-gone brother, Green Snake, but in the end, Smoke Shield emerged victorious, having caused his brother's exile, claimed the woman Green Snake loved, and secured succession to the high minko's panther-hide chair. Smoke Shield had an ugly scar that marred his head as proof that Power never gave its gifts freely.

As he considered that. Smoke Shield fingered the deep scar, remembering the blow his brother had given him. But for it, he would have been a handsome man. Then again, why did a man need beauty when he was muscular, and quick of mind and body? Smoke Shield was in the process of living through his twenty-sixth winter. Despite the ugly scar, his face was tattooed with a Chief Clan bar across his cheeks. Forked-eye designs had been tattooed around each eye—the one on the left a little distorted by his long-healed wound. This day he wore his hair in a tight bun at the back of his head. Three little white arrows, the highest honor bestowed upon a warrior, had been stuck through his hair. A single warrior's forelock hung down over his forehead and was decorated with three gleaming white beads. He wore an eagle-feather cape over his bare shoulders, and a white warrior's apron had been tied at his waist, its long tail hanging suggestively down between his knees.

Smoke Shield stood at the northeastern margin of Split Sky City's great plaza. Just to his left the high minko's mound rose up in a flat-topped pyramid of earth to support the mighty palace where he and Uncle Flying Hawk held sway. Off to his right, and slightly behind him, the tishu minko, a man called Seven Dead, chief of the Raccoon Clan, had his palace. The plaza itself was flat, dominated by the stick-ball grounds that ran east to west just behind the red-and-white-striped Tree of Life — a pole that represented the great tree at the Spiritual center of their world. To either side of that were clay chunkey courts where stone disks were rolled before men attempted to spear them with lances.

Despite the throngs of passing people, busy with their lives, Smoke Shield's attention was fixed on the line of wooden squares that stood empty along the plaza margin. He stood before one in particular. Made of hickory logs, the uprights set deeply into the earth, it was one of five. The square was composed of two uprights with crosspieces lashed across the top and bottom. It left a man-sized frame that would support a human body. Captives were tied inside the open square — wrists to each of the upper corners, ankles to the lower — so that their naked, spread-eagled bodies could be beaten, burned, mutilated, and otherwise abused.

On either side, Smoke Shield could see the other empty squares. Not so long ago, men had hung from them. He frowned, thinking of the captive who had died within the empty frame before him. His name had been Screaming Falcon. He'd once been the White Arrow Chahta's most promising young war chief.

Until I plucked him right out of his house, along with his high minko and the Chahta Priests, and took him prisoner. Smoke Shield had also burned White Arrow Town to the ground and stolen its matron: Screaming Falcon's young wife Morning Dew. Morning Dew had become the matron the instant Smoke Shield killed her mother during the raid. Her brother, Biloxi Mankiller — who had also hung from one of the squares — had been the Chahta high minko. In a stroke, Smoke Shield had decapitated the White Arrow leadership, and dealt the Chahta a stinging blow.

He smiled as he remembered the glorious procession his warriors had made as they arrived at Split Sky City, marching their captives up from the canoe landing, past the Old Camp Moiety Mounds, and around the sacred tchkofa, the Council House where the Sky Hand

Mos'kogee deliberated and conducted their governmental business. Yes, that had been a *glorious* day.

And it would only be the beginning!

He reached out, fingering the wood, remembering Screaming Falcon's misery and horror as he had hung, right here, in this very wooden square. The young man's face had looked lopsided from his broken and swollen jaw, and his flesh had been mottled, blistered, brown, and cracked from where split-cane torches had been pressed against his skin.

"I should have paid better attention to you," Smoke Shield whispered to the empty wood. "Instead I was too preoccupied with your wife."

Pus and rot, what a disappointment. He'd planned the whole White Arrow Town raid around stealing Morning Dew. Once she'd looked at him with the same disdain she'd have given a worm in a fruit. After he'd taken her from Screaming Falcon, burned her town, captured her high minko brother, and wrought every other indignity upon her, she'd just surrendered herself to him without a fight.

What was the point of trying to break a woman who was already compliant?

"I expected more of you, Morning Dew." He cast a glance over his shoulder, across the corner of the plaza to where his first wife's house stood. These days Heron Wing owned Morning Dew. The thought of it rankled. Not so much the loss of his slave, but the way of it.

He turned back, peering closely at the heavy wood square, seeing the dark patterns where blood had stained the wood.

Everything changed that night.

He remembered the fog: thick and clinging, so dense a man could hardly see his hand before his face. All of his irritation had been focused on Morning Dew, on the way she lay under him, as unresponsive to his thrusting manhood as a soggy cloth. And while he was wetting his shaft in Morning Dew, someone was out here in the foggy night, sneaking past the guard to drive a stone sword into Screaming Falcon's heart and then sever his genitals from his body.

"War Chief, I wanted to cut them off myself, just for the pleasure of watching your wife's horrified expression as I handed them to her." Perhaps that would have spurred some sort of violent reaction out of her. But someone had beaten him to it.

Who? That single act of murder had robbed the Sky Hand Mos'kogee of revenge on their victims. No claim had been made by any of the subservient Albaamaha. Not so much as a rumor floated among the Traders. What kind of miscreant would commit such a desperate act and then not utilize it as a means of belittling the Sky Hand?

Smoke Shield ran his finger over the deep pucker of his scar.

It had to be the Albaamaha. They still chafed under the humiliation of serving their Mos'kogee masters. He already knew they had tried to betray the White Arrow Town raid to the Chahta. They *had* to be behind the captives' murders. Anyone else would have bragged about it. Such a triumph would be shouted up and down the trails.

In an effort to discover the culprits, Smoke Shield had taken Councilor Red Awl and his wife, Lotus Root, captive. In a rude shelter, up above Clay Bank Crossing, he and the warrior Fast Legs had tortured the Albaamo mikko, and learned nothing.

Then it had all gone wrong. Red Awl and Lotus Root had escaped. He and Fast Legs had found the mikko later, dead of his wounds; but the woman...gods, where was she?

He reached out and placed his hand on the wood, feeling the polish of years. So many bodies had been tied here. "Screaming Falcon?" he asked softly. "Who killed you?"

If he could only figure that out, he could retaliate. It had to be the Albaamaha! They'd been stewing with revolt for years. He'd caught the Albaamo traitor, Crabapple, who had been sent to warn White Arrow Town. The man had confessed—implicating an old Albaamo named Paunch as the conspirator. So could the mysterious and missing Paunch be behind the ultimate outrage of killing the captives?

"Where are you, Paunch? Wherever it is, I *will* find you eventually."

He narrowed an eye, letting his finger chip some of the caked blood from the square. When he found Paunch, the man *would* talk. Perhaps he even had something to do with Smoke Shield's Hickory Moiety losing the winter solstice stickball game. He had bet everything on that game—and lost it all. His wealth, clothing, shell, and copper...even Morning Dew.

He shot a narrow glance back at his wife's house across the plaza. How had she known to bet against him? In collusion with the Albaamaha? No, that was ridiculous. Heron Wing was much too influential in Panther Clan politics. She'd just bet against him because she knew it would irritate him. Gods, why had he ever married that woman?

"Forget it," he told himself. "Taking her as a wife was your first great triumph. Your attention now must be on breaking the Albaamaha."

He took a deep breath, turning from the empty square. He would have his revenge. And somewhere, up in the north, his most trusted warrior, Fast Legs, was even now running the missing Lotus Root to ground. Fast Legs would already have disposed of Red Awl's body. When the woman was dead—and the stolen weapons she'd taken from Smoke Shield returned—then and only then would Smoke Shield begin to wreak havoc on the Albaamaha.

Fast Legs, what is taking you so long?

TWO

FOR TWO DAYS a freezing drizzle had fallen, coating trees, logs, and the leaf mat with a thin layer of ice. The forest was silent, squirrels, jays, and other creatures waiting it out in warm nests.

Only I am foolish enough to be out here shivering. Fast Legs Mankiller knotted his muscles, seeking to warm himself against the pervading cold. The good news for him was that the weather kept the Albaamaha inside their bent-pole houses. Individuals only ventured out in search of firewood, then hurried back to their snug houses and warm fires.

From the time he was a boy, Fast Legs had always stood out from the rest of his kinsmen. He'd been large for his age, and always the fastest, strongest, and most skilled at stickball, hunting, and use of the bow. And when he had become a blooded warrior—adding the honorific of Mankiller to his name—no one was as steadfast in battle, or as relentless on the war trail. Ropy muscle corded on his body, and he'd had his face tattooed with wedges like arrow points. Despite Fast Legs having fewer than thirty winters under his belt, the high minko himself had presented him with four of the honorary little white arrows to stick through his hair. More than even the war chief had been granted.

As he lay in the ice-clad forest, he wore only a hunter's shirt with a muskrat-hide cape over his shoulders.

Muddy war moccasins clad his stone-cold feet. The staves on his bow gleamed under a rime of ice. Nevertheless, he lay still as a log, peering out at the Albaamaha village where he knew the escaped Lotus Root hid. A distasteful business, this.

Images still haunted him. He would always remember the expression on Red Awl's face as he weighted the dead Albaamo councilor's body and sank it in a backwater swamp. To hide the body, Fast Legs had chosen an abandoned loop of the Black Warrior River, a place where few fishermen went. Using lumps of sandstone, he had weighted the body and eased it over the side of his canoe. The eerie thing was how the man's eyes— shrunken and gray with death— seemed to reanimate as the water swirled over his face.

Fast Legs had stared into the corpse's eyes as the body slowly sank. The effect had been as if the dead man was promising some terrible justice. A fear unlike anything Fast Legs had known was born in his belly.

As he lay in the frozen forest, a shiver that wasn't just the cold ran down Fast Legs' spine. *I was under orders from my war chief.* But he had never really believed that Councilor Red Awl had anything to do with the murder of the White Arrow captives. Fast Legs was pretty sure that he and Smoke Shield had tortured an innocent man to death.

He made a face, feeling cold muscles pull tight in his jaw. "That's the war chief's responsibility," he whispered softly. His job now was the escaped wife, Lotus Root. She'd stolen Smoke Shield's bow and arrows the night she escaped. Fast Legs had been ordered to retrieve them, kill the woman, and make his way back to Split Sky City.

So, here he was, lurking in the forest, awaiting his chance. Too bad that Councilor Red Awl had to be from this far northern village. Fast Legs could look out past the Albaamaha village, just across their northernmost holds, and see the hills that marked the tall line—the rugged country leading up to the divide the Sky Hand shared with the Yuchi enemy. Living in the shadow of a powerful adversary like the Yuchi made things precarious. Just off to his right, past more Albaamaha cornfields, the palisade and protruding roofs of Bowl Town—the northernmost Sky Hand settlement—were visible. How Chief Sun Falcon held this vulnerable outpost together was anyone's guess.

Meanwhile, Fast Legs huddled in the forest, keeping an eye on Lotus Root's bent-pole house with its thatched walls. The dwelling was larger than most Albaamaha houses, but what would a person expect a renowned mikko and councilor to live in?

Killing Lotus Root had to be done right. He couldn't march in, knock her in the head, and march out. No, it had to be accomplished in a way that didn't lend credence to the woman's story. He needed to get her alone, find some way to kill her, and remove the body. The last thing he and the war chief needed was evidence of Sky Hand murder, or a body for the Albaamaha to weep over. Lotus Root simply needed to disappear. But since he had arrived here, she had played the game like a rabbit who knows the hawk's shadow was cast upon her.

During the two days prior to the storm, however, Fast Legs had been forced to retreat from his hiding places close to Lotus Root's village. The forest had literally been swarming with Albaamaha, as if they'd been preparing for the storm. They had spread out like crickets, picking up branches, calling back and forth, chopping at wood. So he had slipped back farther into the maze of trees until they finished whatever it was they had been doing.

Now, with the weather keeping the Albaamaha inside, he had returned. He could see a huge stack of dead wood piled by Lotus Root's house. What on earth would she need that much firewood for?

A fit of shivering left him shaken and miserable. He shifted, rubbing his hands to make warmth, and glanced at the bow and arrows he had fashioned after weighting Red Awl's body and sinking it in the backwater. The bow wasn't his best work, the arrows either, with their crude points; but they'd do to kill Lotus Root. Assuming, that is, that she ever left the shelter of her house.

For two weeks he had been living off the land, trying to sneak close enough to kill her. Each time, the pack of dogs that now lived at her house had set off the alarm, causing him to flee into the darkness.

Twice, he'd sworn that passing Albaamaha had seen him. But in neither case had they raised an alarm. It was almost as if they knew he was there. Worse, he'd observed a constant procession of Albaamaha enter and leave Lotus Root's dwelling. Was that what the firewood collecting had been about? Laying in a supply large enough that she didn't need to set foot out of her house until summer came, or he finally gave up and left?

Gods, have I ever been this cold and hungry?

The distant palisade around Bowl Town seemed to beckon him where it dominated a thin neck of land bounded on three sides by the river. Chief Sun Falcon's tall roof jutted up above the high walls. Fast Legs would be welcomed there, made a place by the fire, and fed real food. But with that delightful shelter would come the question: What are you doing here?

No, too much responsibility rested on him. He *had* to kill the woman, retrieve the war chief's weapons, and get away. Even if it meant turning himself into a wild man to do it.

War Chief, you are going to owe me when this is finished.

Once again he caught himself staring longingly across the distance at Bowl Town. True, he could tell them he was hunting, and they would believe it. But, why, they would wonder, was he hunting here? And why hadn't he announced himself and asked them to join the hunt?

Looking down at his filthy cloak, mud-encrusted moccasins, and feeling his greasy hair, no one would believe he'd just arrived. He looked like what he was, a man who had been skulking in the forest for days. His belly growled, reminding him that he would have to sneak into the Albaamaha settlement and raid their granary in the middle of the night again. Sometime, even the stupid Albaamaha had to realize that someone was taking their corn and squash.

He clenched his teeth to keep them from chattering.

At least he knew she was still inside that house. During those two days the local forest had swarmed with Albaamaha, his greatest fear had been that Lotus Root had slipped away, escaped to another village. But then, after he had sneaked back, he'd seen her. The cursed woman had been walking around the houses as if she hadn't a care in the world. She'd almost been too unconcerned, but perhaps that was the ultimate purpose of the firewood collection, to give him the impression that she had run. Anything to give him reason to give up the chase.

But you don't know me. I am a Sky Hand warrior. And in the end, that knowledge alone would see him through.

He balled his fists, jamming them under his armpits. More than once, he had considered walking in just before dawn, ignoring the dogs, and leaping through the door. He could kill everyone inside and still get away, but it would be messy. Someone would see him. Such a blatant act would give the woman's story credibility. No, she had to disappear without a trace. Reasons could be manufactured for the why of it. The best explanation was that she could no longer live with her lies about the war chief. Guilt had driven her to leave, as it had that miserable Paunch.

Fast Legs made a face. He remembered the Albaamo traitor, Crabapple. The man had been captured trying to reach the White Arrow Chahta. Under torture, Crabapple had screamed out that the Albaamo elder known as Paunch was behind the betrayal. But when the returning warriors had gone to question the man, his house had been empty. Not only had the old man been missing, but so had most of his family, including his Spirit-touched granddaughter, Whip-poorwill.

"But we'll find you eventually, traitor," Fast Legs promised. No old Albaamo man could hide out in the forest for long. Albaamaha didn't have the strength of character and purpose a Sky Hand warrior did.

He shot another glance at Lotus Root's house and froze. The woman had stepped out into the freezing rain. The objects she carried looked like the war chief's bow and his quiver of arrows, although he couldn't be sure over this distance. She glanced this way and that, furtively, as if making sure that no one saw her. In a sprint, Lotus Root darted to the side of the granary, easing around it, hidden from the forest.

Fast Legs was on his feet, almost wobbling on his wooden legs. He took one last glance at the houses, saw no one, and ducked back into the trees. There he sprinted as best he could across the ice-coated leaf mat, his feet slipping and sliding.

Finally! She was taking the western trail. He now knew this bit of forest like he did the plan of his house back in Split Sky City. Why would she be headed west into the forest? There was nothing out there but trees. Perhaps on the way to some secret meeting? Maybe she was going out to hide the war chief's weapons, ensuring that when all was set, she could produce them as proof of her claims?

He didn't care.

Fast Legs circled, cut the trail, and could see scuffed leaves. Like a hunting cougar, he hurried along, careful eyes noting the kicked leaves here and there. Yes, this was fresh, the icy sides facedown where the leaves had been turned by a careless moccasin.

He chuckled to himself, running as fast as footing would permit. There! He caught a glimpse of her ahead of him. She was moving smartly, walking fast. She kept casting nervous glances at the forest around her, but hadn't looked back yet.

As he closed, he fit an arrow in his bow. The wide smile of success bent his lips. She was far enough away that no one would hear her cries. By the time anyone realized she was missing, he'd have her body packed to his canoe, and by this evening, she'd be resting on the bottom of a swamp.

Lotus Root had slowed her pace, staring around uncertainly, as though worried about what might await her in the forest. He closed the distance. Then she turned, seeing him. The woman vented a loud shriek, and ran.

Too late! Fast Legs pounded after her, his thick moccasins slipping on the leaves. She ran as fast as she could, scrambling across the icy ground. The trail went between two gum trees, partially blocked by a fallen log. She clambered over it, slipped on the icy crust, and almost fell, veering wide as she clawed for balance, then raced on up the trail.

When Fast Legs reached the log, he jumped it, landing on his left leg. He barely had time to throw his arms up as the leaves and sticks collapsed under his weight. Momentum threw him forward and down, smacking him face-first into the trail. His bow went flying, the arrow snapped in two. Dazed, he blinked. Shock and disbelief surrendered to a sudden sharp pain.

He stared down, trying to determine what had happened. A hole! He had stepped into a deep hole! He twisted, screaming at the pain. Pushing up, he could see his left leg, bent at a hideous angle where it was thrust down between a series of logs laid sideways in the narrow pit.

Broken! My leg is broken! He swallowed hard, trying to collect himself, pushing with his arms to get his bent right knee under him.

"Don't," a voice called.

Fast Legs looked up to see an Albaamo hunter dressed in brown, an arrow nocked and drawn as he crept forward.

Fast Legs clawed for his bow where it rested an arm's length beyond his grasp.

"If you are not still," the Albaamo said, "I will drive this arrow right through your arm."

"Kill me, you piece of filth!"

"Oh, no," another voice said from behind. "We want you alive."

"And you will live," a third voice called.

Every direction he looked, he could see Albaamaha approaching, each holding a bow, each wary and ready.

Another called, "Lotus Root? We have him!"

The first hunter said, "Drag him out of there. Then fill the trap so that no other poor soul steps in it."

A trap! That's what they did during those two days. They'd known he was there the whole time.

Fast Legs lowered his head, fingers clawing futilely at the frozen leaves in the trail. Across time, space, and through the murky water, Red Awl's gleaming eyes seemed to drill straight through Fast Legs' souls.

———

The man called Trader sat—his dog Swimmer beside him—in Rainbow City's great temple. For the moment he was barely aware of the crackling fire in the large central hearth. The fire cast yellow light over the spacious room, illuminating the clay-plastered walls and the hanging reliefs of carved wood and beaten copper. One consisted of a warrior holding a war club in one hand and a sorcerer's severed head in the other. The hero wore a triangular apron, necklaces of shell beads, and copper ear spools. His hair was pulled back in a bun, pinned with an arrow to mark his victory, and a beaded forelock hung down over the forked-eye tattoos on his face.

Across the room, the three spinning triangles of the Yuchi world—indicative of the three great lights in the sky—were surrounded by the six moons that waxed and waned between solstices, and a final encirclement of clouds. The sky in all of its phases preoccupied the Yuchi, but then they also believed they were descended from Mother Sun, born when drops of her menstrual blood fell to earth.

Trader was young, but twenty-six winters old. He had a smooth face, strong of jaw, with wide cheeks. Two parallel lines had been tattooed across his cheeks and nose; the outline of forked-eye designs surrounded his thoughtful brown eyes. The effect was as if the tattoos were unfinished. Trader wore his long black hair pulled up into a bun and pinned at the back of his head.

Sprung from drops of menstrual blood?

"All people believe something that others consider crazy," Trader said wearily. Years of paddling a canoe up and down the mighty eastern rivers had left him muscular, thick through the shoulders, with strapping arms. He sat cross-legged and ran his fingers along the intricate carvings that decorated a wooden box resting on the split-cane matting in front of him.

At his words, the dog at his side lifted his head, ears cocked, a question in his curious brown eyes. Long black, white, and brown fur gleamed in the firelight. The nose was pointed, a dot of black on a white blaze, and the animal's chest sported a gleaming white bib.

Trader turned his attention back to the ornate box and ran the pad of his index finger along the shape of a human hand that had been carved into the lid. He meticulously traced the outline of the extended fingers and thumb. Fingernails and knuckles were defined, and anatomically correct. What drew attention, however, was the large rendition of a human eye that had been carved in the palm's center. Faded white paint marked the sclera. The brown iris had been inlaid with shell, the pupil a single staring orb of copper. The carving dominated the top of the box. It was surrounded by the interlacing patterns of lines Mos'kogean peoples used to indicate the boundaries of the sky and home of the four winds.

"Which one of my beliefs do you think is crazy, Swimmer?" Trader glanced down at the dog and raised an eyebrow.

Swimmer's furry white-tipped tail batted the matting.

From the doorway a voice called in Trade Tongue, "Some would say that any man who talks incessantly to a dog is missing most of the kernels off his corncob."

Swimmer immediately jumped to his feet, racing off to welcome the man who entered. Born-of-Sun Mankiller—the *bahle gibidane,* or high chief of the western Yuchi, or Tsoyaha, in their own language— was tall, muscular, having seen but twenty-five winters. The man's eyes were tattooed in the familiar forked-eye design, and he wore a striking white apron, the tip of it hanging suggestively down between his knees. In his right hand was a stone mace, its top ground into the shape of a turkey tail—the age-old symbol of authority. Polished copper ear spools gleamed in his enlarged earlobes. A beaded forelock hung down the center of his forehead.

"High Chief," Trader called in greeting as he watched the newcomer bend down and ruffle Swimmer's ears. The dog barked happily, causing Trader to order, "No barks, Swimmer. People are sleeping. It's late."

"It's all right," Born-of-Sun rejoined. "Who is going to chastise me, of all people?"

"The Kala Hi'ki?" Trader suggested, jerking a nod toward the dark hallway that led to the Yuchi High Priest's room.

Born-of-Sun warily eyed the passage. "Yes, well, I suppose it is a wise high chief who treads carefully in the presence of a Powerful man like the Kala Hi'ki." He glanced down. "We'll have to be quiet, Swimmer. But you and I, we will bark later. Maybe outside where we can annoy half of Rainbow City."

The dog yawned, stretching out his front legs, tail swishing happily.

Trader chuckled. "Sometimes, High Chief, I think you would rather be a child than the great leader of the Yuchi."

"How right you are." Born-of-Sun walked over, eyes on the carved and inlaid box before Trader. "The Sky Hand war medicine box." He paused, head cocked. "And inside is no doubt the wondrous copper that I have heard tell of."

Trader gave a faint nod, his fingers still tracing the patterns in the wood. "My people lost this war medicine box long before I was born. I think the Seeker knows more about it than he has told me. I can see it in his eyes, a wistful longing, tinged by a sense of wonder. That it came to me at all is a surprise. Something Power has wagered on."

Born-of-Sun settled himself on the split-cane matting beside Trader and patted the floor to entice Swimmer to lie beside him. "I would hear that story, Trader. From start to finish. Where did you obtain the copper? And how? A piece like that...you must have sneaked it out of some great chief's palace. And the war medicine? What prompted the Kaskinampo to give you, a passing Trader, such a Powerful object?"

"Give?" Trader asked with a chuckle. "Hardly a gift,

High Chief. I Traded for the war medicine, and for a wealth in ..." He paused. "But you want the whole story? From the start to the finish?"

"I would hear it."

Trader fingered the carved ripples in the wood. "And see the copper, too, I suppose?"

"Curiosity is eating at me like a thing alive."

Trader reached down, untying the thick leather straps that both secured the war medicine box and served as shoulder straps, allowing a man to carry it like a pack. Carefully, he lifted the fitted lid, allowing

Born-of-Sun to see the cloth-wrapped square that fit so neatly into the interior.

Trader tilted the box, allowing the heavy slab of copper to thump onto the mat-covered clay floor. Setting the box to one side, his muscles bunched under smooth skin as he upended the heavy slab and slid the cloth sack from the green-streaked metal. In places where he and Old White had used stones to shape the metal, the copper gleamed with a wicked reddish color.

"By Blessed Tso, our Mother, I have never seen such a thing!" Born-of-Sun reached out and ran his hands over the cool metal. "It's one *solid* slab!" He shook his head. "How did you come by it, Trader? A chief would guard such a thing with a horde of warriors. It would rest in the most sacred center of a temple, surrounded by many watchful—"

"I didn't *steal* it! I Traded for it...or rather, the right to dig for it." Trader met Born-of-Sun's disbelieving eyes. "Just because I'm Chikosi Sky Hand by birth doesn't mean I'm a perpetually clever thief! I was up in the Copper Lands, on the western margins of the Freshwater Seas. A man called Snow Otter has lineage claims to some of the copper pits up there. I traded him a shell gorget for the right to mine some of his pits. The deal was that I would be able to keep anything I found."

"You *dug* that out of the ground?"

"I did." Trader smiled grimly. "And barely got away with my life. At sight of the copper Snow Otter was drooling with greed. You could see his very souls change before your eyes. He tried to lull me into dropping my guard—offered me food, drink, even his virgin daughter —but I sneaked away in the night." Trader reached out to touch the cool metal. "It was but the first of the lessons I learned. Greed will make even good men bad, and Snow Otter was never good to begin with."

"How did you keep it safe?"

"By moving. Never stopping in one place for any time, and when I did—like at Red Wing Town—I never left the canoe landing. The copper remained buried in the packs...and I never so much as stepped beyond the sight of my boat." Trader reached out to ruffle Swimmer's ears where the dog lay between them. "Gods, it was torture"! Traders travel around driven by the desire to Trade, to wander around the towns, see what's available, talk to people, hear the gossip. And there I was, virtually chained to my canoe, fearful of someone sneaking a peek at my packs, learning of the existence of that fabulous piece of copper. And the one time I did stop, I had to hide it first, bury it in the forest. And still I worried." Trader shook his head.

"A tough lesson to learn."

Trader nodded. "The next lesson I learned was that with amazing wealth comes incredible loneliness. I could trust no one—well, save Swimmer here—let alone share their fire or companionship. As a Trader I had sought wealth all of my life. With it, I figured to become an admired and influential man. I would have had people look up to me and say, 'Look! There goes Trader! The greatest man on the river.'"

"So you wanted to be a chief after all?"

Trader shook his head. "I could have stayed among the Sky Hand and remained a chief. Granted, I murdered my brother, but I still would have been an influential, if despised, member of my Chief Clan. No, I just wanted to be great, admired, and envied, but without the cares, responsibilities, and dangers of being a chief. Fool that I was, I thought it could be that simple."

"Power never gives something for nothing, Trader."

"As I discovered that night when the Contrary led Old White to my camp." Trader smiled at his memories. "I'd chosen an abandoned village two days' travel south of Cahokia. The place is believed to be cursed with witchcraft. Staying there didn't bother me. I don't believe in Dehegihan witches or their ability to harm me. So there I was, just starting to relax for the first time in days, when I hear voices out of the night. It's the Contrary guiding Old White up the creek to my camp."

"She had camped there before?"

"Oh, no. Two Petals is Oneota, from farther north. She'd never been out of her own village, let alone to the south. She was following one of her visions…and it was leading her straight to me."

"You had your fire right at the landing?"

"Of course not. It was screened by an old house wall, completely out of sight." Trader glanced down at Swimmer. "I was ready to reach down Swimmer's gullet and pull his bark right out of his throat. Thought maybe they'd miss seeing the landing and my canoe in the darkness, but Two Petals directed the Seeker straight to it. As soon as they landed, Swimmer got loose, charging off to bark at them. So, what could I do?"

"You could have killed them."

Trader arched an eyebrow. "I considered it. Especially after the Contrary told me to my face that she knew about the copper. Somehow, High Chief, I just couldn't drive an arrow through her chest. Call me a fool."

"Power would have made you pay if you had."

Trader laughed. "Then I'm lucky that Power loves fools. A terrible storm moved in that night, but as soon as I could, I sneaked to my canoe, loaded all of my goods, called Swimmer, and slipped away." He cocked his head, thinking back. "The thing is, the Contrary told me things before I left...things that haunted my Dreams."

"About?"

"About going home. About my life, people, a woman...things she couldn't possibly have known, but did." Trader shrugged. "I just couldn't get her and the Seeker out of my head. Curiosity will be the death of me one of these days."

"So you went after them?"

"I caught up with them on the Mother Water in the Illinois territory. The Contrary knew I would. Being around her is just downright eerie sometimes."

"And the war medicine?" Born-of-Sun indicated the intricately carved box.

"We were among the Kaskinampo." Trader fingered his chin as he stared thoughtfully at the carvings on the wood. "And there I was, still burdened by the secret of the copper. How do you disguise a piece of copper that big and heavy? All of our packs had to be portaged around the three falls on the Tenasee River — and right under the eyes of the wary Kaskinampo. They have towns at each of the falls and monitor the Trade. So, back to the question: How do you keep a piece of copper like that from being discovered?"

"You found a way?"

"We gambled...and lied a little." Trader cocked a knowing eyebrow. "Copper is heavy. Can't really disguise the fact. So what's heavy and square? Something you don't want anyone to see? We told the Kaskinampo straight out that we were carrying a great stone with Power carvings on it. They didn't even question since we were traveling with the Contrary. We told them we wanted a more secure box to carry it in, something to better hold the Power. And it led us right to the war medicine box."

Trader smiled. "The Kaskinampo chief, Buffalo Mankiller, was most anxious to get us out of their territory. He wasn't any more keen to have Power loose among his people than the Kala Hi'ki was to have us among the Tsoyaha. So he brought us a box...that one there."

"But why the war medicine?" Born-of-Sun asked. "Surely they could have found something less valuable."

"Buffalo Mankiller told us that from the moment they obtained it from you, the Sky Hand war medicine brought misfortune. From the beginning we made it clear to the Kaskinampo that we were headed for Split Sky City and the Sky Hand. The Kaskinampo thought the box should go home to its people."

"For a price," Born-of-Sun added.

"For a price," Trader agreed.

"And what did you Trade?"

"I Traded Buffalo Mankiller a piece of silver, a large nugget from the far north. The man I got it from had obtained it from a Cree."

"Never heard of the Cree," Born-of-Sun admitted.

"They live way far to the north. But Buffalo Mankiller was happy. Value for value. And no sooner had we Traded than the box began to Sing to the Contrary. From that moment on the Kaskinampo almost turned themselves inside out getting us out of their territory and into yours."

"Which you would have passed through but for the Kala Hi'ki?"

"He saw us coming and sent War Chief Wolf Tail to capture us." Trader shrugged. "The rest you know. But I think that Power needed us to come here. Two Petals needed the Kala Hi'ki to help her control her Contrary Power."

"And you, Trader? What did you need to come here for?"

Trader gave him a dry look. "If you will recall, the Kala Hi'ki wanted to torture me to death in one of your squares. When he learned I was born of the Chief Clan of the Sky Hand People, he wished to repay me in kind for what my people had done to him. And you, High Chief, made me wager my life and freedom on the outcome of a chunkey game."

"Which you won."

"Barely." Trader grinned. "Fact is: I had to face my death. The moment I made that decision, I began to understand. Things like copper, status, and glory are distractions. I am only here to serve Power. It will do as it will with me."

"As part of the wager on our chunkey game, you said you wished a runner to be sent to Split Sky City to tell the Sky Hand Chikosi that Green Snake was returning. Is that still your wish?"

"It is." Trader sighed. "I would like the Council to know that I am coming home. Perhaps with that copper, I can make retribution for murdering my brother. After all these years, I would like to make peace with Rattle's ghost and with my clan."

"I have a man in mind. His name is Bullfrog Pipe, named for the magical pipe that slew monsters. He is brave, a man of honor. He will bear the sacred white arrow of peace before him." Born-of-Sun hesitated. "They will honor the white arrow, won't they?"

Trader nodded. "To do otherwise is to incur the wrath of Power. Believe me, the Chikosi take Power very seriously."

"Then I shall send Bullfrog Pipe to you in the morning." Born-of-Sun stared longingly at the copper. "Who knows how this shall play out? But perhaps, if you succeed, we will enter a period that will be good for both of our peoples."

"I think, High Chief, that is why Power sent us on this journey. Somehow, we must make an offering that returns Power to balance. I think red Power has been in ascendance. Perhaps it is time for the white to prevail."

"That may be." Born-of-Sun continued to stare thoughtfully at the copper. "And if it is the case, I am more determined than ever to keep you here. You could still work for the white Power from Rainbow City. And perhaps I could obtain this copper." He shot Trader a sidelong stare. "Do you know how tempting this is? What it would say about me if I displayed such wealth in my palace? Such a piece of copper would literally shout out to the world: 'Here is the greatest chief on earth!'"

"I thought you loved your children."

Born-of-Sun turned quizzical. "My children? Of course I love them! They are my world."

"Then why would you destroy them?" Trader asked. Born-of-Sun might be the high chief of the Western Yuchi, but he loved his children like a fawning grandmother. "Because I think anyone who takes this copper— who tries to own it—will find their souls being devoured by it in the end."

"Is it eating your souls, Trader?"

"It was. Until I thought you were going to tie me inside one of your squares to hang spread-eagle and naked while you Yuchi burned my flesh, cut out my eyes, and slowly sliced me to ribbons." Trader stared thoughtfully at the gleaming metal. "Old White, the Seeker, once told me that no one actually owned copper...that it just passed through our lives. Power wishes this piece of copper to reach Split Sky City. I am only its means of getting there."

"For what purpose, Trader? The Sky Hand are our enemies. You Chikosi have been at war with us ever since you conquered the Black Warrior country. Why should we allow Spirit Power to strengthen them?"

"When we played chunkey, High Chief, I played for peace."

"And ended up a rich man. My people—almost as one—bet against you."

Trader grinned. The winnings, most of the Western Yuchi's wealth, filled two large storehouses. More pots, blankets, jewelry, and baskets of food than he and Old White could ever take with them in their two canoes. "We will give it all back, High Chief."

"All of it?" Born-of-Sun asked, surprised.

Trader sighed. "For most of my life I have served the Power of Trade. As I have so recently discovered, we serve Power's plan. Not our own."

"And what do you think that plan is?"

Trader stared back and forth between the war medicine box and the copper. "I don't know, High Chief. All I know is that I have to get both the copper and the medicine box to the Chikosi at Split Sky City. And once there, I suppose it is in the hands of Power...and the Contrary."

THREE

IN THE DREAM, Morning Dew ran. The pounding of her bare feet on the hard clay plaza was to the beat of a thousand voices screaming their support. She could feel the crowd as she raced through White Arrow Town — sense them, like a giant living creature. The spirit of the moment gave her flying feet speed to rival a deer's.

She knew this day! It had been the happiest of her life. This was the marriage chase, and behind her, Screaming Falcon was running his heart out in pursuit. She could feel his presence, sense the rhythm of his feet in time with the rapid beat of her heart.

With the agility of a cougar she threaded her way through White Arrow Town, rounding buildings, leaping baskets, and darting between buildings. The sunlight seemed to pulse with each tearing breath in her lungs. Still she ran, goaded by the roar of the crowd, jubilant in her speed and cunning.

The Dream was so real it filled her with a bursting joy. All the love that brimmed in her souls rose golden within her. Soon, as was inevitable, Screaming Falcon would lay his hand on her shoulder, symbolically claiming her as his bride. At that moment she would turn and shower the love within her on this most special of men.

From the time she had been a little girl, she had known that this day would come. She and Screaming Falcon had been born for each other. The joining of their lives would begin a mythic union. She knew the truth of that each time her eyes met his. The swelling in her heart, souls, and loins could not be denied. Together, they would bring their people to greatness.

Driven by her endless love, she ran, following the tradition of her people. The longer and harder the chase, it was said, the greater the resulting marriage. And this chase, she swore, would be the stuff of legends.

Onward she pounded, avoiding knots of spectators who had come to share the festive event. Among the crowd were Natchez chiefs or their representatives, renowned Traders, Priests, and the greatest chiefs among the Chahta: the noted high minkos. She barely glimpsed the joy in their eyes as she raced past, felt the pulsing emotion they exuded.

Screaming Falcon and I will remake the Chahta world! Had he not just sacked the Sky Hand's Alligator Town? Had he not burned their southernmost holding and taken its chief and his relatives captive to hang in White Arrow Town's wooden squares? Power favored the Chahta, and with it, she and Screaming Falcon would lead her people to new vigor, prestige, and influence throughout the land. Morning Dew would one day be the matron of White Arrow Chahta, and — with her warrior husband at her side — the world would kneel before her.

The very thought of it made her breast swell, her souls tingling in giddy anticipation.

Onward she flew, rounding the houses and granaries, sprinting down narrow gaps between the buildings, slipping left and right, trying to throw off Screaming Falcon's pursuit. This day would mark the beginning of greatness.

Morning Dew rounded the base of the palace mound, scarcely throwing a glance at the high building atop the earthwork. Then she turned, running headlong down the center of the plaza. As Morning Dew passed the tall pole that represented the Tree of Life, she allowed her fingers to graze its wood, painted in red and white stripes. Arms pumping, she bolted straight across the stickball grounds.

She heard Screaming Falcon as he closed; his breath was blowing like a buffalo's as his feet matched the cadence of her own. And then, as his hand dropped on her shoulder, she experienced a tingling rush that jolted her entire body.

Slowing, smiling her joy, she turned, intending to gaze into his face...and recoiled in horror.

The world went dark, as though a blanket had been thrown across the sun. She was but vaguely aware that White Arrow Town lay abandoned around her, the buildings nothing more than blackened posts jutting up from rectangles of gray ash. Her mother's body lay to her right, arms and legs sprawled, hair spread over the blood-soaked ground. The ugly wound in Mother's head gaped, seemingly alive with maggots.

Corpses littered the earth, broken, blackened with dried blood. Baskets were upturned, pots shattered, pestles and mortars lay on their sides. Dark oily smoke hung low over her head.

Her gaze fixed on Screaming Falcon's face; a cry choked in her throat. He was staring at her, a hollow pleading in his wounded eyes. The swollen deformity of his broken jaw made his head oddly out of proportion. Filth and dried blood matted his hair, and his skin had a pale and sunken look where it wasn't blistered from burning, or scabbed with dried blood.

She blinked, following his arms and legs to the corners of the heavy wooden square where they had been tightly bound with layers of thick rope so that he hung, sagging and spread-eagled like wild meat ready for butcher. Old bruises mixed with new, and trickles of blood leaked from long shallow slices on his naked body. Blistered flesh mottled with gray and red marked the places that burning torches had been thrust against

his body. Where they'd burned the pubic hair from his crotch, the skin was puffed and weeping pus.

She took a faltering step, reaching out, her fingers seeking reassurance that this was no specter. Her eyes locked with his as she touched him. His pain and desperation flowed into her like a cold wave, staggering her on her feet.

"I am so sorry," he croaked from a thirst-dried throat.

"Screaming Falcon?" she pleaded, aware of the chill where her hands rested on his chest. Then there was warmth, sliding down her fingers, trickling over her palms. She looked down, stunned by the blood that coated her hands with sticky darkness.

She was clutching something, a thing alive, that pulsed, spasmed, and then went still. No woman raised in a society of hunters could fail to recognize it. She clutched a human heart.

When she raised her eyes, it was to find Screaming Falcon staring at her through dead eyes, a look of disbelief reflecting from his damaged face. In a slurred voice, he said, "You and your pride brought us to this."

Morning Dew threw her head back. The anguished howl started deep in her lungs, swelling, bursting from her throat with a hideous shriek....

"Morning Dew!"

The harsh voice brought Morning Dew awake. She jerked upright, aware of the blanket falling from her shoulders. She sat on a pole bed built into a wall. "What...I was...Where are we?" Blinking to clear her souls of the images shredding her mind, she stared around the darkened interior of Heron Wing's house. She knew this place: Split Sky City. She was a slave. Screaming Falcon was long dead.

Everything was where it was supposed to be. The pole beds lined the walls, dimly illuminated by the glowing coals in the central hearth. Overhead the thatch roof was lost in the darkness. She drew cool air into her starved lungs, aware of fear sweat cooling on her too-hot body.

"Morning Dew," Heron Wing called again, her voice softer now. "You were Dreaming."

Morning Dew rubbed callused palms into her sleep-heavy eyes. "Yes ..."

"A bad one?" Heron Wing asked.

"I'm all right," Morning Dew insisted. "Go back to sleep." •

"Mother?" Little Stone asked from his bed. "Morning Dew? You screamed. Is something wrong?"

"Everything's fine," Heron Wing insisted gently.

Morning Dew watched the woman across from her sit up. She could feel Heron Wing's piercing stare through the dark. Sense the question that rose inside her.

"It's all right," Morning Dew added, laying her blanket to one side and swinging her feet to the mat-covered floor; anything to forestall Heron Wing's next query. The split cane beneath her soles was warm as she stepped over to Stone's bed. Despite the dim light she could see the little boy's face, make out his wide dark eyes staring up at her. "I'm sorry I woke you." She forced a laugh and lied, "I was playing stick-ball in the Dream. I just made a goal. You know how that is. I've heard you scream, too, just like that, when you made a goal."

"I guess," Stone answered. But she could hear the hesitation in his voice. Heron Wing's son was just as smart as his mother. Nevertheless, little Stone worshipped Morning Dew's ability as a stickball player, and an adoring gleam had filled his eyes ever since Morning Dew had won the women's solstice stickball game for Hickory Moiety.

"Go back to sleep, Stone. Dream of stickball and all the goals you will make."

She could barely make out his smile as she tucked his colorful blanket up around his chin. Then she retreated to her bed, thankful that Heron Wing s other slave, Wide Leaf, was spending the night with her new Albaamo lover. It would save her from suffering the nasty old woman's knowing gaze and thinly veiled comments.

Morning Dew reseated herself on the edge of her bed and pulled her blanket up around her shoulders. A quick glance told her that Heron Wing had lain down again. The woman's blanket rustled, .and the pole bed squeaked as she resettled her weight.

Screaming Falcon... we would have been so happy.

But her brother Biloxi and Screaming Falcon had precipitated disaster when they brazenly raided Alligator Town and burned it to the ground. The White Arrow Chahta had been doomed from the moment the first arrow was loosed.

She clamped her eyes shut at the first stinging tears. What fools she and Screaming Falcon had been. Barely past childhood, they had had no understanding of the Sky Hand. Not of their numbers, strength, or resolve. Knowing what she did now, Smoke Shield's daring raid against White Arrow Town seemed like a bitter blessing. He had broken the White Arrow Chahta with a single blow. In the end that was probably preferable to a slow and lingering death. Pain was better ended quickly.

It was only after Stone's sleep-breath purled in his throat that Heron Wing surprised her by stating softly, "There's nothing you could have done, Morning Dew."

"I know. Dreams are beyond a person's control. I think Stone accepted the stickball story."

"I meant about your husband. Before you screamed, you called out for Screaming Falcon. You couldn't have helped him. You were Smoke Shield's slave. Had you so much as set foot out of the palace, he'd have maimed you, then beat you half to death—if not all the way."

"I know."

"Suppose you had slipped away, managed to cut Screaming Falcon free. Your husband was weak, half-delirious, and captives cut down from the square can't so much as walk until their circulation returns. You would both have been killed in the end: He would have died an even harder death. You would have had to watch it, and then suffer the same." She paused. "For the time being, you may be my slave, but the future is an unknown river. Who knows what you will find at its end, Matron? Remember, I have my reasons for wanting you back with your people one day."

"I know." She took a deep breath. "They still don't have any clue who killed my...the captives, do they?"

"No. Smoke Shield is sure it was the Albaamaha, which if true, may turn into a fire that burns us all. Personally, I hope it was some Chahta warrior who was lucky enough to slip in, kill the captives, and sneak away in that miserable fog."

"You'd think we would have heard if one had."

Heron Wing paused, then asked, "Morning Dew, when you were at White Arrow Town, did you ever hear of any Chahta plotting with the Albaamaha? Perhaps even the silliest rumor of any Chahta clan, no matter how obscure, treating with the Albaamaha?"

"No. We Chahta think even less of them than you Chikosi do. And, believe me, had anyone been inciting them, for whatever purpose, someone would have said something to Mother."

"And among the Red Arrow Moiety?"

"War Chief Great Cougar has his own ways. But not even he would deal with Albaamaha." She shook her head. "Not the man I know."

"You know him well?"

"Well enough."

"Would he have sent a man to kill the captives?"

"Had he been behind it, every Chikosi in the world would know. Great Cougar is never subtle."

"My wish," Heron Wing finally said, "is that we never learn who killed your husband, brother, and the others.

It would be better as a forgotten mystery. But I fear that Smoke Shield will never let it rest. In the end, it could bring us all to grief."

As if you knew the depths of grief! She winced; the very thought had been unkind.

"Grief," she whispered, rubbing her hands as if to sponge them free of blood. "That's all I have left."

An orange-red morning sun hung low over the southeastern horizon and cast its gaudy light over Rainbow City. It colored the thickly plastered house walls, even softening the gray-black of old thatch on the high roofs. Under the crimson light the packed clay of the plaza, with its chunkey and stickball grounds, was made to glow. The sacred red-cedar pole, crafted from the trunk of a mighty tree, seemed to burn with an inner fire. High atop their mounds, the palaces and temples rose proudly against the sky. Even the smoky haze that rose from so many morning fires had a cherry hue. In the distance, beyond the packed houses, elevated corn cribs, and ramadas, the high city palisade made an irregular barrier against the distant sky. A fuzz of winter-bare treetops was barely visible in the distance.

What should have been a lazy morning was anything but. Long before the faintest glimmer of day, people had begun to gather before the two storage houses where Trader's winnings from the fabled chunkey game had been stored.

Old White stood before one of the storehouses. Beside him were Trader and the Contrary, Two Petals. Trader's dog, Swimmer, sat at Trader's feet, ears cocked, watching the proceedings.

Old White was a weathered man, his hair almost snowy. It was said that he had been from one end of the earth to the other. That he had traveled more lands, seen more people, than any other man alive. To many he was known only as the Seeker—a man whose exploits bordered on legend. Nevertheless, he stood tall, his shoulders still broad. On this day he wore a buffalohide cloak that hung down to his knees. Through the open front could be seen a white fabric hunter's shirt belted at the waist, where a large pouch hung. Over one shoulder he carried a sturdy fabric bag, some heavy object pulling down at the cloth. His right hand clutched a Trader's staff made of supple ash, bent over at the top to form a crook, its end terminated in a finely carved ivory-billed woodpecker's head. From the crook hung three white heron feathers. The staff had been carved to represent spiraling serpents, one red and the other white.

For the moment Old White stared thoughtfully at the river of humanity that had formed up along the plaza perimeter. He could see people stretching along the southern boundary in front of the Warrior Clan Palace, past the Men's House, and on to the Winter Solstice Temple. From there they lined the eastern plaza edge along the river's steep bluff, the Healer's temple, and finally the high chief's palace atop its great mound on the northeastern corner of the plaza. The crowd then continued east, edging the chunkey grounds, and extending past War Chief Wolf Tail's house atop its low mound. The crowd was watched over by Yuchi warriors under orders to keep things civil and orderly despite the myriad of old rivalries and slights that always infected a population.

"How many?" Trader asked from behind him.

"One is as good as none," Two Petals said cryptically. One got used to hearing cryptic sayings from her.

"Thousands." Old White shrugged. "I hope we have enough to go around."

"Never enough? Are you sure?" Two Petals asked some phantom only she could see in the empty plaza before them.

"There will be enough, Seeker," the Kala Hi'ki said as he approached from around the storehouse. The old shaman was led by two of his white-robed Priests.

Old White shot him an appraising glance. The Kala Hi'ki wasn't easy on the eyes. As a young man he had been captured by the Sky Hand and hung in a square. The Chikosi had tortured him for days, burning his flesh, gouging out his eyes, severing the fingers from his right hand, and carefully slicing thin strips of skin away. They had even cut the nose from the man's face, leaving two oblong nostrils.

How the Kala Hi'ki had escaped was a long and involved story. Apparently the Yuchi had been cut down by Trader's brother. Rattle had meant to blame it on Trader, but never had the chance since Trader killed him with a war club. Once the Kala Hi'ki was free of the square, it was said that Horned Serpent carried him down into the depths of the Black Warrior River outside of Split Sky City. Horned Serpent then bore him to the Underworld, where it healed his wounds and finally left his broken body where other Yuchi could find him.

Hideously scarred, with a white cloth wrapped around his blind eyes, the Kala Hi'ki stood placidly, his good left hand clasping the mangled remains of his right. The two younger Priests took positions to either side, curious eyes on the still-assembling crowd.

"You know," the Kala Hi'ki added, "that people cannot receive a gift without giving something back. Right now they will be happy to receive something from your winnings on the chunkey match; but after they take it away, guilt will begin to eat at them. Power must be balanced. As the line shortens, it will lengthen again."

"This could take all day," Trader said with a sigh.

Two Petals softly said, "Days are such funny things.

How can one last so long and be so short?" Her eyes darted around as though searching for something just beyond her vision. Her hands twitched in oddly synchronous movements. "It is already done. See, just over there. All finished. Like standing here tomorrow afternoon. No one around."

Old White arched a white eyebrow, but was happy to see that the two young Priests no longer started to fidget when the Contrary was speaking .in riddles. He rubbed his old wrinkled face and checked to make sure that his gray-white hair was still pinned tightly in the bun at the back of his head.

No time at all? He sighed as he stared at the crowd, feeling each of his fifty-some winters. An ache lay deep in his bones, in the small of his back, and in the stiffness that had settled in his knees. What a thousand desert suns had done to brown his skin, another thousand freezing blizzards had finished. Endless high Plains winds had lined his face, only to have the creases chiseled deep by unforgiving ocean breezes. Northern snow fields had etched the corners of his eyes into a squint that had fixed under shimmering heat waves rolling off desert pavement.

"Thinking of the past?" the Kala Hi'ki asked.

"Always," Old White replied. "All that a man is comes from the past. What he will be in the future is only a fantasy, a Dream."

"You did not need to travel to the ends of the earth to learn that."

"No."

"And they call you the Seeker?" the Kala Hi'ki asked. "I find that to be a divine joke."

Old White turned, fingering his Trader's staff. "I don't see the humor."

When the Kala Hi'ki smiled, the effect on his maimed face was gruesome. "What do you carry in that heavy canvas bag hanging from your shoulder?"

Old White looked down at the travel-stained fabric bag. "My past, Kala Hi'ki."

"It is a heavy burden to bear."

"What does my past have to do with my name being a joke?" Old White asked warily.

"Because you weren't seeking. You have always been driven." The Kala Hi'ki's ruined smile thinned. "You enjoy keeping the secrets of your past, Seeker. Whatever terrible thing you did, it has hounded you from one end of the earth to the other. And the harder you run to escape, the closer it barks at your heels."

An eerie shiver ran through Old White. "For a blind man, you see just fine."

"I am the Kala Hi'ki." The Yuchi turned his sightless eyes toward Old White. "Horned Serpent gave me the gift of life...and sight."

Old White swallowed hard, remembering the time the Kala Hi'ki had removed the bandage from his face. There, exposed in the fire-light, were two large crystals—allegedly gifts from Horned Serpent—embedded in the sockets where the man's eyes should have been.

"If you can see that well, you know why I keep secrets. If you don't, explaining won't sharpen your vision."

The Kala Hi'ki nodded. "You are a stronger man than I, Seeker. I would rather hang on a square again than bear your burden."

Old White caught Trader's suddenly sharpened expression. Old White waved it down. "All in time, Trader. Assuming we live that long."

"Living is just dying. Only backward." Two Petals frowned at something in the air above the plaza. "How can light just hang in the sky like that? Meanwhile, these people are happy to swarm around. Hungry as bees. Waves upon the shore, forever lapping and lapping. Can't go meet my sister with all these goods piled in a warehouse. No, they've got to be turned upside down first. Can't send a wooden bowl south if it's in the north. She'd never know us for who we are. Seeds in the soil. Messengers can't die until they're sent."

"What?" Trader asked.

"Forget it," Old White told him, glad to have the subject changed. He raised his staff, and the waiting Yuchi grew quiet. He could feel the rising expectation in the crowd. At that moment, Born-of-Sun, followed by War Chief Wolf Tail, came striding across the plaza. The Yuchi high chief was dressed resplendently, fans of turkey feathers at each shoulder, the point of his apron hanging down between his knees. A bearhide cape was perfectly draped over his shoulders, and sunlight glinted off the copper headpiece pinned to his hair.

Born-of-Sun wore an expression of solemn dignity until he stepped close, winked at Trader, and shot Old White an amused smile. In a low voice he asked, "Are you ready for this? If we avoid a riot it will be a miracle."

"Riot, riot," Two Petals sang. "All is chaos."

"Ready," Trader replied. "Seeker? Do you wish to do the honors?"

Old White cried out to the crowd, "Greetings! I am Old White, known as the Seeker. With me is Trader, and the Contrary, Two Petals. As you know, we came to Rainbow City under the Power of Trade!" He took a breath as a cheer went up. "At the height of the winter solstice, you watched a great game of chunkey played between Born-of-Sun, high chief of the Tsoyaha, and Trader. The stakes were Trader's life and freedom against his promise to seek peace and well-being between the Yuchi and Chikosi. The game was close, tied at twenty apiece, when Trader's final cast shattered his lance upon the stone!"

People called out, stamping their feet, shouting in applause.

Old White lifted his Trader's staff, the feathers waffling in the breeze. When the crowd began to quiet, he continued, "You Tsoyaha wagered everything on your chief, knowing Born-of-Sun was the finest chunkey player among you. Power, however, favored Trader in this contest among equals."

A few hoots and jeers broke out.

Old White grinned. "Trader, the Contrary, and I are humble Traders, and it is not right that we three should hoard our winnings. Power seeks balance. We serve the Power of Trade. So we would Trade."

"Trade what?" someone called.

"The goodwill of the Tsoyaha in return for this mountain of winnings!" Old White pointed to the two storehouses full of blankets, jewelry, pots of corn, beans, and dried squash. Wooden dishes, colorful fabrics, shell-inlaid wooden boxes, bows, lances, several canoes, rolls of matting, and the wealth of a nation lay piled within.

A roar went up from the crowd.

"What do you think, Kala Hi'ki?" Born-of-Sun asked.

"I think our children's children will talk of this day, High Chief."

Old White turned for the first of the presents, handing it to Two Petals. The piece was a finely crafted Illinois bowl. The artisan had carved it from a single piece of black walnut, thinning the wooden bowl and rubbing it with oils to accent the grain. The handles were in the form of a raccoon's head on one end with the animal's ringed tail protruding on the other. It rested on four lifelike feet; but for being wood, the toes and claws might have come from the real thing. He had obtained the bowl in Trade, given it away during the solstice celebrations, and now Trader had won it back. For a moment Old White stared at the intricate carving of the muzzle and admired the masklike face that had been so finely rendered. Wonderful workmanship. Then he turned to Two Petals. "Here. You do the honors. You're Contrary: Say something…cryptic."

"As if she could say anything else?" Trader asked from the corner of his mouth.

"You Dance with your feet on your head, Seeker," Two Petals announced as she took the bowl from his hands. "Try and be rid of this bowl, Trader. It will finally rest with the one you love."

Old White watched Trader roll his eyes and shake his head.

FOUR

"I AM NOT TIRED. Not at all. What need do I have of sleep?" Two Petals asked herself with a sigh as she stared up into the night sky. The young woman had hollow eyes, her face lined with fatigue. Her head kept nodding, and she'd jerk before blinking stupidly.

Trader laughed as he puffed reflectively on his pipe.

Old White sat with a buffalo robe around his shoulders, his hands extended to the flames. Firelight played across his aged features. Was it just the exhaustion, or was his face more drawn, his eyes sadder? Trader drew from his pipe and wondered.

"Storm is coming," Old White noted, glancing up at the clouds.

"Cold wind from the north, dark clouds moving up over it from the south." Trader gave the sky a slit-eyed appraisal. "My guess is freezing rain come morning. Should make travel miserable."

Old White grunted in humorless agreement.

Trader suspected the old man wanted nothing more than to sleep for three days straight. Then he, too, looked up at the night. Dark and tortured, it threatened rain. Heavy clouds—menacing and swollen—were rolling up from the gulf. The air carried the scent of moisture, and here, so close to the earth, it had grown thick, cold, and still after having blown down from the north that entire day.

The three of them sat around a crackling fire, backs to logs that other travelers had drawn up at the terraced campsite. Their two canoes rested at the edge of their vision, where the creek flowed. Thick ropes were tied from the bows to the trees in case rain raised the creek waters high enough to float the craft.

The morning of their departure from Rainbow City, the canoe landing had been packed with enough people that the crush knocked over a ramada. Too many volunteers came forward to pull them upriver. A lottery had to be held. They hadn't pushed the canoes out into the Tenasee River's water until almost midday, but the paddlers made up for it, arriving at Cane Break Town just after dark. Then it all started again.

Trader laughed as he stared at the fire. "I don't think a single Yuchi has what he started out with. We could have saved a lot of work if we'd just told everyone to switch households."

"I've never seen such a thing," Old White agreed as he reached for his own pipe. "They'll be talking about us for years. Kind of pleasing, actually."

The Yuchi men who were traveling with them had a roaring fire a stone's throw to the south. They, too, looked exhausted, having expended unflagging energy towing the two canoes upstream. Word had traveled upriver like a wind-borne leaf, and as the party passed, people would appear on the banks, waving and calling greetings. The Yuchi paddlers had waved back, then expended their efforts against the current, making a show of their strength and energy for the spectators.

They had been on the river for four days, now. Travel had been slow because it seemed that a Yuchi town lay at the end of each day's journey. And, at each, they had been honored, feasted, and kept up late into the night, telling stories. Mostly, it was Old White who related his adventures as the Seeker. Night after night, the old man stood beside a fire in some crowded Council House, his sonorous voice eliciting gasps of disbelief from his listeners. But Two Petals had drawn her own crowds, evoking awe and reverence as people asked her questions, listened intently to her backward answers, and then struggled to interpret the Power behind her words.

Trader glanced down at Swimmer, flopped on his side, paws twitching as he chased something in his. Dreams. Then Trader looked out at the Gray Fox River—their route up to the portage that would take them to the headwaters of the Horned Serpent.

"I have a question." Old White lit his pipe and puffed.

"For me or Two Petals?"

"I am Contrary, now," she said through a yawn. "You no longer see Two Petals."

"Right," Trader replied. "I forget. It will take a while."

Old White blew smoke toward the fire. "That last cast at the chunkey game. You gave me a look, trying to tell me something. I thought you were going to miss on purpose."

Trader expelled a weary -breath. "Honestly, I didn't know what would happen. I was torn, Seeker. Born-of-Sun made me a very good offer. We could have stayed at Rainbow City, Traded from there, built lives. They would have made Two...the Contrary welcome among them."

"It surprised me that you didn't look worried. From the way you and the high chief were talking, congratulating each other, I wasn't sure that you had your heart in it."

"Oh, I did, Seeker, believe me. When I'm on the chunkey court, I play to win. I really wanted to see which of us was better." He laughed at himself. "The night before the match, I was all tied in knots. Worried like I had never been worried before. Then, when I went out to practice, Born-of-Sun joined me. We talked, and I suddenly realized, the best thing to do was enjoy myself. So I did. I gave myself over to fate. If I were to lose, it would be the will of Power. And as a result, I played brilliantly. I can't remember enjoying a game more."

"And that final cast?"

"That look I gave you, it was surrender. I didn't know what was right. Should we go on to Split Sky City and face whatever terrible thing awaits us? Or was it better that we stay with the Yuchi? So I was trying to tell you: 'Here it is.' Then I made my cast. But just at the last moment, I closed my eyes, letting the lance seek its own path. I didn't make that throw. I let Power do it."

"And shattered the lance."

"Which I regret!" He gestured with his pipe stem. "That was the best lance I'd ever made. It will take time to craft one as good."

Old White nodded, a look of relief on his face. "The Contrary knew. She tried to tell me. Stone would shatter wood."

Trader sighed, remembering his complete calm. "We are destined to arrive at Split Sky City."

Old White blew smoke up at the threatening sky. "What did you think of that messenger, Bullfrog Pipe? Was that his name?"

Trader shrugged. "I made him memorize my message word for word. He was quick. He had it after two attempts. We talked some about how long it would take for you and me to Trade our way through the Chaktaw and make our way up the Black Warrior to Split Sky City. Assuming we don't have some unforeseen problem, he should arrive sometime before we get there."

"I'm still not sure that later wouldn't be better."

"We talked about this."

"I know. I'd just like to be sure that the Sky Hand honor the white arrow."

"Seeker, anyone who refuses to honor the white arrow would bring disaster down on their heads. No, Bullfrog Pipe will be quite safe. And once his message is delivered, the Council will be expecting us to come from the north. I was explicit. Bullfrog Pipe is only to tell them that I'm coming to make restitution for Rattle's death."

"Well, it will lay the groundwork for our final meeting with the Council."

For a long time, they sat and smoked, each lost in his thoughts. Trader noted that Two Petals had drifted off to sleep. She looked so delicate in the firelight. Her glossy black hair hung around her; a peaceful expression had settled on her smooth face. Lately she had come to his Dreams. More often than not, it ended in some erotic Dance in which her naked body hovered just beyond the reach of his straining manhood.

It's just that you're a man and she's an attractive woman. Forget it, she's Contrary.

"The Kala Hi'ki says that a Horned Serpent lives under Split Sky City in the Black Warrior River," Old White said suddenly. "He told me the story of his escape. According to him, he died, and Horned Serpent took him to the Underworld and healed his wounds. Then it left him on the banks of the Tenasee for his people to find."

Trader lifted an eyebrow, happy for a distraction. "Then, maybe we'd better not go to Split Sky City."

"Oh?"

"You've heard the stories. Horned Serpents are supposed to be enamored of copper. There are legends that if you can follow one down to its lair, you would find a huge cache of copper. I've heard that for copper, Horned Serpents will do great favors, grant wishes and Power to anyone who can meet their price." Trader narrowed an eye. "Even drag an enemy's canoe underwater and drown someone."

Old White gave him a tired sigh. "Beware, Trader. Sometimes I think you covet that copper more than your own life."

He chuckled. "That's all right. Giving up the copper might be worth it if I could see a real Horned Serpent. In all my travels, I should have seen at least one. Several times, I thought I had, but closer investigation proved they were just submerged logs. How about you? Ever seen a Horned Serpent, or Tie Snake?"

Old White shook his head. "Not without the help of Spirit plants or a high fever." He paused. "But then, I never tried luring one in with copper, either."

They enjoyed a companionable silence before Old White added, "I have gone to places—caves, springs, empty canyons—where people have sworn Spirit beasts lived, but none ever appeared to me in this world. Over the years, I've grown skeptical. On the other hand, it doesn't matter where you go, people believe these things. Whether it is Sedna, at the bottom of the sea, or Nanabush in the far northeast, none have appeared to me." He smiled. "When the *Katsinas* came to me to tell me to go home, my souls were floating with the Power of a cactus button."

"I don't know that plant."

"From the far south, in the desert, north and west of the Azteca. The Huichol call the Spirit *Peyote*. I have some if you would like to try it sometime. But the point is: I think the world of the Spirit beasts lies side by side with ours. Remember our discussion of the Healer's bits of bone? We are separated, kept apart by some barrier I do not understand. One must pass through the portals to move from this world to the next. In the case of the Kala Hi'ki he had to die first. Because he did, he sees out of that world into ours."

"So, they can see us, but we can't see them." Trader nodded. It figured. All of life had rules. "Is that why Power is sending us to Split Sky City? Because we can do what some Spirit cannot?"

"That would be my guess."

"How are we supposed to know what to do?"

Old White glanced at Two Petals. "Ask the Contrary. She sees things we do not. Hears voices beyond our human ears. Through her, they will tell us when the time comes."

Trader nodded, remembering Old White's misinterpretation of the stone and wood statement during the chunkey game. "If we are smart enough to understand."

Old White was nodding off, his eyes half-closed.

Trader yawned. "Time to sleep."

But after he rolled into his robes, his Dreams were troubled. In them, he killed his brother over and over.

———

Two days of freezing rain had left Split Sky City sodden, cold, and miserable. People had huddled around their fires in an effort to avoid stepping out into the cold. Ice had rimed pestles, ramada roofs, and any other object left outside. It had coated the ground, making travel difficult. Finally, the weather had broken, the clouds retreating to the north. At first opportunity, Smoke Shield had called out his Hickory Moiety men.

The Albaamaha councilor called Amber Bead stood at the edge of the plaza and watched the Chikosi war chief berate his warriors as they raced back and forth on the stickball field. Then he glanced up at the sky, seeing the puffy white clouds scudding away. The ice melted, dripping into puddles from thatched roofs and making travel under the trees a nasty endeavor. The Hickory Moiety stickball players were having a miserable time of it, slipping and sliding more than running, catching, and casting. Most of the men were soaked, streaked with grass stains, and splotched with mud.

Mikko Amber Bead was old, nearing fifty winters. He wore an old white hunting shirt, the image of Tailed Man—one of the Albaamaha culture heroes—hanging down over it from a thong on his neck. Faded starburst tattoos could be seen on his withered cheeks. His feet were clad in grass-stuffed moccasins for warmth. That morning he'd pulled his hair up in a conservative bun and pinned it with a turkey-bone awl.

For the last ten winters he had served the southern Albaamaha clans as their voice in the Chikosi Council. Most thought him little more than a Sky Hand lackey, having but a faint idea of the role he played in his people's resistance. Amber Bead liked it that way. As long as the Chikosi considered him to be their little lapdog, he learned things. Most of what he learned he had been able to turn deftly against the conqueror's interests.

"You run like a bunch of women!" Smoke Shield cried in frustration.

"Yes, but the women won," Amber Bead added smugly to himself. He cast a glance back over his shoulder and shook his head. Of course the Hickory warriors were practicing. They'd just lost the most humiliating game in recent memory. Rumor had it that Smoke Shield had bet everything, even down to his shirt, and lost it all. Even his slave, Morning Dew—his prize from the White Arrow Town raid—was now Heron Wing's possession. The very thought of Smoke Shield's loss brought a light-hearted joy to Amber Bead's breast.

Amber Bead tried to see the pattern in all this. One moment Smoke Shield is at the height, and the next, here he is, at the bottom. Rumors were circulating that Flying Hawk had given the man half of his clothes so that he didn't have to appear in public wearing a slave's shirt.

But what did that mean for the future? Fact was, losing a stickball game was of only passing interest. Great wealth was gambled every season on the games. Clans were destitute one season, wealthy the next. It was the flux of things, dictated by Power. Fortunes rose, and in an instant they vanished.

None of it meant that Smoke Shield wouldn't be confirmed as high minko should anything happen to Flying Hawk. That it hadn't yet was either a tribute to Smoke Shield's affection for his uncle—which Amber Bead doubted—or the knowledge that he might face embarrassing questions prior to the Council's approval.

That being the case, just what was Smoke Shield waiting for? He had had only limited success so far in whipping the Council into a fervor against the Albaamaha. When it came to politics, the enemy closest to home was the one you wanted to pick on. The threat was more immediate than, say, blaming the Charokee far off to the northeast.

Amber Bead wound his way through the clutter of houses and out the south gate. He nodded pleasantly to the warrior stationed there, and had almost reached his house when a travel-stained young man stepped out, calling, "Mikko? Could I speak with you?"

Amber Bead noted the mud, the soggy moccasins, and the soaked cape the man wore. The youth had his damp hair in a tight bun, pinned with a wooden skewer. Other than a belt pouch, he carried no other pack.

"Come from far, have you?"

The man nodded, a haggard look about him. "Mikko, I am Bull Fish, of the Bobcat Clan. I come from Bowl Town. My mother is Slick Pole, of the Flat Rock lineage. I have news for your ears only."

Amber Bead wasn't sure, but the man's legs seemed to be trembling. Exhaustion? "Come. My house is this way."

He took the lead, but from the corner of his eye he could see that loose-jointed walk characteristic of an exhausted runner. At his door, he glanced this way and that, ensuring that no one seemed to be paying attention, and gestured young Bull Fish in. The fellow nodded appreciatively and lowered himself by the hearth, extending cold hands to the warm air above the coals.

"If you will give me a moment, I'll add some wood to that. Have you eaten?"

"No, Elder. I came here as fast as I could."

"Just a moment then." Amber Bead tossed some wood on his fire and stepped out the door, using the trip to his niece's house next door as an opportunity to look around and ensure that no one was lingering close to his walls.

After borrowing half a cooked turkey and a bowl of beans, Amber Bead returned, taking a final look around. No one lurked behind the screen of his latrine, or behind the woodpile.

Entering, Amber Bead found his guest gratefully absorbing the fire's heat. Bull Fish looked up, abashed. "Excuse me, Mikko, but I seem to be leaving mud on your floor. I should take these moccasins off."

"Do not worry about the floor. The matting will sweep clean. What's the point of having kin if they can't care for an old man's house? But do take your moccasins off. Use that stone there and prop them so the heat dries them. Meanwhile, eat, and then, when all is well, you can tell me your story."

He watched the young man toss an offering of meat into the fire, and then utter a prayer for the turkey's soul. He did the same for the beans, thanking the Spirit of the plants.

Well, at least he's devout. From Bull Fish's clothes, and the wooden image of Tailed Man that he wore on his necklace, Amber Bead could readily believe he was from Bowl Town. A great many interesting rumors were circulating out of the north these days.

When Bull Fish finished, he tossed final offerings to the fire, smiled weakly, and said, "If I may, great Mikko. Might I use your toilet?"

"Out back." He nodded approval. "Oh, and while you're out there, you might just take one last look around."

Bull Fish hesitated, momentarily confused, then caught his meaning. "Of course."

Amber Bead waited, collecting his thoughts. Something about the young man's manner spoke of great excitement. As if he'd been bursting with news. Ah, well, all in good time.

When Bull Fish reentered, he propped his bare feet before the fire, and sighed. "The food will make me sleepy. I ran all night."

"To tell me what?"

"You have heard the allegations about Red Awl's capture and murder by Smoke Shield?"

"I have." Amber Bead leaned forward. "You must understand, while I do not put such a thing beyond Smoke Shield's capacity for stupidity, it will take more than just producing his weapons and Red Awl's widow standing up to make accusations. We need the body. Some sort of actual proof of the deed."

Bull Fish smiled. "You have heard that Fast Legs was the second warrior?"

"I have, but the mysterious Fast Legs is missing."

"Not anymore." Bull Fish lowered his voice. "We *have* him!"

Amber Bead's heart skipped. "You killed Fast Legs? Gods, if this doesn't play out right that could turn on you like grabbing a cotton-mouth's tail! Who knows of this thing?"

The young man raised a cunning brow. "Elder, please, we are smarter than that. He's alive. Oh, granted, his leg is badly broken, but his black heart is still beating in his chest."

Amber Bead sank to a seat, stunned at the implications. "How did you do this thing?"

"First we set a trap, and then we lured him into it.

Lotus Root was incredibly brave. We let the fool believe he was undiscovered. He even took the food we set aside for him in our granary. The plan was, if nothing else, we'd poison it."

"Where is he now?"

"In a hunter's shack a couple of hands' travel west of Bowl Town. We are taking special precautions, keeping an eye on the Chikosi. If any of them take off to hunt, we'll have plenty of warning. We've made sure that Chief Sun Falcon doesn't suspect a thing."

"Fast Legs didn't consult with him?"

"No." Bull Fish frowned. "That was odd, too. You'd think that he would have gone there, demanded Lotus Root, and had Sun Falcon do his dirty work for him. Sun Falcon is Chief Clan, after all, a cousin to High Minko Flying Hawk. Instead Fast Legs lurked out in the forest like the animal he is."

"There is a reason Sun Falcon wasn't alerted. He knows nothing of this. No one does. Smoke Shield did this against the orders of the Council. Don't you people hear anything up there?"

"Our representative to the Chikosi Council is *dead*, Mikko!"

"Keep your voice down. You are welcome to your passions. I have my own. But that doesn't mean shouting them at the top of your lungs is either smart, or necessary."

The young man looked chastened.

Amber Bead considered. "So, we have War Chief Smoke Shield's bow and arrows, Lotus Root's accusation, and Fast Legs. Better yet, no one knows. The question now is how do we use it all?"

"We sneak our mikkos from up and down the river to see this man, hear the accusation, and inspect the war chief's arrows, that's what. Then, when the time is right, our people storm the Chikosi, and they serve us for a while."

Amber Bead felt the corner of his lip quivering. "Is that how you people see this playing out?"

"Mikko," Bull Fish pleaded, "it is our time! This is a sign, sent by Abba Mikko above, for the Albaamaha to reclaim our land."

"I see. Tell me, has Sun Falcon acted in some atrocious manner in the last couple of moons? Anything I wouldn't have heard about?"

"He's still the same arrogant Chikosi he ever was."

"But he hasn't beaten any of our people? Raped our women after dragging them from their husbands' beds? Hasn't defiled any of our temples?"

"No. He's just arrogant. Thinks we're beneath him. He even has Albaamaha who grovel and go whimpering at his feet. Those people, we tell nothing."

"How many Albaamaha do you know who go groveling?"

"Too many!"

Amber Bead nodded. "Yes, my young friend, and that is exactly the problem. Unlike some Chikosi, Sun Falcon is a just man."

Bull Fish glared up. "We thought you were on our side! Red Awl was the one who constantly called for patience, who wanted to compromise. Look where that got him! We heard you were the one who chafed under the Chikosi burden basket."

Amber Bead fingered his chin, nodding. "Chafe? Oh, yes, I do. Am I willing to undermine the Chikosi at any opportunity? Definitely. Here's the thing you must know: If we strike at the Chikosi, we will be crushed. This is exactly the sort of thing Smoke Shield is hoping for. An Albaamaha revolt would shoot him onto the high minko's stool up there in that palace yonder. It would solidify the Council's support."

"We outnumber them!"

"But they are better warriors."

"We trapped Fast Legs! The fool ran right into it."

"You manipulated one tired man in the forest." Amber Bead raised his hands, stalling any outburst. "I am not your enemy. Do not mistake me. I do not like the Chikosi. I want to see them gone from our country, but that time hasn't arrived. They must be weakened, made vulnerable. We just avoided one calamity; I would not instigate another."

"They are vulnerable. You proved that when you murdered their captives."

"I murdered their captives? Is that the story told up-river?"

"Who else? It is thought that you had Paunch do it. He's missing, isn't he? What better person to sneak in through the fog and drive a knife into the captives' hearts?" '

A cold chill ran down Amber Bead's back. "First, let me make this painfully clear: I had *nothing* to do with the captives' deaths! You must go back and tell everyone who will listen. No Albaamaha had a hand in that action. And it certainly wasn't Paunch! He's out hiding in the forest somewhere because the Chikosi think he had something to do with Crabapple's attempt to warn White Arrow Town of Smoke Shield's raid. Do you understand?"

"Then who did?" Bull Fish seemed perplexed.

Amber Bead sighed, fully aware of the danger he was in. "To the best of my knowledge, the Chahta did it. And, in the end, I fervently hope it was them. Let the Chikosi distract themselves raiding Chahta towns. I need you to make sure that everyone upriver knows it wasn't us. And, in Abba Mikko's sacred name, do not attach my name—or Paunch's—to it in any way."

"Why? It strengthens your position among our people."

"And will get me hung from one of their squares if the Chikosi hear of it." He shook his head. "No, even if I could have done it, I wouldn't. Listen. *Understand.*

The Chikosi consider me to be an old, amenable fool. I make sure they think of me that way. No one suspects the old dog that sleeps by their door to be a wolf. If they blame me for the death of the prisoners, you will get some lackey appointed in my place that will lick their hands, and wag his tail at any Chikosi order that comes along."

"Then why do you resist using Fast Legs against them?"

"I don't. I just can't figure a way to do it right now without getting our people killed." He looked at the perplexed young man. "Don't you see? We need them weakened before we strike."

"Our Albaamaha could take Bowl Town in a single night. We outnumber them. All we have to do is sneak in, unlatch the gate, and kill them in their houses."

"You have planned this?"

Bull Fish nodded. "All we need is approval from the mikkos. And when enough people have heard Lotus Root's story about how Red Awl was killed, we will have it."

By the Ancestors' bones, the man was right. They probably could take Bowl Town. Red Awl had been a respected man there. But what about Wind Town? Chief Buffalo Killer and his Albaamaha depended on each other. How many would side with the rebels? Yes, the Albaamaha could take towns up and down the river, but how could they crack Split Sky City's hard shell? The fact was, they couldn't.

How do I buy time? "Your people are committed to this?"

"We are."

Amber Bead broke out in bitter laughter.

"What do you think is so funny?"

"I have waited all of my life to see our people united against the Chikosi. And now, when the gods have finally granted me my wish, it is at the worst time possible. The joke is a cruel one."

"I see no joke here. We have the means to destroy the Chikosi."

Time. He needed time. That and a convenient miracle. "I need you to take this message back to your leaders: I sit in the Chikosi Council.

I hear things, know things, that they do not. I am in the unique position to know when the Chikosi are the weakest. Will they be willing to wait for word from me before they strike Bowl Town? If they will, I will do what I can to throw the support of the southern Albaamaha to their side. But here is my condition: If you act before the time is right, I will urge the southern mikkos to side with the Chikosi. I will do this not because I do not share your goals, but to save the lives of my people from senseless slaughter."

"You would act against your own people?" Bull Fish cried incredulously.

"I would act *to save my people,* you fool!" Then he lowered his voice. "You have my message."

Bull Fish glared at him through hostile eyes. "I will take that message to my leaders. They will send you an answer by the full moon."

Amber Bead nodded. At least he had some time, but how on earth could he forestall a conflagration and still be rid of the hated Chikosi?

FIVE

WHAT DID *I ever do to offend Power so?* The question rolled around in Paunch's head as he huddled in his damp shirt and nursed the small, smoky fire he had built in a hollow behind an old log. The smoke rose, blue and lazy, to trail off through the trees. Around him the forest dripped and waited, silence only broken by the occasional birdcall and the chatter of an irritated squirrel.

He and his granddaughter, Whippoorwill, had made camp on a ridgetop a day's walk east of the Horned Serpent River. They had chosen this place, a gloomy flat dominated by huge black oak. Around them the great trees rose toward the sky, their high branches interlacing into a weave that allowed but faint light to penetrate to the forest floor. The trunks were huge, many having the diameter of his long-gone house back in Split Sky City. Walking among them left him with the same feelings his Albaamaha Ancestors must have felt when they first emerged from the Below World into this one. For the first time, Paunch could understand their awe and wonder.

He glanced uneasily at the rising smoke, worried that its odor might attract a wandering scout.

"We are far from any of the trails," Whippoorwill told him. "There is no point of vantage here; the forest is old. Power almost sleeps here."

"I wish I could be as sure as you are. How many times have we escaped by a hair's breadth? This country is crawling with scouts. Half of them are Smoke Shield's, looking for any sign of retaliation from the Chahta for the White Arrow Town raid. The other half are Chahta, watching the Chikosi watching them!"

Whippoorwill gave him that eerie, liquid-eyed look that sent his souls scurrying. "You knew the risks when you sent Crabapple off in that foolish attempt to warn the White Arrow. I told you about Dancing close to Death. Are you enjoying the feeling?"

"No." He sighed, rubbing his smudged face with callused hands. "It seemed like such a good idea at the time. If the White Arrow were warned, they would be ready for Smoke Shield and his warriors. They could have crushed him, taken the Chikosi war medicine, and dealt the Sky Hand a blow from which they would never recover. Weakened, we could have won our freedom."

The faintest of smiles bent her full lips. "You knew nothing of freedom. But I think you have found the faintest hint of understanding." She spread her arms in a movement so delicate it reminded him of swans' necks. "Here it is, Grandfather. Freedom. No man stands over you with a war club telling you what to do. I see no Chikosi here to bully you or seize your food."

"There's no food to seize."

"Ah, freedom has already lost its luster. And you are but so recently free."

He rubbed his face harder. She'd always been such an odd child. "Why aren't you home, married, with a child on your hip?"

"I am betrothed."

He stared at her through slits in his fingers. "Curious. I don't remember that. Every time we've approached a solid young man's family, either he, or you, has said no. Usually, he says it so quickly you don't have a chance." She was such an attractive young woman, tall, with long black hair that fell to her waist. When she passed, young men cast envious glances at her full bust, long legs, and round hips. Her face was nicely formed, with high cheeks and a tall forehead. She had a perfectly lush mouth and delicate nose. But all it took was a single glance into her large dark eyes and any man worth spit would turn around and run. Whippoorwill's eyes always reflected midnight, as from seeing into worlds that no human wished to view.

"My husband will come."

"Along with this mysterious sister you talk about?" He shook his head and dropped his hands in defeat. "You have no sister. Your mother died just after you were born. The way you talk, it sends shivers down my spine." A large cold drop of water spattered on his back as it fell from the melting ice in the trees. He flinched at the impact. "As if I didn't have enough to shiver from. I just want to go home."

"The Chikosi will not have forgotten you."

"I know." He stared glumly at the forest giants around them. "Thank the Ancestors for Amber Bead's warning. But for him, I'd be dead now. They'd have hung me in a square." He winced at the very thought. "And I'd have told them everything. Amber Bead would be dead, as would you and the rest of my line. Our people would have been made to suffer. All for me."

"Power isn't finished with you, Grandfather."

"Saw that in your Vision, did you?" He recalled the day he'd made her Dance with Sister Datura and scry the future in a well pot. Looking into the depths of the bowl, she'd seen something that she refused to relate to him. Odd as she was, she'd been even odder after that day.

"Then tell me, how much longer do we have to scurry around out here? Will I ever see home again?"

"Oh, yes, Grandfather. You shall even be there before I am." She smiled, the effect eerie in her young face.

"All we have to do is survive the Chahta. Then, after we meet my sister, you shall be headed home."

"What about you?"

"I'll come. But only after I swim down to find the dead."

"Dead? What dead?" By the Ancestors, he dreaded it when she said things like this.

But she didn't answer. Instead her eyes were fixed on an opening between the gigantic trees.

"What do you see?"

"The black wolf," she whispered softly. "He has just dropped by to assure me that all is well."

But try as he might, Paunch could see no wolf on the empty leaf mat.

SIX

GROWING OLD CAME AT A PRICE. High Minko Flying Hawk considered that as he dressed in his room. His bones and joints ached, and over the last couple of years, old injuries—like the one in his left knee—had grown progressively worse. Now, on cold mornings, he could hear bone grating in his knee when he stood.

His fingers had lost their dexterity, and the mere act of tying his apron around his waist was clumsy. Nevertheless, he straightened it and cinched it snugly to his thickening hips. Next he wound his hair behind his head, fixing the thunder-arrow copper headpiece with its pin. That came from long practice. His thick gray hair had to be wound tightly, just so, to support the weight.

Finally, he draped a cougar hide over his shoulders and picked up his turkey-tail mace. Made of chipped stone, then polished to a gleam, the thing was heavy. So many of the trappings of authority grew burdensome with time. Just like the weight of responsibility that caused a droop in his shoulders. His confirmation as high minko, or supreme chief of the Sky Hand, had been ten winters past. In that time, he had fought both to control his notorious rages and to manage his people. Through it all, he'd struggled to shape Smoke Shield to follow him.

He passed Smoke Shield's room, and gave it a sidelong glance. Would the man never come to his senses?

What kind of fool—especially a potential leader—bet everything on a stickball game when he hadn't managed to get his team together for regular practice? Even Smoke Shield had to understand that Power was watching, ready to reward those who followed its ways.

Yes, but he had the White Arrow Town raid to plan and execute. That, at least, Smoke Shield had done brilliantly. Still, had he been more interested in Power and drawing it to his aid instead of wetting his shaft in a new slave woman, perhaps he wouldn't have gambled away all of his possessions.

The fact that Flying Hawk had divested himself of his own clothing to replace what Smoke Shield had lost prickled like bull nettle under his skin. And what had become of Smoke Shield's comely Chahta slave? He'd lost her to Heron Wing! His wife, of all people! Gods, that story was told with amusement around many fires.

He will come around. I did. Yes, he thought with a sigh, his nephew just needed to feel the weight of responsibility for his people. Then he would understand. When Smoke Shield's selfish drive had to act for the people's good instead of his own, it would all come together.

Carrying his stone mace, he stepped into the great room and found Sun Falcon Mankiller waiting for him. The Bowl Town chief stood, hands behind his back, his eyes on the Seeing Hand carving that hung behind the three-legged stool.

The sight of the carving brought a shiver to Flying Hawk. But a handful of nights past, he'd walked out after a terrible nightmare and seen a tear streaking down from the corner of the great eye that filled the palm. Even now he could see a slight stain, as if the wood had discolored along the tear's track.

Did it weep for my people?

"Greetings, old friend." Flying Hawk shook it off and walked forward, clasping the chief's elbow. "I must admit, seeing my cousin so soon after the solstice comes as a surprise. What is so important that it brings you in person instead of a messenger?"

Flying Hawk seated himself painfully on the stool, wishing he had another cougar hide to cushion his old bones. The cool stone mace rested heavily on his lap. With a tingle in his spine, he was painfully aware of the Seeing Eye in the hand relief behind him.

Sun Falcon touched his forehead in respect and looked around. "Are we alone, High Minko?"

"Only my slave was here. When he told me you had arrived, I sent him to fetch suitable food. Some of our hunters found a bear denned up in the top of a hollow standing tree. They set fire to it and shot the bear as he crawled out. The meat is excellent. It will be heated and brought here."

"And the war chief?"

"Off to some purpose or other." Flying Hawk gave Sun Falcon a weary grin. "He dislikes the jokes made about his team's performance in the recent games."

Sun Falcon's expression didn't change. "Then he is not close by?"

"I could send for him if you wish?"

"No, for the moment let us just talk."

"Then I am your willing audience." He paused. "Do we need black drink, or perhaps the pipe?"

"No." Sun Falcon paused, as if suddenly unsure of himself. "High Minko, what do you know about the disappearance of Red Awl?"

"Not much. Only that he was called home, but never arrived. Since then I have heard stories, most of them wildly speculative, but nothing with any meat on the bones. I remember your concerns at the solstice Council. You were concerned about relations with the Albaamaha."

Sun Falcon lowered his voice. "Were there any special instructions, things that perhaps a high minko would have wished to accomplish without either the Council or the chiefs' knowledge?"

Flying Hawk frowned, his unease growing. "Very delicately put. May I ask why?"

"You know our position in the north. Chief Buffalo Killer and I are both on the frontier with the Yuchi. Any raiders coming down from the north, be they Yuchi, Charokee, or Shawnee, will attack us first. Because of that, we have somewhat closer relations with our Albaamaha. When raiders come, we are their shield."

"And they your eyes and ears." Flying Hawk nodded. "I am well aware."

"Because of our codependence, our relationships with the Albaamaha are different from those down here, closer to Split Sky City."

"Spit it out, Sun Falcon. I'd think you were negotiating a marriage."

"Mikko Red Awl was chosen to represent the north in the tchkofa Council because he had a basic understanding of our mutual problems. He was fully aware of the threats we face, and that we needed to work together for the betterment of both of our peoples." Sun Falcon looked up. "I need to know if you sent Smoke Shield and Fast Legs to waylay him for some purpose. If you did, I will understand."

Flying Hawk shifted on his stool. "I sent Smoke Shield on no such mission. I know he was obsessed with the death of the captives, but the Council and I were specific in our instructions that no action should be taken against the Albaamaha. We decided to wait, watch, and learn before we pursued anything." He paused. "Are you telling me different?"

Sun Falcon took a nervous breath. "One of my Albaamaha — a man I trust, and who trusts me — came to me yesterday morning. You have heard the rumor about Red Awl's widow, Lotus Root, supposedly having Smoke Shield's weapons? You have heard that she claims that Smoke Shield and Fast Legs took her and her husband prisoner? The story is that they tortured Red Awl, trying to make him reveal the names of the traitors who sent the Albaamo Crabapple to warn White Arrow Town. Have you also heard he demanded to know the name of the Albaamaha who killed the captives?"

"Something, yes. But I thought them nothing more than rumors." He felt a tightening in his chest.

"My informant tells me that the Albaamaha suspected that Fast Legs was stalking Lotus Root outside Bowl Town. He also tells me that they laid a trap for him." Sun Falcon swallowed hard. "High Minko, if my informant is correct, the Albaamaha have captured Fast Legs. Alive."

Flying Hawk stared in shocked disbelief. Captured Fast Legs? Impossible! No Albaamaha would dare! They...No, he knew his cousin. This wasn't some wild story.

"Smoke Shield would not have done such a thing. I was *clear* about the Council's decision regarding the slain captives. He told me he understood that."

"But not about finding the Albaamaha traitors?"

Flying Hawk closed his eyes, a sudden sense of desolation within. "No. I told him they were his to hunt down."

Sun Falcon reached out frantically. "And he suspected Red Awl, of all people?" The chief took a deep breath. "If he did this thing, High Minko, he has poured coals on dry kindling. From the moment of Lotus Root's return, my Albaamaha have retreated to their villages.

People who once nodded when they passed me now look away, a darkness in their eyes." He paced uneasily back and forth. "The next thing I hear is that they have captured Fast Legs, that he was stalking Lotus Root....Gods, this could burn out of control."

"If this thing with Red Awl actually happened," Flying Hawk corrected. "Smoke Shield knows the ramifications of such a rash action. He wouldn't have crossed me and the Council this way."

Sun Falcon stopped short, staring back over his shoulder. "The war chief had gone hunting, hadn't he? Wasn't that the story? And when he returned without his weapons, without his cape, wasn't there some story about having them stolen in the forest?"

Flying Hawk narrowed an eye. "Would you call my nephew a liar?"

Sun Falcon stiffened, but said, "And that scab on his lip? He claimed to have fallen during the hunt, but the joke was that one of his women must have bitten him."

"Enough!"

Sun Falcon drew a deep breath, meeting Flying Hawk's hard stare. "High Minko, if there is so much as a cast-off nutshell of truth in this, we have a problem."

Flying Hawk fought down the old rage. Once, years ago, he would have thrown the man out, ordered him away and told him never to return until he had a civil tongue in his mouth. Now he forced himself to breathe easily, to keep the tremble out of his hands.

Taking his time, he said softly, "You find Fast Legs, wherever they've hidden him. You find him, and get him back. No matter what has happened, one of my warriors has been taken. That is unacceptable."

Sun Falcon gave him an unwavering stare. "I will do what I can, High Minko. Who knows what Fast Legs will have told the Albaamaha? If the stories are true about what they did to Red Awl, I'm not sure Fast Legs wouldn't have been subjected to the same treatment. In the meantime, I would appreciate any warriors you could send my way. I would like them to sweep up from the south, searching the woods as they come. Any excursion from Bowl Town will be observed, and warning will be given. They'll have moved him by the time my warriors even get close."

"I shall have warriors in the forest by morning. Keep as many as you need to secure your town. Feed them from the Albaamaha's stores." He pointed his mace at Sun Falcon. "Whatever happens, don't you dare let any of the Albaamaha overrun your town until we get there."

"Not while I'm alive," he answered. "If you will excuse me, High Minko, I think I had better be getting back."

"You are excused." He sat with closed eyes, not even bothering to look as Sun Falcon strode out of the room. *Smoke Shield, tell me you have not done this thing.*

Moments later, a slave entered bearing steaming plates of bear meat and sweetened corn gruel. Flying Hawk, however, no longer had an appetite.

SEVEN

THE AIR inside the sweat lodge was close, dark, and hot with steam. Smoke Shield reached into the water bowl and cast droplets onto the hot rocks. After two days of hard play, his team was beginning to look like more than a bunch of overgrown boys with racquets. The passing was better and catches were made with grace instead of looking like a poor attempt at swatting mosquitoes.

Why couldn't they have looked this good in the game?

The problem was that Fast Legs was still missing. Obviously he had hidden Red Awl's body successfully. The Albaamaha would have combed that entire area as surreptitiously as possible at their first opportunity. Smoke Shield would have heard rumors of the wailing and funeral processions. At least Fast Legs had done that much. So, why...?

"Smoke Shield?" his uncle's stern voice called from outside. "Are you there?"

Smoke Shield made a face. How often in the past had he heard *that* tone in the old man's voice? Now, what? Another lecture about how the wise always kept a little something in reserve in case Power didn't favor them that day?

He sighed, collected himself, and stepped out into the cold day. It only took a glance to see that this was more than a gambling lecture. "What's wrong?"

"Red Awl," Flying Hawk said coldly. "Do you wish to become high minko someday, or just remain a buffoon for the rest of your life?"

He felt his heart begin to pound. "Do not call me a buffoon, Uncle. Buffoons don't take towns like White Arrow without losing a warrior."

"Fast Legs has been captured by the Albaamaha. They are holding him somewhere outside of Bowl Town. At least that's Sun Falcon's guess. It seems our Fast Legs was trying to kill Lotus Root. You remember her? The Albaamo woman who bit you on the lip while you were warming your ridiculous throbbing shaft inside her?"

Smoke Shield's heart began to hammer. *Fast Legs, you stupid imbecile!*

"I want this taken care of," Flying Hawk said, glancing toward the Men's House to see who was within earshot.

"I will call the tishu minko, have him cry for the warriors and—"

"No." Flying Hawk gestured at the Men's House. "How many of your stickball players are in there? From the sound of it, nearly all?"

"Perhaps twenty."

"Take them. Now. Cross the river and start up the west bank. As you reach Basswood Creek, spread them out. You need to sweep the entire forest like a game drive. Find Fast Legs, get him back, and kill the people holding him. Do it efficiently, mercilessly, and quickly. As soon as you do, find a way of disposing of the bodies. Bury them, burn them, sink them in the river. I don't care. But I don't want any evidence left behind. Then, when you are done, you leave as many warriors as Sun Falcon requires in Bowl Town."

"But I can't—"

"You could start this mess; now you can finish it." He leveled the mace. "And if you cannot do this thing, and do it with the same brilliance you showed at White Arrow Town, I will tell the Council everything. How you ignored their will and spurned the direct orders of your high minko. Do not cross me this time, because by the blood of my brother, I will *ruin* you!"

Flying Hawk turned, stalking back toward the Great Mound.

Smoke Shield stood stupidly, a slow resentment beginning to burn in his chest. He stomped into the Men's House, seeing his warriors lounging, smoking, dipping food from the pot of mashed beans and smilax root. "Get dressed. Get your weapons. We have work to do."

"What work?" Greenbriar asked. "I was thinking we did pretty well today."

"The Albaamaha are on the verge of revolt at Bowl Town. They have taken Fast Legs captive and are torturing him. I have just received our orders from the high minko. There is no time."

He stared at their stunned faces, some holding food only halfway to their mouths.

"I said now," he barked. *"Move!"*

———

The camp was a good one, as was indicated by the broken pottery, the ash-stained soil, and the old fired rock from countless hearths before theirs. The canoes were pulled up above flood stage if it rained hard upstream. Most of the grass had been mashed flat in the months since it had gone dormant in fall. Firewood necessitated a bit of a hike into the forest, but could be had for the taking once past the scavenged area.

The waterway consisted of a narrow winding channel that was deeply cut into the yellow soil. Most of the route was overhung with trees, branches, and vines. But as the major link between the Tenasee and Horned

Serpent Rivers, enough traffic moved through that most of the offending logs, branches, and shrubbery had been cut away.

Trader looked back at the low hut they had constructed for the Contrary.

"You two men are different," she had told them. "You have no need to fear a woman's moon. But I do."

That had been uttered no more than a moment after the last of the Yuchi had waved and vanished on the path leading back over the divide to the place where they had stashed their canoes.

The parting had almost been sad, the Yuchi lingering, offering advice, fingering the pieces of shell, bits of copper, and Oneota figurines they had been given for their service. Each would have been more than happy to have labored for days without compensation, just to have the honor of saying they had helped the Seeker, the Contrary, and Trader make the journey up to the winding headwater. Then they had worked like slaves to portage the heavy packs and canoes the hard day's travel over the divide trail.

After making sure the canoes would float, Trader had led the way here, to this streamside camp. Once sure it would fit their needs, they had lashed the fallen walls of a hut together, and covered it for the Contrary's privacy.

"So," Trader asked Old White, "do you fear a woman's moon?"

He shrugged. "Must be something to it. A great many people have ways to avoid it." He paused. "On the other hand, I've been amongst folk who could care less. They never seem to sicken or be tainted by it. I have heard women say that they enjoy it. It's their free time when they don't need to fuss over babies, cook for the men, or do hard work. Instead they can sit inside, catch up on the news with friends, and do whatever makes them happy."

Trader placed his pipe stem between his lips. "That may be. I think I'd worry though. Even if I didn't believe it, I'd still be suspicious."

"You were raised with the notion. It becomes part of the souls the way a log is part of a wall. No matter what, you will always believe that a woman's Power is separate, distinct, and in opposition to a man's. It always goes back to the white and the red. A man's semen is white, the color of order and harmony. The woman's blood is red, the color of chaos and creation. The two major Powers of life, always sawing back and forth in an attempt to find balance."

"And you, Seeker? You were raised believing that, too?"

Old White smiled faintly. "Yes, even when among the peoples who don't pay any attention to a woman's monthly cycle, I still get the soul shakes."

"How many peoples have you known? Did you keep track?"

"Too many to count," he said. "And you get out along the western ocean, there's a different people in every bend of the creek. Good country, too. Food everywhere, just for the picking up. Climate's nice. No winter until you get up north. The mountains run right down and drown themselves in the sea. Beautiful land. People there live in towns like we do, but they fish, go out on the ocean and hunt whales, seals, walrus."

"Whales I've heard of. What are the others?"

Trader sat rapt as Old White tried to explain, then drew the beasts in the dirt with a stick.

"They could be like our Spirit monsters." Trader gestured with his pipe. "Perhaps that's where some of our legends come from."

"Perhaps," Old White agreed. "But unlike your Horned Serpent, they don't crave copper." A pause. "Yes, I've seen some amazing things. Way up in the Western Mountains, I've crossed ridges with oyster shells cropping out of the rocks. Way up there, higher than any mountain you've ever seen, and a half year's walk from the ocean. Oyster shell. The peoples who live there were as baffled by an oyster as you are by a seal."

"You've led a wonderful life, Seeker."

The old man shrugged it off. "A lonely one at times." He glanced down at his feet, wiggling them in his moccasins. "These have carried me farther than any living man. Some of it was glorious, some downright miserable." He tapped his carved wooden pack box. "I keep my memories in here."

"Do you do that with some incantation?"

Old White smiled wistfully. "No. And if anything ever happens to me, I entrust the box, and the memories, to you."

Memories in a box? Trader sucked on his pipe. He didn't think so. All those marvelous things were locked away in Old White's head. And if he was right about going home to die, who would ever know the stories, sights, and places locked in the old man's souls? No one, at least not until a person died and found Seeker's ghost in the Land of the Dead. Even then there would be such a collection of souls around Seeker that it wouldn't be worth the effort to fight the crowd in order to hear the stories.

"Have you given any thought to what we're going to do when we reach the Chaktaw?" Old White used the Yuchi pronunciation of the name.

"Depend on the Power of Trade, I guess. Why wouldn't they honor it?"

Old White pointed at Trader's face. "You have the markings of a Chief Clan tattoo on your face."

"It was never finished. I killed my brother before they could complete the job."

"It still says Chief Clan."

"I'm just Trader." He stared at the fire. "If anyone questions it, I'll talk about my time among the Natchez. About Trade up the Father Water. It's not like they can trick me by asking questions about local politics. I don't even know who the clan chiefs are these days."

Old White arched an eyebrow in acceptance. "What about when we reach home?"

"What were you thinking?"

Old White stared at the fire. "I was thinking we'd just be ordinary Traders. Camp out below the palisade, listen to the gossip. No one will know me." He glanced at Trader. "They might not even know you. You told me you're not an identical twin, and ten summers have surely changed you. The sun has left you darker; the weather has aged your face." He paused. "Thing is, but for the tattoos, we'd pull it off smartly."

"I'll give some thought to explaining the tattoos. I've seen the like over most of the country. The cheek bar, the forked eye. As you noted so aptly, mine was never finished with the intricacies that make the Chief Clan tattoo so distinctive."

"Learned the design from Cahokia," Old White noted. "A long time ago. Maybe it won't be an issue. Maybe tell them you got it among the Caddo."

"I speak pretty good Caddo."

"After we're there for a while, if it seems wise, maybe we'll have the tishu minko call the Council. By then, assuming that no one recognizes you, Bullfrog Pipe will have delivered his message. We'll have a feel for how your message has taken root. Then, when the Council rituals are done, we'll tell the entire story. We can give them something to talk about for a long time to come."

They would indeed. He glanced at the war medicine box, and thought about the copper it contained. *We'll both leave them talking.*

"Split Sky City is a big place. It'll be pretty easy to disappear into the crowd. If my return is the talk of the place, we can take steps to avoid anyone recognizing me." Trader shot a sidelong look at Old White. "You're Chief Clan, too. What if someone recognizes you?"

"They won't. It was a long time ago.".

"Why have I never heard of you?"

"Because I'm dead." Old White smiled at Trader's expression. "At least that's what everybody thinks." He glanced at his heavy fabric bag, a thoughtful expression on his face.

"But you never got tattooed."

"Wasn't there that long. I was just a boy."

"Stolen?" Trader asked. "You were captured in a raid?"

Old White stretched. "I think I'll turn in."

"You're not going to tell, are you?"

"No. Not yet."

"Will you tell me why?"

Old White stared absently at his feet. "Part of the deal I made with Power once. That, I think, you can understand." He glanced at Trader. "I learned some things in Rainbow City. I think you're in for a surprise, too. But that's another thing I think Power wants you to find out on your own."

"What surprise?"

"Oh, you'll find out when we get there."

———

Smoke Shield looked at the score of warriors who crouched around the fire. Each and every one had been part of the White Arrow Town raid. He could see the admiration in their eyes as they watched him. It vied with the worry and disquiet that had accompanied their rapid departure from Split Sky City. He had allowed them to speak to no one—not even wives or family. Some feral instinct had led Smoke Shield to order his warriors out by ones and twos, each with the story that they were headed out in different directions to hunt. Each had been told to wear hunting clothes, to carry their war clubs and shields sacked, so as to elicit no undue comment.

The rendezvous was here, at Tie Snake Spring. Little more than a seep, the spring lay under a ridge in a recessed bowl eroded out of the exposed sandstone. The trickle of water was home to a stand of tall oak, hickory, and beech. In the sheltered bottom, he had built a great fire and waited for his warriors to assemble. As they listened, he outlined the plan that had come to him as he had trotted, fuming, up the trail.

No, this wasn't a punishment as Flying Hawk had intended, but an opportunity. Power had practically breathed the plan into his souls.

He paced before the flames, studying each man. They waited, fully aware that something big was happening.

"Do you trust me?" he asked, worried that he might have shaken any faith they had in him during the solstice stickball game.

One by one, they nodded.

"Good," he told them. "Because I am the man who led you to

victory at White Arrow Town. I am the man who planned and executed the attack."

"War Chief?" Bear Paw asked.

Smoke Shield turned to the wide-faced burly warrior. "Yes?"

"Is it true that the Albaamaha have taken Fast Legs?"

"It is. He was on the trail of the man who killed the captives." He added, "Your captives, taken at White Arrow Town." Now, to lay the seeds of his plan. "These are dangerous times, my friends. The Albaamaha are cunning. You all witnessed their perfidy when we captured the traitor, Crabapple, and made him divulge how he would have led us into disaster. You have felt the burn of Albaamaha treachery when you looked upon the dead captives, robbed away from us by a sneaking Albaamaha plot. In you, and you alone, I can confide what Fast Legs and I discovered."

He measured their response, seeing frowns and uncertainty coupled with curiosity. "What we are about to do must be done with great care and caution." He pressed his palms together, as if in stern deliberation. "What would happen if we attacked the Albaamaha outright?"

"They would rise in revolt," Three Scalps said softly.

"Correct." Smoke Shield smiled. "So here is what the high minko has ordered us to do. We are to sweep north as if in a game drive. In the process, we are to find and free Fast Legs. Now, if we do this as Sky Hand warriors, it will inflame the Albaamaha even more. We will play into the hands of the malcontents, drive them to irrational action, and have a major uprising on our hands."

"So, what do we do?" Bear Paw looked perplexed.

"You all have seen Chahta arrows? You have seen how they dress?"

All around the fire, warriors nodded.

"For this action we shall become Chahta. We shall paint our arrows in their colors. Wear our hair in their style, and paint our faces in their triangular designs. When we leave a corpse behind, it shall be under their sign, carved into a tree. A few survivors will be allowed to escape, and they will carry the word that it was Great Cougar, the Chahta war chief, who has made this raid." He looked around. "When we attack, each man is to affect the Chahta accent. Slur your words the way they do. Speak disparagingly of the Sky Hand."

He noted the surprise, unease building behind their expressions.

"Oh, yes, I see your hesitation. You think that by doing this, you will spurn the Power of our ways, anger your Ancestors. But think about this: In the end, we strengthen ourselves! Do you believe that Power is so simple it does not recognize the ruse? Do you think for a moment that our souls are not shining and pure in our motives? I tell you, yes, they are! By the cunning of our plan, we shall stand out, attract Power to our cause with the results we achieve!"

Some were nodding to themselves.

"Think of it! We will deal the Albaamaha a blow! Shake their confidence in themselves, remind them who keeps the wolves from their doors! At the same time, we eliminate the discontents, behead their leadership, and clear the way for war against the Chahta in the Council. Once the Albaamaha are cowed, desperately seeking our protection, we can strike with our full might against the Chahta. Once we have broken them, they, too, shall be as the Albaamaha." He thumped his chest. "Servants! Yes, I say servants. They shall toil in their fields and pay us tribute! We shall rule the Horned Serpent River Valley. And you, my fine champions, shall see your relatives sitting atop their mounds."

He could see the gleam that had come to their eyes as they imagined it. Each and every one had lost a relative at some time in the past to Chahta warriors. If he could lead them to believe that retribution could be had for all past slights, and offer them the hope of greater prestige, they would be his.

"That is the future...if we can pull off this charade. But it will be difficult. When we strike the Albaamaha we will only attack isolated farmsteads and ambush individuals out away from their villages. You must show no mercy, remembering instead Crabapple and his treason. The lives you take in the next couple of days will save hundreds of others. You are forestalling a revolt. You must keep that in mind. By killing a few Albaamaha, you are removing the risk to your families, your kin, and clans."

He turned slowly, meeting their eyes, one by one. "Are you brave enough? Do you have the hearts to make this come true? Can you, great Sky Hand warriors, act like Chahta for just two days? Can you convince yourselves enough to convince the Albaamaha that they are being killed by Chahta warriors?"

One by one, they nodded, expressions set with resolve.

"Then let's get about it. You all have your paints; it is time we become Chahta. Then, when this is all finished, we will share our people's rage over this terrible incursion into our territory." He gave them a grim smile. "Do this thing, prepare the hearts and minds of our people, and I shall lead you all to the greatest glory. In the end, we shall rule as did the great lords of Cahokia."

They were nodding to each other. Yes, they believed him.

The Albaamaha shall rue this day!

Paunch was asleep, Dreaming of steaming dishes of pumpkin and sweet squash. He was sitting at home, in his tight little house, a fire crackling before him. To one side, a freshly roasted turkey had been browned in the fire; the aroma of the meat carried to his nostrils.

"They are coming," Whippoorwill's voice intruded.

Paunch stared down at the feast, but each time he tried to reach out, his arms might have been made of stone. Try as he might, it took all of his effort just to lift his arm, and when he did, it rose ever so slowly, as if stuck in thick pitch.

"You had better wake up. It's time," Whippoorwill's voice intruded again.

Paunch blinked, his mouth awash in saliva.

The cold leached back into his body, masked by the pleasure of the Dream. He could sense the pangs in his belly, as insistent now as they'd been when he struggled to reach those tantalizing dishes.

He groaned, rolled over in his filthy cape, and stared out at the morning. Their camp lay on a rise, just below the crest of a low ridge. They had moved here, closer to the Horned Serpent River, figuring on robbing isolated Chahta fish traps. Morning sun lanced through the high branches, indicating the time was just after sunrise. Somewhere an ivory-billed woodpecker hammered a staccato against resistant wood.

"Did you say something?" He glanced at Whippoorwill. She sat, back straight, hands neatly in her lap. Her long hair hung down to frame her oval face. She had a faint smile on her lips, a Dreamy look in her large eyes.

"They are coming," she replied simply. "It is time."

"They who? Time for what?" When she went eerie on him like this, it set his nerves on edge.

"What we've been waiting for."

He stared at her. "Waiting for? I've been waiting to go home! I'm cold to the bone, hungry like I've never been, and my joints hurt. I'm starting to believe the Chikosi square would come as a relief. It would be painful, sure, but they'd feed me until it came time to die."

"You will eat soon enough."

He growled to himself and sat up. His hair was full of sticks and bits of leaves. Their fire had burned down to white ash. He mumbled to himself and reached for the small gourd they kept water in.

After gulping the cold liquid, he stood, shivered, and stretched. "I don't see how you can sit there so calmly after all we've been through." Then her words sank in. "Who's coming?"

"Sitting calmly is the best way to wait," she told him simply. "They are already here. All around us."

"Yes, right." He walked over to the edge of their small camp, pulled up his shirt, and reached behind his breechcloth. He sighed as he urinated behind a fallen log. "All around us." What could that mean? He stared out at the forest, surprised to catch movement out of the corner of his eye.

He squinted, rubbed his eyes, and stared harder. His sharpening vision was enough to make out a partial face, one eye peering past the bole of a tree.

"Someone's out there," he said nervously, refastening his clothing and ducking down. "We've got to go."

"That is correct," she told him in a knowing voice. "They're here. If you run, they'll kill you."

"Who?" He peeked over the log to find a Chahta warrior peering back at him. "By Abba Mikko! They've found us."

"Just surrender. It will be all right." She was perfectly composed as she said, "They smelled the fire."

"Gods, do you know what they'll *do* to us?"

She nodded serenely. "Of course. I've seen it all."

"What? When?"

"When this all started. Come, gather your things and let's walk out to meet them. Do not resist."

"Blood and muck!" He felt something sink down in his empty gut. As he stared this way and that, he could see other warriors, each creeping forward, wary, arrows nocked in their bows.

"We give up!" he cried, raising his hands high. "We're not armed.

We're just…just out hunting!" With no weapons? How did he explain that?

He stood, scared like he had never been. Watching as the warriors closed in around them. To his dismay, Whippoorwill just smiled, as if nothing in the whole world was going terribly wrong.

EIGHT

SMOKE SHIELD LOOKED BACK at the soft soil. His tracks stood out perfectly as he left the collapsed remains of the Albaamaha farmstead. He could see the woman's body, sprawled half out of the doorway, her dead arms reaching for the corpse of her little girl. The child lay where he'd struck her down, the back of her head caved in from the blow of his war club.

On either side, one of his warriors trotted, eyes searching the forest for additional prey. They did look like Chahta, their hair up in the side-sitting bun affected by the enemy. Their painted faces were done up in the Chahta pattern of red and black. Painting the arrows to resemble the Chahta's had been easy. Restitching their moccasins was a little more time-consuming, but the tracks looked right, and would have fooled him had he found them on a forest trail.

Smoke Shield's advantage—as he'd laid it out to his warriors— was that they knew the lay of the land, and how to approach the isolated farmsteads. That knowledge allowed him and his warriors to avoid the commonly traveled trails, to sneak through the thick patches of forest, and to remain unseen.

He'd seen the resistance in Bear Paw's eyes the first time they'd chanced upon a lone Albaamo man. Killing him had gone against the grain, but once that first one fell and they took his scalp, the subsequent killings had been easier. The added advantage lay in the

Albaamaha's belief that Sky Hand scouts would have given a warning had a raid been imminent. None of their victims was suspecting a thing.

He had ordered no farms to be burned and wanted no smoke to give away their location. Others would stumble upon the dead soon enough. Hopefully, by the time the alarm was raised, it would be behind them, long after the fact.

He saw it all in his mind, as if he were Eagle, looking down upon the land. Four separate parties of five were moving north, attacking farmsteads, then hurrying on after taking scalps and mutilating the dead. Speed was essential.

His warriors would loop wide around Thunder and Burned Wood Towns, keeping to the forest and seldom-used trails. Similarly, they avoided the hamlets where numerous Albaamaha lived, having no hope of overcoming that many people in such a short time.

"Minimize the risk of discovery," he had told his men. "Strike and run! We want to be well ahead of pursuit. Remember that the alarm will be raised at any moment. Pursuit will be coming behind us, and these are our people—Sky Hand warriors motivated to find the intruders. You know their hearts as well as I do. Our only hope is to be ahead of them, to have time to become Sky Hand again before we finally meet up with them."

And that was the beauty of it all. No one would ever know. In the confusion, his warriors would look as if they, too, were searching for the Chahta.

But that was later, after they had finished their sweep. After they had found Fast Legs, and rescued him from his tormentors.

They took one of ours! The knowledge festered like a deep splinter. It drove him onward, fueled his rage at each Albaamaha farmstead. After all these years, had the Albaamaha learned nothing of Sky Hand vengeance?

He trotted on. Another farmstead lay just past this belt of trees. The place had been built at the edge of the fields, easy to approach. As he glimpsed it through the boles, he smiled. Smoke was rising from the fire out front. He could see a man, a woman, and three or four children. The woman was pounding corn in her mortar, the pestle rising and falling in time to a rhythmic thump, thump, thump.

He broke from the trees, with Bear Paw and Lightning Arrow on either side. The dogs began to bark, but by then he was racing around the house, his bow drawn. They had no chance.

———

The journey down from the hills had been difficult in places. Trader, Old White, and Two Petals periodically had to step out and wade, dragging the canoes through shallows, until the channel deepened. But as the terrain opened into swampy bottoms, the route had grown easier. Now, with the confluence of several streams, they had both current and enough draft to make the descent into the Horned River Valley easy. The soils here had taken on a yellow hue where they were exposed in the river bank.

Trader leaned his head back, drawing the familiar scent of the swamplands into his nostrils. Beyond the trees and backwaters, the gum, bald cypress, and tupelo gave way to oak and hickory.

They passed the first small Chahta farmstead, waving and calling greetings as they passed. Old White had made sure to hold his staff high, the white feathers waving. Despite calls to make land and Trade, they passed on, leaving the disappointed family staring after them.

"Well, we passed the first Chaktaw," Old White called. "No one's shot at us yet."

Trader grunted, glancing at Swimmer. "And to think we were worried about the Yuchi." He shrugged as he took a stroke with his paddle. "You think we should have at least stopped for news?"

"I suspect we'll find out soon enough," Old White responded. "What do you think, Two Petals?"

She didn't react where she sat, facing backward in Old White's canoe.

"Hey, Contrary!" Trader called. "Are we headed for bad times among the Chaktaw?"

"The worst," she replied. "It will all be so simple." She glanced his way. "They think he's in two places, you know."

Trader scowled at Swimmer. "Now that was a big help. He's in two places? Which ones?"

Swimmer gave him a knowing look before he deigned to lift himself up on one of the packs and scratch at a persistent flea.

Evidence of settlement continued to grow. Here and there they passed lines of sticks protruding from the water where fish weirs had been constructed. An occasional canoe was pulled high on the bank next to trails that led into the forest, probably to farmsteads built farther back, where the soils were better for growing corn.

At midday, they rounded a bend and almost ran full-tilt into a canoe carrying two young men. Swimmer barked happily, his tail wagging as he sniffed at the air, trying to suss out the newcomers. After fending off a collision, Trader called, "Greetings!" in Mos'kogee tongue.

"Greetings yourself!" one of the youths replied. looking them over with interest. "You are Traders?"

"That we are ...from the far north by way of the Father Water to the Tenasee. We are in Chaktaw lands, correct?"

The second youth nodded. "You have been in the north. The proper pronunciation is Chahta. I am Crawfish and this is Bobwhite. We live near here." He cocked his head. "You speak our language well, but with an accent."

Trader nodded, glancing at Old White, who had nosed his canoe close. Two Petals seemed oblivious.

"It's been a long time. I'm out of practice."

"How far to the next town?" Old White asked. "We would greet the chief and Trade."

The boys grinned to each other. "A half day. It's Feathered Snake Town. The chief is White Bear Mankiller. You'll see the landing on the right. A lot of canoes. Then it's a short walk up the trail."

The second boy gave the first a pleading glance, only to have his friend shake his head. "No. We can't go with them. Uncle would skin us if we don't check the fish traps."

Trader grinned, reached into one of the closest packs, and retrieved a beaded turtle effigy, its top done in brightly dyed quill work. This he tossed across. "For your information. If your family can spare the time, we will see you at Feathered Snake Town."

The two boys almost capsized as they squabbled over the stuffed leather turtle.

"We'll be there!" the second promised.

When they had left the boys behind, Trader was still grinning. "Let's hope all the Trade goes like that."

Old White used his paddle to parallel Trader's course. "They didn't seem uneasy at the sight of strangers."

"They're still little more than boys. When I was their age, I never worried, either. The young think they'll live forever."

"Hmm!" Old White grunted. "I remember being a boy. Forever is shrinking by the day."

The next canoe they encountered was occupied by two fishermen, their craft piled with a folded net. They, apparently, had no demanding uncle, and immediately changed course to travel with the Traders to Feathered Snake Town.

"What is the news?" Old White asked. "We've been up north, and only heard rumors."

"We are at war with the Chikosi," one of the men replied. "They attacked White Arrow Town, downriver a ways. There have been meetings with the chiefs, all trying to decide how to respond. Most vote to ambush the trails; others wish to carry the fight to the Sky Hand."

Trader glanced uneasily at Old White, who seemed to be digesting the information.

"What brought it on?" Trader asked, trying to sound only mildly curious.

"Our warriors attacked one of their towns. They retaliated." The fisherman shrugged. "How do these things ever get started?"

The second said, "It's downriver. Maybe it won't come here."

"Great Cougar might have something to say about that." The first shrugged. "I just fish and farm. The warriors, they live in the towns. Out here, we just want to be left alone."

By the time the sun was slanting in the sky, Old White and Trader had collected a small flotilla of canoes, all interested in the Traders from the north, anxious to hear the news, spend a night with relatives at Feathered Snake Town, and, if possible, Trade. Several of the young men, anxious to bear word, sped ahead, paddles flying.

When Trader nosed his canoe into the landing, it was already crowded with people. More were on the way, appearing one by one on the heavily traveled trail that led up from the landing to disappear into the trees.

Willing hands laid onto Trader's gunnels, dragging his birch-bark craft high onto the bank.

"Easy, Swimmer," Trader coaxed. "These are friends."

But he noticed that none of the Chaktaw were anxious to get too close to the growling dog.

Old White's canoe was similarly hauled up onto the beach, and the old man climbed stiffly from his seat, raising his staff high and calling out in Mos'kogee, "We come under the Power of Trade, and would see your chief. I am Old White, called the Seeker. With me is Two Petals, the Contrary. This man is Trader."

Trader stepped out, flexed his cramped legs, and lent Two Petals a hand. She turned, staring at the crowd. In Trade Tongue, she said, "When the world changes, there is no thunder, only the wonder of it. Look, they don't know their lives are about to be altered forever. That's for the future. It lies between them and me like a fine net."

One or two, who perhaps understood Trade Tongue, stared awkwardly at her.

Trader sighed, and said, "We are pleased to be here."

The crowd parted; a muscular man of perhaps thirty winters stepped through. He wore his hair in a warrior's bun pierced with a multitude of miniature white arrows. To have earned such honors, this was no ordinary warrior. One hand held a polished war club that sported two copper blades inserted into the wood. A red apron hung about his hips, the point falling between his knees. His face was tattooed in a forked-eye pattern, his cheeks and chin done in black diamonds. A bobcat-hide cloak hung around his shoulders.

He stepped forward, hard eyes on Old White. Then he turned his inspection to Two Petals, and finally Trader. He seemed to hesitate as he studied Trader's tattoos. In a perfect accent, he asked, "You are Sky Hand?"

Trader shook his head. "I am called Trader. Recently from the far north. I have lived among many peoples. Your friends among the Natchez, the Caddo, and Tunica know my name. We come under the Power of Trade, and would stop here for that purpose."

The warrior considered, glancing sidelong at Swimmer in the canoe, then taking mental note of the packs. He seemed to be adding up the validity of the claim. Fact was, spies, if that was what he assumed them to be, would not carry a wealth of northern goods.

"From the far north?" the war chief mused. "Have you things from there to Trade?"

"We do," Old White replied, holding his staff a little higher.

"Forgive me," the warrior said. "I am Great Cougar Mankiller, of the Red Arrow Moiety. I am war chief of the Chahta. It has been some time since Traders such as yourselves have come among us. Let alone from such a great distance. Further, relations with the Chikosi have become a little strained. Just today we captured two Albaamaha spies."

Two Petals smiled wistfully, saying, "Hello, my sister."

"Our purposes are only dictated by Power," Old White assured while shooting the Contrary a sidelong glance.

"And where do you come from, woman?" Great Cougar asked Two Petals. She stared openly at the crowd, as though seeing them through some transparent veil. She kept reaching out with questing fingers, as if encountering something only she could see.

"She does not speak any tongue of the Mos'kogee," Old White told him. "Sometimes she will answer in Trade Tongue, but being Contrary, her answers and responses are backward."

"What is her native tongue?" Great Cougar asked, looking somewhat unnerved by Two Petals' continued preoccupation with the space before her.

"Oneota, War Chief. A people of the north."

"I have heard of them." He glanced again at Old White. "And which people do you come from?"

"Many," Old White replied. "I am known as the Seeker."

"The Seeker?" Great Cougar lifted an eyebrow. "There are stories about a man called the Seeker. They say he has traveled the entire world. The Caddo speak of him with reverence. It is said that only last spring he was with the Natchez."

"The Natchez high chief, Spotted Serpent, made me welcome during my journey upriver."

"I have heard stories of that." Great Cougar smiled suddenly. He turned, ordering, "Inform Chief White Bear that we have guests. Prepare a feast. Someone fetch two warriors to guard the Traders' possessions. Make sure their belongings are undisturbed." Turning back, he remarked, "As Traders, you will wish to have certain packs taken into town. My people will bear them."

"We are honored and humbled," Old White said, bowing slightly.

Trader shot a glance at the thick fabric bag that held the war medicine box and his precious copper. Just leave it here? Take a chance that Great Cougar's warriors were as good as their chief's words?

"Dance with the Power, Trader," Two Petals said suddenly. "Just tuck your desires to your chest. Spin around and around with them until all is lost. The tighter you clutch wealth, the sooner it will slip away."

Trader gave her a worried glance, seeing curiosity behind her eyes. *Entrust it to Power? Just like that?* Then he remembered the image of his arcing lance on that last cast of the chunkey game.

He called Swimmer to his side and considered the pack he wanted, letting his finger hover over the bag that hid the war medicine box as if in indecision, then pointing to another. After it was lifted out by a burley Chaktaw, they formed up, walking up the bank and into the trees. People followed along behind and on both sides, chattering excitedly.

Trader forced himself not to look back at his canoe with its hopefully guarded cargo.

I must be mad to trust a Contrary.

Just beyond the trees, where the high soils were better drained, they crossed into an open patch of fields dotted with small farmsteads. The bean and squash vines had already been burned in anticipation of planting season. The trail led across the floodplain to a palisaded town now silhouetted against the evening sky. Behind the walls, several high roofs could be seen, and the carved images of Woodpecker, Falcon, and Cougar rose from the center poles, darkly silhouetted against the sunset.

Trader followed the war chief through a narrow defensive entry to the town. Inside he found the usual clutter of steep-roofed houses, ramadas, standing mortars, and granaries. Men, women, and children accompanied by dogs flooded into the open spaces, surprised and delighted by the arrival of Traders. More than once Trader growled a command at Swimmer to keep him close. It was a constant chore since his dog wanted to pee on every passing post or wall.

They wound through the houses and stepped out onto a plaza, its clay surface swept clean. A stickball ground, chunkey court, and two ominous wooden squares lay between him and the palace atop its man-high mound. In the middle stood a single pole, representing the Tree of Life, its red and white spirals barely visible in the fading light.

They climbed the wooden steps that led up the low mound to the palace and passed through the palisade. Two guardian poles stood in the narrow courtyard and had been carved and painted to resemble snarling panthers. Great Cougar motioned them to wait as he stepped to the open doorway, calling, "Great Chief White Bear Mankiller, I come to announce the arrival of Traders."

"Let them enter and be welcome," a voice called from inside.

Trader followed Old White and Two Petals into the warm interior. There a blazing fire in the middle of the room illuminated a man seated on a three-legged stool covered with the traditional cougar hides. He was old, white-haired, with a lined face. Upon his head rested a beaten copper headpiece formed in the shape of a falcon, its wings spread. A stone war club lay heavily atop his white apron, the latter arrayed so the point hung down between his knees. Necklaces of white shell beads draped his breast, and a bearskin cape was thrown back over his sagging shoulders.

The wall behind him was adorned with a panther relief. Real cougar teeth had been inset in the jaws, and claws reached out from the grasping paws. Copper inlay added to the effect, the entire thing meticulously carved.

Around the room, benches were set against the walls. Masterfully carved wooden boxes had been neatly stowed beneath them along with pottery and baskets. The matting on the floors was new, clean, and covered here and there with hides.

Old White stopped just before the fire, lifting his staff and calling out the traditional greetings before invoking the Power of Trade. Then he made introductions, and finally handed a bag of tobacco to the war chief, who in turn carried it to the chief on his stool.

"The Seeker?" White Bear said in amazement. "You are actually him?"

"I am, Great Chief." Old White bowed.

"Spotted Serpent has told me of you. He says that you relate the most remarkable stories."

Trader glanced to the side as the packs were deposited. People were filing in, taking places on the benches around them. Some, to Trader's amusement, were scuffling, trying to get a better vantage. One look from Great Cougar was all it took to chasten them. At least until he turned his glance on others.

A muscular young man emerged carrying a heavy stone pipe, also carved to represent a crouching panther. This he carefully placed on the matting before the chief; then the man inserted a long and ornately carved stem. The chief handed him the sack of tobacco, and the young man shook the leaf into the bowl in the animal's back. Careful not to touch it with his fingers, he used a small wooden pestle to tamp the bowl. Next he lit it with a twig kept to the side for that purpose.

White Bear stepped down from his stool, took the stem in his mouth, and drew. As he exhaled he raised his head, Singing his prayer for health, Power, and good fortune.

Old White and Trader followed the ritual. Then, to everyone's amazement, Two Petals walked to the pipe, took the stem, and blew with all her might. Burning tobacco erupted from the bowl, sending sparks and embers in a cascade.

The young man stared in horror before he came to his senses and began stamping the smoldering leaf out with his foot.

The silence was complete, everyone staring in disbelief.

"Thank you, Contrary," Old White said smoothly. "Power has received your gift."

White Bear's mouth hung open, his eyes on Two Petals.

"Wait! This is *not* an offense to Power! Hear our words!" Trader cried, stepping forward. "Our apologies, Great Chief. She is Contrary, and follows the rules of that Power. I would have you understand that if you speak to her, anything she says will be backward. If she is happy, she will tell you she is sad. When hungry, she claims to be full. Should you find her speaking to empty space, it is to someone, something, that we in this world cannot see."

"This is true?" White Bear asked. "You are Contrary?"

Two Petals looked absently around the room. "It's all lies. There's no such thing as a Contrary." She sniffed. "Whatever that smell is, it's awful. I wouldn't feed that swill to a raccoon."

At the sudden looks of consternation, Old White simply sighed.

For his part, Trader sniffed, catching the odor of venison, steamed mussels, and sweet corn on the air. Old White stood easily, adopting a faint smile as he translated Two Petals' words for anyone who didn't speak Trade Tongue.

White Bear's mouth worked, as if searching for words. He walked forward and stared incredulously at Two Petals. In Trade Tongue he said, "We only serve filth here. If you want good food, you'll have to go elsewhere."

"I wouldn't touch good food if I was full to bursting," she replied. Then one of the women at the side of the room caught her attention. She pointed at the woman's abdomen. "It's a boy."

The woman, who apparently didn't know Trade Tongue, gaped

when White Bear translated. She placed a defensive hand on her stomach. "You know?"

When Old White translated the woman's question, Two Petals shrugged. "Contraries know nothing. Nothing at all. But that boy is going to marry well."

"So, it's really a girl?" the woman asked after the translation, then glanced at the man beside her. "I just realized myself. How could she know?"

"Don't know a thing," Two Petals insisted. "Actually, I don't even know a great many things."

Sensing incipient panic, Trader glanced down at Swimmer and spread his arms wide. "I think we should stop this for now. The Contrary's answers can be disconcerting in the best of times. And," he laughed, "sometimes a man may not want his wife pondering too deeply on the meaning of her words." Some of the men chuckled; the women looked less sure. "The Seeker and I will make the Contrary available to any who wish to speak with her later." He looked around, adding, "And in a more private setting conducive to maintaining marital bliss."

"I concur." Old White raised his staff. "It can be upsetting when she tells a person that their toenails will grow backward." He sighed wearily. "And believe me, traveling—as Trader and I do—in her company is not without its travails." He used his staff to point at the packs. "We have brought Trade from the north. Our goods include furs, medicinal plants, some copper nuggets, pigments, and crafts the likes of which you have rarely seen. Among our Trade are relics obtained in far-off Cahokia. If your chief agrees, we will be happy to Trade tomorrow morning in the plaza."

"We are honored by your offer to Trade." White Bear was staring at the charred places in his matting.

"But, there is more," Old White told them. "I am Old White, the Seeker. The stories you have heard are true. I have crossed the world from ocean to ocean. I have lived among peoples so distant their names have never been uttered among the Chahta." He raised a finger. "But I warn you now: These stories are not freely given, but in Trade."

"Trade for what?" Great Cougar asked skeptically.

Old White turned, inclining his staff toward the war chief. "Why, in Trade for some of that wondrous cooking all of us but the Contrary are delighted to smell. For food, and of course in Trade for your kind hospitality." He smiled. "If I conduct myself correctly, we shall all believe ourselves the better for the bargain."

Trader lifted an eyebrow. It had been smoothly done.

White Bear clapped his hands. "Then let us begin with black drink. We will follow it with a feast, and then, Seeker, you had better be as good as the stories say you are."

Old White smiled.

Trader knew it would be like shooting carp in a mud puddle. Then he cast a nervous eye toward Two Petals. If she'd blow backward through a lit pipe, what would happen if someone offered her a sip of the sacred black drink?

NINE

FLYING HAWK MADE his way to the tchkofa, touching his forehead respectfully as he passed the guardian posts at either side of the entrance, and climbed the wooden steps. With each, his knee grated and burned. At the palisade on the summit, he nodded to the guards and passed the clan totems staring down at him with baleful eyes.

He entered the dim tunnel that led inside the main room and walked around the circumference to his stool. The eternal fire was burning in the central hearth, and offerings had been placed on the altar.

Once he had settled himself on his stool, a young man motioned, and Vinegaroon, minko of the Old Camp Moiety and Skunk Clan chief, emerged from the covered hallway that led to the Old Camp council room on the south. At the same time, Tishu Minko Seven Dead, chief of the Raccoon Clan, led a procession from the northern hallway and the Hickory Moiety's room.

The moiety representatives filed to their respective sides of the chamber and seated themselves. The young Priest, dressed in white, knelt, tamped tobacco into the Eagle Pipe bowl, and lit it.

Flying Hawk, as high minko, took the first puff before offering a prayer to invoke Power. He asked it to guide him in finding a solution to the current problem.

Then, one by one, the others took the pipe stem and exhaled smoke toward the high smoke hole, letting it mingle with the sacred fire's as it rose to the sky beyond.

This was the part of being high minko that Flying Hawk liked least. Any squabble among the moieties that could not be brought to a satisfactory conclusion eventually ended here, in the tchkofa, to be decided through an appeal to his authority. Mostly it involved property, divorce, or some petty boundary dispute.

He glanced at Blood Skull. The man was Seven Dead's brother, the second war chief, and Smoke Shield's sworn enemy. Flying Hawk detested him. "It is my understanding that you represent the accused."

"Yes, High Minko."

"And, Vinegaroon, you represent the aggrieved party?"

"That is correct, High Minko." Vinegaroon rose and pointed to a short man who looked uneasily in every direction except toward Flying Hawk. "This is Fine Clay, a man of the Hawk Clan. I believe you are familiar with his work?"

Hawk Clan specialized in the finest pottery made at Split Sky City. While they made cooking vessels and other utilitarian pottery, they were most noted for the fine ceremonial ware used in rituals, for gifts and Trade, and for purposes like burials, weddings, and other special events. The Hawk Clan potters sought out the finest of clays, ground, and washed it. They made their own temper, and mass produced bowls, jugs, jars, and other ceramics. Each was carefully decorated, incised, and fired according to rituals and processes that were strictly guarded by the clan.

"I know his work," Flying Hawk agreed. "I have one of Fine Clay's jars, one that has Flying Serpent depicted on the side."

For the first time Fine Clay looked up and smiled.

Vinegaroon cleared his throat, saying, "The matter before us today concerns one of Fine Clay's molds."

"I don't understand," Flying Hawk said. "I thought the molds were the property of the clan."

"That is normally the case." Vinegaroon clasped his hands before him. "However, Fine Clay made this mold, ground it out of stone, and used it to make a certain style of jar."

"Explain this."

"Yes, High Minko. You've seen how many of Hawk Clan's bowls are quickly and efficiently produced? Instead of making each one by taking clay and flattening it with a paddle and anvil, the potter makes a mold, usually a half or third of the finished pot. In a mold the clay can be formed quickly and exactly each time, and to the same dimensions. Each piece of the pot is then removed from the mold and joined to its mates, perhaps a bottom, top, and neck. Only three seams need to be joined to create the whole."

"I am familiar with the process. What seems to be the trouble here?"

Vinegaroon spread his hands wide. "Fine Clay made a new mold. Ground it from stone, and formed it for his own purposes."

"I went to the hills up north," Fine Clay interjected. "I collected the stone myself. Then I ground it down, High Minko. I made it just so. When it was finished, I didn't like it. So I Traded it to Burnt Hand." He pointed to a man sitting beside Blood Skull.

"I see." Flying Hawk glanced across at Burnt Hand. "Is that correct?"

"Yes, High Minko." Burnt Hand made a gesture, and Flying Hawk could see the scar tissue on his left hand for which he'd received his name. "The trouble is that now he wants it back."

"No," Fine Clay insisted. "I don't. The Clan does. They say it's theirs."

Flying Hawk looked at Vinegaroon, who pointed to Black Tail, the Hawk Clan chief who had sat quietly so far.

Black Tail sighed, and rose to his feet. "High Minko, Fine Clay is a member of the clan. He knows that what we make is unique. Of course, any simpleton can craft a pot. We offer the finest pottery available. We do not dispute that Fine Clay made the journey on his own to find the stone for his mold. He put days of labor into grinding it to the shape he wanted."

"I didn't like the way the jars looked when I was finished," Fine Clay muttered. "Then, when Burnt Hand saw the finished jar, he liked it. I Traded *my* mold to Burnt Hand for seven white shell-bead necklaces."

"And where are the necklaces now?"

Fine Clay spread his hands wide. "They were a gift to Redbud's family." At Flying Hawk's raised eyebrow, Fine Clay added, "She's a Crawfish Clan woman. My wife. The seven necklaces were a wedding gift."

Flying Hawk nodded. The seven necklaces were now scattered far and wide, having been distributed to who knew where among the woman's relatives. "So Hawk Clan wants the mold back, but ownership of the mold is at question."

Black Tail shifted uncomfortably. "High Minko, Fine Clay knew perfectly well that any mold he made would become property of the clan. That is our way."

"But no one liked the finished jars that came out of the mold!" Fine Clay protested. "I didn't even like them. The balance was wrong, the neck too high and thin. They were"—he made a face—"ugly!"

Flying Hawk sighed. "If no one liked the way the jars looked, why does anyone care if Fine Clay Traded off the mold?"

"Because," Blood Skull interjected, "Burnt Hand gave the mold to his cousin in High Town. Now she's making jars on the mold. Her jars are being Traded up and down the river. When we sent a runner to ask if she'd give the mold back, she said no. It was hers now."

Flying Hawk shot a look at Black Tail. "You're telling me that now this woman is making jars, and you want the mold back?"

"That is correct, High Minko. It wasn't Fine Clay's to part with in the first place. The mold belongs to the clan."

"Even if you don't like them."

"Even then." Black Tail crossed his arms.

Flying Hawk leaned back on his stool and straightened his leg to ease the pain in his knee. "Fine Clay, did you ask anyone if you could Trade the mold?"

The man stiffened indignantly. "Why should I? It was my mold. I made it myself. I got the stone for it. I collected the sand, did the grinding. My clan did none of that labor. Worse, when I finished it, they made fun of the jars."

"They were ugly jars," Black Tail insisted.

Flying Hawk turned to Blood Skull. "You say the jars are in demand now?"

The warrior spread his arms helplessly. "People seem to like them. They are being Traded up and down the river. The workmanship is good, and while they tend to tip over easily, they are different enough that they stand out."

Flying Hawk considered the claims. "Very well, it will be settled this way. The mold will be returned to Hawk Clan."

"What?" Fine Clay cried. "Why?"

Flying Hawk gave him a narrow-eyed squint. "Because you are a member of your clan. You may have quarried and shaped the stone molds, but your clan taught you the skills. I don't care that they didn't like the jars that came from it. From now on, when you make something, you owe part of that skill to the people who taught you the craft." Then he pointed to Black Tail. "Hawk Clan, however, will send seven strings of quality white shell beads to Burnt Hand in repayment of the Trade. And as to Burnt Hand's cousin, Hawk Clan will send her all the jars she wants, made from those very same molds. In return, you will receive a tenth part of all her Trade."

Black Tail threw his hands up. "Why give her anything?"

"Because," Flying Hawk growled, "they are your molds, but you didn't like the jars. Burnt Hand's cousin, on the other hand, realized that people liked them. For that, she is to be rewarded. The tenth part of her Trade is to pay you back for the labor of making her jars."

"A tenth isn't enough," Black Tail protested.

Flying Hawk leveled a finger. "Hawk Clan let this thing grow out of control. Perhaps next time your—"

"High Minko!" a warrior cried, bursting through the entrance. The man was out of breath, sweat running down his face. "It's the Chahta! *We're under attack!*"

———

You are not holding your racquet correctly," Morning Dew told little Stone. The boy insisted on clutching his racquets the way he would an ax. "Move it forward in your hand like so." She repositioned the little boy's hand on the polished handle. Since the day she'd made the winning goal in the great solstice game, he'd taken to staring at her in outright adoration.

At first she hadn't been sure what to make of that, but how could even the most hardened woman ignore such a look of worship in a boy's eyes?

"It's harder to hold," he insisted after trying a couple of swings.

"That's because your muscles aren't used to it." She smiled down at him. "You must trust me on this. A racquet is a living thing. It must be gripped firmly, but not so tightly that you squeeze the life out of it. Here, let me show you." She took the racquet from him, showed him how her fingers laced around it, and how it seated in her palm. "There, see? Now, watch. Do you see how by twisting my wrist I can make the hoop turn?" She flicked the racquet this way and that. "The racquet must become part of you, an extension of your arm. It must be flexible, capable of easy control."

He took the racquet back, trying to mimic her motions.

"That's the way."

"Holding it this way is hard."

"That, my young warrior, is why you must practice. My mother made me hold my racquet for hands of time." She smiled at him. "I hated her for it. My arms hurt, but you know what?"

"What?"

"There are times in life that you must work steadily, bored the entire time, and with your muscles aching." She knelt to eye level with him. "What you must always keep in mind is that for that one moment of glory, you must pay with boredom and practice. The harder you work, the more you dedicate yourself, the greater you will be when that final test comes."

He avoided her eyes, staring stubbornly at his little racquet.

"Stone, you can't help it. It's just the way life is. You have been told the stories, how everything worthwhile requires your dedication. To be young is to have souls like butterflies. They want to flit this way and that. It's hard, at your age, to keep that concentration when so many other things distract you. It's even hard when you are grown. But to win at stickball, to triumph at the end, you must cling to this one thing. You must believe in yourself and know that you will grow proficient very slowly."

"I will?"

"You can become the greatest stickball player in the history of your people. But only if you carry your racquet with you at all times. Learn to live with it in your hand. Not today, but within a moon, you will be amazed at how you can outplay your friends. Only after all that time will the rewards become apparent."

"All right."

She rose, patted him on the back, and turned to see Heron Wing standing in the doorway. The woman's eyes were thoughtful, a curious smile on her lips.

Morning Dew looked down at the basket of laundry she had been carrying up from the river. Still wet, it had been heavy. And, yes, perhaps she had looked forward to taking a moment to rest as she talked to the boy.

"Sorry," she said. "Stone distracted me."

Heron Wing nodded. "Feel free to distract yourself like that any time you wish." She glanced after her son, who was trotting out past the pestle and mortar, his racquet clutched diligently as Morning Dew had shown him. "I hope he listens to you. When I tell him things, the words flow out of his ears like water through a hole in a pot."

"You are his mother."

Heron Wing shrugged. "And you are his hero."

"For the moment."

Heron Wing looked after her son. "I am hoping he will be a good chief for Panther Clan when he becomes a man. He's a bright child. I think he inherited his father's cunning, but I hope that I can influence him to use it for our people in better ways."

"Let us hope he finds your wisdom." Morning Dew bent, picking up the wash. It had been her first task since leaving the Panther Clan's Women's House. For four glorious days she had sat close to the fire and allowed herself the luxury of thinking about the last three moons. Her biggest surprise had been relief that had crept unheralded into her life. In that space of time she had been plummeted from the height of authority and prestige to the depths of despair. She had found a courage she didn't know she had, and then been rescued, brought here, to this foreign woman's house. To her surprise, she had realized that she admired Heron Wing.

Now, looking at the woman, she wondered, *Will I ever be as great as she is?*

"Yes?" Heron Wing asked, reading her expression.

"Nothing."

"It must have been something. You were looking at me with the strangest eyes. Almost a longing. Is something on your mind?"

"Does it bother you that Pale Cat sits on the Council and you don't?"

Heron Wing looked startled. "Why should it? I'm proud of my brother. He's a voice of reason on the Council. Actually, it amazes me that he can serve as *Hopaye*, fulfill his duties to the Council, and still be such a good uncle to Stone."

"You Chikosi amaze me. I know of no other people who keep their women so removed from leadership. Among the Chahta, women sit in our Councils."

"As does Night Star in ours."

"But she is the exception, partially because of her age, partially because she's a dwarf."

Heron Wing arched an eyebrow. "Then, you think I should sit on the Council?"

"As capable as your brother is, you would be a better voice for your clan."

"You have decided this, have you?"

"Sometimes people are blinded from being too close to things. Only when viewed from the outside does the shape of an object become clear."

"And what about your own people, now that you've had a chance to—"

The hollow blare of a conch horn carried on the clear morning air. Heron Wing turned, staring south toward the high minko's palace. There, at the gateway, stood Seven Dead, the horn held high to his lips.

"Warriors!" his faint voice called. "Chahta raiders are west of the river!" Then he started down the steps, taking the steep stairway three at a time.

Chahta! Here! Morning Dew stared off to the west, unable to see past the houses, palaces, and palisade. Her heart began to race, excitement building within her. *Rescue!*

"Not so fast," Heron Wing said firmly. "Think this thing through."

Morning Dew gasped, turning anxious eyes toward Heron Wing. "My people."

"Yes, but how many?" Heron Wing propped a hand on her hip. "Tempting, isn't it? Were I you, I'd be thinking that I could run, take a canoe in the confusion, and duck into the forest west of the river. Maybe, with a little luck, I could find those raiders."

Morning Dew bit her lip, having just thought that very thing.

"But then," Heron Wing added, "if it was a big war party, the scouts would have seen them coming. Slipping a small party past the scouts would be easy. But hundreds of warriors? The kind of war party necessary to deal us a real blow? No, that kind of force would have been detected. Were I you, I would decide that by the time I could reach the forest—assuming I could find a fast-moving, small force—they would be long gone. Another thing to consider is that this might be a false alarm. There may be no Chahta out there, just some nervous scout's imagination. Either way, in an unfamiliar forest crawling with warriors, how would I avoid recapture by those hundreds of Chikosi scouring the woods for Chahta?"

"I would have thought of that." Morning Dew sighed. "You're right."

"Yes, and I would stay here, knowing full well that when my time comes, I would finally go back to my people with my heel tendons uncut."

Morning Dew dropped the basket, almost spilling the contents she had worked so hard to wash. "Why? Why do you care?"

Heron Wing smiled, amused at her distress. "Because you have just begun to discover yourself, Morning Dew. Take a while longer. Learn a little more about yourself. You have the time now, and soon events may not leave you with such a luxury."

———

As the raid progressed, Smoke Shield was firmly convinced that Power rode his shoulders. They were closing on their quarry. The broken hills west of Bowl Town were the perfect place to hide. Thick timber, deep drainages, and broken ridges filled the land. While hidden nooks and crannies lay in every direction, the main trails were few and far between. Anyone wishing to hurry could only follow a few specific routes; otherwise they would become bogged down in rugged country, hampered by brush, deadfall, and steep slopes.

The first clue came from a forest trail. Here the leaf mat had been disturbed. Too many feet had been up and down the trail in recent days. Smoke Shield crouched, fingering the damp leaves. Around him, silent as cougars, his warriors settled into watchful wariness, their dark eyes searching.

Which way? Smoke Shield looked back down the trail toward Bowl Town. No, that would lead back to town. Whatever the people traveling the trail were after, it was farther west. He rose, pointed, and began easing down the trail, sniffing the breeze for telltale hints of smoke.

As he went, he noticed that here and there individuals had stepped away, the signs of travel lessening. He stopped, cocking his head as he searched the surrounding trees. The ridge here had flattened, but to the north and south, it fell off in steep ravines. His practiced eye immediately noted that the ground under the hickory, walnut, and pecan trees had been thoroughly collected. None of the fall nut crop remained atop the leaf mat but for occasional moldy or squirrel-chewed specimens. Nor did piles of deer scat indicate the animals had browsed heavily here. That meant the nuts had been collected long ago, probably just after they fell in the fall.

So if people weren't splitting off to collect nuts, what were they doing?

Hiding their trail, of course.

He smiled grimly, motioning his warriors forward in an arc. He had almost grown used to their appearance, could almost make himself believe he was Chahta himself. So far all had gone as he had planned. Only that morning had they allowed an old Albaamo man to "escape" after hearing the warriors call Smoke Shield "Great Cougar" in a mangled Chahta accent. By the time the morning sun rose, he and his warriors would appear at Bowl Town, dressed once again as Sky Hand. No one would be the wiser as he joined forces with Sun Falcon to search the forest for Chahta raiders.

As the ridgetop continued to widen, the trail virtually disappeared.

Close! He signaled a halt, cocking his head, listening. To the north, a squirrel chattered a warning call. Disturbed by a man? Who knew? He turned in that direction, using hand signs to line out his warriors.

His heart began that familiar excited beat in his chest. A euphoric feeling, almost elation, danced about his bones and muscles. Every sense seemed sharper. Step by step, they made their way forward to the lip of the ravine. One by one his warriors lined out, dropping low, peering over the steep edge. Below him lay a tangle of fallen trees, most covered with moss. Grape and greenbriar wound up from the brown forest floor in a maze-work of thick vines. A mockingbird called in the distance, and sparrows tweeted.

He could see nothing. Perhaps the squirrel's call had been a ruse?

At the point of rising and turning back, a signal was passed down the line from Bear Paw's position. Makes Calls—a warrior of the Raccoon Clan—caught Smoke Shield's attention. He pointed to his nose, and made the wiggling fingers sign for smoke.

With the grace of a panther, Smoke Shield rose, crept low across the ridge, passing his warriors, to Bear Paw, who gave him a smile and shrug, repeating the "smelled smoke" sign and pointing down into the steep ravine.

Smoke Shield turned, signaling his warriors to start down. They eased over the edge, each taking his time, placing a foot, checking the purchase, and lowering himself. A cottontail broke cover, bouncing and darting down the slope.

The warriors stopped, each studying the ground below them, bows at the ready, arrows nocked.

The faint whiff of smoke came, only to be lost as the breeze eddied through the trees.

Smoke Shield slowly resumed the descent. At the bottom, they found a trail winding among the roots, leaves, and dead saplings. Here a great many feet had trod. Smoke Shield aligned his warriors and started forward.

He caught the first glimpse of the hut, a shabby thing. made of branches bent over and covered with bark. A fine blue haze rose through cracks in the roof. He caught a faint snatch of voices; then the forest resumed its normal winter silence.

Smoke Shield signaled for his warriors to spread out, then crouched, waiting for them to move slowly and surely into position. Periodically he cast glances behind him, ensuring that no traveler came walking up the trail behind him to sound the alarm.

He could feel the first cooling of perspiration as he waited, heart thumping in his chest.

Yes, this is it. He could almost smell Fast Legs' sweat and fear from inside the little hut.

At that moment, a man walked out, calmly stepped to the side, and opened his breechcloth to relieve himself. He stared out at the forest, unconcerned. The man was an Albaamo, wearing a brown hunting shirt, his hair in a poorly tied bun.

Smoke Shield crouched lower, hoping that none of his warriors were visible.

Finished, the man fixed his clothing and turned back to the door, scratching just behind his ear as he ducked into the low hut.

Moments later, a robin chirped from up the ravine, Bear Paw's signal that he had reached his position. Smoke Shield raised himself, catching a glance of War Heart where he waited in his position. The man nodded, and Smoke Shield gave him the signal to advance.

He watched as one by one his warriors filtered down to surround the hut.

Lying flat on his back, Fast Legs panted for breath. He stared up at the daylight filtering through cracks in the bark roof. In the agonizing time since the Albaamaha brought him here, he had memorized every feature of the ceiling. He knew each bent branch, and the knots of twine that bound them together. When the Albaamaha dropped hot rocks on his belly and twisted his broken leg, he grunted as he studied them, forcing his screaming brain to imagine the intricacies of the knots.

Weary, he blinked, wishing desperately for a drink of water, knowing the futility of asking. His leg had been turned into a repulsive thing, fragments of bone lancing out through bloody and bruised flesh. It had swollen hideously, and pus leaked from the punctures. The smell of it had caused him to throw up.

Now, he tried to remember it as it had been, whole and muscled, the smooth skin intact. No matter what, he would never walk again, never run like the wind.

I *am a dead man.* The knowledge did little to soothe him. Even if he survived this terrible hut, the evil infection that had slipped into his leg would finally kill him. He would die, fevered, crying out as his souls slipped in and out of his body.

"Just kill me," he whispered again.

"When the time is right," the big Albaamo told him. "Red Awl was my brother. You foul weasel, he tried to work with you. For that, I will make you suffer until the end." He raised an eyebrow. "Of course, if you promise to tell your story to the mikkos, we will be happy to tend to your wounds. We have potions, things you can drink to deaden the pain."

Fast Legs drew another breath. Gods, he couldn't take this much longer.

"All right." His voice sounded like something far away, the hoarse rasping from another throat than his. "I'll tell you everything."

"Smoke Shield planned this?"

"Yes. The whole thing."

"Why?"

"To find the Albaamo who killed his captives. He knows you sent Crabapple to betray us to the White Arrow Chahta."

"And if he fights us, the Chikosi will unite behind him?"

The second Albaamo, a small wiry man, had crouched beside him. The man grinned as the big one spoke.

Fast Legs jerked a quick nod.

"And where is Red Awl's body?" the first asked.

"In a backwater."

"You will show us where?"

"Yes."

The man straightened, saying, "You will tell the mikkos everything?"

"Yes." What did it matter? He was dead anyway. No matter what he said, the Albaamaha would suffer in the end. Sky Hand warriors would put them down, hunt every last one of them to earth and kill them.

The man chuckled to himself before saying to his companion, "You see? They're not so tough. A man hanging in the square has the crowd to play to, but out here, alone, deep in the forest, there is no one to impress."

He turned, made a half step, and grunted, bending slightly.

Fast Legs stared in amazement at the bloody arrow that protruded from the man's gut. He watched the Albaamo reach down and wrap his fingers around the feathered shaft. The man stared in disbelief. Then a second arrow drove deeply into his chest. He turned, dazed, and toppled. Fast Legs screamed as the man's body landed on his broken leg.

Unable to see, Fast Legs heard the thin Albaamo shriek as he ran for the door. The fellow's shadow darkened the entrance; then a meaty snap—the impact of a war club—could be heard.

The dying Albaamo lying on Fast Legs kicked, whimpered, and writhed. Fast Legs blinked in the half-light, still trying to understand. He froze, staring at the silhouette that loomed over him. He knew that hairstyle: Chahta.

Then the impossible happened: The enemy warrior spoke in Smoke Shield's voice. "So, old friend, you would tell them everything?"

Fast Legs swallowed down his dry throat. He could feel the dying

Albaamo's warm blood leaking onto his body, trickling down his naked sides.

"I'm sorry," Fast Legs gasped.

"So am I," Smoke Shield said, straightening.

Fast Legs tried to gather enough breath to scream as the war chief's club rose, hanging for a moment against the patterns of light cast by the ceiling. Then it arced down, blasting lightning through Fast Legs' brain.

TEN

THE SOUND of laughter brought Lotus Root to a sudden stop. She glanced around at the narrow ravine, looking this way and that up the steep, tree-choked slopes. The forest lay dormant around her, the only patches of green being the holly that eked out an existence on the forest floor.

She had been in the Albaamaha Council House until just before dawn, listening as the men planned their attack on Bowl Town. It would come the following morning, leaving her just enough time to make the journey up to the hut, and then back before the attack. Once they had the town, Fast Legs could be dragged back, presented to the entire village as proof of Chikosi treachery.

Laughter? Her people knew better. They had been schooled in the need for silence.

She stepped off the trail, wary now, mindful of the fact she had already been stalked by at least one Chikosi warrior. She picked a path off to the side, stepping over roots, bending low so the food sack that hung from her shoulder slipped down.

She used a secondary trail, one the deer had made, keeping the thickest of trees between her and the main route. When she reached a fallen log, she stopped, seeing the soil where a squirrel had dug it up. There, imprinted, was the plain track of a moccasin. She knew that stitching, had seen it before: Chahta!

But what were they doing here?

As her fear built, she glanced around at the trees, and heard another sharp bark of laughter from the direction of the hut.

Her mouth had gone dry, but somehow she managed to creep forward, settling herself behind the bole of a great tree where she could just see the hut.

Chahta warriors, five of them, stood in a knot before the hut. Two of them had bent to the task of dismembering bodies. She could see their stone-headed axes as they rose and fell, chopping legs from torsos. Then the men bent, using knives to separate the resisting sinew and tendons.

One of the others had walked a short distance away, using a stick to dig a hole where the dirt lay loose at the foot of the slope. Only when he had hollowed out a fair-sized hole did he take a brown fabric bag and stuff it in, using his foot to press it down. Then he carefully scooped the dirt back before he reached for leaves to scatter over the ground and hide the disturbance.

In horror she stared. *How could this have happened? Out of the entire forest, how did they pick this place to attack?*

She blinked at sudden tears, aware that all of their plans lay shattered. Sick, she crouched there, watching as the last of her people's Dreams were cut to pieces.

Tonight, there would be more than just mourning for her two fallen comrades. Their best chance to unite the people in revolt was dead before her. No one would believe now.

Then the two warriors straightened. They, with their companions, undid their hair and began retying it. The two warriors who had done the butchery walked over to the small seep and began washing the blood away. Others used cloth to wipe the Chahta paint from their faces.

One—a muscular man—turned in her direction, smiling. A deep scar disfigured his familiar face.

Lotus Root froze. *Smoke Shield!*

Unable to believe, she watched as some of the men seated themselves, pulled off their moccasins, and began undoing the stitching that had been laced across their soles. For the entire hand of time it took, she continued to stare. Before her eyes, the Chahta turned themselves back into Chikosi warriors.

The weather was perfect, warm and sunny, with a damp breeze blowing up from the south. Trader sat in the sun before a ramada just below Chief White Bear's mound. The plaza was dotted with people, many of whom had come in from the surrounding farmsteads. Most simply spread blankets and watched. They were, after all, farmers and hunters. What little they had consisted of everyday pottery, locally produced fabrics, and crudely made clothing and accoutrements. Knowing this, Trader had brought little knickknacks, drawings on birch bark, pressed flowers—things that only had value because they came from the far north. Such items could be had cheaply, and in bulk. Many were given away for a couple pots of shelled corn, or a smoked turkey.

There was method behind it, of course. Trading two jars brimming with shelled corn for a birch-bark drawing, he had amassed a huge stock of corn. This, along with the rest of the local goods, he would Trade for a single copper effigy from one of the clan leaders at a later date. And, after all, a clan leader with a lot of corn might find salvation several moons later if the crops failed. It was cheap insurance against drought, famine, floods, or corn blight.

That morning, first thing, Trader had trotted down to the canoes, Swimmer running happily beside him. There, he had checked to ensure that the guards were on duty. His anxiety about the packs had been for naught. Everything was just as he'd left it. With the briefest touch, he could feel the carved surface of the war medicine box through its protective fabric.

"No one has tried to bother anything," one of the guards told him.

"We thank you for keeping an eye on things."

"Our people are not thieves." The guard had said it proudly.

"No, they are not," Trader lied, knowing full well that Chaktaw only "borrowed" other people's possessions.

To ensure continued vigilance, he removed two small gourd cups obtained from the Yuchi. Each had the image of a bullfrog carefully incised and painted on the outside. "These are for the two of you. A token of appreciation for your time and inconvenience." He smiled. "When we have finished our Trade here, there will be more."

Both warriors grinned, lifting the beautiful cups to admire them in the light. "Thank you!"

"The Seeker and I could ask for no better service than that which you provide."

Still, as he had turned to start back, it was all he could do to keep from glancing over his shoulder at the hidden box with its wealth of copper inside. Gods, the thing was like a curse, forever tempting him to keep it close.

He continued to dwell on the copper as he sat behind his Trade goods in the plaza. The only relief from nagging worry was the Contrary's assurance that it would be safe. *Does Power really guard it?*

Trader could only hope. But Power, as he had known since boyhood, was a fickle thing at best. One never knew when it might be tempted to teach the unwary some sort of cryptic lesson—like not to covet an incredibly valuable piece of copper.

He glanced across at Old White and scratched Swimmer's ears as his latest Trade partner, a fisherman who had offered a pouch of fresh-water pearls for an Oneota mat, walked away. Old White was demonstrating a Cahokian gorget, a beautiful thing made of wood with a chunkey player engraved on its surface. The clan chief he dickered with had shaken his head, unable to come up with an acceptable offer. The man walked away, a perplexed look on his face.

Trader had seen the like before. Time would tell, and the more the man thought about that Cahokian gorget, the sooner he would be canvassing his relatives, seeking a way of obtaining the necessary goods to finally make a bargain. Some relative, or friend, or in-law would have something that would finally meet Old White's price.

Trader stretched, rubbing the back of his neck. The stories and feasting hadn't ended until dawn was breaking. Now he yawned, aware that most of the people seated in a large semicircle were taking the opportunity to gossip, enjoy the sun, and socialize with their neighbors.

Trader closed the flap on his pack and rose to walk over to Old White. "Things have slowed. I might go up and catch a nap."

Old White nodded. "Last time I looked, Two Petals was sleeping soundly on one of the benches." He, too, climbed unsteadily to his feet, laying the cover back over his pack. Under the ramada, neatly arranged jars, baskets, and folds of hides were proof of his morning's work. He called out, "Trader and I are taking a break. We will return after a rest."

The people nodded and smiled. Some climbed to their feet;

others remained sitting in the sun, happy for the chance to avoid their household chores. Most everyone had seen the goods, and most of the easily obtained pieces had been snatched up. When the Trade continued, it would be for the most valuable items, the ones that would necessitate a family or clan pooling their resources. It was an old game. Trade wasn't the sort of thing that happened rapidly.

They walked slowly toward the stairway, Swimmer padding along beside Trader's heel. At the steps they paused, seeing a warrior checking the posts that made up the two squares. He was inspecting the knots.

"Is someone going to be hung?" Trader asked.

"Two Albaamaha slaves that we found skulking in the forest." The warrior frowned at the knots. "Mice like to chew the bindings. They crave the salt from sweat and blood. Once, when the lashing hadn't been checked first, we hung a captured Yuchi, only to have the whole thing fall apart." He gave them a wistful shrug. "I don't think Power was impressed with us that day."

"And the Yuchi?"

"Our *Alikchi Hopaii* set him free. We beat the Yuchi for good measure, then chased him naked from our lands with the promise that if he ever came back, we would double-check the knots before we tied him in the square."

"Lucky Yuchi," Old White said as they made the climb to the palisade gate, nodded to the guardian panthers, and stepped inside.

The shadowed great room was warm, its desultory fire burned down to coals. As they stepped in, it was to find two bound captives — an old man and a slim young woman — seated before Chief White Bear's stool. To one side stood Great Cougar, his war club in his hand, a scowl on his face. At White Bear's right sat his sister, Clay Bell. The Red Arrow clan matron was a gray-haired woman, her face lined with age. The faded tattoos around her mouth and chin were nothing more than smudged dots.

She nodded to the Traders, then turned her wary eyes back to the Albaamaha prisoners.

To Trader's surprise, Two Petals was sitting bolt upright on her bed, feet firmly planted on the floor. She had fixed her knowing eyes on the captives. From time to time, the young Albaamo woman turned, meeting Two Petals' gaze. In that instant, time seemed to slow.

Trader shook it off and walked over to seat himself beside the Contrary.

"What's happening?"

She shook her head. "They speak so fluently in Trade Tongue, I can understand everything."

Trader studied the captives, then looked at Great Cougar. The man was caressing his war club, and from the red bruises on the old Albaamo man's naked shoulders, he'd used it a time or two.

Old White made a face. "It might get too noisy in here to sleep."

"I swear!" the Albaamo man cried. "I had to leave. They were looking for the people who had sent Crabapple to warn White Arrow Town."

Clay Bell thrust her jaw forward. "And you expect us to believe that you would do this thing? Warn the Chahta?"

The old Albaamo straightened, glaring back at her. "We don't like the Chikosi any more than you do. We just want them to leave."

"You do understand that we cannot believe any of this," White Bear said softly. "An Albaamaha plot to betray a Chikosi war party? You work for them. In return they protect you from other enemies. It is an old arrangement."

"One many of us would change," the Albaamo protested.

Trader stepped over to Great Cougar. "What is the story behind this?"

The war chief gave him a sidelong glance. "One of our minkos down south, Biloxi Mankiller, and his war chief, a man named Screaming Falcon, decided to raid a Chikosi town last fall. They were successful, but before anyone could anticipate retaliation, the Chikosi attacked. It was masterfully done. They sneaked in at the end of a wedding, somehow remained undetected, and penetrated the palisade. They killed many, burned the town, and took the leaders captive."

"And you, of course, will raid them as soon as you can collect your forces?"

Great Cougar turned inquisitive eyes on him. "Why would you wish to know this?"

"Trade is difficult when it is done in the middle of a war. To be forewarned is to be prepared." Trader raised his hands. "The Chikosi will be prepared. Surely they have scouts out."

"A great many." The war chief tapped his club against his palm. "Our scouts watch their scouts watching our scouts, although we hear there is some sort of commotion over there. Warriors are boiling through the woods. I just received a report this morning while you were Trading. We have sent an alert to the towns farther inland. At first sign of a group of Chikosi headed in our direction, we shall lay our trap for them."

Trader frowned. "It doesn't make sense."

"What doesn't?"

Trader indicated the captives. "They have scouts throughout the forest, you said."

Great Cougar grinned wide enough to show broken molars in the back. "You can't throw a rock along the ridgeline without hitting a Chikosi scout."

"Then why would they send out an old man and a young woman to spy on you? Unless things have changed in the years since I traveled among the Chikosi, they wouldn't entrust as important a task as scouting to any of the Albaamaha. It's just not in their nature."

White Bear had been listening, his fingers rubbing the line of his jaw. "I had wondered that myself."

Trader added, "The Chikosi used to have good relations with the Chahta."

"How long has it been since you were among them?" Clay Bell asked, her sharp brown eyes on Trader.

"Ten summers or more." He made a vague gesture.

"Flying Hawk can't be trusted," Great Cougar muttered. "He has settled down some over the years, but he is still a volatile and shifty man. This latest trouble started last summer when their war chief, Smoke Shield, paid us a visit. He walked among us like one of the lords of Cahokia come to life. I did hear that there was trouble when he was in White Arrow Town. That might have been the excuse Biloxi used to raid Alligator Town."

"Biloxi was too young to be high minko down there." White Bear gave the captives an irritated glare. "The fool never consulted any of the upriver towns. He just made his raid, and now look what has happened!"

"This Smoke Shield is war chief?" Trader mused.

"For the moment. Unfortunately, he will be high minko soon," Clay Bell said with disgust. "And you think we have trouble now? It will be nothing compared to what's coming when he is confirmed. Their Council must have maggots in their heads to even consider it."

Trader was watching Two Petals and the Albaamo woman exchanging glances. Gods, it was as if Power swirled in the air every time their gazes locked. He could almost feel his scalp prickling.

"You will go there?" Great Cougar asked. "To Trade among the Chikosi?"

"That was the original plan," Old White declared.

"Perhaps we should conduct our interrogation of the Albaamaha where your ears, which clearly have no maggots, cannot hear."

Trader shifted his attention from the Contrary to the conversation. "War Chief, you have our word. We are bound by the Power of Trade. Anything you wish us to keep secret, anything that you ask us to be bound to, we will keep to ourselves. To betray that information would be to betray the Power we live by."

"Traders do like to gossip," White Bear noted.

"For which reason you plied us with question after question last night," Old White said from the side. "Did we tell you anything about the disposition of Yuchi warriors? Or where they might have a weakness?"

White Bear arched an annoyed eyebrow. "To my complete irritation, you did not. You only spoke kindly of those sneaking vermin."

"As we will speak kindly of the Chahta should we venture to Split Sky City," Old White insisted. "I have been at this business for many summers, Great Chief. I have been whipped, beaten, derided, cajoled, threatened, and bribed to provide information about many peoples' enemies. The reason I am here today is because even when certain mad individuals demanded that I break the Power of Trade, I did not." He gave them a mild expression. "I would hope that here, among the noble Chahta, no one will give me reason to reconsider that vow."

"Reason how, Seeker?" Clay Bell asked.

Old White steepled his fingers. "On occasion, extreme measures were used by the more enthusiastic of my past questioners. In doing so, they broke the rules of Trade, spurned its Power. What I would have withheld from their enemies, I parted with most readily." He paused. "You see, the Power of Trade binds us all. And Trader and I are of the old way of thinking."

"Point made," White Bear said with a nod. "Very well, I accept your integrity. And I will tell you this to tell to the Chikosi in turn: We are preparing for them. They will not catch us asleep as they did at White Arrow

Town. If they cross the hills in force, they may manage to have initial successes, but we have warned our people. We *will* retaliate."

Trader shook his head. "I have seen this before."

"As have I," Old White mused. "Nothing good ever comes of it. Not when peoples are prosperous." He looked up. "This isn't a matter of leaving starvation behind and moving into better lands. Nothing would be served by a prolonged war between your peoples."

"Many of us feel that way," Clay Bell agreed. "But something must be done about the attack on White Arrow Town. Some seek vengeance for the people killed, the damage done. Power is out of balance. The ghosts of the dead must have revenge."

Trader added, "Reparations could be made on both sides. Chahta sending gifts for the dead at Alligator Town, the Chikosi reciprocating for the dead at White Arrow Town. Power could be brought back into balance."

"That," White Bear said, "takes wiser heads than the ones at Split Sky City."

Old White remained thoughtful. "Do the majority of the Chahta seek war?"

"Most would prefer to avoid it. Any prolonged fighting will only serve to weaken us," Great Cougar said stiffly. "And once weakened, the Yuchi lie just to the north. They couldn't resist the opportunity to come here, seeking captives, booty, anything to add to their own Power."

At that point, Two Petals rose. She walked over and pointed at the captives. In Trade Tongue she stated, "You must want these people very much."

White Bear glanced at Clay Bell, then back at Two Petals. "What do you mean when you say we want them?"

"You're not going to Trade for them."

"They are spies!" Great Cougar said stiffly. "We don't Trade for spies. We teach them lessons."

"I don't think they're spies," Trader said in reply. "I think they're telling the truth. Albaamaha wouldn't flee into your territory unless there was no other place for them to go. Look at the man—he's half-starved. By the gods, he's got leaves in his hair." Trader bent down, looking the old Albaamo in the eyes. "How long have you been living in the woods?"

With a heavy Sky Hand accent, the old man said, "Too long." He looked up as if to see Breath Giver himself. "I was only joking about being hung to a Chahta square"

The girl turned large dark eyes on Two Petals. "We were waiting for you, Sister."

Trader started. He really got a good look at her, concluding that she was pretty—if thin. He was well aware that her eyes had the same Dreamy quality that Two Petals' had. In terribly bad Albaamaha he asked, "Waiting for Two Petals?"

"And for you. It was in the vision," the young woman said simply. "The three of you will bring Power back into balance."

The old man barked, "What are you saying?"

Trader's ear struggled a bit over the Albaamaha.

The captive said calmly, "They are the ones, Grandfather. Power has sent them."

Trader rocked back in surprise. "Power sent us?"

"So it would seem." Old White arched a quizzical brow.

Then Two Petals spoke in Trade Tongue. "I can see them dying on the Chahta squares. When they do, blood shall run from so many bodies. The future of hundreds now pulses in their veins."

Trader shot a glance at Old White, but the old man's eyes had taken on a hard gleam. He asked White Bear, "Will you Trade for the captives?"

"They are not his to Trade," Great Cougar insisted.

"They belong to me. I captured them. By hanging them in the squares, we will call Power to our side in the coming struggle. Their blood will give heart to my warriors—a foretaste, if you will, of things to come." Two Petals and the Albaamo woman both threw their heads back and laughed in unison.

———

Lotus Root willed herself to walk out from her hiding place in the trees. The Chikosi masqueraders had long since vanished, but it wouldn't be long before others arrived, come to collect the bodies.

She placed her feet carefully, ensuring that she left no tracks for keen-eyed warriors to find. She winced at the sight of the hacked and mutilated bodies, pausing only long enough to spit on Fast Legs' dismembered corpse.

"Odd, isn't it?" she told the man's scalped head where it lay rolled on its side. The skull was caved in. "This is the fate you wished for me."

No answer came from the parted lips, no reaction from the death-grayed eyes.

She picked her way over to the place where the warrior had buried the sack. Easing the leaves aside, she pulled the tamped dirt back, found a corner of the sack, and pulled. The bag was oddly heavy, and she could see that blood and grease had stained its sides.

Shooting a frightened glance over her shoulder, she tightened her grip on the sack and climbed the steep-sided ravine. Topping out onto the flat she ran south as fast as she could, keeping to the deep leaf mat, trying not to disturb the cushioned footing with her smooth-soled moccasins.

Only when she had crossed the flat and reached the cover of a deadfall did she bother to stop, catch her breath, and stare at the sack. Opening it, she looked inside. At first she thought it was some kind of animal skins. And then the realization hit her: Scalps! The Chikosi had buried a sack full of human scalps!

ELEVEN

THE EVENING WAS BEAUTIFUL, the air still warm. In the southwest, the sun sent rays of light through puffy clouds, burning the edges yellow, gold, and red to contrast with the deeper purple of the cloud bodies. A few brave insects flitted here and there, wings shining in the light.

Old White followed the trail up from the canoe landing, assured that all was well there. He passed through the trees and into the fields. The people he encountered nodded pleasantly, calling greetings. They carried jars to be filled with water at the river, and some had packs on their backs.

Women were preparing the evening meals, cooking over outside fires. The smell of woodsmoke lay heavy on the air. Children laughed and played. For the moment, life was good.

He reflected on that as he approached Feathered Snake Town and glanced up at the sky. What were the purposes of Breath Giver when he Created the world? All of this could vanish come spring. Where people now lived, loved, played, and worked could become a battleground if Flying Hawk massed his warriors and sent them here.

In the old stories, all the Mos'kogee people had been one, a large nation that migrated eastward from across the Father Water. Driven by the availability of new land, they had come and conquered, or driven off, the local peoples. While crossing such vast territory, his people had split, some staying, others moving on, until Chahta, Sky Hand, Ockmulgee, Tuscaloosa, Coosa, and so many other nations had grown from the original stock.

The Chahta are our cousins. These people, the ones he now saw — but for a chance of the past — could be his relatives. But if things went badly, blood would be spilled in a terrible war. He knew his Sky Hand people. They trained constantly for war. It was fed into them along with their mothers' milk. Among all the peoples he had visited, only the Azteca had a more proficient military: They marched in massed armies of thousands, each a trained warrior, capable of taking commands in battle.

Sky Hand warriors only traveled in hundreds, but what they lacked in mass and organization, they made up for with a fierce spirit. They would cut a swath through the Chahta lands. In the end, however, the Chahta would call on the Pearl River villages to the west. Where the Sky Hand filled the Black Warrior River basin, the Chahta sprawled over a large territory. If something finally united them, like a war of retribution against the Sky Hand, they would pose a worthy adversary.

The final resolution would boil down to attrition — and who could find allies. The Natchez, surely, would side with the Chahta. But who would help the Sky Hand? Not the Yuchi or Pensacola. The Coosa and Tuscaloosa would probably make excuses and remain home. They, after all, would have no stake in a war off to their west.

So, there it was, a grueling conflict pitting a better, smaller Sky Hand force against a larger, poorly organized Chahta resistance. And just to the north the Yuchi lay in wait. Born-of-Sun's people would sense an opportunity.

There will be no winners here.

That notion preoccupied him as he entered the defensive gate and made his way through the houses inside the walls.

People smiled, waved, and called greetings as he passed. He touched hands with large-eyed children who ran out to greet him, and entered the plaza. He was passing the Men's House when Great Cougar emerged from the sweat lodge, his skin dripping with perspiration.

Just the man I wanted to see. Old White stopped to watch as the war chief raised a water jar and poured the cool contents over his glistening body.

"The perfect temperature," Old White noted, taking stock of the war chief's muscular body. He was tattooed over most of it, scarred here and there.

The man used a cloth to dry himself and nodded. "A warrior must be clean. The body is the home of the souls, and must be maintained like the temple it is."

Old White nodded as the man dressed himself and flipped his wet hair back. The long warrior's lock that hung down over' his forehead had been pulled through three white shell beads. His copper ear spools gleamed.

"I was just thinking of what war would do to the people here," Old White said. "If you fight the Sky Hand, who do you think will win?"

"We will." Great Cougar flashed him a smile. "Power will side with us." He used the cloth to slick away the remaining dampness on his brawny arms.

"I suppose that if you asked the same question to Flying Hawk, he would give you the same answer. People, no matter what their beliefs, always believe Power, the gods, fate, whatever, sides with them."

Great Cougar walked over, expression reserved. "I have fought the Chikosi before. Beaten them, too. That was some time ago. They've grown soft since then, only skirmishing with the Yuchi."

"And your Chahta haven't grown soft as well?"

Great Cougar chuckled to himself. "What is your purpose here, Seeker? Really? Oh, I know the reasons you've given, but I think there is more. Especially when that odd woman you brought with you is so obsessed with my Albaamaha captives."

"Do you think we are Sky Hand spies, too?"

"The thought has crossed my mind." He studied Old White through narrowed eyes. "Trader speaks with a Sky Hand accent. His tattoos remind me of theirs. The pattern is Chief Clan, but unfinished."

Old White pointed. "I see forked-eye designs on your face. I have seen them on the faces of the Caddo, the Natchez, the Yuchi, and so many others. The falcon eye design spread out from Cahokia long ago, as did the cheek bar he wears. Seriously, don't you wonder why a man of his age would only have the design, not the finished tattoo, if he were Sky Hand?"

Great Cougar grunted noncommittally. "I think the three of you are full of secrets."

"On that we agree." Old White gave him a mild smile. "But on my honor, we are not here to seek an advantage of the Chahta."

"But you are concerned about us going to war?"

Old White shrugged. "I was just wondering at the reasons for it. War in general, I mean. I was just contemplating how happy everyone is. All around Feathered Snake Town, people are simply living, dealing with their everyday problems. If this thing between you and the Sky Hand goes wrong, it will change those lives."

Great Cougar glanced up at the failing daylight. "War serves its purpose, which is to keep a people in balance with life. You asked if we had become lazy during our years of relative peace? Perhaps we have. We are part of this world, Seeker. Look around you."

"Believe me, I have. And in more places and for more summers than you have."

"And you see the deer, agile of foot, keen of senses, because he knows the cougar stalks the shadows. So, too, does the passenger pigeon remain fast and darting in flight because the falcon sails high on the currents, awaiting the unwary. People who live in comfort become easy prey when they forget that predators wait on the fringes. Power must balance, Seeker. The white Power of order grows stagnant, soft, and weak. When it does, the red washes in, bringing with it the strong, who pick the bones of those unprepared for its ways."

"Do you not seek that balance yourself, War Chief?"

"I am dedicated to the red Power, Seeker. I leave the white for others to cultivate."

"I see." He reached into his pouch. "What do you think of this?"

He handed across a shining copper gorget. The image had been beautifully rendered, showing a crouched warrior over a kneeling captive. The warrior's head was up, as if looking to the sky. Forked-eye designs surrounded his large eyes, a beaded forelock hanging over his forehead. In his right hand he held a long knife pressed against the captive's exposed throat. The string it hung on had been beaded with perfectly cut shell disks.

Great Cougar held it up to the light, a gleam in his eyes. "I have never seen the like. It's magnificent."

"It came from Cahokia. I have no idea of its age, or who might have worn it. Perhaps one of the very lords who once ruled there."

"You would Trade this?"

"For the right Trade."

Great Cougar reverently fingered the piece. "I have an engraved cup for black drink, a large thing made from a huge conch. The workmanship is wondrous. It was Traded to me by a Pensacola, who in turn Traded it up from the Calusa. It is my most prized possession. A moment." He turned, trotting off behind the Men's House.

Old White smiled to himself. *Yes, well chosen indeed.*

Of all his Trade, he had thought of this piece, one of the items given to him by Silver Loon. Of their combined possessions, it seemed the most likely—excepting of course Trader's copper and the medicine box—to pique the surly Great Cougar's interest.

At that moment, Great Cougar dashed back from his quest, a large white conch shell cradled in his hands. The shell cup was among the largest Old White had ever seen. Nearly as long as his forearm, it had been carefully cut in half lengthwise, leaving the outer wall of the shell, the columella removed. It tapered to a long thin point on one end. The design etched into its outer surface was of geometric lightning patterns surrounding the narrow image of a seated cat.

Old White took the shell, uttering an admiring "Ah!" In the far north, this cup would fetch half a canoe load of copper, several packs of prime lynx hides, or even one of the very rare white bearskins.

He glanced at Great Cougar, who again held the Cahokian gorget up to the evening light. The man seemed to be entranced.

"Hang it around your neck," Old White suggested. "I may be wrong, but you can almost feel the Power pulsing within it."

Great Cougar reverently looped the gorget string over his head.

"I have heard," Old White added, "that something of a person's Spirit remains with a cherished possession. When I hold that piece, it is as if I can touch the essence of a Cahokian lord. Imagine the emotions, the pride that once beat in the wearer's heart." He paused. "Fascinating, isn't it?"

Great Cougar stared down at his chest, fingering the rim of the copper gorget. Finally, almost breathlessly, he asked, "Do we have a Trade? The gorget for the cup?"

Old White considered, running his fingers over the intricate design. He had, he decided, never seen such a marvelous piece. It tempted him, affecting him the same way the gorget did Great Cougar.

"Let me propose something else, a way for you to keep the gorget...and the cup."

Great Cougar gave him a suspicious look. "And that would be?"

"I would Trade the gorget for the Albaamaha captives."

"Before or after I hang them on the square?"

Old White arched an eyebrow in censure.

"Why?" Great Cougar asked as he removed the gorget. He hesitated, unwilling to hand it back.

"Because for reasons I cannot understand, the Contrary wants them."

Great Cougar's expression was guarded. "You would give up that cup because the Contrary wants the Albaamaha?"

Old White made a face. "It pains me to do so, but yes."

"In Breath Giver's name, why?"

Old White chuckled, amused at himself. He did covet the cup. "From the time that I found the Contrary among the Oneota, she has never ceased to amaze me. She sees the future. When she speaks, it is with that knowledge, which is why everything she says is backward. She is watching us from the future. Even with my experience, I can hardly imagine how she thinks."

"What could she possibly want with an old Albaamo and a skinny woman?"

"Honestly, I have no idea. That she desires them is enough. Of course, you can refuse the bargain. In that case, I have done my best."

Great Cougar gave him a crafty look. "You could offer more."

Old White waved it off. "Well done. You are worthy of being a Trader yourself. But no. Were I to offer you everything I owned, you would wonder why. That question would eat at you, feed the suspicions you already have about us. I can hear the thoughts that would churn between your souls: If they would Trade so much, the captives must be worth a great deal to them. But why?' And the answer you could not help but arrive at would be that despite the evidence we carry in our packs, we did not travel down from the north. Instead, you would convince yourself that we were indeed Sky Hand spies, come to discover your war plans."

"Perhaps you would Trade the cup for the gorget now, and something else for the captives later?"

"Perhaps I might Trade the captives for the gorget now, and something else for the cup later."

Great Cougar continued to run his fingers over the relief on the copper gorget.

Old White handed the cup back, saying, "This need not be decided at the moment. Keep the gorget for a while, War Chief. Wear it until you make up your mind." He handed the cup back reluctantly. "Even if you do not decide to take my Trade I don't see why you shouldn't wear such a piece for the time being. You know...just to look at it in the sunlight tomorrow and marvel over the workmanship, as I have."

"You would trust me with this?" He had tucked the cup under one arm and now raised the gorget.

"War Chief, you are a man of honor. Take it home, see how it looks in the firelight. It is my pleasure to share it with a man who will admire it as much as I."

Old White smiled to himself as Great Cougar turned, headed back in the direction of his house.

"Now," he mused, "how do I get that cup away from him?"

The Albaamaha had been assembled just outside Bowl Town's palisade. They stood uncomfortably, watching with sullen eyes as Smoke Shield stood beside Chief Sun Falcon. Behind him, Smoke Shield knew the gathered Sky Hand warriors shifted nervously; his warriors held their weapons high, though Sun Falcon's did not. The latter looked uncomfortable with the proceedings. The evening sky glowed in the west, sunlight sending bars of light through the distant clouds.

"Where is Lotus Root?" Smoke Shield demanded. "She has made charges against me. I have searched her house, only to find it vacant. Let her come forward and make her allegations known!"

The crowd remained silent, eyes down, hands clasped before them.

Smoke Shield had literally paraded his warriors back and forth through their village, looking in houses, searching granaries. He had read their hard looks, seen the anger they tried so diligently to hide. But what could they do? As many as they were, they dared not challenge his war-hardened warriors. If anything, his men had tried to provoke a response, having freshly washed Albaamaha blood from their hands.

But the Albaamaha had refused to rise to the bait.

Cowards, all of them. The thought drifted between Smoke Shield's souls like smoke.

"Come on," he chided. "How can this woman speak her poison behind my back, yet refuse to face me?" He spread his arms. "If she has cause, let her tell all of us. I am not afraid to answer her questions."

They stood uneasily.

Sun Falcon was shooting Smoke Shield sidelong looks, clearly displeased at this turn of events. Let him be. Who cared what the Bowl Town chief might think?

"Will someone tell me where Lotus Root is?"

In the long silence, no one spoke.

"That is an order!"

Finally, an old man, one of the Albaamaha mikkos, stepped forward. He cleared his throat. "War Chief, she is not here."

"Not here," Smoke Shield replied thoughtfully. "Well, she certainly wasn't up at the hut. Her body wasn't among those the Chahta killed." He raised a knotted fist. "We tracked the raiders for a distance and saw no woman's tracks among theirs, so they didn't take her."

The old Albaamo hung his head. In a voice barely audible, he said, "She may have feared for her life, War Chief."

"And why is that, Mikko?"

"Because...because a Sky Hand warrior was stalking her."

Smoke Shield nodded. "Ah, Fast Legs."

Sun Falcon broke the silence. "Some of us would wonder what he was doing up at that hut, War Chief."

"I sent him," Smoke Shield said firmly. "At the first hint of rumors that I had killed Red Awl, I asked him to come and find out if Red Awl was indeed dead. My instructions were that he be discreet. That he learn what was being said about me without upsetting people. The last thing I wanted was for him to barge in like a hungry bear and demand explanations. Had he done so, do any of you think he would have heard the truth? No, it was better that he look and listen."

He saw some of the Albaamaha glance uneasily at each other. Among others, the only response was the tightening of jaw muscles, the hard knotting of fists.

Smoke Shield propped his hands on his hips. "When we found the bodies, they had been cut apart by the foul Chahta cowards. But I can tell you this! My warrior had a broken leg long before the Chahta killed him. Could anyone tell me how that happened?"

Silence.

"Come on, people, talk. The news of a Sky Hand warrior taken captive would have been up and down the trails within moments."

"Captive?" the old mikko asked. "Has the war chief not considered that his warrior might have fallen in the forest and our people took him to shelter to help him?"

"Oh, indeed I have." Smoke Shield lifted a hand, staring absently at his fingers. "The thing is, Fast Legs had obviously been in that hut for days. More than enough time for the kind Albaamaha to send a runner to Chief Sun Falcon for aid. But then, I don't suppose any of you would have wanted Sun Falcon's warriors to see Fast Legs. The scars where hot rocks had been dropped on his flesh were scabbed. No fast-moving party of Chahta raiders takes the time to torture a single hurt man. So I can well understand why no word was sent to Sun Falcon. Fast Legs would have told them everything, pointed out the people who had tortured him. And what would you have done then?"

"War Chief," Sun Falcon said softly. "Do not take us to a place we cannot back away from."

Smoke Shield gave him a scathing look before turning back to the crowd. "Very well, some want to find a solution to this. I can understand why, with the Chahta roaming our woods, killing our people. So be it, but I will tell you this! I swear on the red Power, I do not know where Red Awl is." *And I pray that Fast Legs hid his body so no one will ever find it.* "If he is dead, I swear on the souls of my Ancestors, I didn't see it happen. Didn't order it done. I have no idea how to find him, even assuming he is dead." He paused. "Sometimes I wonder if he really is."

A couple of Albaamaha shot him glances from under lowered brows.

"So let us bring an end to this. Let Lotus Root make her false accusations and I will respond to them. I could be persuaded to let this thing drop if the people who took my warrior and tortured him will step forward and announce themselves. I will leave their judgment to Chief Sun Falcon, taking no part in it."

He spread his hands. "So no one knew what was going on up there in that ravine? Is that what I am to understand from your silence? Or do you all fear some terrible reprisal in the night?" He grunted disgust. "Then let the guilty come forward tonight, alone, so that none of the innocent ones are implicated because of kinship or ties of friendship."

Smoke Shield pointed at the darkening woods. "We cannot afford dissent! Not now. The Chahta have just reminded us of who the enemy really is. Think of their timing. We are consumed with rumors and false charges, weakened by our distrust of each other. As that festers, here come the Chahta, seeking scalps." He lowered his pointing finger. "Meanwhile, do not forget who raced out into the forest to drive the raiders off! Remember that Sky Hand warriors stand between you and the enemies of both of our peoples."

His gaze fixed on a pretty young woman. Her dress conformed to a perfectly proportioned body. Long dark hair hung over her shoulders, and he liked the look of her oval face, uptilted nose, and downcast eyes.

Perhaps he would pay her a visit later. The young man she stood beside would have to make do with a string of beads for compensation.

TWELVE

THE MORNING WAS CLOUDY, a smell of distant rain borne by the southern breeze. In winter, Trader had come to realize, it often warmed before a storm. The warm air enhanced the muddy smell of the river as he and Old White stood at the Feathered Serpent Town landing. Around them, a crowd of people had come to say farewell. They wore their finest dress, and he caught the smoky odor rising from their clothing. Trader saw to the loading of his last pack after reassuringly patting the war medicine box, undisturbed the entire time.

Old White was in the process of handing the two erstwhile guards small sacks of tobacco, saying, "This is narrow leaf, mixed with a plant called kinnikinik. It only grows in the far north, up toward the Western Mountains. Save it for special occasions, for there is no other like it anywhere in this part of the world."

Chief White Bear stood beside matron Clay Bell, watching thoughtfully. "You are sure you will not stay?"

"We are Traders, Great Chief." Old White bowed slightly. "As much as we have been delighted with your kind hospitality, and enjoyed our time at Feathered Serpent Town, we serve the Power of Trade. It now calls us downriver. Given what you have told us, there is good reason to believe that we might brighten some lives in White Arrow Town."

"They may not have much to Trade. Most of their goods will be needed to obtain food to replace what the Chikosi burned."

Trader signaled Swimmer into the canoe. "We shall do what we can for them. Part of the Power of Trade is to balance need with demand. If it builds goodwill, I think we can take a loss this time." He grinned. "But next time we pass through, we'll expect to get it back."

Two Petals had fixed her eyes on the trail heading up for the trees, as if waiting for something. She might have stood alone on an empty shore, completely oblivious to the activity around her.

Old White turned to Great Cougar, who was fingering the shining copper gorget. "War Chief, as much as it grieves me, I must ask for that back. Perhaps next time we come through we can come to an agreement."

"Are you sure you won't take the cup in Trade?"

"Oh, don't you worry. I'll be back for that."

"With the gorget?"

Trader watched, curious as Old White shrugged. "Who can say? Some chief downriver might find the bargain right. Trade is never a sure thing."

Great Cougar sighed, the fingers of his right hand still caressing the metal. He made a gesture with his left, and two warriors emerged from the trees. Led by ropes, the Albaamaha captives followed, their hands tied behind them. Even across the distance, Trader could see the relief on the old Albaamo's face. For her part, Two Petals smiled, appearing suddenly to be back in this world.

The slender Albaamo woman had a slight and beguiling smile, as if she'd known all along. Her eyes seemed to enlarge as she stopped before Two Petals and said, "I am ready, Sister. My steps follow your Dance."

Two Petals—unable to understand a word of Albaamaha—replied in Trade Tongue, "He wails in grief. You will hear his call through the water."

The Albaamo woman nodded. "I will find him."

There is more to this than the Contrary has told us. An eerie shiver traced down his back. But then he should have known enough to take it in stride.

"I would take it badly, Seeker, if I were to learn that you told the Chikosi our war plans," Great Cougar added.

Old White smiled. "War Chief, assuming that they have any brains at all, they already know you are going to lie in wait for them, attempt to disrupt them in your own lands, and then kill as many as you can."

"I never told you that."

"No, you didn't. On my word as a Trader, Flying Hawk shall learn as much about your plans as you have learned of the Yuchi's."

Two Petals stepped into the canoe and watched the Albaamaha climb into Trader's boat. "Our Dance grows faster. Bones will rise from the water before copper sinks," she muttered in Trade Tongue.

Trader shot a nervous glance at his copper, then took his seat, lifting the paddle and letting the Chahta push his birch-bark canoe into the current. Swimmer was sniffing curiously at the Albaamaha, eliciting smiles from the young woman; the old man pulled back as if afraid of being bitten.

"Swimmer, these are our new slaves," Trader told the dog. To the Albaamaha, he added, "Don't mind Swimmer; he won't bite you if you don't bite him." Then in Trader Tongue, he asked, "Do you have names?"

Both gave him blank stares, so he repeated the question in Mos'kogee.

"I am Whippoorwill," the woman said, smiling brightly at him.

"Paunch," the old man admitted. He kept casting nervous glances back at the Chahta who pushed Old White's canoe out. Two Petals was seated as usual, facing the rear, an oddly satisfied smile on her face. Then Paunch whispered, "By Abba Mikko, I don't believe this. I thought I was dead for sure."

"Well, I'm not one to dash anyone's hopes, but there's no guarantee as to how this whole thing will play out." Trader jerked his head back toward the landing. "That's only one town. We've several more to pass before the confluence to the Black Warrior. And perhaps you noticed that people are a little nervous here?"

"Did the Seeker actually Trade that gorget for us?" Paunch asked incredulously.

"He did." Trader gave him a scowl. "Though I can only hope you're worth it. If you have to thank anyone for your lives, thank the Contrary."

"My sister is remarkably Powerful," Whippoorwill told him as she glanced across at Two Petals. "She Dances with time, her feet beating the sacred rhythm of the stars, moon, and sun."

Sister? Trader narrowed an eye. Whippoorwill couldn't speak a word of Trade Tongue, but she seemed to have understood Two Petals' talk about underwater wailing?

Gods, not another one!

———

Great Cougar stood on the canoe landing, letting the river water lap at his toes. The Traders' canoes — followed by a ragged flotilla of fishermen and the curious — rode the currents toward the south.

"Do you think they suspect?" Clay Bell asked.

"I do not. No, if anything they think we're being absolutely practical in our plans for defense." He shrugged. "Perhaps they won't even carry their stories to the Chikosi, but I doubt that's the case. They may indeed have come from upriver as their goods and that birch-bark canoe indicate, but they asked too many questions. For whatever reason, they have an interest in our plans."

"You played that artfully, War Chief," Clay Bell said softly. "It would have been different several days from now. The warriors will be coming."

"I just hope I delayed the Traders long enough for the runners to get downriver to warn the other chiefs." He sighed, fingering the copper gorget. "The Seeker played a good game to obtain the Albaamaha spies. I wonder if he'll get his value's worth?"

"They are up to something," Clay Bell agreed. "We had better get back. We have work to do. The coming days are going to tax our energy. Hiding so many warriors is going to be difficult."

"Oh, yes. But Power is with us; I can feel it. If we do this right, they'll never know we're coming." The hard part would be moving so many warriors in silence and stealth. But the last thing the arrogant Chikosi would expect was a major assault on Split Sky City. He had a plan for the Chikosi scouts. They were already bored, watching for a raid that never seemed to come. His scouts were watching their scouts. Some had even taken to calling back and forth to each other. It was a weakness he could exploit.

Great Cougar smiled. "When I asked that old Albaamaha if his people had been cutting pine logs, he had no idea what I was talking about."

Clay Bell smiled. "Then those rotted palisade walls at Split Sky City haven't been replaced yet."

"Too bad," Great Cougar mused. "I suspect a Chahta wind is about to blow them down."

———

Wake up," Heron Wing said as she nudged Morning Dew's shoulder.

"Huh?" She blinked, finding the room in total darkness. Only the faintest of red eyes marked the hot coals in the hearth.

"Shhh! Don't wake Stone."

Morning Dew sat up, her hair spilling around her.

"Get dressed." Heron Wing added, "We're going out."

"It's the middle of the night."

"That's the whole point."

"The point of what?" Morning Dew asked as she pulled a long-sleeved dress over her head.

"Plotting."

"We're plotting in the middle of night?" *I'm confused.*

"All good plotting is done in the middle of the night." Heron Wing led the way to the door, and then stepped past the hanging.

Morning Dew followed her out, wishing she'd learned to keep better track of the stars to tell the time; but when she looked up at the inky sky it was to see an infinite black. Instead, a faint drizzle settled from the darkness. She hurried along, following Heron Wing's dark shape as she wound through the maze of mortars, ramada poles, and fire pits to the edge of the plaza.

"Careful," Heron Wing said after tripping. "It's dark as pitch out here."

"Where are we going?"

"Pale Cat's. No matter what, you are to speak of this to no one. I have a specific reason for asking you along tonight. We need your expertise." "We do?"

But Heron Wing said no more as she made her way along the edge of the plaza. How the woman found her way was remarkable. Morning Dew had to stop several times, calling out to reorient herself.

"Take my hand." Heron Wing reached back, grasping Morning Dew's. The surefooted woman led her on a winding course through the Panther Clan houses, past the charnel house with its unmistakable smell of decomposition, and to the base of the *Hopaye's* ramp. Step by step they felt their way to the top, entered the palisade, and finally, with the glow around the door to lead them, crossed to the Panther Clan palace.

Morning Dew looked around owlishly as she stepped inside. A central fire illuminated the room. The usual carved relief of the Seeing Hand covered the back wall. A tripod sat in the north; numerous boxes, packs, jars, baskets, and other vessels had been stowed beneath the wall benches. Unique for the room, carved wooden statues of panthers, bears, falcons, woodpeckers, raccoons, and rattlesnakes were spaced evenly between the benches. Many had a polished look, as if people had leaned on them for support.

Pale Cat and the diminutive Night Star were seated before the tripod. A ceramic pot hung over the fire, steam rising from the surface. Just to Pale Cat's left sat the Raccoon Clan warrior Blood Skull, a fabric pack by his side. *Blood Skull, the man who captured me out of my own house.* For an instant she was back in White Arrow Town. Then came the memory of her husband's body slamming into the hard ground. She remembered stepping out the door, seeing Screaming Falcon's body on the ground. And then she flinched at the memory of Blood Skull's muscular arms clamping around her body.

She forced herself back to the present, stifling the urge to fly at the man.

Pale Cat stood, his smile at Heron Wing's entrance fading. "You brought Morning Dew?"

Blood Skull asked, "Heron Wing, why? We have serious things to discuss here tonight. This isn't a social visit."

When Morning Dew planted a foot to turn back, Heron Wing reached for her hand, pulling her forward. At the same time, she said, "No, this isn't a social visit.

We're here to discuss the Chahta. If we're going to know their will and aims, we are best served hearing them straight from the Chahta themselves. Having only one White Arrow matron available for that purpose, I brought her along."

"She's a slave!" Blood Skull protested. "A captive!"

Morning Dew fought the building urge to spit at him. *Stop it! Heron Wing's right. You are a matron. Act like one.*

Heron Wing seated herself to Night Star's right, dragging a resisting Morning Dew down beside her. "Very good, warrior. Your sharp wits—having just been demonstrated—can now be put to good use helping us form some plan of action."

Night Star gave Morning Dew a distasteful scowl before she turned her squinty eyes on Heron Wing. "I hope you aren't joking, Niece."

Morning Dew forced her heart to cease its pounding. A smart woman might learn something from this. She did her best to relax.

"Far from it, Aunt. I'm deadly serious here. We are discussing the future of our people. Specifically, we are trying to figure out what the Chahta raid means." She glanced at Blood Skull. "If it really is a raid."

"Precisely," Pale Cat agreed, thoughtful eyes on his sister. "Do you trust her that much?"

"I do." Heron Wing turned to Morning Dew. "Tell them what you want most."

Morning Dew read the firm look in Heron Wing's eyes. *Yes, yes. I'm a matron. Gods, you could be my mother.* And then she stiffened her resolve. "I want to go home to my people. No matter what my present status, I am still Chief Clan, the matron of the White Arrow Moiety of the Chahta."

"So," Night Star asked, "that being the case, why should we trust you?"

Morning Dew was aware of Heron Wing's evaluative expression. *She wants to see what I'm made of.* "I'm not sure you should." She indicated Blood Skull. "Acting as second to Smoke Shield, Blood Skull and his warriors killed many of my relatives, including my mother. As I was his captive, he was the one who gave me to Smoke Shield. He was the man who tied my brother, High Minko Biloxi, to the square, tortured him, and would have killed him." Her heart skipped. *Gods, get over it. Be the woman Heron Wing thinks you are.*

"In fact, it was my brother"—she swallowed hard—"and his war chief who started this thing with the Alligator Town raid. You did to us what we did to you." *Think! Don't let your heart rule your souls.* "The fact that Heron Wing brought me here tells me that you need to know the hearts of the Chahta. So I will tell you." She paused, looking from face to face. "Assuming, that is, that we are working to bring this problem between our peoples to a sane conclusion."

Heron Wing was smiling like a fox who had just caught a bobwhite.

Night Star watched her with midnight eyes.

Blood Skull lifted a skeptical eyebrow.

Pale Cat had an amused look on his face as he nodded to his sister.

Night Star clasped her small hands in her lap. "You could be a potent enemy."

"I could also be just as potent an ally." Morning Dew met the woman's stare. "...With the right persuasion. Why don't you tell me what you need to know about the Chahta, and why? After that we can iron out the details about why we should or should not trust each other."

Night Star glanced at Blood Skull. "Objections?"

"Yes," the Raccoon Clan warrior muttered, "but for the moment I'll keep them to myself."

"Very well," Night Star relented. "You just returned from hunting the Chahta raiders, Blood Skull. What did your warriors find, and why are you concerned?"

He glanced suspiciously at Morning Dew, then withdrew a blood-stained arrow from the sack beside him. "The raiders moved from south to north, starting their sweep just west of us and ending outside of Bowl Town. They attacked only small farmsteads, killing Albaamaha. As best we know at this early date, twenty-three were killed. Two survivors, both Albaamaha, claimed that the raiders were under War Chief Great Cougar. They heard him called by name. The trackers found four parties of five warriors apiece."

"And what is the problem with that?" Pale Cat asked.

Blood Skull twirled the bloody arrow in his fingers. "Our scouts saw nothing on the ridgeline, no trail, no evidence of passage. We can't backtrack the raiders, nor could Sun Falcon's trackers find where they turned back west."

"So they were very skilled."

"Were they?" Blood Skull handed the arrow to Morning Dew. "Look at it. Can you say for sure that this is a Chahta arrow?"

Morning Dew took the light shaft. About the length of her forearm, it had been broken, as if snapped from the body it entered. "The colors are right. The white band indicates it comes from our Deer Clan of the White Arrow Moiety."

Blood Skull nodded.

Morning Dew frowned at it. "Honestly, I'm no expert on arrows. Men don't like women around their weapons."

Blood Skull took it back, asking, "How many Chahta Deer Clan warriors live at Feathered Serpent Town?"

Morning Dew frowned, trying to think. "Some, I'm sure. Probably men ..." She shook her head. "No, that doesn't make sense. It's a Red Arrow Town. But that's not to say Great Cougar couldn't have had volunteers from some other place."

"My thoughts exactly." Blood Skull stared at the arrow. "I wouldn't have given it any thought. But I broke this shaft off from where it was sticking out of a woman's back. I was about to throw it away, angry, enraged at the Chahta. Then something caught my eye. The problem is with the notches cut here in the fletching." He pointed to two small nicks. Each was repeated on the three split feathers tied to the shaft. "Bear Paw notches his arrows in this fashion."

"Bear Paw?" Night Star asked. "He's one of your kinsmen."

"I know. I hunt with him. All Raccoon Clan hunters leave a distinctive notch, or perhaps a zigzag line scratched in the shaft, something, to tell whose arrow actually killed the game. Normally we paint a blue ring on our shafts, the sign of our clan. This arrow, if you'll notice, has been rubbed with fine sand right around the white ring. The wood is pale, as if the old color had been sanded off."

"That's hardly conclusive," Pale Cat said.

Blood Skull looked up. "Four parties of five apiece. But just before the Chahta raid, Smoke Shield left with twenty warriors on some errand for Flying Hawk. The thing is: Bear Paw was with them."

Heron Wing asked, "You think Smoke Shield's warriors did this?"

Blood Skull turned his eyes on Morning Dew. "Tell me, *Matron*, you know Great Cougar. Does this raid sound like something he'd lead?"

Did it? She frowned at the arrow. "No," she said softly, feeling the oddness of it. "Great Cougar isn't a man of half measures. Nor is he impulsive. The Red Arrow war chief I know will bide his time, build his strength, and come at you in force. He believes in war, and he believes in winning. He told me once that a good war chief goes to war with the intent to smash a pot with an ax."

Blood Skull nodded, the first thawing of his reservation. "That is the man I know, too."

"This is madness," Pale Cat whispered. "Are we seriously considering the notion that a band of our warriors—led by our war chief—is running amok, killing innocent Albaamaha?"

"He is after something," Heron Wing said thoughtfully. "I've seen it in his eyes." She glanced up. "You know I have ears among the Albaamaha. Most of you have at least heard the rumors that Red Awl is missing. Among the Albaamaha the story is passed that Smoke Shield and Fast Legs waylaid him, that Smoke Shield tortured Red Awl and raped his wife, Lotus Root, up at the sandstone quarry above Clay Bank Crossing. According to the Albaamaha story, Lotus Root escaped with Smoke Shield's weapons, and bit him on the lip in the process. At the solstice games, Fast Legs, one of Hickory Moiety's best players, was missing."

Blood Skull nodded, looking at Pale Cat. "At the Council he was adamant that the Albaamaha were betraying us. He accused them not only of sending Crabapple to warn White Arrow Town, but also of killing the captives."

Morning Dew drew a breath, stilling herself.

"Yes?" Heron Wing caught her reaction.

In a whisper, she said, "I wouldn't put vendetta beyond Smoke Shield." She glanced hesitantly at Blood Skull. "You were there. You know why he really attacked White Arrow Town."

Blood Skull refused to meet her eyes, focusing instead on the arrow.

"Enlighten us," Night Star said dryly, her eyes like knives.

"To take me," Morning Dew told the dwarf woman.

"Because I spurned him last summer. All that planning to make the raid a success was diversion. The attack on Alligator Town was only the excuse."

"We are to believe that?" Night Star scoffed. "He did all that just to capture you?" She chuckled. "You seem to have a pretty high opinion of yourself, *Matron.*"

Morning Dew stiffened. "Chieftess Night Star, you don't know the man like I do. He is cunning, deceitful, and very, very clever."

Night Star continued to chuckle.

"Do not laugh," Blood Skull said with dark purpose. "It is just as Morning Dew says." He sat back, somehow chastened. "It was perfectly planned. For all Smoke Shield cared, I could have killed Screaming Falcon— the man who planned and conducted the raid on Alligator Town. He meant nothing to Smoke Shield; My explicit orders were to capture Morning Dew alive. It was all orchestrated, right down to the giving of the captives in Council that night."

Heron Wing drew a deep breath. "Nothing said here surprises me. I've lived with Smoke Shield." She lowered her eyes. "I know the depths and ramifications of his cunning as none of you do." Thought lines creased her face; then she added, "I think he is fixing his mistake."

"What mistake?" Pale Cat asked.

"The one he made with Red Awl. He realized that he picked the wrong man. Then, somehow, it went awry. The woman got away. He sent Fast Legs, his accomplice, to find her. I've heard a rumor that Fast Legs was taken by the Albaamaha."

"What?" Night Star cried. "Are you sure?"

"Of that"—Heron Wing shrugged—"no. But something has been brewing up at Bowl Town."

"Sun Falcon said as much." Pale Cat shifted, eyes on the fire. "He said there had been a change among the Albaamaha up there."

"And that was where the supposed Chahta raid was headed. That was where the killing ended." Blood Skull slowly shook his head. "What I do not understand is why nineteen of our warriors would participate in this."

Heron Wing lifted a hand. "Wait, you said Flying Hawk sent them out?"

Blood Skull gave a shrug. "I was playing chunkey some distance away. Flying Hawk spoke to Smoke Shield following a stickball practice. While I wasn't close enough to hear, I could tell by the way Flying Hawk and Smoke Shield acted that it wasn't a pleasant conversation. Immediately afterward, Smoke Shield led some of the men out, supposedly to go hunting. They carried large packs with them. Each group headed off in a different direction."

"The high minko knows," Night Star said. "Someone brought him word."

"That is speculation," Pale Cat countered. "Surely he wouldn't order our warriors to dress up like Chahta?"

"Maybe." Blood Skull raised his eyes. "I heard that Sun Falcon made a quick trip down from Bowl Town. The men paddling his canoe didn't even have time to cage a meal before he had them back in his canoe and paddling north." Blood Skull rubbed his hands together. "You don't believe that nineteen of our warriors would murder Albaamaha? I do. Those warriors trust Smoke Shield...were with us on the White Arrow Town raid. He led them to a singular victory. They saw Crabapple, heard his confession. They know some Albaamo tried to betray us. They trust him, all right."

"But you don't?" Heron Wing noted.

Blood Skull lowered his gaze. "It is no secret that my clan has held Flying Hawk and his nephew in low regard for a long time now."

"Since Flying Hawk killed his brother." Night Star jutted her oversized jaw as if to make the point. "People say there's bad blood there. It goes back to the night of the great fire when Bear Tooth and the matron burned to death. A lot of people still think it odd that only Flying Hawk and his brother survived that night. Some have even speculated—given all that's happened—that Flying Hawk himself set that fire. That to keep the secret, he killed Acorn."

"Who was Acorn?" Morning Dew asked.

"His twin brother," Blood Skull told her. "Most people still knew him by the name Acorn. He was just becoming a man."

"Everything went wrong starting that night," Night Star insisted. "Flying Hawk might look like a ripe persimmon from the outside, but he always had a worm eating out his insides."

Morning Dew said, "The current problem isn't Flying Hawk. He finally made peace with my people. We didn't like him, but he finally came around to the idea of leaving us alone." She met their eyes, one by one. "Flying Hawk is old and he's tired. I've been in the palace. I've seen the look in Smoke Shield's eyes when Flying Hawk lectures him."

"So?" Pale Cat asked. "That's what uncles do."

"Smoke Shield is chafing, angry, and the White Arrow raid has given him a sense of invincibility."

"Right up to the solstice games when he lost everything," Blood Skull countered.

Morning Dew shot a look of thanks at Heron Wing. "But that wasn't his fault. He made five of the goals." She straightened. "Here's what I think: Flying Hawk hears of something wrong upriver. He tells Smoke Shield to fix it. So Smoke Shield takes matters into his own hands again. By deceiving us into believing it's a Chahta raid, he throws the Albaamaha off-balance, dampens their ardor for revolt. The raid also affects the Council— distracts them from Smoke Shield's misdeeds and focuses them on the Chahta threat. Suddenly attention is shifted from the missing Red Awl to outside enemies.

When the Council thinks of the Chahta, they think of Smoke Shield's raid again." She shook her head. "How brilliant."

Pale Cat mused, "And if something happens to Flying Hawk, the Council *will* confirm him to be high minko. What then?"

Night Star said, "He will plunge us into war. He will do it as a means to increase his prestige and authority. He will lead us to destruction with his plotting."

"The problem is," Heron Wing noted, "who—with the exception of those present—is going to believe any of this?"

THIRTEEN

AT THE SUGGESTION of some Chahta who had accompanied them partway downstream, Trader made camp on an old levee of the Horned Serpent. Behind them a shallow swampy backwater was full of bald cypress, tupelo, and sweet gum. Hanging moss drooped from the branches, and white herons waded in the shallows. In summer it would have been riotous with fish and swarms of insects. The mosquitoes were already humming in loathsome columns, kept at bay only by the grease-based lotion Old White had concocted of spruce, larkspur, and red root. A fire not only gave them warmth, but cast its cheery light over the camp. Trader sat with his back propped against a tree and listened to the last of Paunch's story. He kept noticing that young Whippoorwill continued to give him her large-eyed attention.

Why is she so obsessed with me? Not that he minded an attractive woman's intimate stare, but gods, the woman had just met him.

In his mind he couldn't help but compare her with Two Petals. Where the Contrary had a fuller body, wider in the hips with more pronounced breasts, Whippoorwill carried herself with a slender grace. When she moved it was almost as though she were ethereal. Whippoorwill had washed her hair, allowing it to flow around her in soft black waves. The effect was to make her face even more delicate and feminine. For the moment she watched him with a curious attention that missed no detail. Her large dark eyes seemed to drink of his very soul.

Trader muttered to himself, turning his attention back to the conversation.

"And then the Chahta captured us," Paunch finished. "You know the rest of the story."

Old White tapped the dottle from his pipe, expression lined. "It wasn't wise to try and warn the White Arrow."

Paunch lowered his head. "I know. It was my fault. Our mikkos had decided against it. I have no one to blame but myself."

Trader had translated most of the story to Two Petals, but near the end, she had finally looked at him, saying, "I'm hanging on each of your words, each one echoing in the Spirit world. Is it because the world's hollow? What do you think of the Chahta arrows sticking in the dead? It's all a mystery."

He'd glanced uneasily at her, chalking it off as one of her peculiar moments.

Old White sighed, slapped at a mosquito, and studied his pipe in the firelight. "Lucky for you that the Contrary chose you, Paunch."

Paunch shook his head. "My Power is bad. It has led me to poor choices." He glanced at Whippoorwill. "It has plugged my ears when they could have listened to wiser counsel." He paused. "How has this happened to me? I have gone from a happy man to a prisoner and slave."

Old White shrugged. "Your fate belongs to the Contrary."

"But it was you who Traded such a precious gorget to save us." Paunch looked confused.

Old White replied, "I did it for her, for Power. So, Paunch, I wouldn't be too quick to think Power had turned against me, were I you."

He nodded. "I am not the same man who once plotted against the Chikosi. Looking back, it wasn't so bad, having a full belly and never having to worry about being hung in a square."

Two Petals said, "Everything in its place, threads woven."

In Albaamaha, Whippoorwill added, "The weave must now be pulled tight."

Trader and Old White crossed knowing glances, wondering if Two Petals was referring to Paunch's declaration, which—not speaking

Mos'kogee—she couldn't understand, or if she was talking to one of her Spirits. The way Whippoorwill followed the Contrary's speech was a puzzle to both of them.

Trader shifted to a different position on the tree, blowing smoke up at the mosquitoes. "How did relations grow so strained between the Albaamaha and the Sky Hand?"

"They are arrogant conquerors." Paunch spread his hands. "Look, I realize you are foreign Traders, but you must understand: This land was ours once. We came here just after our emergence from under the World Tree. The Chikosi took our heritage from us. How can resentment not fester? They just sit there, behind their walls, imposing their will through their mighty warriors. We are the ones who sweat in the sun, raising their food, building and repairing their towns."

"I thought you had a voice in their Council," Trader remarked.

Paunch looked at him. "You have only passed through. Seen only what a Trader would see. Yes, once we did have a voice. But that was long ago, back before the great fire, when Makes War was high minko. In my lifetime I have seen things turn against us. We have become even more meaningless than ever. Flying Hawk worked to silence our voices. The Ancestors alone know what our fate will be when Smoke Shield is made high minko."

"Smoke Shield," Trader muttered. "I keep hearing his name."

Paunch declared, "He's Chief Clan. They're all sired of weasels mated with foul-tempered badgers."

Chief Clan? Trader and Old White glanced at each other, expressions amused. Paunch missed it. Whippoorwill didn't, a curious smile gracing her lips.

"It's a large clan," Trader noted. "There are many lineages."

"I hope Horned Serpent crawls out of the river and devours them all," Paunch growled. "I remember my uncle telling me how things were better in the old days. Before Flying Hawk. We might have been two peoples, but at least we were granted a little respect."

"Back before the great fire," Old White mused.

Paunch nodded. "People always bemoaned the fact that Flying Hawk and his dead brother were the only ones who survived that night. But even before that, so the stories say, things were turning against us. It started with the loss of the war medicine and the death of High Minko Makes War. Then Midnight Woman, the Chief Clan matron, married that War Chief Bear Tooth, and things went bad." Paunch made a face. "I think Power wanted to be rid of them all. That's why the Great Palace was burned that night. Power tried to kill them off, but somehow, it missed Flying Hawk and Acorn." He grunted. "Although Flying Hawk finished half of Power's work later. Too bad he didn't kill himself after he drove a rock into his brother's head."

Trader swallowed hard, having stiffened, his ears burning as the man talked. It all brought back memories— that look in his dead brother's eyes that he had fled from so long ago.

About to speak, Trader happened to glance at Old White, and the words stopped in his throat. The expression on the Seeker's face was like a lightning-riven mask.

"Time to turn in," Old White said with odd defeat.

"The currents eddy and flow," Two Petals added ominously. "No one can stop the river."

"It lives, and a flood is coming," Whippoorwill added in Albaamaha.

Trader blinked, shook himself, and knocked out his pipe bowl. He gestured to Swimmer and took his bedroll before heading off into the darkness. After the talk of dead brothers, the nightmares were sure to come. This night, he wanted to be by himself.

I walk under the trees, moonlight playing through the branches. I can feel them as they come alive. The first of the sap is waking, beginning to flow toward the branch tips. Soon, they will bud. The flowers, so delicate and fine, will enlarge inside the buds, swelling until they burst the shell. Soon they will unfurl and send their sweetness into the air. Pollen will spread with the sweet aroma, finding new homes. The seeds will be fertile.

I look down at the patterns of moonlight crisscrossed with branches. I am a being of the forest. I, too, feel the call. It Dances with me, swaying with each careful step I take. I let myself flow with the forest, feeling the dormant world around me beginning to stir.

For the first time, I am stirring with it. Coming alive in a way I never have before. What will it be like to take the seed, to begin the process of new life?

I stop, seeing the dog, his white-tipped tail arcing in the pale light like some curious creature.

I kneel down, hearing the man groan in his sleep. Moonlight caresses his smooth face, reveals the movements of his eyes. His Dreams are tortured, set free to plague him by careless words.

Straightening, I pull the dress over my head, letting it settle onto the ground. I throw my head back, and the moonlight casts its magic over my naked body. I trace the shadow patterns of branches over my skin, running the tips of my fingers along the designs cast by new life. I shift slightly so that the shadows lay across my breasts, and center over my womb. The warm rush in my loins quickens.

As I lift the edge of his blanket, he stirs, still half locked in the Dream. He blinks, struggling to wake. My cool fingers find his lips, stilling the question that rises in his throat. With my other hand I reach down, feeling him already hard under his shirt and breech-cloth. Perhaps that is why I must act now, to counter the Power of his Dream with my own.

He watches me, mystified, as I untie his breechcloth, letting it fall away from his slim hips. Freed of restraint, his shaft is bathed in the soft light. I let my fingers slip down its firm length. At my touch, his body stiffens, growing as hard as his member.

My hair falls around us as I straddle him. I have seen this moment, waited for it. Brother Moon has timed my body for him. My blood rushes, heart beating with anticipation as I place the point of his shaft into my moist sheath. As I settle, the length of him fills me. The sensation is new, urgent, and wonderfully uncomfortable. I stare down into his moon-filled eyes, savoring the miracle.

His mouth opens as I begin to rotate my hips. His hands rise, closing on my breasts, rolling them with each motion my desperate loins crave.

For the moment, we are eternal, playing our part in the endless ritual of life.

When he finally arches against me, I tighten, awed by the Power of his release jetting inside me. The rising tingle is my only warning before a pulsating rush of pleasure shoots lightning through my hips, up my back, and down my legs.

When it is finished, when I can breathe again, I roll to the side, trapping his fluids inside.

Why? The question fills his eyes.

"Because you are the future," I tell him softly.

———

Two Petals stood naked in the moonlight, bathed in the soft white radiance. She had been drawn to this open spot, free of the shadows cast by high branches. The moon filled her, glowing on her skin, her nipples no more than dark dots on her round breasts. She raised her arms, letting the light flow over her. A faint breeze shifted her long dark hair where it hung down her back.

She heard the soft steps approaching from behind and waited until they came to a stop to her right. Just as in the Dream, she relived the moment as Whippoorwill raised her arms to the moonlight. They stood silently, side by side, arms raised, naked bodies illuminated by the glow.

"We have Danced the first steps," she whispered.

Whippoorwill's hushed voice spoke—the Dream inside Two Petals' head saying, *"We are bound."*

Even across the distance, Two Petals could hear the sweet Song of her husband. It wound over the hills, through the trees, and across the leaf-strewn ground. She felt herself sway with it, and closed her eyes, letting the musical strains mingle with her souls. I *hear you, husband.*

In time to the Albaamo woman's voice, the Dream said, *"He knows you are coming. Have you Dreamed a way to obtain the copper?"*

"Yes." She sighed, lowering her arms as the Song faded. An empty longing opened in her souls. "It will be difficult. Tricking a clever and suspicious man is perilous at best, but he has weaknesses."

"He and deceit are old companions. He breathes treachery with every heartbeat."

"There are things I must learn in order to distract him."

"Use them well. His slightest suspicion will mean disaster for all." Whippoorwill lowered her arms. Her long black hair seemed to gather the darkness as it hung over the rounded globes of her buttocks. The woman's slender legs were firmly braced, her bare feet on the leaves beside a rolled dress.

Two Petals said, "Trader and Old White will need you when the time comes."

"I *know.*"

Two Petals turned her gaze to the forest, seeing the black shape slipping through the shadows. A large black wolf stepped into the moonlight and fixed luminous yellow eyes on them. The animal lowered his head in canine greeting.

"Your guide has come."

They shared one final glance, bits and pieces of visions and Dreams flowing between them like colors of light.

"In the future, when you Dance, Dance for me."

"Always," Whippoorwill's Dream voice replied.

Then the woman reached down, lifted her dress from the leaves, and slipped it over her head. She walked to the wolf, each step airy. The Spirit animal turned to match her pace, and they disappeared into the shadows launch didn't know what to make of the Seeker. He had heard of the man—who hadn't? But he'd always believed him to be a legend. And that was a problem. How did a lowly Albaamo farmer deal with a living legend? Especially one who had used a priceless copper gorget to purchase said farmer and his granddaughter's lives?

For the moment, unable to think of anything else, he cooked breakfast.

The sun was casting its first faint rays over the trees and into their camp on the levee. Paunch shot nervous glances at the roll of blankets where the old man was sleeping, wondering what Dreams hovered inside that old white head. Trader and his dog had slept farther out, away from the camp. But then—for all Paunch knew— perhaps he always did.

Whipporwill's blanket lay empty, and that worried him no little bit. But then, she'd always been odd. She often rose in the middle of the night and walked off.

Tell me that this is one of those times she will show up at just the right moment.

He glanced again at the Seeker's sleeping form. How, he wondered, was he going to explain Whippoorwill's odd behavior to her new master?

And then there was the Contrary. She was another matter. She sat across the fire from him, watching with really spooky eyes as he stirred the boiling freshwater mussels and added dried grapes, red currants, and pawpaws.

"Wish you could talk," he said. He cursed himself for not learning Trade Tongue, but as a farmer what use did he have for the languages of the elite? For most of his people it was enough just to know a smattering of Chikosi. "I wish Amber Bead was here. He can talk Trade Tongue."

And that got him to thinking. Was the old man even alive? Had so much gone wrong in Split Sky City that the Chikosi had discovered his duplicity and hung his old friend from the square?

"Too much for an old man to know" he muttered, glancing again at the Contrary, wondering what she was seeing. Just an old slave? But by Abba Mikko's eyebrows, did she have to give him that dark-eyed stare? He avoided looking at her. Meeting her eyes was like looking into midnight. Each time he felt his souls sway, as if their hold on his body had suddenly come adrift.

The Seeker rolled onto his back, yawned, and made a face. When he sat up, his brightly colored blanket fell away.

Paunch watched him climb stiffly to his feet, arch his back, and step over to the side. He relieved himself, looking up at the morning sky, stretching. Then he replaced his breechcloth and stepped to the fire before squatting to extend his hands.

The Contrary said something incomprehensible, and the Seeker glanced at the rumpled blanket where Whippoorwill had slept.

He turned curious eyes on Paunch. "I think the Contrary is telling me your granddaughter is gone."

"Elder, don't panic." Paunch spread his hands. "She does this. The girl has never been right." He tried to smile reassuringly. "Power has always touched her. She'll be back before we go. She wouldn't just leave me."

The Contrary laughed.

The Seeker asked some question, and the Contrary replied.

Paunch swallowed hard, saying, "I've got breakfast cooking. A good meal for us. Something to keep the gut happy for a long day."

The Seeker sighed. "You aren't planning on running, are you?"

"Who? Me?" He shook his head vigorously. "Oh, no. I've had my fill of hiding out in the forest." He forced himself to keep his attention on the fire. *By the Ancestors, Whippoorwill, get back here and set this man's souls at ease.*

The Seeker frowned at the flames, shot a quick glance at the Contrary, then asked, "I would know more about the situation with the Albaamaha. Who leads this uprising?"

Paunch scratched his head. What did he say? It wasn't like the man really cared, did he? "Why would you want to know?"

The Seeker gave him a reproving look. "We're Trading our way down the river. Can you think of a reason that I wouldn't have at least some interest in the local politics?"

One thing was sure, as long as he belonged to the Traders, he wouldn't be scrambling for his life. A single glance at the canoes had told him that untold riches lay hidden in those packs. And who knew? They might end up among the Koasti, relatives of the Albaamaha. Once there he might have a chance of slipping away with Whippoorwill. The two of them could make a home for themselves. Whippoorwill could Heal, maybe tell fortunes. Things were looking up.

"Very well," Paunch said. "The mikkos are dissatisfied, but most are cautious, afraid to wake the Chikosi bear's anger. But people work like slaves, only to pack their harvest away to Chikosi granaries. Those people breed like rabbits. The man who most wants to see the Sky Hand weakened is Amber Bead. The stupid Chikosi think he's a doddering old fool. Amber Bead is clever, though. He keeps his ear to the ground. He was the one who hatched the plot to send Crabapple to White Arrow Town." He winced. "I had already sent the boy before I heard that the mikkos disapproved."

"And you told me that he ran right into the war party?"

Paunch nodded. "He wasn't much more than a boy. He must have confessed everything under torture." He stared down at his hands. "It was my fault."

"How close to an uprising are the Albaamaha?"

"I cannot tell, master. Much will have depended on what has happened while I was in hiding." He looked up. "But I don't think you want to Trade with the Chikosi. I have heard that the Koasati have marvelous things: shells, yaupon, remarkable wooden goods. Is it true that stingray spines and hanging moss are valued in the northern Trade? The Koasati have them in great abundance."

The Seeker stifled a smile. "Yes, it is true."

Paunch used a stick to stir the stew. "I can help you. Albaamaha and Koasati are related. According to the story, we were the same people once, back before we emerged from beneath the roots of the World Tree. They came out on one side of a root, and we on the other. Trading with them would be like Trading with brothers. My skills could be of good use to you."

The Seeker nodded. "That is pleasing to know."

"Whippoorwill and I will act tirelessly to help you make back the value of that gorget." He gestured with the stick. "Do not think for a moment that we are ungrateful for your actions on our part."

His stomach was growling at the smell of the stew. By Abba Mikko's eyebrow, he'd dreamed of such while eating bugs and nuts in the forest. Traveling with the Traders would have him putting on fat in no time.

Trader came walking in, a perplexed look on his face. He was scratching his hair, his blanket rolled under one arm. The dog was pacing at his side, tail swinging. The man glanced around, noted Whippoorwill's flat blanket, and lifted an inquiring brow.

"Do not worry," Paunch cried brightly. "I'm sure she's out in the forest. You know, attending to women's things."

Trader started. "It's not her moon, is it?"

"No, no. She passed that not so long ago. Just before the Chahta caught us."

Trader seemed to take a relieved breath.

"Nothing to worry about," Paunch continued. "She'll tell me before she has to go into seclusion."

The Seeker said something in Trade Tongue, and Trader shot a glance at the Contrary, who spoke softly. At that Trader turned, staring out at the woods for a moment; then he rushed down to the canoes where they lay beached at the foot of the levee. He took quick inventory of his packs, and muttered to himself in obvious relief.

Paunch felt fingers of worry clutching at his souls as he furtively searched the woods. *Come back, Granddaughter. This is starting to worry them.*

Trader said something reassuring as he strode up the incline, and squatted beside the Seeker.

"We were discussing the Albaamaha," the Seeker said in Mos'ko-gee. "The ringleader is a mikko called Amber Bead. But Paunch tells me the Albaamaha are split. Some want revolt; others are afraid."

"What would it take to start an uprising?" Trader asked, eyes on Paunch.

"One atrocity by the Chikosi and the whole country could erupt," Paunch told him darkly. "You can't trust their Council or leadership. Most of them are thieves." He paused, seeing unease rising in Trader's expression. "The Seeker and I were just talking about heading downriver and Trading with the Koasati."

"They have stingray spines and hanging moss," the Seeker said mildly. "Things of great value in the northern Trade."

"I see," Trader said with equal aplomb.

"You know this Amber Bead well?" the Seeker asked.

"Oh, yes. An old friend. Kin of mine, actually."

Trader and the Seeker were giving each other knowing stares.

"Could we Trade with him?" the Seeker asked.

"He wouldn't have much to Trade." Paunch gestured at the canoes. "The kind of goods you carry can't be parted with for a few baskets of moldy corn. No, for good value, you would want beautiful shell, things from farther south that would make you a handsome return in the north."

"Which the Koasati have," Trader replied, nodding. "I think I understand." He paused. "But wouldn't the Chikosi have those things, too?"

"Trust me." Paunch affected ease. "They're as crooked as a sassafras root. We've been dealing with them for years. No one knows how sneaky they are better than me."

Trader nodded, a grim set to his lips as he found his bowl and scooped up some of the stew. After a taste he said, "Paunch, you'd make a lousy Trader, but your stew is pretty good."

No one said more as they ate, but Paunch couldn't help staring out at the trees.

Whippoorwill? Where are you?

After the meal was finished the Traders began packing.

"I'll be right back," Paunch called. "Just need to use the trees for a moment."

He hurried down the slope, eyes on the swamp. Under his breath, he muttered, "Whippoorwill?"

The empty forest showed no sign of her.

"You coming?" Trader called from behind him. "Or are you going to run like your granddaughter did?"

Paunch hesitated. Go after her? For what? More hiding in the forest?

He rubbed his belly, full to bursting since he'd eaten enough for two. No, there was no turning back. If he was to have any chance, it would be downriver, among the Koasati.

As he turned back and plodded up the slope, he asked himself, *Girl? What have you done?*

———

For two days Smoke Shield had played war games within sight of Bowl Town. He had his warriors working in tandem with Sun

Falcon's. They ran, made mock attacks, charged and shouted from behind a line of shields. Archery practice consisted of the one group releasing a volley of arrows, only to have the second group run forward and release theirs. Like overlapping waves, they practiced the advance technique, well aware that Albaamaha eyes were watching.

He had each warrior demonstrate his skill with a war club, often matching equally skilled opponents to hack at each other with sticks of wood, practicing blocking, striking, and parrying.

The message was clear: If you do not submit, we will turn this on you.

But threaten as he might, no offer of information was made as to the whereabouts of Lotus Root. Sun Falcon's few remaining informants reported that for all intents and purposes, she might have walked to the edge of the world and fallen off.

Thus it was that a somber Smoke Shield led his warriors back into Split Sky City. He tried to come to some conclusion as to the effectiveness of his efforts. The Albaamaha in the north had seemed pacified. None of their inscrutable faces had told him anything except that they were beaten. Not cowed by any means, but they understood the doom he could rain down upon them.

"Not a word," he had warned his nineteen warriors as they neared the city. "What we did was special, a thing of Power. You do not tell your friends, your uncles, or brothers. From this moment forward, our part in the Chahta raid did not happen."

"What of purification?" Bear Paw asked. "We have been bloodied. There is no alternative but to retire to the Men's House. There we must fast, drink button snakeroot, and purge our systems of pollution."

"We will do that," Smoke Shield told him. "But the story is that we do so because we have been in the presence of Albaamaha corpses. Our story is that some terrible Chahta Power may have been turned against us. We tell no one of what we did. *No one!* If any of you speaks of this thing, you will answer to me." And then he had made them all swear, binding themselves to the most terrible of oaths.

Only as he led them up from the canoe landing, Singing, stamping, and clapping their clubs against the sides of their war shields, did he wonder if anyone would remember hunters leaving, and warriors returning.

People formed up on both sides, watching them, cheering. Smoke

Shield thrust out his chest, leading the procession with the same arrogant pride he would have had he just razed a Chahta town.

Three times they circled the tchkofa; then he led his procession to the Men's House. He could see Flying Hawk standing at the high palace gate. The high minko shaded his eyes with a hand, watching like a mute sentry from atop the mound.

Upon entering the Men's House, Smoke Shield ordered the fires to be built up, and the sweat house to be made ready. He pointed to one of the youths lingering outside the door, ordering, "Send for the *Hopaye*. My warriors must undergo purification rituals to ensure that we bring no evil into the city."

The boy left at a run.

As Smoke Shield had expected, Flying Hawk appeared in no more time than it would have taken the old man to descend the stairway and cross the plaza. The high minko entered, smiled at the warriors, and indicated that Smoke Shield should follow him out to the sweat house. He shooed the boys away from the fire they were making, and gestured Smoke Shield into the dark and cramped interior.

Leaving the flap open so that he could see if anyone approached, Flying Hawk asked, "Well?"

"I have seen to the situation. Fast Legs will tell no one of his activities. No one is the wiser."

"And the woman?"

"Gone. No one knows where." Smoke Shield cupped his hands. "She is too conspicuous. If she shows up, we will hear. My suspicion is that she will mysteriously disappear some night if she has the temerity to raise her voice."

"And your missing arrows?"

Smoke Shield shrugged. "Missing, with the woman, I presume."

Flying Hawk stroked his chin, reflecting. "There was no Chahta raid, was there?"

"Oh, yes, Uncle," Smoke Shield replied. "And a very cunning one, too, I must add. May Breath Giver bless Great Cougar, for he solved a lot of our problems with his audacious attack. The Albaamaha are cowed, but unfortunately Fast Legs, and the kind Albaamaha who found him hurt and were caring for him, are dead. It's a shame that Fast Legs and his helpers cannot come forward and tell their side of the story. Chief Sun Falcon and Bowl Town are secure, and the Chahta raiders have been driven off."

"Though no one can find their trail."

"Odd, isn't it, that they seemed to simply disappear from the land?"

Flying Hawk watched him with flat, emotionless eyes. "Someone will talk."

Smoke Shield shook his head. "Even the ghosts of the slain Albaamaha think they were killed by Chahta. As to my warriors, they have their own reasons to keep their tongues. These are men who followed me into White Arrow Town. They fully understand the Albaamaha threat. They understand the gravity of our situation here."

Flying Hawk vented his irritation with a clenched fist. "You play with fire!"

"And I put it out with my piss when I am done." Smoke Shield glared at the man. "The green shoot that started up when the Albaamaha sent that courier to warn the Chahta has been clipped off short. No leaves will sprout from this, Uncle. The Albaamaha have been paid back for the murder of the captives. They have been given a lesson on our strength and prowess. No one can lay this at the doorstep of the Sky Hand; meanwhile the plotters among the Albaamaha know that there is a price to be paid for treachery. Those who were innocent have been reminded that only our warriors stand between them and the enemy."

"As long as none of your warriors talk."

"They are my *picked* men. Their loyalty is to their people. But it would harm nothing if upon their leaving the Men's House, their high minko rewarded their dedication to the people with a grand feast and gifts."

"That will be done."

"Good." Smoke Shield smiled. "Because, Uncle, you have a stake in this, too. Each and every one of those warriors believe down in their souls that this Chahta raid was done with your blessing. They think *you* ordered it."

Flying Hawk gave him a chilling look. "And why would they think that?"

"Because that's what I told them."

Flying Hawk was no one's fool. He understood very well the trap Smoke Shield had laid for him. Wearily, he said, "Very well, I will go and make my report to the Council." Flying Hawk pointed a finger.

"But if any of this turns sour, you are on your own. You understand that, don't you?"

"Nothing will go wrong, Uncle." He smiled, feeling Power hovering in the air around him. "Nothing can stand in my way now."

Not even you.

FOURTEEN

AMBER BEAD SAT before his hearth. His house was dark—the fire burned down to coals. He watched the draft coming in from the door cast different patterns in the coals.

Flying Hawk had dismissed the Council after making his report. Warriors had combed the country to the west, some even skirmishing with the Chahta scouts watching vigilantly on their side of the divide, but no one had found the route taken by the raiders.

Twenty-three of my people are dead. The knowledge was like a splinter under the skin. It was as if the Chahta had known exactly where to strike. *And then they killed Fast Legs and his captors.*

Hearing that had been like a stab, followed by curious relief. Perhaps Power had balanced, removing his people's greatest asset and threat, while claiming twenty-three lives as payment. Fast Legs would never reveal what had been done to Red Awl. That spear of revenge had been forever broken, and with it any possibility of an Albaamaha uprising stemming from Red Awl's blood.

"A disaster averted, an opportunity lost." He pulled at the loose skin under his chin.

For the moment, his people's ardor was cooled, damped in the blood of twenty-three victims. This night, in the farmsteads, people lay in their blankets, wondering when the Chahta would strike again; who would their victims be next time? In contrast, they had seen grim parties of Chikosi warriors trotting past, searching relentlessly for the intruders.

He stiffened at the soft scratching at his doorpost.

"Who is there?"

"Mikko?" a woman's voice called.

"Come in."

He watched as the door hanging was pulled back, and then a furtive figure slipped in. In the dim light he couldn't make out the woman's identity. She carried a fabric bag that hung down almost to her knees.

"Are you awake?"

"I am. Just sitting here. Thinking."

The woman walked forward, bowing respectfully. Her hair was shorn, the sign of a recently made widow. Walking up, she laid the bag carefully on the matting and seated herself.

He squinted in the faint light. "Lotus Root?"

"Yes, Mikko."

"By the Ancestors, where have you been?"

"Taking the long way here, avoiding Chikosi warriors."

He could see that she was filthy, mud spattered, and exhausted. The pretty young woman he had once known had vanished, replaced by this hard-eyed creature. Bursting with questions, he instead reached for a bowl of beans and lotus root, placing it on three stones to warm.

"People have been looking for you."

"That is why I have come in the middle of the night. Is there a place here where you can hide me?"

"There are many." He paused. "You have heard that Fast Legs was killed by the Chahta?"

She gave him a level gaze. "Oh, yes, Mikko. I know the lie well. I saw it happen." And she reached down, patting the bag with a tender hand. "These are the scalps of our people. The ones the Chikosi sought to hide. I brought them here, along with Smoke Shield's bow and arrows."

Amber Bead stared at her in the dim light. "The scalps of…But the Chahta…How is this possible?"

In a haunted voice she said, "Power has given us the means to destroy the Chikosi. And by the ghosts of these murdered people, I swear, I *will do it!*"

Deep in her voice, in the set of her shoulders and the passionate glow of her eyes, he recognized pure hatred mixed with a deep-burning rage.

The smell of steaming hickory oil mixed with the pungent odor of woodsmoke as Morning Dew lifted the heavy pot. Loops had been molded into the rim, and cords had been run through. When the thongs were laced over the sticks of a tripod, the bowl could be hung over the fire, its height adjusted by the position of the tripod legs to control the temperature. She now used the cords to carry the vessel over to a larger pot over which she had placed a loosely woven fabric.

Moving the heavy pot into position, she shortened the cords to pour the hot mash of ground hickory nuts and oil into the larger vessel. Stepping back, she laid the pot to one side and lifted the edges of the fabric, using it to strain hickory pulp from the oil.

The hot fabric she then placed into a shallow bowl, allowing it to cool. Later, when the temperature was right, she would wring the last of the oil from the cooked meats. The meats she would use with white acorns, walnuts, and ground goosefoot seeds to produce a heavy bread.

Hickory oil was used in cooking, oil lamps, wads to be placed on torches, and any number of other uses.

Sometimes it even served as a dip to be soaked up with lotus-root bread.

Wiping her brow, Morning Dew stepped around to the doorway. There in a tall-necked bottle, a cool drink of sassafras tea slacked her thirst. She was replacing the bottle when she saw Wide Leaf, her head bent close to Heron Wing's. The old slave nodded, gave Heron Wing a quick hug, and turned, leaving around the back of the house.

Heron Wing stared thoughtfully after her, then, wiping her hands with a rag, she turned, seeing Morning Dew. She sighed and started forward, brow lined.

"News from the Albaamaha?" Morning Dew guessed.

"Something is up. Wide Leaf only caught a whiff of it. Amber Bead has a visitor. Someone so secret, he doesn't want anyone to know."

"And who could that be?"

"Wide Leaf has no idea, but she says that young men have been dispatched to most of the Albaamaha mikkos." She looked back in the direction Wide Leaf had taken. "I hope to the gods that she's careful."

Morning Dew reached for the tea bottle again. "Drink?"

Heron Wing took the bottle and raised it to her lips. She didn't even seem to taste the sweet tea, her gaze instead drifting toward the plaza, resting for a moment on the tchkofa. She seemed to ignore the two men practicing on the chunkey court. A knot of children were watching, shouting encouragement. "Whatever it is, Wide Leaf says that tension and speculation have grown overnight in the Albaamaha village. No one seems to know what's happening, but it's important enough that Amber Bead has left for the hills. He was gone before sunrise."

"Amber Bead?" Morning Dew wondered. "I thought he was just an old man."

Heron Wing gave an absent shrug. "I've always thought he was more; but then, what do I know?"

"I think you know a lot."

"Most of the Council ignores him for the most part."

Morning Dew considered that. "I don't know him."

"Maybe none of us are supposed to."

"Meaning?"

"I'm not sure." Heron Wing waved it off. "Perhaps it is nothing."

"The Albaamaha could suspect what we do, that the raid was a sham."

"Let's go for a walk."

"To the Albaamaha village?"

"No. I was thinking of the canoe landing. Maybe we should go poke around among the Traders. If anything is happening, that's where the rumors fly."

"What about my hickory oil?"

"It should be cool by the time you return. No one will bother it."

Morning Dew slipped inside, finding capes for both of them, then matched Heron Wing's stride as she started across the plaza.

"You and Wide Leaf have been together for a long time."

Heron Wing smiled. "She raised me. I asked her once if she'd like to go home to the Koasati, but she just smiled. She told me she's been here for most of her life. She's not sure she'd know anyone down there. Honestly, it was a relief. Allowing her to be a spy worries me, though. People know we're close."

"You didn't send her?"

"It was her idea. For years now, she has shared my counsel. Offered her own, in fact." She made a face. "Once, years ago, I didn't listen to her advice. I've never made that mistake again."

"What advice was that?"

"She told me that if I married Smoke Shield, I would regret it."

Enough said there. "You seem to inspire loyalty from your slaves."

Heron Wing laughed. "I have found that I can get more out of people by treating them with respect, listening to their ideas, and helping them than by ordering them around." A pause. "It's a skill that has served me and my people well over the years."

"You would have made a formidable matron yourself."

"No. Then I'd have to spend my life tied up in plotting, mischief, and politics."

Morning Dew chuckled. In a more serious tone, she said, "I want to thank you for everything you've done for me. But for your advice, I'd be dead now. Or worse, broken and beaten. If I ever leave here, I hope that I can act with your wisdom and skill."

They touched their foreheads as they passed the Tree of Life pole with its red-and-white spiral. To the right, the high minko's palace rose as if to challenge the skies. A team of young girls were practicing stickball, passing, running, their long black hair flying out behind them. A group of boys watched, more interested in the girls than the game.

They passed Minko Vinegaroon's massive mound, not as high as Flying Hawk's but with a larger building atop it. Not only did the structure serve as the Skunk Clan chief's, but its large council chamber was used to conduct most of the Old Camp Moiety's internal business. At its base were the houses of the Skunk Clan leaders, their granaries, and society houses. Winding through these, Heron Wing called greetings to people.

Occasional dogs and children stepped out to watch them pass. The workshops where shell was processed sent the familiar onion odor into the air as men and women cut, ground, and incised beads and gorgets. To the northwest stood the charnel house. When a member of the Skunk Clan died, he was taken there, laid out on benches, and his flesh carefully removed from the bone. Only after the proper rituals were completed were the bones given to relatives for final burial.

Morning Dew, though familiar with the scent of death, had never particularly cared for it.

Just past that they walked around the stoneworking shops where men ground and polished sandstone, granite, and claystones. Most of Split Sky City's pipes, statuary, axes, adzes, and war clubs were finished here. Two lineages—with workshops across from each other — specialized in shaping sandstone disks for paint palettes.

Winding through tightly packed houses, Heron Wing led the way down the slope to the canoe landing. Morning Dew tried to remember the last time she had been here, walking in a half daze as she climbed the slope, her mind on captivity and the fate of her husband and family.

It seemed like a lifetime past. That day she'd been unable to see much for the press of people who had come to watch the returning warriors enter the city in triumph. Now, on an average day, the beach was lined with canoes drawn up parallel on the sand. The ground was black, stained from old campfires, rotting refuse, and almost glittering with flakes of stone, bits of broken pottery, and rocks spalled in the fires.

Ramadas were placed haphazardly: occasional shelter for Trade goods brought in from up and down the river. Here visitors from the other towns landed and displayed whatever goods they had brought with them. The blankets laid out on the ground created a colorful patchwork, their surfaces crowded with wooden bowls; boxes; folds of fabric; jars of corn, beans, squash, dried fruits, nuts; haunches of meat; hides; tools; and the other minutiae of Trade.

Heron Wing slowed as they passed a blanket set out by an Albaamaha family. A line of fish had been laid out, the dead eyes starting to dry, mouths agape.

"A good catch," Heron Wing noted.

"Power was with us, great lady," the fisherman said. His wife looked up, nodding, unsure what to say in the presence of a high-born Chikosi.

"Where are you from?" Heron Wing asked, bending down to inspect the largest of the catfish.

"Our farm lies south of Hickory Town. Just to the south."

"Ah, you were away from the Chahta raid."

"Oh, yes," the man said quickly. "Fortunately, they went north. But we're closer to the river, safer for the most part. Could I interest you in the fish?"

"No, not today, but he's a fine one. I wish you the best of Trade."

"And to you," he said, and touched his chin.

One by one, they passed the blankets, talking, praising the goods.

"What do you think?" Morning Dew asked.

"I think whatever Wide Leaf heard, it hasn't made it here, yet."

Morning Dew looked around, then stopped to inspect a wooden bowl. It was a beautiful thing, made of walnut, carefully hollowed out, polished, and waxed to a sheen that accented the perfect grain. The handles had been formed in the shape of a raccoon's head on one end, its tail on the other, rings rendered in the carving. The four five-fingered feet had been cunningly carved into the bowl's legs so that it stood free.

"You like that?" a young Sky Hand man asked.

"It's beautiful."

"So are you," he said brazenly. "And for you, I would make a special Trade. Just a little something and a smile are all it would take to send my souls into flight."

"What kind of something did you have in mind?" Heron Wing asked.

The man shrugged. "I am Gray Squirrel, of the Deer Clan and Old Camp Moiety. From up at Thunder Town. I just Traded for this bowl. But for the Chahta raid, I'd have brought it down sooner. I obtained this most special bowl from a friend of mine. He's half Yuchi, half Sky Hand. Now, he lives on the other side of the divide. He's got a Yuchi wife, you see."

"Yuchi?" Heron Wing asked, impressed. "It's good work for the Yuchi."

"They do all right," Gray Squirrel agreed. "But this bowl isn't Yuchi. It comes from the Illinois way up on the Mother Water. Look at the excellence of this workmanship. You don't see the like among the Yuchi." He cocked his head, looking shrewdly at the bowl. "Now, a piece like this would make a wondrous gift...perhaps something to give at a marriage, or perhaps for a special occasion like the Busk Feast. Then again, maybe you have a cherished uncle, someone who has spent most of his life as a teacher and guardian."

Morning Dew ran her fingers over the smooth wood. "What news did your Trader friend tell you of the Yuchi?"

"The most incredible things." Gray Squirrel sat back knowingly. "They are bursting with news."

"Not about Chahta raiders, I hope." Morning Dew carefully replaced the bowl and picked up a wooden cup decorated with the Seeing Hand design.

"No, not the Chahta. The big news on the Tenasee is that Traders came through from the north. Remarkable Traders, like in the old days. That's where this bowl came from. It cost me a shell cup that my Yuchi friend has been admiring for years. These Traders brought all kinds of wondrous goods, and the blind Priest up there…you've heard of him?"

"I have," Heron Wing agreed. "The one who escaped from us summers ago."

"Yes, he's the one. He saw them coming."

"I thought you said he's blind." Morning Dew, herself, had heard of the Kala Hi'ki. The greatest of the Yuchi Priests, he lived at Rainbow City.

"Nevertheless, my Yuchi Trader friend told me the Priest saw them coming. Who knows? Perhaps he actually got word from the Kaskinampo. Those people are thick with each other."

"And these Traders?" Heron Wing asked absently, her eyes straying to the next blanket.

"That's the remarkable thing. One was a Contrary, a woman. She sees everything backward. The other is supposed to be the legendary Seeker. You know, the man who has traveled all over the world. But the biggest thing was a chunkey game."

Heron Wing had taken a half step, her attention on the next blanket. She was interested in Albaamaha rumors, not Yuchi ones. Still, Morning Dew hesitated, loath to leave the magnificent raccoon bowl. "Chunkey is chunkey," she said.

"Not this game. The young Trader played for the Traders' lives against Chief Born-of-Sun. They had to play to twenty-one. And on the last cast, the young Trader made the cast of a lifetime." Gray Squirrel grinned. "He shattered his lance on the stone."

"I thought you said there was only a Contrary and the Seeker?"

Heron Wing was clearly impatient, but too well-mannered to drag her away.

"Ah, but there is a third." Gray Squirrel reached down, lifting the bowl, fully aware that Heron Wing wanted to take herself to the next blanket. "And here's the odd part. The young Trader, he's Sky Hand."

"Sky Hand?" Morning Dew asked, reluctant not to reach for the bowl one last time. What did she, a slave, have to Trade for such a piece?

"He goes by the name of Trader—that's how he's known on the river—but according to what my friend told me, his name is really Green Snake."

The gasp caught both Morning Dew and Gray Squirrel by surprise. They both turned to see Heron Wing, mouth open, staring wide-eyed.

"I'm sorry," Gray Squirrel asked. "Do you know this Green Snake?"

Heron Wing stepped back on shaken legs. "What did you hear of him?"

"The story told up on the Tenasee is that he's traveling with the Seeker and this Contrary. He and Born-of-Sun played chunkey at the solstice. The Yuchi wanted to keep the Seeker and the Contrary. But this Trader, Green Snake, won the match."

Heron Wing seemed to have trouble finding her voice, and the look of confusion on her face left Morning Dew staring in disbelief.

"Did...Did you hear anything else about him?"

Gray Squirrel hesitated, apparently unsure how to use this newfound interest to his best advantage. "I heard that he's Sky Hand. Supposedly Chief Clan, which is why Born-of-Sun ... Are you all right?"

Heron Wing's eyes had lost focus, her hand going to her breast. A pinched frown lined her brow. She reached down, running her fingers along the raccoon bowl's smooth wood, touching...what?

"What would you Trade for the bowl?" Morning Dew asked, distracting Gray Squirrel.

"Oh, it would take a lot," Gray Squirrel replied, sensing his advantage.

"A moment ago, you just asked for my smile and a little something," Morning Dew reminded, flashing him her best smile.

"This bowl came straight from Green Snake's canoe," he shot back, no doubt guessing that such information could drive his Trade higher.

Heron Wing slipped a trembling hand into her belt pouch. She withdrew a small copper pendant, one of the hanging scalp designs that featured a spinning four-legged spiral, below which hung a narrowing tail of copper. The design was indicative of the four directions of the turning heavens. It had been hung from a shell-beaded thong.

He took it, frowning. "I don't know ..."

"That belonged to War Chief Smoke Shield," Heron Wing said, swallowing hard. "I won it from him during the solstice games. He in turn received it from the *Hopaye* Pale Cat. It was a marriage gift."

"I'm not sure," Gray Squirrel said cautiously. "This could be from anyone."

Morning Dew pointed a finger. "Under the Power of Trade, that is the truth. Take the copper pendant. As it had belonged to Smoke Shield, you can Trade it for *ten* bowls among the Yuchi."

"That bowl comes from —"

"Take it, or leave it," Morning Dew insisted, holding her hand out for the pendant.

"It is a Trade," Gray Squirrel said, clutching his fingers around the pendant. Heron Wing reverently lifted the bowl, staring at it as if it were precious beyond belief.

"Oh, and one last thing," Gray Squirrel told them, sure they wouldn't back out now. "If you can believe the stories the Yuchi tell, this Green Snake is supposedly on his way here."

"What?" Heron Wing asked anxiously. *"Here?"*

"That was the rumor. He, the Seeker, and the Contrary are Trading down the Horned Serpent. They're coming here. According to my Yuchi friend, it's something about Power."

Heron Wing had clamped her eyes closed, clutching the bowl to her chest.

"Excuse us, Gray Squirrel." Morning Dew took Heron Wing's arm, steadying her. "My friend isn't feeling well."

She led Heron Wing away from the puzzled Thunder Town Trader. Heron Wing looked shocked, as if someone had just punched her hard in the stomach.

"I'm going to take you home."

"He's alive," Heron Wing whispered. "Gods, he's still alive."

Evidently, Morning Dew thought, *and coming here.*

But who was Green Snake? And if a distant Trader could have

this kind of effect on the rock-solid Heron Wing, did Morning Dew really want him arriving?

———

Word of their coming had spread. As Old White and Trader made their way downriver, they were met at each town landing. People were lined up, some under ramadas, all with their best Trade displayed. At no town were any of Trader's party allowed beyond the landings, though the Chahta made up for it with feasts, Singing and Dancing, and perfect hospitality.

"You'd think they didn't trust us," Old White had noted wryly.

"You have already seen everything," Two Petals told him cryptically. "There is nothing left. It is all so apparent."

"What is?" Trader had replied indignantly. "They're hiding something."

"They are showing us everything," she'd insisted. "Naked, without clothes. You can even see the bones."

White Arrow Town, the southernmost Chahta settlement, was a mess. Old White's party had landed below the town, finding not one, but four grim-eyed warriors guarding the landing. They had nodded, reluctant, but still honoring the Power of Trade. One had run to fetch the war chief, a man named Otter Mankiller. He had looked suspiciously at their cargo, then at Paunch, and said, "The old matron gives you leave to Trade. A place has been made for you." His stern orders ensured that the guards would allow no one close to the canoes and their precious cargo. Trader ordered Swimmer to stay with the packs, just to make sure. He didn't look like much of a guard dog, but then, dogs, like men, could be deceiving.

The town itself was in a state of chaos. Burned buildings had been torn down, and most were in the process of being rebuilt. Rings of charcoal marked where granaries had been incinerated; most consisted of charred posts rising in black spikes toward the sky.

Atop the high minko's mound, a group of slaves labored to dig old posts from the hard clay, sending them rolling down the steep slope to the ground below. These in turn were scavenged for firewood. One thing White Arrow Town had plenty of was partially burned firewood.

They had set up in the plaza, doing their best to stay upwind from the newly rebuilt charnel houses. The odor was disquieting to the senses.

Despite a large crowd when they laid out their goods, Trade had been desultory at best. Most had come to look, to marvel at the goods, and hear the news from upriver. But the people—at least those who weren't in a kind of daze—had little to offer. Trader found himself substantially undercutting value, unable to resist the hollow-eyed women, their hair shorn in mourning, or the thin children who tagged about their legs. By noon most had wandered off, having more pressing concerns to attend to. Now the Traders sat alone, even the children called away by their mothers.

"I think we should head south in the morning," Old White said. "This place doesn't need us right now."

"Have you noticed something?" Trader asked softly.

"The lack of men?"

"Most of the building is being done by women and children."

"Maybe the men are out cutting wood, chopping grass for thatch; and by the gods, they've got to hunt, fish, and collect to feed themselves."

Yes, that made sense. Things in White Arrow Town were difficult enough, let alone finding food.

"You should see them," Two Petals remarked.

"Who?" Trader asked, following her gaze out to the plaza. "The men?"

"All the people. Laughing, running. And what a feast. It's the grandest marriage in a long time, you know."

"Marriage? Where?" Trader asked.

"Right there," she said. "Look at her run! He's hard-pressed to catch her."

"Who, Contrary?" Old White asked in turn.

"Trader's wife," she replied calmly.

Trader shot Old White a skeptical look, shrugged, and went back to making a count of his goods. Not many of his pressed weasel-hide bags were left. Up in the north, weasels turned white for the winter. Skinning them, with their thin hides, was an art. He had opened one of the packs for Trade, figuring that the small skins might be unique to a people whose local weasels remained brown year round. The notion had been that the White Arrow Town people could use them for Trade with their neighbors for items more relevant for their survival, like food and clothing.

He glanced up at the setting sun, and began to carefully replace the remaining hides in their pack. People were already turning to the chores attendant to cooking the evening meal. From what he could see, most of the pots were filled with a watery stew. Not as many people were in town, most having moved out to farmsteads near the forest to hunt, or to camps along the river where fishing and trapping waterfowl was easier. The normal food stocks had been burned during the attack.

They were lacing up the packs when a single warrior happened to stop by. "Greetings. I heard that Traders were in town. Not much to Trade, I suppose?"

"Oddly," Old White answered, "we are pleased. The goods we offered will help. Little things from the north that people can tempt their neighbors with."

The warrior looked at the collection of little stick figures, wooden beads, occasional bits of shell, packs of hanging moss, and carved bone. The Trade looked dull and lusterless beside the few northern goods displayed.

"My people appreciate the gesture," the warrior said, squatting. He looked out at the plaza, where solitary individuals passed. "I have heard kind things said. Most know that you took a loss on their account. I think many are embarrassed by their current circumstances."

"White Arrow Town will come back," Trader told him. "I know the Chahta. By next fall, after a good harvest, the heart will be beating here again."

The man chuckled without humor. "Let us hope so. The future, however, is a grim place."

"Why is that?" Old White asked.

"I've been scouting in the forest. Keeping an eye on the Chikosi. We watch them; they watch us. Sometimes we shoot an arrow at someone who gets too close. Mostly we shout curses at each other." He gave them a curious glance. "I heard that you came from upriver?"

"We did."

"You saw Great Cougar?"

"We did. Traded for that lazy Albaamaha over there." Old White pointed to where Paunch lay sleeping on a blanket beneath a ramada.

The warrior seemed to digest that, then asked, "Was Great Cougar planning a raid?"

Old White's bushy eyebrow lifted. "Just the opposite. He's organizing his forces to ambush the Chikosi when they attack in spring."

"That's what I thought." A pause. "Odd."

"What is?" Trader asked. "It seems a sound defense. Here you can ambush them on your home ground. Lead them into traps and generally make them miserable."

The warrior took out a little stick he'd stuck in his belt. He drew doodles on the clay as he said, "One of the Chikosi, the man who was watching me watch him, said that Great Cougar had raided the Sky Hand lands east of the divide and killed some Albaamaha. This Chikosi...he promised revenge."

"Great Cougar did this?" Trader asked.

"That's what the Chikosi said. According to him, it was several days ago. Just after the rains."

"If Great Cougar did, he is indeed a great warrior," Old White noted, "for he was able to do what every war chief wishes more than anything else: He was in two places at once. We were guests in his palace during that entire time."

"I thought so. It must be some Chikosi plot, but for the life of me, I can't understand what it would be. What do they gain by threatening retaliation for a raid we didn't commit?"

"What else did you hear from the Chikosi?" Trader asked, reaching over for his last weasel skin.

"Threats of what they'd do to us. Some kind of nonsense about our 'ally Albaamaha' and how we couldn't weaken them that way."

"The Albaamaha are your allies?" Old White asked.

"That's news to us." The warrior retraced his doodle. "An Albaamo is just a Chikosi hand-licker. After what happened here, we'd just as soon kill every last one of them."

"You lost someone?" Old White asked.

"Two brothers, their wives, and some children. I've taken my nieces and nephews in. My wife was fortunate; she got through the gate. It will be a stretch, but we'll keep food in their mouths." He glanced up, lines forming around the corners of his eyes. "Hard to do when I have to spend half my time out in the forest."

"Here." Trader handed him one of the remaining weasel skins. He explained how northern weasels changed color and how the northern chiefs had entire cloaks made only of the white tails with their black tips. "Take it. If you can get to some of the Pearl River towns, that hide should Trade for enough corn and beans to fill those young bellies you're worried about."

The warrior ran his finger over the soft fur. "I have nothing to Trade."

Old White replied, "We are now bound by the Power of Trade. Someday in the future, when things are better, you can give us something in return."

The warrior smiled wearily. "Someday. Yes, Seeker, I will do that." He stood, replacing the stick in his belt and rubbing the fur. "For now, I pray that Power hovers around you, and protects you from any evil. I thank you."

Trader watched him walk away. "Great Cougar was raiding the Albaamaha? How?"

Old White shrugged. "It was only talk between "two warriors in the forest. The Chikosi must have been mistaken."

"Oh, very wrong," Two Petals said. "He has made a bad mistake. Just wait; we'll see the truth of it come out of his mouth like vomit."

"Who made a mistake? This warrior, the Chikosi, or Great Cougar?"

"None of them." Two Petals' hands were making their synchronous twitching.

Trader scratched the back of his neck. Not for the first time did it strike him as strange that a person could get used to such talk. "I suppose I'd better go over and kick Paunch awake."

Old White nodded. "I'm wondering if it wouldn't have been better if he'd run away with his granddaughter. At least then we wouldn't have to feed him."

"Away? Oh, no. She's running straight toward us," Two Petals said thoughtfully. "Running forward, running, running, right into the future."

A shiver traced down Trader's spine. He had an image: an almost mythical female, bathed in moonlight, rising and falling, a look of wonder on her face as she rode his hard shaft. Even now he wasn't sure that it hadn't been a Dream.

Trader asked, "You think we should have gone after her?"

Old White shrugged. "Ask the Contrary. She was the one who told me to let her go."

"You should have run her down," Two Petals agreed. "That way you could have stopped the future. Chopped it off clean, like a root from a seedling." She glanced at Trader. "What Power you wield, Trader."

He barely kept himself from cringing at her tone. "I'm just me."

"Isn't that what I said?"

To change the subject, he picked up his pack, walked over, and nudged Paunch awake. "Can you carry our packs down to the canoes?"

"Of course, young master," Paunch said with a yawn. "I guess I must have dozed off."

"We would never have guessed." Trader dropped his pack and went back to where Old White was lacing his closed.

They watched as Paunch began picking up their Trade, ready to follow him back down the path to the landing, when a boy ran up, his hair tangled, skin smudged with soot.

"You are the Traders?" he asked, as if there were any others in the town.

"We are," Old White said easily. "And who might you be?"

"I am White Cricket!" The boy tapped his skinny chest proudly. "The old matron would like to see you."

Two Petals laughed to herself. "Let us pull another thread tightly into place. Can't they see how this fabric is forming?"

Trader shared Old White's mystified look.

"Very well," the Seeker said, and followed in the boy's wake.

Trader ambled along behind, passing the corner of the high minko's mound. The lad led them to a newly constructed house, its walls freshly plastered; the thatch roofing looked ratty. Normally grass was cut in the summer when it was lush and green, allowed to sun dry, and then bundled into shocks before being tied to the roof poles. Winter grasses were brittle, did not compress well, and barely lasted a season. This had been a rush job, just enough to keep the occupants sheltered until summer, when the place could be reroofed.

"Aunt?" the boy called at the door. "I've brought them."

"Let them enter," a reedy voice called.

Trader followed Old White into the house, Two Petals coming behind.

The room was barely furnished, the poles for the roof and bed freshly cut. No matting lay on the beaten-dirt floor. A puddle-clay hearth contained a small fire. Blue smoke rose to pool under the roof and leak out the eaves. A single wooden box rested just this side of the hearth, its carved sides decorated with the cross-in-circle emblem of the sacred fire. Pearls had been inset into the design, and sections of shell gleamed whitely where they had been inlaid into the dark wood.

An old woman sat on one of the benches, her gray hair pulled up and pinned in place with eagle feathers. She had a bearskin cape over her shoulders, and wore nothing but a long skirt that hung down just past her knees. Too many summers had withered her flesh, stooped her shoulders, and left her breasts sagging like empty sacks. Her eyes, however, ensured she wouldn't be mistaken for an empty husk—they burned with a fevered intensity, as though fiery souls inhabited the used-up flesh.

"Greetings," Old White said. "I am known as the Seeker."

"So I have heard." She gave him a thoughtful scrutiny. "I knew you, once, long ago. You shared the Great Sun's fire among the Natchez. I was at that feast. Twenty, perhaps twenty-five winters past? You had come from the far southeast, telling tales of Traders from the islands out in the gulf. As I recall you brought a wonderful tobacco that you Traded. You said you were headed west."

Old White smiled. "I remember that night. People wouldn't let me sit down. They wanted to hear more. I had to answer question after question."

Trader gave him a dull look. When was that ever *not* the case?

"And now you are here," the old woman mused. "I am called Old Woman Fox now."

"And when I met you among the Natchez, you were called Fast Red Fox. Your husband was a subchief from one of the western Towns. I hate to say it, but that was nearly forty winters past. You were with child, as I recall."

Trader masked his surprise. Old White had a good memory; the woman was nodding. "My daughter. Odd, isn't it, the way Power works? You were there before my daughter was born, and now you are here just after her death. As though to mark both ends of her existence."

"Power moves us all, Matron." Old White paused. "The boy, White Cricket, called you the old matron."

"I surrendered that position to my daughter. Now they have given it back to me. It has fallen to me to see to the supervision of things.

Then, when the men return, we can go about the business of confirming a new high minko to replace my grandson."

"You have my sympathy, Matron," Old White said gently. "Though things appear grim now, Power will balance. It always does."

She waved it away. "Please, Seeker, do not trifle with platitudes. Fortunes come and go. I have seen enough to know that Power is like water in a cup. Sometimes the slightest of movements can slosh it from one side to the other. Momentum builds, and with the right timing, a wave is generated well out of proportion to the initial movement."

"I have often thought so myself."

She gave the three of them a careful inspection. "You are going to the Sky Hand to Trade?"

Old White spread his hands wide. "We do not know, Matron. There is a certain temptation to visiting the Pensacola. Some of our goods would Trade for their most coveted pieces of shell."

Her eyes glittered. "Do not play me for a fool, Seeker. I have lived too long, known too much of life. I brought you here for a reason."

"And what might that be, Matron?"

"I want you to do a little Trading for me."

"We are at your service."

"My granddaughter was taken during the raid. She is known as Morning Dew." She gestured toward the box. "That is all that I have, all the wealth I could muster from my clan. Under the Power of Trade, that is yours if you can get my granddaughter back."

Trader glanced at the box, worth a fortune by itself. He stepped forward, opening the lid to find copper effigies of Eagle Man, and beautiful pottery jars that were decorated with water panthers; they were filled to the brim with pearls. Gleaming copper ear spools, long chert blades, and copper ax heads composed the rest.

"Matron," Old White began, "like I said, we may not be heading up the Black Warrior."

She ignored him, saying, "The other captives the Chikosi took are dead—but for some of my grandson's wives. They are from other clans who can do what they will to get them back. My concern is Morning Dew. I need you to find her and Trade whatever you must for her freedom." She whisked her fingers at the box. "If that is not enough, I can find more, later. That was all I could come up with on such short notice."

Old White shot a casual glance at Trader. "We will do what we can, Matron. On the Power of Trade, I can only give you my word."

"The word of the Seeker is enough for me," she said firmly. "You must find my granddaughter, and have her out of Split Sky City by the coming of the equinox moon. That is my only condition. Beyond that, I could care less what you Trade, or how you get her, but have her out of the city by that date." She smiled, her toothless gums pink. "Do that and I will grant anything you ask of me."

"A Trade is a Trade," Two Petals whispered. "The knot is drawn tight." Her glowing eyes had fixed on Trader's. "Much more, and you won't even be able to wiggle."

"How's that?" he asked.

"Isn't it tight in there?"

"Tight in where?"

"In that sack Power is closing around you."

FIFTEEN

LITTLE STONE WAS asleep when Morning Dew checked him. He had his blanket tucked up under his chin. She had sat with him, holding his hand, Singing a lullaby about squirrels and acorns she had heard as a child. Now she disentangled her fingers, folded in the edges of his blanket, and turned to attend the fire.

As she added two pieces of wood, she glanced at Heron Wing, sitting to the side, the raccoon bowl clutched to her breast. For most of the afternoon, she had sat thus, asking Morning Dew to turn away the steady stream of visitors coming to discuss clan business, to ask advice about the suitability of certain marriages, or any of the other problems that Heron Wing was constantly consulted about.

During that time, Morning Dew had finished processing her hickory oil, and now had four jars of the precious liquid sealed and stowed under the sleeping benches. She had cooked supper, fed Stone, and entertained him with stories of how Wind lost his four sons and killed a monster by blowing through a bullfrog

Pipe-Now, her chores at end, she replaced the last of the supper plates and made up Heron Wing's bed. Then she walked over and seated herself next to the woman. "Do you want to tell me the story?"

"About Green Snake?" Heron Wing asked softly.

"I remember something about Smoke Shield's brother. You and

Wide Leaf were talking about him once. Green Snake is that man, isn't he?"

Heron Wing nodded. "We never even knew if he was alive or not. The night he struck down Smoke Shield, he ran away. No one ever heard of him again. The name Green Snake might have blown away with the wind. He never came back, never sent word."

Green Snake. He may have been aptly named. The thin, bright green snake of the forest was a special Spirit helper to both the Sky Hand and the Chahta. The delicate little creature was known to be filled with Power, and to harm one was considered the worst of bad luck. Any act against the little green serpent could ruin a man's Power for the rest of his life.

"I loved him." Heron Wing glanced at Stone, sleeping in his bed. "He should have been the father of my children."

Morning Dew sighed. "And now he is reportedly traveling in the company of the Seeker and a Contrary? Coming here? Why?"

Heron Wing shook her head. "I don't know. Breath Giver help me, I can't even imagine it." She turned frantic eyes toward Morning Dew. "For years, I have told myself that he's dead to me. I have Dreamed of him, hoped that he was with some far-off people, that he had found peace and happiness. It was better than thinking he was dead." She paused. "More than one person wondered if he had been killed in the fight with Smoke Shield. Even I have often wondered if Smoke Shield hid his body somewhere."

"Did you ever ask Smoke Shield?"

"Green Snake's blow had knocked the souls out of his body for four days. They were going to carry him to the charnel house, but he woke up first." Heron Wing paused. "Years later, I only asked once. At the mere mention of Green Snake's name, Smoke Shield flew into a rage. He gave me a backhanded slap and told me never to mention him again. Said that if I did, he'd kill me. Then he ripped my clothes off and took me, hard. When he came, he looked into my eyes, telling me at the same time that I was his. And his alone."

"Too bad that blow to the head didn't finish him off. It would have saved all of us a difficult time."

"But why, after all these years, would Green Snake come back now?"

"I don't know."

Morning Dew sat silently, staring at the fire. What would this new twist mean? She glanced at Heron Wing, seeing her desperate long-ing. The woman looked as if someone had wound her guts around a stick and was pulling them from her body.

"This isn't the time to let your concentration falter, Heron Wing. If you'll recall, something happened among the Albaamaha. Someone is trying to blame the Chahta for this raid. Red Awl's widow is missing. This whole country is about to erupt, and Smoke Shield is in the middle of it. You need all of your wits about you. The people need you."

"Yes, yes, I know." Heron Wing pinched her eyes shut. "That's how I got into this mess. The people needed me. The clans needed me. So I married Smoke Shield. I have given everything to the people." She laughed brittlely. "You know, if Green Snake had just come to me, I would have run off with him. All he needed to do was ask."

"Perhaps that is why he is coming now? What if he has finally learned that his brother lived?"

"A Trader," she said softly. "All these years. Do you think he Traded here, camped right down there on the landing, telling no one who he was? He would have been so close. But I never knew. Do you think he ever walked up, saw me from a distance?"

"Maybe."

She stared down at the bowl she caressed. "If he asked about me, people would have said, 'That's Smoke Shield's wife.' That would have driven a stake into his heart. Nothing would have hurt him more. That's why he never came to me."

"You don't know that."

"Oh, yes, I do."

"Were I him, believing I'd killed my brother, I would never have come back."

Heron Wing looked at her. "I would like to believe that."

"It makes more sense," Morning Dew said positively, unsure herself.

"If he does come here, what will I say to him? How can I look him in the eyes?"

"You will do it. And you will do it well."

"Easy for you to say."

"No, that's just the way it is, Heron Wing. No matter what might lie between the two of you, you are a clan leader. Your brother is

Hopaye. Your aunt is the Panther Clan chief. You will be who you must be."

"Is that my own medicine turned against me?" The faintest smile crossed Heron Wing's lips.

"What do you think?"

"I think somehow, some way, you have become my finest friend, Morning Dew." Then she shook her head. "When he left, my souls went with him."

"Then perhaps it's time you got them back."

Heron Wing stared down at the raccoon bowl. "No one must know." She stiffened. "Do you think that Thunder Town Trader will tell?"

"By morning, he'll be gone upriver again. I don't think he had any idea who you were. It wasn't like you were dressed like a clan leader. Your skirt is stained with hickory oil. To him, it was just a Sky Hand woman and her slave come down to Trade. Nothing more."

———

A hard day's travel had taken Old White's party to the confluence of the Horned Serpent and Black Warrior Rivers. Most of the route lay through hilly country where the Horned Serpent flowed quickly, allowing them to make good time. At the confluence they had camped with a party of Pensacoloa Traders for the night. The place was a levee that rose above the swampy ground.

After an active Trade, in which they divested most of their Chahta goods and several prized northern pieces for quality shell, yaupon, stingray spines, sharks' teeth, and several packs of pelican feathers, they started up the Black Warrior River.

At first travel was easy, the broad current lazy, but as they entered the hills, the current that had helped them on the descent of the Horned Serpent fought against them. The route consisted of criss-crossing the channel, forever searching for the slower backwaters and shallows. Progress dropped to a snail's pace.

Good camping spots, however, were abundant. They had pulled up on one such—a low terrace covered with sweet gum, bitter acorn, and cottonwoods.

Paunch, who could at least cook, had made them an excellent meal of catfish and freshwater mussels he had harvested from shallows along the river. Old White had carefully laid his wooden pack and the fabric bag with its hidden contents by his side. He now kept them close, ready at hand for reasons of his own.

At the fire that night, Trader spoke in Trade Tongue so the Albaamo couldn't understand. "Something doesn't make sense." He glanced at Old Woman Fox's ornate box where it rested among the Trade.

"A great many things don't make sense," Old White agreed, packing his pipe and lighting it. "Like trying to have a normal conversation with Two Petals." He puffed reflectively, blowing the blue smoke up to annoy the hovering cloud of mosquitoes. For the most part, the little beasts were discouraged by an unguent rubbed on their skin. A few brave insects, however, were foolish enough to land, bite, and then be slapped flat.

"Let's lay this all out in sequence." Trader filled his own pipe. "First, we land at Feathered Snake Town, and Great Cougar, though skeptical, makes us welcome. He acts as the perfect host, even urges us to stay longer. Then, as we travel downriver, people are nice, but firm in keeping us away from the towns."

"And why do you think that is?"

Trader smiled warily as he reached down and ran his fingers through Swimmer's long black hair. "He was giving his messengers time to alert the other chiefs, to assemble their Trade, and then get us back on the river as soon as possible."

"All but at White Arrow."

"Correct." Trader glanced at Two Petals, who listened and smiled, as if amused. Curse it all, life would be so much easier if she'd just come out and tell them what her visions had shown her.

Old White arched an eyebrow. "And we are allowed into White Arrow Town to Trade because Old Woman Fox wants to have some private time with us. She does this to ask us to get her granddaughter back."

"She is obsessed by that," Trader agreed. "Meanwhile, we learn that Great Cougar was supposedly raiding the Sky Hand at the same time he was feasting us and being a good host."

Swimmer flopped over on his side, stretching so that Trader could scratch his belly.

"All the while, he's letting us believe he's making defensive preparations for a Sky Hand attack."

Trader sucked at his pipe. "Which we both agree is the smartest way to handle any Sky Hand retaliation. With warning, he can fortify his villages, position his warriors, and hopefully break up the raiding party before destroying it piecemeal."

"But the men were missing at White Arrow Town," Old White mused. "Sure, they might have been out hunting and fishing, but during the whole day we were there, did you see any men coming in with game? Did you see loads of fish being carried up from the river?"

"I saw some women unload a basket of fish from a canoe as we were leaving," Trader said. "But no, you'd think with that many people, some man would have come in with a deer, opossum, turkeys, or what have you."

"So, where are the men?" Old White blew another cloud of smoke up at the mosquitoes.

"And why is Old Woman Fox so insistent that we get her grand-daughter out of Split Sky City before the first new moon after the equinox?" Trader shot him a clever look, answering his own question. "Because Great Cougar did his cunning best to mislead us. But the Sky Hand have scouts everywhere, enough so that they are exchanging jabs with the Chahta scouts. Each side knows the other is watching vigilantly."

"My guess," Old White mused, "is that Great Cougar is somehow counting on that."

"He plans to use the large number of Chikosi scouts against the Sky Hand?" Trader looked up at the sky, now clouded over. Around them, the forest was dark. Somewhere in the river, a fish splashed, and an owl hooted in the trees behind them. "He could make a feint. Display a mass of warriors in the south, draw the Sky Hand strength in that direction."

"Possible."

"Or he could send a large band through the forest, looping around the rough country to the north, bypassing most of the scouts."

"Also possible."

Trader looked at Two Petals. "What is our future, Contrary? Are we the deciding factor? What does Power want us to do?"

Her hands were fluttering in that odd way of hers. "The current is strong, isn't it? Traveling like this, paddle, paddle. This is your river, Trader; only you can ascend it." She paused before adding, "She knows you're coming. Her heart is torn."

"Who knows? She who?" Trader asked. Gods, you ask her one question, only to receive a different answer.

"Why, both of them, of course," Two Petals stated positively, as if only a fool wouldn't understand what she was talking about.

"Well," Old White mused as he knocked his pipe out and pulled his fabric bag close, "we've time to think about it." He glanced at Paunch. "I just wish he was younger. It would be nice if he could paddle like a youth instead of just splashing water about."

Trader knocked out his own pipe. "Maybe that's all any of us are doing, Seeker. Just splashing aimlessly toward something we can't even imagine."

"Finally," Two Petals said with relief. "I wondered why it was taking you so long."

Trader rolled out his bedding, climbing beneath the thick blanket into relative protection from the swarm of mosquitoes. He lay there, aware of the dying fire and the night sounds in the forest. A fox yipped and squealed somewhere. He could hear a beaver gnawing on one of the cottonwoods at the water's edge.

Ever since nosing into the Black Warrior's waters, he'd been on edge, his nerves pulled tight. *I am going home.* For the first time it was real.

He tried to imagine what it would be like to land below the city. A disturbing mixture of anticipation mixed with dread in his breast. Images replayed of that last night, of running from the Men's House in a blind panic, how he'd stolen a canoe, pushing it off into the waters of this same river. That time he'd gone north; now he returned from the south: full circle. Headed back to the place his Dreams had died.

I am not the youth who fled. I return a different man. But was he? Had all those years on the rivers made him into someone he hadn't been that night when he struck down his brother?

He swallowed hard, clamping his eyes shut at the wheeling images. After losing everything, what kind of fool ever believed he could get any of it back? Would he have to look into Flying Hawk's eyes, see the censure for becoming what his uncle had insisted that he not be?

And Heron Wing? What would her reaction be? How did he tell her what he had gone through? How did he tell another man's wife that he was sorry?

He heard the rustle of fabric and looked up. Two Petals stood over his bed, her face turned down, hair spilling around her. She dropped to her knees, pulling her dress up over her head.

"What are you doing?" Trader whispered, uncomfortably aware of her naked body as she reached for his blanket.

"I don't understand," she said, sliding in beside him and tugging on his shirt. "This would feel better sleeping by itself tonight."

He grudgingly pulled his shirt off, feeling her cool skin next to his. "Two Petals, are you sure this is a good idea?"

She ran her hands over his chest, tracing the lines of rib and muscle. One by one, she rolled his nipples under her fingers. The effect was electric. "There is no such thing as a good idea. They fly like birds, lighting here and there." Her fingers slipped down across the ripple of his belly, twining in his pubic hair before tracing around his tightening scrotum. He drew a deep breath, tensing.

"Two Petals, you don't have to—"

"We've Dreamed this. Both of us. Over and over. This time we don't have to. You can help me learn what I need to know." She gripped his hard shaft, tightening her hold until he gasped. "Is this distracting?"

"Gods, *yes!*"

"I have to learn."

"Learn...what?" His concentration was shredding.

"What they know."

"Who?"

"All those distracting women." She bent down, taking his nipple in her teeth, teasing it gently.

Distracting women? What women?

Then his thoughts fluttered off—as lost as Two Petals' rhetorical birds.

In the dim morning light, Old White looked into his fabric sack. He let his gaze rest on the smooth lines of the object inside; then he laced the sack tightly closed again. *Soon,* he thought. And what would the reaction be when he removed it for the final time? He turned his gaze to the war medicine box, hidden in its bag. So many things were coming together, a convergence of Power that he could but imperfectly comprehend.

He laid his bag aside and stirred the fire, having coaxed some of last night's coals to life, and added kindling. As the flames leapt up and snapped at him, he caught movement from Trader's bed, and saw him slip naked from the covers. Swimmer rose from where he'd bedded down on Trader's shirt, stretched, and waved his tail. Trader shooed the dog off and pulled the wadded shirt over his broad shoulders. Two Petals' face was obscured by the dark swirl of her black hair where it spilled over the blanket.

Trader turned, saw Old White watching, and stiffened. Mortification filled the man's face as he fled down the slope to relieve himself. Moments later, he walked uncertainly up the slope; Swimmer, taking time to pee on grass stems, followed behind. Trader glanced at the sleeping Paunch, and continued awkwardly to squat on the other side of the fire.

"Two Petals came to my bed last night."

Old White cocked his head, using his stick to stir the fire again. He reached out and gave Swimmer his customary morning petting. "I wonder, when a Contrary cries, 'Yes! Yes! Yes!' does it mean 'No, no, no'?"

"She did?" Trader looked like he'd just swallowed a live frog.

"Um-hum."

"Oh."

"She wasn't the only one."

"Sorry."

Old White gave him a curious look. "Then you are a lesser man than I would have been."

"Look, she came to me. Talking some nonsense about learning about distraction."

"Don't be so defensive. She's a woman. You're a man. I've seen the way you look at each other; I'm just surprised it has taken this long."

"It was her choice," Trader said lamely.

"Could I give you a word of advice?"

"Of course."

"She's not a normal woman."

"I discovered that last night."

"Believe me, I'm well aware," Old White said dryly. "But I'm not referring to repeated athletics."

"What then?"

Old White met Trader's nervous eyes. "I would warn you not to expect any change between the two of you."

"I don't understand."

"Well"—he prodded the fire—"generally when a man and woman couple, it changes the way they regard each other. The act serves to alter their relationship...a shared intimacy that comes across in looks, in how they behave toward each other."

"I am fully aware of that." He shot a sidelong look at Two Petals. "You think she'll be different?"

"She's already *different*. What I'm saying is that I wouldn't be upset if she acts like she always has. Last night may have changed the way you feel about her, but don't expect her to reciprocate. Do you see where my canoe floats? I'm betting she won't have the same emotional reaction you do. Last night wasn't about love, or a bonding between a husband and wife. It was something else, something Power led her to."

"Oh."

Old White watched Swimmer scratch after a flea. "In short, don't expect her to wake up beaming with affection for you, ready to hold hands and smile into your eyes. Expect her to wake up as a Contrary, that same distance in her eyes, uttering the same confounding statements." He paused. "That's a guess, of course, but I'm willing to bet it's a good one."

Trader frowned down at the fire, nodding. "Yes. I think I already knew that."

"But you hadn't really thought it all through?"

"No." He glanced up, a shy smile on his lips. "Thank you, Seeker. I would have ended up there eventually, but you probably saved me some discomfort."

Old White nodded, thinking about the times he'd dealt with Power, how it had affected his relationships with the women it haunted.

Trader glanced out at the river, the water silvered with the dawn. "What about when we arrive at Split Sky City? Have you given that thought as well?"

"We land, act like Traders, and see what the situation is." He smiled. "I must confess, the noise wasn't the only reason I didn't sleep last night."

"Me either." He flinched. "Well, I mean until Two Petals showed up." He shook his head. "Setting foot in Split Sky City is going to be the hardest thing I've ever done. I was lost in that, all knotted up." He glanced again at Two Petals. "You think that's why she came to me?"

"Perhaps. Contrary ways have their own logic. She knows things we don't." He paused. "Thinking about turning back, were you?"

"The notion of going down to Bottle Town and spending this spring with the Pensacola has a certain appeal." He hesitated. "Like staying as far away from the Sky Hand as possible."

"And never having to face ourselves," Old White agreed. "But that's what Power is insisting on."

"Why?" Trader asked the familiar old question.

"We'll find out when we reach home." His lips curled evilly. "Assuming anyone but me has the energy left to paddle a canoe against the current."

———

Smoke Shield stared at the map he'd drawn on the palace great room floor. He had pulled back all the mats, then used a pointed stick to draw in the rivers. Each Chahta town was represented by a bowl, cup, or jar.

Flying Hawk perched on his cougar-hide stool, staring down thoughtfully. The firelight cast a golden glow across the floor, and dark shadows wavered behind the bowls. He looked up thoughtfully at the carving that hung on the wall across from him, of a warrior bearing a head. It had been taken from the Yuchi years before he was born and incorporated into the legends of his people. The story his people had started to tell was that in the beginning times, Morning Star had killed his own father and finally carried the head up to the stars where it now rested, a constellation.

But the Yuchi, from whom we obtained it, don't believe a word of it. So how many other stories that people now believed had been born just that way, adopted as an explanation? Just like Smoke Shield's imaginary Chahta raid?

What surprised him was that the Council had swallowed the whole thing. All but Blood Skull, Pale Cat, and Night Star, who had just listened, skepticism easy to read on their faces. Not that that surprised him; if he or Smoke Shield claimed the sun rose in the east, they would insist on believing it was a Chief Clan plot.

And now I am part of it. That knowledge bothered him. Why it should was no mystery: Smoke Shield had plotted it. The man had always had a facile way with the truth, and that it seemed to work for him made Flying Hawk wonder.

Power has always favored him. But perhaps that was part of the problem. All of his life, Flying Hawk, too, had leaned toward the red, the tumultuous and creative side of life. His violent rage had led him to kill his brother. Subduing that passion had taken most of his life.

When he looked at Smoke Shield—still scowling down at his map —he wondered if the man ever would, or even should, for that matter.

"The problem is the number of warriors we must use," Smoke Shield said absently. "By my best figures, we can take nearly a thousand. With a force that size, moving rapidly, we can overwhelm their eastern villages."

"But you have to feed them, keep them together."

"Food is the problem," Smoke Shield agreed. "Unless we can rope the Albaamaha into a caravan to pack food for us."

"Too risky. They'll melt away into the forest unless you have nearly as large a force to guard them."

Smoke Shield nodded absently. "How did the lords of Cahokiadoit?"

"They didn't have to travel cross-country. They could use the rivers, especially when traveling south. They could load large Trade canoes to carry their provisions. In our country, war must be conducted across ridges, mountains, and valleys. East to west. Warriors can only carry so much on their backs. An army's movement is curtailed by the food supply each man can carry. If you add an additional slave per warrior, you can extend the range, but only by another couple of days' travel. The slaves have to eat, too."

Smoke Shield traced the route of the rivers with his stick. "It would take too long to send canoes down the Black Warrior and then back up the Horned Serpent. The Chahta would have fair warning of our movement." He shook his head. "No, it's too easy to ambush canoes on the rivers. Down in the narrows, where travel upriver is slow, they'd be spread out, easy to pick off one by one."

"So we are restricted to striking overland." Flying Hawk pointed with his stone mace. "Your only chance is to take the first town by surprise and raid its food supplies. In early spring, there will be little extra available in the countryside. Even the isolated farmsteads will have emptied their granaries."

"Hunting during travel is out." Smoke Shield stated the obvious. "It's much too time-consuming, and with that many men combing the landscape, someone will see them. The alarm will be raised."

"So you are back to striking fast and quickly to take a town. But realistically, you can only do that once. Someone will escape and raise the alarm."

Smoke Shield twirled his stick in his fingers. "What if the Chahta were already weakened and looking the other way?"

"Meaning?"

"We let the Yuchi strike first."

"I see," Flying Hawk added dryly. "Of course. You'll send a runner to Born-of-Sun asking him to kindly raid the Chahta in order to further your war plans?"

"Don't be flippant, Uncle." Smoke Shield grinned. "You know how cunning Great Cougar is. He's just killed a bunch of Albaamaha and escaped our pursuit. What would happen if he attacked a Yuchi town? How would Born-of-Sun react to an unprovoked Chahta raid? Especially if a couple of captives managed to overhear Great Cougar planning to make even more attacks, then 'escaped' to bear the news to Born-of-Sun?"

"He'd immediately mass his warriors and attack Feathered Serpent Town." Flying Hawk felt a cold rush along his spine. "But it wouldn't be the Chahta. It would be your picked warriors, the ones who faked the Chahta raid on the Albaamaha."

"You begin to understand." Smoke Shield gave him an oily smile. "Great Cougar, knowing nothing of the raid, would still have the majority of his scouts watching us. His north will be relatively unprotected. He won't be expecting a blow to come from the Yuchi. There is a good chance that Born-of-Sun will achieve success and break Great Cougar's back. The Yuchi will go home feeling vindicated, having restored the balance of Power. The Chahta will feel obliged to strike back as soon as possible to avenge their dead, their honor, and to restore the balance of Power. If they do, that many more warriors will be sent north."

"And what does this gain us?"

"The Chahta will be reeling." Smoke Shield smiled.

"What if I sent a warrior to Great Cougar, someone— perhaps

Blood Skull—with a white arrow. It could be a secret mission to tell the Chahta that we will not attack. That we have only recently learned the Albaamaha raid was done by the Yuchi. The Chahta will believe that, knowing full well that they didn't raid us; and they will have just been struck by the Yuchi. Reassured, Great Cougar will recall all but a handful of his scouts on our border. A few of those remaining can be eliminated, just enough to make a hole. Then a thousand of our warriors pour through and descend on Feathered Serpent Town."

"Using a white arrow to mislead an enemy—"

"Forget the white Power, Uncle. I serve the red." Uneasy with that, Flying Hawk fingered his chin. "How do you feed these thousand warriors? Any grain stores the Yuchi don't burn will be stripped to feed the Chahta warriors heading north in a counterstrike. You can only carry enough food to reach Feathered Serpent Town. Your warriors will be running on empty bellies."

"Not if we pre-position food," Smoke Shield replied. He pointed to a place on his map. "This is three days' travel northwest. There's a large meadow where a fire cleared a ridgetop. A good spring lies just below. I've hunted there; the place draws buffalo as well as elk and deer. Two hundred Albaamaha could leave Bowl Town, travel three days to the meadow, drop their packs to be left under guard, and hurry back to Bowl Town. We can tell them that we're building a town up there, or some such lie. Clear Water Creek Crossing lies just below the ridge, and the channel down to the Horned Serpent is almost passable by a small dugout canoe. The Albaamaha might even believe it." He shrugged. "If their bellies are empty by the time they make it back to Bowl Town, what do we care?"

Flying Hawk nodded. The plan was brilliant. Why hadn't he thought of it years ago? Because he would never have thought of dressing Sky Hand warriors up as Chahta. Even now the notion bothered him. It reeked of abusing Power and angering the Ancestors.

Flying Hawk asked, "So, you arrive on Great Cougar's doorstep and take the town. What next?"

"We clean out the local Chahta, kill everyone we find, and burn every farmstead in the area. We are there to destroy, Uncle. To weaken their eastern settlements. The planting season is coming; we want to disrupt it as much as we can."

"You still have to deal with the fortified towns farther to the west along the Pearl River."

"No, I don't. They will only be thinking of defense, and reluctant to act. If you were a chief, and the Yuchi had just raided your neighbor, would you be willing to weaken your defenses by sending warriors off to fight in the west?" He seemed to be seeing the future reflected in his map. "The important thing is to burn Feathered Serpent Town, destroy the farms in every direction, and fight until we have used up the food reserves. Then we withdraw across the Horned Serpent." He tossed his pointed stick at the bowl representing his objective. "I need to leave that country in ruins. And then we have to look like we're falling apart, disorganized. Perhaps let the counterattacking Chahta warriors win some small victories."

Fascinated, Flying Hawk leaned forward. "And just what does that gain you?"

"If I'm lucky, a pursuit that I can ambush and destroy. I want the few terrified survivors running back, telling anyone who will listen that the Chahta are defeated. I want them sowing panic." He walked over and picked up his stick. "Meanwhile, I need you to continue sending me food, here, at the Clear Water Creek Crossing. As many Albaamaha as you can find, all carrying the heaviest packs they can." Flying Hawk shook his head. "But you will already have won."

Smoke Shield continued to study his map. "We pursue the panicked survivors back west and take the next town to the south. For the most part the country will be defenseless. There we restock and move to the next town. In a matter of days, we can destroy every farm and town in the northeast. Any war parties from the south or west will be coming in disorganized groups. We can destroy them, or choose not to fight. The thing is we will have food and they won't. When the time is right we retreat across the river, have a cooked meal at Clear Water Creek Crossing, and come home to a triumphant greeting."

"Just what will this accomplish in the end?"

"Two things. First, we will have dealt the Chahta a terrible blow, killed a great many of their warriors, and burned some of their most important towns. Second, the survivors of the ambushes will flee, beaten, starved, and terrified. They will spread that terror among the other towns off to the west." He looked up. "Uncle, if we can continue this, support raid after raid, we can drive the Chahta out of the Horned Serpent Valley and take it for our own."

Flying Hawk nodded. "As long as we don't pull too many

Albaamaha from the land, they can farm while we fight. Assuming, that is, they don't pick that moment to revolt."

Smoke Shield tapped his stick. "Would you rise up against a people whose warriors were winning victory after victory?"

"Perhaps not." But he wasn't sure.

"We could take some of the Albaamaha mikkos with us. Hostages. The reason given, of course, will be that we wanted to honor them for their people's support of the war. We could give them enough gifts looted from the Chahta to even make the pretense seem real."

Flying Hawk considered the plan as Smoke Shield had laid it out. The whole thing was intricate, well thought-out, and workable. He could see flaws, of course—no war party ever functioned according to the plan—but Smoke Shield, if anyone, could make this thing work.

I could be high minko over half the world. The notion startled him.

Smoke Shield's half-lidded eyes were fixed on his. "Think of it, Uncle. If we can trick other peoples into destroying each other, we can move in when they are at their weakest. Split Sky City could become the new Cahokia."

Flying Hawk turned his attention to the map, seeing all that country, imagining the wealth and prestige that would accrue to the Sky Hand, and to himself. Gods, it was tempting. He could imagine his brother—see him staring worriedly at Smoke Shield.

No, you would never have seen through his arrogance to the brilliance. But if this could be done, if the Chahta could be finally broken, Flying Hawk's actions that long-ago day would be vindicated. People would speak of him and Smoke Shield in turn as the greatest high minkos to have ever lived. The disaster of that long-ago fire would be forgotten, seen as a blessing instead of a curse.

They will finally understand that there was a reason why I survived and none of the rest did.

"You have two problems," Flying Hawk noted.

"And that is?"

"Gaining the Council's support is your first problem."

Smoke Shield snorted. "For the moment they are incensed by the Alligator Town and Albaamaha raids. There is no love for the Chahta. Why would they turn down the chance to obtain the Horned Serpent Valley? We will lose some warriors, obviously. If I plan this right, it will be from among our enemies here. For example, I think the Chahta will take their wrath out on Blood Skull and his white arrow.

But the others will be thinking of establishing new chiefdoms in the Horned Serpent farmlands."

"Then there is only the second to worry about."

Smoke Shield gave him a sloe-eyed look. "And what would that be?"

"Power."

"Power?" Smoke Shield laughed, tossing his stick into the air. "I *am* the Power! It hovers around me, red and beautiful. Watch me. I'm going to carry it with me and let it wash all over the Chahta!"

"You will be sending a white arrow to Great Cougar."

"A white arrow? That's what you are worried about? What threat could white Power have for me? In all my life, it's never hindered me. Not once."

Yes, I know.

But then, when had it ever hindered him, either?

SIXTEEN

"MASTERS, I have to tell you, this is a bad idea." Paunch looked back and forth from Trader to Old White.

To Old White's way of thinking, the old Albaamo' had just reason to worry. Outside of a definite talent at cooking, he wasn't good for much else. The man was an old farmer. He knew beans, corn, and the turning of the soil. That he had dabbled in politics had been to his misfortune. The old man would have required more than just a dislike of the Sky Hand to have defeated them.

They had bypassed Alligator Town, accepting Paunch's word that the rebuilding center had nothing of value that hadn't already been carried off by the Chahta. Instead they had called greetings to both Albaamaha and Sky Hand who passed or shared their course. Some had Traded across the canoe gunwales, offering food or pottery for small things. During those visits, Paunch had fidgeted studiously, rubbed his hands, and tried to keep his face hidden.

"Cut your hair," Old White said.

"Cut my hair?" Paunch reached up, fingering his gray-white locks.

"Who will know you?" Trader asked. "You're dressed in a Chahta-style hunting shirt, and if you keep your mouth shut, act like a mute, no one will look twice at a Trader's slave."

"But...cut my hair?"

"That or you could hang from a Sky Hand square."

Old White read the man's expression, dashing his hopes when he said, "Running off didn't get you much last time, either."

Paunch made a face.

"I can only wonder how your granddaughter is doing."

"She will be fine." He sighed. "She lives in the shadow of Power. I've never understood that girl, I swear, master."

"She seemed to know what she was doing," Trader mused, his eyes lost in thought. Then he glanced at Two Petals, who sat by the fire, whispering softly and listening to the air. Her hands were fluttering like butterflies.

"I just hope that no man has found her." Paunch shook his head. "Oh, the young men watched her, admired her; but then she would turn those odd eyes on them, seeing down to their souls, and they'd find other interests. And right fast at that."

"So she never married?" Trader asked, suddenly curious.

"No. My clan even tried a couple of times. She always broke it off, usually before she could even meet the young man."

"The child was more important to her," Two Petals said absently. "It was worth waiting for. That boy's a strong one. She knows how important he is."

Paunch, of course, missed it, not having the language, but Old White could see Trader suddenly turn pale.

Gods, had he lain with her, too?

"Trader?" he asked in Natchez, knowing that neither Paunch nor Two Petals had any fluency in it.

"She came to my bed that first night, Seeker." He knotted his hands together. "I swear, I made no gesture, hadn't even thought of it. Then there she was, leaning over me in the moonlight. It seemed like a Dream then, and it still does."

"You have the worst luck when it comes to getting a good night's sleep." He glanced at Two Petals. "You think she's right? That you planted a child in her?"

"How could I know? Maybe. It depends on where she was between her moons."

Power again. Flowing around them, using them.

Old White fingered his fabric sack, feeling the outline of the object within.

"Master?" Paunch asked. "I hate to keep bringing this up, but do you know what they will do to me?"

Old White growled, "Shut up! Gods, don't you know who I am?"

"A very Powerful Trader, yes, but the wrath of the—"

"Will be *nothing* compared to what I will do to them if they bother you!" Old White ground what few teeth he had left, glaring at the man.

Trader fought a smile.

"Listen, *farmer,*" Old White snapped. "I have sat in the company of high chiefs. I have stood on the heights of Cahokia. I have climbed the steps of the Azteca sun temples. I have Danced with the *Katsinas* in high Oraibi. The Great Serpent Chief of the Natchez calls me friend. Sorcerers and Dreamers listen with respect when I speak. No petty Sky Hand high minko is going to cross me."

He watched Paunch shrink down before him. Gods, he hoped that his words would be prophetic.

In the silence, he asked, "Now, Albaamo, you once mentioned Amber Bead. When we arrive at Sky Hand City, I think it would be best if we meet with the man."

Paunch blinked, taking to fingering his hair again, as if wary of having it cut. "You would see the councilor?"

"I would. We will need to know things when we arrive at Split Sky City. Some we can learn at the canoe landing; for other things we must have additional sources."

"Only a few threads remain," Two Petals said softly. "All is coming together. What a curious weave it is."

"Instead of all this weaving," Trader muttered, "have you ever thought about taking up pottery?"

"Just so it isn't squares that she's filling in," Old White added in Natchez. He had the beginnings of a plan coming together, but it would necessitate their being able to move unfettered through Split Sky City.

———

It was one thing to have a wish come true, but quite another to know what to do with it. That notion perplexed Amber Bead. He sat beside the river and looked up at the sky as a rain shower passed to the west. Around him, several Albaamaha women used discarded pieces of cloth to make salt pans. Salt was one of the prized Trade commodities, and Albaamaha women specialized in making the pans used to evaporate seawater. This was a fortuitous arrangement. The right kind of clay was available along the lower Black Warrior Valley to produce the pans. The Pensacola, down to the south, didn't have much in the way of clay. Most of their soils were sandy silts washed down from the great rivers, and the few hills around them were made of crumbling sandstones.

The Chikosi and Albaamaha needed salt; the Pensacola needed drying pans. It worked out neatly. To make the pans, Albaamaha women hollowed out a shallow bowl shape in the river sand to the dimensions needed for the salt evaporators. When the basin was shaped just so, old fabric was laid smoothly inside the basin.

This provided the mold. Wet, tempered clay, mixed to just the right consistency with river water, was carefully pressed into shape, making a bowl as thick as a woman's little finger. The interior was smoothed with a round pebble to create a slick, burnished surface impermeable to water. Then the whole was allowed to sun dry.

After the bowl was sufficiently dry, two women stood on either side, lifting the fabric carefully, using it to free the shallow pan from its mold. The fabric was then peeled off, leaving its impression in the bottom of the clay. The wide shallow bowl was left to dry further, and finally fired.

Amber Bead watched the process—enjoyed the sun peering through the partly cloudy sky—and pondered his problem. He had come here because no one looking for sage advice or demanding definitive answers was likely to think of this place. They would be looking in the seats of authority, around the tchkofa, near the chiefly palaces in Split Sky City, or around his abode just outside the walls. The last place anyone would think of searching for him would be down near the river where women were making salt pans.

He had Lotus Root hidden just outside of Bird Town, close enough to be handy should he need to call on her, far enough away that no one looking specifically for her would stumble upon the woman while she was out using the latrine.

All he had told his cousins was that she was a recent widow, up from the south, and could she stay with them for several days? The story that he and Lotus Root had concocted was that her husband had been killed in the Alligator Town raid. Her house had been burned, her family killed. Having no house to mourn in, she was here. When her mourning period was over, she would look over the local supply of husbands, and perhaps make a new start in the Bird Town locality.

Amber Bead's cousins knew enough not to pry. They had already been inspected once by Chikosi warriors just after Paunch disappeared.

Paunch? Now there was a problem he hadn't had time to ponder much recently. He looked off to the west, wondering just where his overeager friend and pretty young Whippoorwill had vanished to. The forest was crawling with warriors. Chahta scouts were watching the trails, and Chikosi were keeping track of them. At least they were when they weren't dressing up as Chahta and killing Albaamaha.

He sat on the log, his butt growing sore, his back bent, chin propped as he watched the women chatting and forming their clay.

Chikosi dressed as Chahta. And Smoke Shield right in the middle of it. Now that was a thick knot to pick apart. As Lotus Root had told her story, he hadn't even been amazed, though the sight of those twenty-three Albaamaha scalps had sent eerie shivers up his spine. Blessed Ancestors, didn't the woman fear for the safety of his aged souls, even if she didn't fear for her own? Scalps were Powerful things, often carrying the essence of their previous owners' souls. And here she came, traipsing around with them, heedless of the screaming and angry ghosts that followed after, howling for revenge for their untimely deaths.

The very thought of it made his souls cringe.

We have the proof to act against them. But how? Only that morning he had heard that within weeks, the high minko would be calling warriors to Split Sky City. They would come in the company of the chiefs from up and down the river to discuss the proper action to be taken against the Chahta for their supposed raid.

"That part, at least, makes sense." So, too, did the sudden reluctance among the Albaamaha to antagonize the Chikosi further. Both peoples seemed to accept that Great Cougar had magically penetrated the Chikosi defenses, cut a swath along the western hills, and then vanished just as mysteriously into the thin air, leaving tracks only where he wanted them seen.

"It's easier to believe that," he mused. Great Cougar had every reason to raid in response to the White Arrow Town massacre. "But a few people are uneasy with it." He'd seen that at the Council meeting. One of the advantages to being present but rarely called upon to comment was that he had spent years studying his enemies. Each Chikosi chief had his own particular habits. Vinegaroon chewed his thumb when he was frustrated. Blood Skull's nose flared when he thought someone was lying to him. When Black Tail disagreed, he wiggled his right foot. Two Poisons began rocking his head when he was unimpressed.

Amber Bead had seen outright hostility in Night Star's eyes as she listened to Flying Hawk's report, and Blood Skull's nostrils had gone so wide they looked like round eyes. Pale Cat, too, had averted his eyes, a habit he had when displeased with what he heard.

The rest of the Council, however, had accepted the entire story.

As did a great many of the mikkos he had communicated with.

"So, what do we do?" he mused, watching a great white heron wing silently north over the river. The bird flew so effortlessly, its wings barely flapping, its neck bent double.

"There you are!" a voice called.

Amber Bead turned, gasped, and leapt to his feet. "High Minko!"

Flying Hawk walked down the slope to the beach, favoring his bad knee. The women had stopped to gape, their actions frozen.

"Oh, it's all right," Flying Hawk called in passable Albaamaha. "Go back to work. I'm just here to chat with my old friend." They remained frozen, looking more like deer caught in a hunter's surround than reassured.

Flying Hawk sighed as he reached the flats, walking over to Amber Bead. "This is a good place. Came here to think, did you?"

"Yes, High Minko. How...How did you know?"

"I have my ways."

The words touched his souls like ice. *What else does he know?* He couldn't help it; his eyes went to the surrounding trees, wondering if even now he was being spied upon.

"Oh, relax," Flying Hawk muttered. "One of my warriors went past in a canoe a half a hand's time ago. He saw you sitting here. It was just luck that I mentioned I needed to speak with you." He paused, looking out at the river, seeming to ignore the women who still watched with worried eyes. "Yes, a nice place indeed. I won't tell. I have my own places to disappear to. Men like us need them."

"Yes, High Minko."

Flying Hawk looked at him, eyes speculative. "It has recently been brought home to me that I do not pay enough attention to you."

"You have other concerns more pressing than worrying about an old man like me."

"Perhaps, but recent events have brought it to my attention that there have been problems in our relationship with the Albaamaha."

"There have?" He tried to stifle the fear that had hunkered in his gut.

"This thing with Red Awl." Flying Hawk shook his head. "I have heard Smoke Shield's side of the story. Some of it I believe; some I don't."

"Really?" he asked, intrigued in spite of his better judgment.

"Whatever it was, it's over, Councilor." Flying Hawk clapped a hand to his knee as he seated himself on Amber Bead's log. "Then the Chahta raid brought things into focus for me."

I'm sure it did. Everything was back to normal. Flying Hawk was scheming.

"We cannot allow the Chahta to treat us this way. Not the Sky Hand, and not the Albaamaha."

"No, we can't."

Flying Hawk lowered his voice. "I am planning on dealing with them, but in due time." He looked at Amber Bead. "In order to do this thing, I need Albaamaha help."

"I see."

"I need you to think something over for me: What would it take to get five hundred men for several weeks just after the equinox?"

"Five hundred men? You wish to build something? Ah, the rotting palisade!"

"Oh, curse the palisade. Yes, yes, it needs repair, but I have something else in mind. A fortified settlement up on Clear Water Creek Crossing. There is a ridge there, burned off at the moment, with good soil. It sits just at the head of navigable water."

Amber Bead blinked. "You wish us to build you a town? Way up there? How far away is that?"

"Three days' hard pack overland."

"How will you defend it?"

"With warriors," Flying Hawk said, amused. "Don't look so shocked. And, no, your people don't have to build the whole town, not right away. For the moment, I just need enough food packed up there to keep a small band of warriors. I want to use the location for a warriors' camp. They will be able to run patrols through the forest, keep us from being surprised like we were this last moon. At the same time, we will put in some gardens. My people tell me the soils are good for corn. If we can hold it through the summer, we can put up a palisade after the next harvest. For that, I would need additional workers."

"A town at Clear Water Creek Crossing?" The idea still amazed him.

"A first step," Flying Hawk countered. "If we can defend it, a second town can be built a little farther downstream. Eventually we would have a line of forts down that valley, a way of buffering attacks against our people here."

"So, for the moment, all you want is for us to pack up enough food to keep your warriors from hunger?"

"That is correct." He looked out at the river, lost in thought. "This wouldn't just be for us, Amber Bead. Your people would be working for their own protection. Can you ask the mikkos to approve this thing?"

Amber Bead kept his face toward the river, realizing the women had managed to get back to at least a semblance of working, though they had grown suddenly awkward and clumsy in their movements.

"And perhaps, when this is all finished, you could join me?"

"Join you, High Minko?"

"I was thinking of fishing."

"Excuse me?"

"At the ponds. The old borrow pits where we took dirt to build the mounds. Those are kept stocked just for the chiefs to fish. I would be happy to have you join me." He nodded his head thoughtfully. "It would be an occasion like this. A chance for us to talk without having to be so formal."

"It would be my delight, High Minko." *I would rather dive down and be eaten by a water panther.*

"Good. Anything you need, Councilor, just ask."

Amber Bead tried to fit all the pieces together, and it came to him. "I will ask the mikkos to come here, High Minko. I am much more likely to get a satisfactory answer if I have them all in one place, and being just outside the walls of Split Sky City, well, it will lend a certain gravity to the discussions."

Flying Hawk smiled. "Excellent idea. Perhaps you can tackle the problem of Red Awl's replacement while you are at it? I'm sure someone suitable can be found."

"Of course, High Minko." *We will discuss a great many things. And Lotus Root can tell her story to the assembled mikkos.* "I will make preparations immediately."

Flying Hawk sighed. "If only I could count on everyone the way I do on you."

"Oh, you can, High Minko. I assure you."

———

Finding a replacement for the bow Lotus Root had stolen hadn't been easy. Smoke Shield had used the bow Fast Legs had given him during the Chahta raid, but it hadn't really suited him. The bow Smoke Shield now held was a good one. Made of imported Osage orange-wood, it was a tightly grained stave. He had often admired the bows that came through Trade from the west. This one was perfectly balanced, just the thing he needed to replace the weapon Lotus Root had made off with.

This piece had been offered by a Trader down at the landing, a fellow from Thunder Town who claimed to have obtained it several years ago. The Trader complained that the pull was too heavy. Smoke Shield had found a suitable string made of gut that appeared to be the correct length. Now he slipped the loop over the notches and bent the bow stave behind his leg. Grunting, he slipped the upper loop into the grooves and settled the string into place. Lifting it, he tested the pull.

It took effort, but with this, he could drive an arrow clear through a man. The next thing would be to shoot it.

"New bow?" Flying Hawk asked as he entered the palace great room. He was winded, puffing from the long climb up the Sun Stairs.

"I Traded with a Deer Clan man from Thunder Town."

"Don't lose that one," Flying Hawk said darkly.

"Uncle." A surge of frustration began to build. "Don't try—"

"High Minko!" A warrior burst into the room. "A canoe has just landed. It is a Yuchi! He brings a white arrow."

Smoke Shield's rage filtered away. "A white arrow? He is a messenger?"

"Yes, War Chief. He wishes to address the Council."

"Go and alert the tishu minko. Tell him to call the Council," Flying Hawk ordered.

"No!" Smoke Shield reached out, placing a restraining hand on his uncle's arm. He gave Flying Hawk a warning look. "Bring him here, Black Hand. The high minko and I will see him alone."

"Alone, War Chief?"

"He carries a white arrow, does he not? We will be perfectly safe. The high minko and I will hear his message, and then, having time to consider it, will bring him before the Council." He gave his uncle a wink where Black Hand couldn't see. "We are better forewarned as to his intentions. That way we can inform the Council before he makes his announcement."

"Do it," Flying Hawk ordered.

No sooner had Black Hand turned and left than Smoke Shield hurried to the door, looking out. Reentering, he waved down Flying Hawk's question and asked, "Is anyone else here?"

"My slave."

"Send him away."

Flying Hawk's eyes had narrowed. "What are you plotting this time?"

"This Yuchi may just turn out to be the solution to a very large problem."

———

The Yuchi messenger, known as Bullfrog Pipe, held the sacred white arrow before him as he started forward. Split Sky City wasn't what he had expected. As he followed his guide up from the canoe landing— bearing the white arrow so that all could see—people flocked out to watch his progress. The sight of this many Sky Hand and Albaamaha —all watching him with hostile eyes—was daunting. They cleared a path for him, making way for his escort, the warrior called Black Hand.

He had not expected to see such a large city, nor the great buildings, let alone so many of them. Several thousand people had to live here, just inside the palisade alone. And he had passed seven substantial towns already. More, he knew, were downriver.

That he was escorted by only one warrior was heartening. A guard of twenty would have left his heart hammering in his chest, and fear sweat beading on his brow. It was one thing to proudly claim the honor of bearing Trader's message back in Rainbow Town. It was another to be here, alone, in a sea of hostile Chikosi faces. The eerie thing was the silence with which they watched him; but then, the Tsoyaha and Chikosi had been enemies from time the Mos'kogee had first migrated into this land.

He had seen the high minko's mound from the river, as he looked up beyond the escort of warrior-laden canoes that followed him downriver. Perched on its high mound, the place might have been the home of gods, rather than men.

Now, as he passed along the northern base of one of the moiety mounds, the sight of the high minko's structure atop its stupendous earthen mound amazed him. To the north, burial mounds and charnel houses rested atop the finger ridges overlooking the river.

The path skirted a deep drainage; the slope had been dug away to make climbing nearly impossible. A force of attacking warriors would slip and slide trying to storm it, subject the entire time to a hail of arrows. He looked down to see a tangle of brush and pointed logs at the bottom. No stealthy approach from that direction.

Black Hand led him around the head of the ravine and to the western wall of the great mound. This they skirted, people following along behind him like a human river. He peered again into the depths of that sheer-walled ravine.

If they kill me, throw me down into that mess, no one will ever find my body. It was a sobering thought.

I *am* Tsoyaha! The knowledge lent him courage. He held his head up straight, remembering how his people were born of the sun. When he cast his glance skyward, it was to see Mother Sun, beaming down on him with love and admiration.

The way led to a flat along the northern base of the mound. Here a small plaza had been leveled, a clay chunkey court running northward to the edge of the bluff.

At the long stairway, he took a deep breath, then started up, following in Black Hand's steps.

He climbed and climbed, counting the wooden steps as he went. The knowledge of how high this was awed him. Nevertheless, aware of the crowd that had gathered below, he forced himself not to look back.

Only when, breathing deeply, he reached the high gate did he stop and glance down. Below him the people looked like colorful dots. Beyond the bluff with its charnel houses and mounds, the river gleamed in the light like a wide silver band. Beyond the opposite shore, endless fields, dotted with tiny distant houses, stretched to the far forest. Rolling up from the south came a solid black line of clouds, flickers of lightning at the fore. It looked like he'd just beaten a nasty storm to Split Sky City.

"Stunning, isn't it?" Black Hand asked in Trade Tongue.

"I've never seen anything like it."

"Come, the high minko awaits you."

He followed Black Hand through the gate, finding the area enclosed by the palisade to be suddenly cramped, the building taking up most of the space. Two fierce-looking eagles had been fashioned for guardian posts. They watched him pass with malevolent eyes. He rounded the corner of the building, finding that the entry faced east.

More guardian posts confronted him with threatening visages.

At the Great Palace door, Black Hand called in Mos'kogee, "A Yuchi messenger, High Minko."

"Send him in," a voice answered. "Guard the door, Warrior. No one must pass."

"Yes, High Minko."

Bullfrog Pipe saw surprise and no little disappointment on Black Hand's face. Bullfrog Pipe mustered all of his courage and stepped inside. As he entered the room, he held the white arrow before him as if tendering an offering.

The room was impressive, but not more so than Born-of-Sun's. Only the huge carving of the Seeing Hand on the rear wall startled him. That single eye seemed to be looking right through to his souls. The old Yuchi relief on the opposite wall reassured him. When had the Chikosi stolen it? What tales of woe and suffering could it have told?

He walked forward, taking a position before the fire. There he raised the white arrow over his head, the slim shaft resting on his open palms. "I am Bullfrog Pipe, of the Chief Society, and born into the Bear Clan. I come here as a messenger of the Tsoyaha. I am sent by High Chief Born-of-Sun. I bear my high chief's blessing with words to be given to the Council of the Sky Hand." He spoke in flawless Mos'kogee, one of the reasons he had been chosen for this great task.

The high minko was an older man, white haired, with a gleaming copper headpiece supported by a tight bun pulled severely behind his head. He wore a spotless white apron, its point hanging down almost to his knees. A stone ceremonial mace rested in his hands. This would be Flying Hawk. He looked oddly worried, worn, and old. His face was lined, as if the weight of leadership had grown too great.

The man who walked off to his right was young and muscular; a terrible scar marred the side of his face. He watched Bullfrog Pipe with a curious intensity in his black eyes. The scarred man stood stiffly, as if his back were immobile. A thick thong was pulled into his throat, as though it were tied too tight. He, too, wore a white apron. Something about him didn't seem right. Even standing the man radiated the bunched energy of a cougar ready to pounce.

The high minko spoke. "I am Flying Hawk, high minko of the Sky Hand Mos'kogee, of the Hickory Moiety, born of the Chief Clan. You are welcome here." He indicated the scar-faced man. "This is War Chief Smoke Shield, also of the Hickory Moiety and the Chief Clan. We wait to hear the words of the Yuchi high chief."

"Bullfrog Pipe?" Smoke Shield asked. "What kind of name is that?"

Bullfrog Pipe shot the warrior a sidelong look. Why did the man insist on standing off to the side? Or was this some silly protocol the Chikosi adhered to? "It is a name of great honor. Among my people, it is told that in the beginning days, Wind sent his four sons off to the west. Many days passed but none returned. Wind became concerned. He, himself, went west, taking a bullfrog pipe with a pipe stem made of a snake. When he reached the land of Stone Man, he realized that this was the being who had harmed his four sons. Though Stone Man tried to trick Wind, he cunningly evaded all of Stone Man's sorcery. Because Stone Man was made of rock, no weapon could kill him. To achieve that end, Wind built a smoke in his bullfrog pipe, and using sacred tobacco, blew the smoke through the pipe, onto Stone Man. When Stone Man inhaled the smoke, it killed him. Thereafter, Wind was able to retrieve his sons from the waters where Stone Man had drowned them."

"Ah." Flying Hawk nodded. "Yes, I have heard that story. Your people must have great respect for you to have given you that name." He arched an eyebrow. "I would hope that you do not consider me to be Stone Man."

"No, High Minko. Though our peoples are enemies, my message is carried in peace. With my chief's blessing, I bear the words of another party for your people."

"And what might that message be?" Smoke Shield asked mildly.

"I am supposed to deliver those words to your Council."

Flying Hawk made a dismissive gesture. "And so you shall, brave Yuchi." Then he smiled warmly. "Very well, we can all relax now." He stepped down off his tripod, walking forward, taking Bullfrog Pipe's hand.

"Be welcome here. I have sent for food and drink. You must have had a long trip. Tell me about it."

Bullfrog Pipe met the man's warm smile with his own. "I thank you for your greeting, High Minko. It was a long trip. I ran overland from the Tenasee to the headwaters of the Black Warrior. There, I bartered with one of your Traders for a canoe. When I encountered your people on the river, I called out to them in friendship, and extended the white arrow of peace to show them my intentions were honorable and protected by the white Power. I am proud to be bound by that Power."

Flying Hawk nodded. "Though our peoples are enemies, you will receive the treatment of an honored guest." He stepped over to one of the wall benches and retrieved a wooden gorget carved in the shape of a water cougar, its back sprouting wings. This he handed to Bullfrog Pipe. "I offer you a token of our respect. Take this as a gift. When you return to your people, you can show them that we treat your chief's messengers with respect and honor."

Bullfrog Pipe studied the piece. Hung on a deerhide thong, it was beautifully carved.

"Our woodworkers are among the finest," Flying Hawk said frankly. "This comes from a man named, fittingly enough, Wood-pecker. His pieces are in great demand all the way down to the gulf. Some have been Traded as far as the Calusa."

"It is beautiful, High Minko."

Flying Hawk smiled happily. "It pleases me that you like it." He paused. "Now, about this message, what can I do to help you?"

"I need but deliver it to your Council. That is all."

Flying Hawk's brows lifted in amusement. "Oh, no, my friend. Our politics are anything but as easy as that. Your chief would not have sent us a message if he didn't expect a favorable outcome." He slapped the heavy mace against the palm of his left hand. "If this is a peace offer, I may be able to anticipate the objections of some Council members. If this concerns territory, others could be approached with certain discretion and made more amenable." He shot a knowing look at Bullfrog Pipe. "That is, if I agree with your chief's objectives."

"I see what you mean, but no, High Minko. My message concerns none of these things."

"You said that you carried another's message through your chief. Could it be from the Chahta? We are looking for a way to smooth our relations with them. A prolonged war will do neither of our peoples any good."

"No, it is from one of your people, actually."

From his expression, Flying Hawk expected any answer but this. "One of my people?"

"He and his party came to us just before solstice. The Kala Hi'ki saw them in a vision. The Trader is a man of your moiety and clan. He played the most remarkable game of chunkey! I, myself, lost many of my most prized possessions betting on the high chief to beat the Sky Hand man. They played evenly, High Minko. Right up the last cast, when Green Snake splintered his lance on the stone. It was a thing of Power."

"Green Snake?" Flying Hawk said in disbelief. "Did you say Green Snake? *My nephew?*"

"Yes, my message is to inform your Council that Green Snake is returning to his people."

Flying Hawk actually staggered, his legs seeming to go weak, his expression dazed.

Bullfrog Pipe stepped forward, steadying the old man's elbow. "High Minko, are you all right? Can I—"

He caught the barest of movement behind him, thinking that Smoke Shield, too, was rushing forward to steady the old man. The whistling of a war club cutting the air was his only warning—then lightning and pain blasted through his head. His skull snapped and jerked at the impact. He had a momentary feeling of falling; then his body bounced on the matting, his vision blurring, the world growing ever more gray and distant....

SEVENTEEN

FLYING HAWK STUMBLED away from the falling Yuchi, barely catching himself before he toppled into the fire. In the process, he dropped his mace. The war club's slapping impact as it broke the Yuchi's skull rang in his ears. He'd had misgivings when Smoke Shield hung the strap of his club around his neck, letting it dangle down his back.

Unable to stand, Flying Hawk sat weakly, staring incomprehensibly at the dying Yuchi. The man's arms and legs twitched, his open eyes staring with disbelief. His mouth formed a questioning O as his sight dimmed and the pupils expanded. Blood was leaking from the back of his head, pooling bright and thick on the matting.

"What did you do?" Flying Hawk whispered.

"I killed him!" Smoke Shield said through gritted teeth. "Green Snake? Living among the Yuchi? He's up there...spreading his poison? No one must know this."

"Green Snake?" Flying Hawk asked in amazement. "After all these years?"

"High Minko? Is something wrong?" Black Hand called from the doorway.

"The high minko is attacked!" Smoke Shield bellowed before Flying Hawk could gather his wits. "Quickly! Run and fetch the *Hopaye!* Go now, man! Hurry!"

Black Hand turned and vanished.

"But, I am not wounded."

Smoke Shield bent down, peering into his eyes. "It will have to be a flesh wound, enough of a gash to enrage our people."

"Why?" He was shaking his head. *Green Snake? He is alive among the Yuchi? Coming home, after all these years?*

"Because we were looking for a reason to make war on the Yuchi, remember?"

The Yuchi? I thought we wanted them to attack the Chahta.

Smoke Shield closed his eyes as if struggling for control, his shoulders trembling. "Green Snake! Gods, what evil is he spinning against us?" Flying Hawk could hear the man's teeth grinding. "Why now, of all times?"

"He still lives," Flying Hawk whispered. "After all these years without word..." He glanced at Smoke Shield. "I honestly had come to believe that you killed him that night. That somehow you had hidden his body."

"I only wish, Uncle."

"Green Snake lives."

"No!" Smoke Shield thrust a hard finger in emphasis. "You will say *nothing* of this. Not yet. This is our secret, Uncle. No one is to know until the time is right."

The smoldering anger in Smoke Shield's eyes was warning enough. *He's thinking of killing me. Blaming it on the Yuchi.* "Yes, yes, you're right." Fear focused his wits. "Quickly, go through the Yuchi's things. Yes, there, that knife. Someone will be here soon." He pointed. "Here, across the chest." He met Smoke Shield's hot eyes. "But not too deeply, Nephew, or I shall scream loudly enough that they will know I died long after the Yuchi did."

A faint smile crossed Smoke Shield's lips. "Does that mean you don't trust me, Uncle?"

"You shall be high minko soon enough without rushing things along. Crushing the Chahta will leave no •opposition to your confirmation."

The slash was lightning fast. It didn't even begin to sting until Flying Hawk looked down. Blood was welling from a deep but clean cut across his breast.

Oh, yes, we shall have our warriors. Once again, Power has played right into Smoke Shield's hands.

Flying Hawk considered, a slow smile growing. "I am glad I am not your enemy."

"Yes, Uncle. I know."

Then feet pounded outside, accompanied by rising shouts. Flying Hawk looked at the dead Yuchi. The man's blood was soaking the white arrow. *He came here under the white Power of peace. May Breath Maker help me. What have we brought down on ourselves?*

But then Flying Hawk had no time to worry about offended Power. He looked up to see the great room filling with angry people.

"Yuchi treachery!" Smoke Shield bellowed. "The high minko is wounded!"

As Flying Hawk was lifted, he thought, *Green Snake is alive!*

But what did it mean?

Somewhere in the distance, thunder rumbled, as though the heavens were enraged.

———

Homecoming was not what Old White had anticipated. They rounded the final bend to see Sky Hand City rising at the end of a southerly loop of the Black Warrior, its high palaces obscured by sheets of falling rain. The gray skies continued to pelt them with the misty downfall. Even Paunch put his back to the paddie, anxious to reach the shelter of the ramadas at the canoe landing.

All those years of deserts, forests, mountains, and seacoasts, and here he was, wet, cold, and miserable, wishing only to reach that place and stand under a shelter with a fire to warm and dry his old bones.

They followed the backwaters, catching occasional glimpses of farmsteads where the roofs could be seen above the banks. Then Trader's canoe pulled ahead, angling across the lazy current toward shore. Two Petals, sitting backward, looked glum under a bark rain hat. Swimmer, perched high atop the forward packs, appeared more like a drowned wood rat than a dog.

Old White and Paunch dug in with their pointed paddles, shooting their craft across rain-stippled waters to the bank.

Home. "Gods," he mumbled, shivering. "Get me out of here."

Trader stepped over to offer him a hand. Old White's cramped legs almost folded under him. He braced himself on the gunwale. "Just a moment. Let me get some blood back in my legs."

"Paunch," Trader ordered, "move those packs up to that ramada there. No one seems to be using it for the moment."

Two Petals was looking around the landing, seeing the long rows of canoes, some inverted to keep the rain out. Irregularly placed ramadas had been built for just such occasions as this. Most had packs, baskets, jars, and other wares beneath. Under a few, people were tending fires, avoiding the leaks in the roofs and staring out at the rain and the newcomers.

Old White finally trusted himself to take a step. He shouldered his carved wooden pack and his bags, then slogged his way up to the ramada Trader had indicated. White breath hung in the cold air. The feel of the heavy weight in his bag was a reminder of the long-ago past. Did it know where it was, the full turning of the circle that had taken him so far away, now coming to completion?

He cast a glance up at the Skunk Clan Council house, its gray roof almost camouflaged against the sky. Lightning lanced out and vanished. A short ten breaths later, it boomed over the land.

Trader did most of the work, lugging the heavy packs up from the canoes, making three trips for every one that Paunch and Old White managed. Two Petals carried some of the lighter items, and Swimmer, as usual, carried none.

With their goods stowed under the leaky ramada, Trader crossed to a pitch-roofed shelter where an Albaamo bartered dry firewood.

Old White puffed and rubbed his cold arms.

"My life is in your hands, Seeker," Paunch reminded, shooting frightened looks up toward the city.

"We may all freeze to death before that, you fool."

"I think freezing is easier than dying on the square."

Two Petals was sitting hunched up, her hands twitching as she stared absently at the city.

"What do you see up there?" Old White asked gently.

"They are watching us with empty eyes." She shrugged. "It must be confusing to see with such clarity."

He squinted up through the rain. The beaten soil was silvered with water. Rivulets of it ran in patterns down the landing, carrying charcoal, mud, and refuse with it.

Trader came at a run, a bundle of wood covered in matting under one arm. His expression was grim when he arrived.

"They ask too much in Trade?" Old White asked dryly. "Or are you just that displeased to come home to so much fanfare and excitement?"

"The Yuchi messenger is dead," he said grimly. "The story is that he tried to kill the high minko. The whole city is in shock. There's a meeting at the tchkofa as we speak. According to the firewood Trader, people are just up there in the plaza, standing in the rain, waiting to hear what the Council has to say."

Old White considered that. "Born-of-Sun will be enraged."

"The Council will vote for war," Trader agreed.

Two Petals looked up, shivering as she clutched her knees to her chest. "Weaving is such an art. So many strands have to go into it. Each one has to be laid with careful perfection. Now, the warp and weft must be made tight so that the story it tells cannot leak through."

"We're worried about treachery, and she's talking about weaving." Trader dropped the wood in a clatter.

"One and the same, I would suppose." Old White looked up at the storm. "The messenger would have come under a white arrow. You and I know that Born-of-Sun sent no assassin. This is the work of Flying Hawk and Smoke Shield." He glanced at Trader. "It would appear that they don't want you back."

Trader raised a rain-dewed brow. "I was smart enough to ask if the Yuchi had delivered any message before he died. The wood Trader didn't know of one."

"We must be careful." Old White gratefully knelt as Trader opened one of their jars, removing tinder. Then he uncapped another, pouring ash from their last fire until he found a hot coal. Teasing it into the tinder, he bent, blowing gently. The coal brightened, and smoke began to curl into the air. Old White almost sighed with relief as the first tiny flicker sprang to life.

"I am no longer sure how to proceed." Trader looked questioningly at Two Petals. "Do they know they are looking for the Seeker, a Contrary, and me, or do they expect us to arrive in some grand armada? Accompanied by Dancing, Singing, and marching warriors?"

"Oh, you are expected, all right," Two Petals said between chattering teeth. "You look so proud, seated in the Yuchi palace. You shouldn't laugh so loudly, or eat like a starved wolf as they ply you with food."

"So perhaps we're not expected?" Old White tried to decipher her words. "Is she saying that they still think we're with the Yuchi?"

"Not there, no," Two Petals told him. "You'll see: Every eye will be on you as you enter the city."

Trader looked out at the rain, his dashed hopes as damp as the weather.

"I think I should go up first," Old White decided. "One old man won't stir much interest." He chuckled to himself.

"What's so funny?"

"Endings and beginnings. I was thinking of the night I left Split Sky City."

"And?"

"Beginnings and endings are always the same."

"Gods," Trader muttered. "You're making as much sense as the Contrary."

"Yes. I know." He listened to his knees crack as he knelt down to the growing fire. Its heat soothed his fingers. Within moments, they were all crouched over the flame, letting the heat and smoke battle the chill.

Old White watched as Trader—ever vigilant about such things— finally straightened, picking through the packs and opening the precious furs. One by one, he sorted them, taking any that were damp and laying them out to dry before they could mold.

There lay the most valuable of their wealth, outside of the metals. Skins of wolverine, two arctic foxes, northern beaver, lynx, and pine marten. They had been well tanned, pressed, and, so far, had made the trip in perfect condition. Then Trader opened yet another pack, one Old White hadn't seen. He stared in disbelief. "Are those what I think they are?"

"Something called ivory." Trader lifted one of the two large teeth. "They were Traded down to the freshwater lakes along with the white fox skins. The Trader was from a northern forest people." Trader looked at the tusks, and shrugged. "He said they could be carved. I just hope these Chikosi are smart enough to know what they're worth."

"We're not supposed to say Chikosi. It's derogatory." Old White shook his head. "That ivory you hold, it comes from one of those walruses I was telling you about. And yes, they can be carved. Worked with the same tools as people use on stone."

He cocked his head. Had any Trader ever brought wealth like this to the Sky Hand? He glanced at the square fabric covering the war medicine. "We should make sure the box doesn't warp. It's waxed, but this is a pretty hard rain. You might want to dry it before curious eyes come peeking this way."

Trader muttered, glanced surreptitiously around, and removed the cloth bag from the copper-heavy box. He found a moderately dry cloth and soaked pooled water from the hollows of the engraving. Then they held the protective fabric over the fire, drying it.

Only after ensuring that all of their Trade was safe did they resume their huddled stance over the fire, hands out to the crackling flames. For a long time, they were silent, each locked in his thoughts.

Trader finally mused, "So Great Cougar is coming with a war party, Born-of-Sun will be coming with a war party, and no one knows but us. What kind of joke is Power playing on us?"

Two Petals laughed softly, but said nothing.

"We'll find out soon enough," Old White decided. "But perhaps the storm was a gift. No one has seen us arrive, and the people are distracted. We couldn't ask for a better way to come home. We have time to blend in before anyone comes looking for us." People packed shoulder to shoulder inside the tchkofa—and these were just the chiefs and high-ranking personages who had been readily at hand. A great fire burned in the hearth, sending sparks toward the high smoke hole. Rain battled the heat, showering down from the opening, hissing as it met its adversary. Occasional gusts sent droplets this way and that, to sprinkle the occupants.

People tended to crowd back, away from the fire's heat and unpredictable rain, making the press in the rear even more unbearable.

Pale Cat stood beside Night Star, trying to find some rational explanation to this sudden change of events. He glanced behind him, seeing Heron Wing, her damp hair hanging in strings over the shoulders of her wet dress. Her expression was pinched, concern behind her eyes.

Smoke Shield pranced out, unflinching as raindrops turned his way. A terrible rage seemed to fire his gaze as he glanced about the room. "The high minko could have been *murdered!* This is treachery most foul! And it was sent to us under a white arrow!" He lifted the bloody shaft, holding it up in the firelight for all to see. "The Yuchi weasels tried to *assassinate* our high minko! There can only be one response."

War. Pale Cat glanced behind Smoke Shield to where Flying

Hawk sat, his breast stitched by Pale Cat's own hand. The cut had been deep, glancing off the bone in places. Flying Hawk would battle infection, and it would leave a nasty scar.

But something hadn't been right. He could sense it.

The fact was, Flying Hawk should have been enraged, but instead he simply sat like a lump. The man had appeared dazed, not even flinching as Pale Cat drove his copper needle into Flying Hawk's flesh and closed the wound. As if numb, the high minko had stared off into the distance, seeing something long gone and wistfully lost.

"I agree." Two Poisons, chief of the Deer Clan, stepped forward, his face passionate. "This is an affront not only to us, but to Power!" He looked around. "Chiefs, all eyes are on us! Not just here among our people—who look to us for leadership—but Power, too, waits, watching, looking to us for a response. We *are* Power's strong right arm. This must be avenged. Power must be brought back into balance."

Voices of approbation called out, feet stamping. The chiefs nodded, including Night Star. Pale Cat looked down at his diminutive aunt.

The Old Camp minko, Vinegaroon, took the floor. "Skunk Clan votes for war." He looked around. "Two Poisons is right. There can be no other alternative. We have done nothing to deserve this foul and treacherous attack on our high minko. The Yuchi have grown too arrogant, too vile for us to take any other course."

The tishu minko, Seven Dead, stepped forward. "Raccoon Clan votes for war. If this Council agrees, I will make the call for warriors." Behind him, Blood Skull, too, was nodding, but there was hesitation behind his hooded eyes.

Yes, you smell it, too, don't you, old friend?

Again feet stamped in assent.

Pale Cat laid his hand on Night Star's shoulder and stepped out. He looked around at the familiar faces, read their anger and disbelief. "I am *Hopaye*. No one knows the ways of Power better than I do. No one knows the risks of offending Power—let alone in so blatant and outrageous a manner. A man bearing a white arrow has tried to kill, and then been killed himself." He paused, letting that knowledge sink in. "What remains unanswered here is why."

He met their eyes, pair by pair. "We must respond to his atrocity. On that we all agree, but the question still remains: Why? Why would the Yuchi high chief—like lightning from a blue sky—purposefully abuse Power in a manner that will surely turn many of his own people against him? This action will lead to the deaths of many of his people. Why?"

Even Smoke Shield seemed at a loss for words.

"This question must be answered." Pale Cat stepped back to his place, eyes on Flying Hawk.

For a moment, no one spoke; then Smoke Shield stepped forward, stating, "There is no *why*. These are Yuchi dogs! They have no regard for Power and its ways! Think! How often in the past have they raided us for no apparent reason? How many times have they stolen our relatives, hung them in their squares or burned them as offerings to the sun and sent their screaming ghosts wailing into the darkness? How many of our daughters have they taken away, and corrupted with their evil seed? These people have no truth as we do. This latest atrocity is just another example of why we must finally, and forever, teach them to behave as Power has decreed for all men!"

Again the applause, but Pale Cat kept his face expressionless. Throughout the tirade, not once did Flying Hawk look up, or nod his approval. Instead, he seemed removed, oblivious, as though some more important consideration preoccupied his souls.

But what?

Then Blood Skull stepped forward and raised a knotted fist. "I, too, call for war." He glanced at Smoke Shield, nodding slightly. "I have served the war chief as second on many raids. I will be happy to do so again, but I would have us ponder this: Before we go to war, we *do* need to know why. If this is truly the act of some rot-infested souls, we need to stamp it out, make an end of it. If, on the other hand, this is some tragic mistake, we must know that, too."

Blood Skull glanced around, avoiding the glowering Smoke Shield's eyes. "What if this is not what it seems? What if this Bullfrog Pipe acted alone? For the purposes of revenge? What if, in fact, it was his idea alone to perpetrate this foul deed?" Blood Skull spread his hands. "What if our reaction here tonight is to serve some schemer's purpose, and the Yuchi chief, like us, is being lured into a bloody conflict that will blind us to some other person's plans?"

Growls of discontent rose from among the spectators.

Blood Skull finished, saying, "If the Yuchi chief did this thing the way we are currently led to believe, we have no choice but to drive a fiery lance through his heart. I will drive that lance myself. But I want to do so knowing that it wasn't just some lone demented Yuchi, driven by his own twisted Spirits, who plunged us into this."

In the uproar that followed, Pale Cat saw the look Smoke Shield gave his second. It burned with undisguised loathing and hatred.

Flying Hawk, however, finally raised his eyes and focused his attention on Smoke Shield. A look of premonition and misery lay behind them.

Now that is most interesting.

Lightning flashed, its hot light lancing through the smoke hole in a strobe of blinding white. People started, smiled uncomfortably, and then the deafening crack of it shook the building around them.

Morning Dew had never liked lightning and thunder. She had been a little girl, believing herself safe in the palace at White Arrow Town, when a bolt of it hit the roof, shattering the center pole and raining bits of burning thatch down on top of her. A hard rain—like this one—had drowned the fire before it even got started. She had been left cowering, huddled into a little ball beneath one of the benches. Meanwhile people ran about, stamping on flames and screaming in panic while rain lashed the great room.

Now Morning Dew waited, hating the fear in her gut, but being brave for little Stone's sake. For the duration of the storm, she had crouched beside Stone's bed, holding his hand, trying to control her desire to flinch at each lightning strobe, and soothing his worry as thunderbolt after thunderbolt cracked and banged around them.

She looked up at the roof, illuminated by the flicker of the fire. Bits of soot had rained down from above when the house shook under the impact of nearby thunder.

"Why is there thunder?" Stone had asked.

"Power is on the move, little one." She tried to give him a reassuring smile. "The snakes call the thunder, just as they call the rain. That's why you should never kill them. Thunder, lightning, and rain are their particular Power. It goes back to the beginning times, to just after Crawfish brought land up from the deep waters to make the earth. That's when snakes first crawled out of the Underworld. Where they went, the water followed. Even to this day, that's why you find them around springs and rivers."

"But thunder comes from the sky."

"That's right. That's why snakes are so Powerful. Even though they are beings of the Underworld, they can call the clouds and rain. It's just the way they are. Power must always balance, Stone. It is part of the harmony of our world."

"Oh," he said, seemingly unconvinced.

She glanced uneasily at the door, wondering what was happening in the tchkofa.

Like the rest of the city's population, she, Stone, and Heron Wing had been standing at the foot of the great mound, sections of matting over their heads for protection. People had been frantic for news. It wasn't every day that a Yuchi tried to murder the high minko. Speculation had run rampant. Rumors passed from lip to lip. In some, Flying Hawk was dead; in others, he remained unhurt. Heron Wing had waited for each bit of gossip, Morning Dew, holding Stone's hand, close behind her. They had watched as Pale Cat made his way carefully down the rain-slick stairs. The *Hopaye* had called out that Flying Hawk was fine, waving down the shouted questions. Then he had walked up to Heron Wing, saying, "The Council is called. Come with me."

Heron Wing had nodded, turning to Morning Dew.

Forestalling her, Morning Dew had said, "I'll take Stone home. Make sure he has supper and is put to bed."

Heron Wing had just nodded, her mind no doubt on why Pale Cat would insist she be in the tchkofa with him.

Morning Dew tucked the blanket around Stone's chin. A Yuchi messenger had tried to kill Flying Hawk? In the name of the gods, why? In the entire time she had been in Split Sky City there had been no rumors of trouble along the northern border. To her, the act was that of a madman. Of course the Sky Hand would respond; they'd mobilize every warrior on hand to march north. This would not be any petty border skirmish, but a long, drawn-out war, with large armies marching back and forth. Pitched battles would be fought, towns burned, and a great many souls sent weeping to the afterlife.

She listened to the night, hearing the soft patter of rain. The worst of the storm appeared to have passed.

Stone's eyes had grown heavy now that the terrible thunder had faded. Only the rolling distant rumbles of it came out of the north.

Morning Dew heard wet steps beyond the door and looked up as Heron Wing stepped in, her clothing soaked, her hair in limp strands over her shoulders.

"What has happened?"

Heron Wing stepped over to the fire, struggling out of her wet dress. She dropped the soggy garment onto the matting and shivered as she hovered, naked, over the flames. "The vote, as expected, is for war."

"You don't sound happy."

"I'm not." She bent, throwing another piece of wood on the flames.

Morning Dew stood, stepping over to pick up the dress before she leaned out the door to wring the fabric.

She reentered and placed the dress on clean matting to dry. "Could I get you something? Make you tea?"

"Yes, please. We don't have much time." She glanced at Morning Dew. Water droplets beaded on her normally serene face; they sparkled on her long lashes. Her eyes, however, were troubled. "Night Star would like to talk to us. We're to wait until most people have gone home."

"So there's more to this than meets the eye?"

"Perhaps."

Morning Dew nodded as she went about warming the tea. As it heated, she studied Heron Wing. The woman's stomach remained flat, her waist narrow above rounded hips that tapered into muscular thighs. Her high breasts with their dark pointed nipples remained firm and provocative.

I hope I look half as good at her age, she thought.

"Something bothering your souls?" Heron Wing asked, giving her an appraising look.

Morning Dew smiled. "Just thinking of the future."

She waved it off. "More to the point, why would the Yuchi high chief send an assassin to kill Flying Hawk? Is there some reason I don't know?"

Heron Wing's classic brow arched as she took the tea Morning Dew poured. "You and Pale Cat think a lot alike. He is wondering the same thing. Something happened in the palace when he was stitching up the wound in Flying Hawk's chest. He smells a skunk among the raccoons. That's why we're called to Night Star's."

"And you want me to go? What would I know about Born-of-Sun?"

"I haven't the foggiest idea. Have you ever met him?"

"Once, long ago. I was still a girl, he just barely a man."

"I see. And?"

She laughed. "I thought him one of the most unusual young men I'd ever met. He speaks fluent Mos'kogee. He was charming, intelligent, and had a smile that made my heart flutter."

"A rogue?"

"Hardly. I thought he was responsible beyond his years."

"That is his reputation." Heron Wing chugged the tea, shivering again, but most of the moisture had been wicked away by the fire. "Find me something warm and dry to wear. We don't want to be late."

"And Stone?"

"Wide Leaf will be here soon. I saw her in the crowd outside the tchkofa. She had to attend to some things first. I don't think she'll be—"

"I'm here, I'm here," the old woman called as she stepped in through the door. "By the Ancestors, it's a wet one out there. You be sure to wear a rain hat." She stepped forward, dress dripping on the floor. "Bless you, lady. That fire is the finest thing I've seen in years."

Heron Wing pulled her dry dress over her head, saying, "I don't know how long we'll be."

"See you when you're back." Wide Leaf gave a toss of her hand.

Morning Dew followed Heron Wing out into the night. Once again, it was pitch black. This time, beads of rain spattered down on the piece of bark she held over her head.

"I would have you think," Heron Wing said. "Could Great Cougar have thought this up? Could this be a way of distracting us, diverting our attention away from the Chahta?"

Splashing through the puddles, Morning Dew considered the idea. Heron Wing had a clever mind. Could that indeed be the case? She remembered the man, keen-eyed, smart. He was a devout warrior, attending all of the rituals and ceremonies.

"No," she stated firmly. "The Yuchi came under the white arrow of peace. Great Cougar—cunning warrior that he is—would never abuse Power in that way."

"You're sure?"

"As sure as I am of anything."

"But," Heron Wing mused, "if someone else abused the white Power, Great Cougar wouldn't hesitate to strike, would he?"

"Make no mistake about Great Cougar. He will use any advantage given him in war." She stopped short.

Heron Wing made a few steps, then turned. "What?"

"One thing you do not want to try and do is lay this at his doorstep. I tell you, he is an honorable man. If the Sky Hand were to accuse him of misusing Power in this way, it would goad him to any length to destroy you. There could be no hope of peace until an apology was offered."

"Then," Heron Wing mused, "we must try and ensure that no such charges are made."

Morning Dew looked up at the night. "Gods, has the whole world gone mad?"

"Apparently so," Heron Wing agreed. "Though only Power and the gods know how we can stop it."

EIGHTEEN

IN THE PITCH BLACK, Flying Hawk climbed step by step as he made his way up the steep Sun Stairs. The wood was wet, slippery. Many of the steps slanted downward and were even more treacherous. As soon as the weather improved, he would have workers out to reset them. It was a constant labor, made more pressing in wet weather when the squared logs turned in the damp soil.

Three warriors traveled with him, offering their hands, warning him when the steps were sloping. *Three warriors. Perhaps I should have more.*

Was it his imagination, or did he hear dark wings beating in the air above him?

He glanced up into the night, feeling the patter of rain on his head and shoulders. Images of a Dream came back to him. In it, he'd seen his dead brother's body as it had been the day Flying Hawk had killed him. He had still clutched the stone he'd used to pound his brother's brains out of his head. That's when the mysterious Spirit Being had come. The Being was handsome, a glow surrounding his body.

"You have done everything," the Being had said. *"All that will be, you have wrought to obtain the high minko's chair."* And then he had said, *"In the end, it is a struggle between brothers."*

At the time, Flying Hawk had thought that referred to him and his own brother. Now, hearing that Green Snake was alive and returning to the Sky Hand, could it have been something else?

After that, the Spirit Being had extended arms that turned into mighty black wings and leapt into the air. The sound they had made was exactly like what he had just heard. He shot a nervous glance into the storm-thick night sky. *Are you up there, even now, watching me?*

At a sudden pain, Flying Hawk raised a hand to his chest. Oh, he remembered that Dream. Unable to sleep, he had walked out into the great room and stared at the large carving of the Seeing Hand. The hair had stood at the back of his neck, for he would have sworn the great carved eye in the hand's palm had been crying.

Was it crying for me? Or for my people?

He shook off the premonition, wondering where Smoke Shield had disappeared to. Even with three warriors, if Smoke Shield was up there, he could "accidentally" bump one, sending the whole lot of them tumbling down the long ramp, or off of its sides. The younger warriors might only end up with broken bones, but it had the probability of killing an older man like him.

Green Snake is alive, among the Yuchi! And now they were going to war with them.

Fleeting images of a bright-eyed boy flashed from his souls.

Ah, Green Snake, I never did right by you.

He had been the first hope. Smart and quick of wit and body, Green Snake had been what neither Flying Hawk nor his brother, Acorn, had been. It was as if Power had granted his line a second chance, drawing the distinction more clearly between Smoke Shield and Green Snake: red and white, two versions of the same boys. Choose between them. But even that chance had ended in disaster. It all went back to the night of the terrible fire. Power had been shifted long ago, taken by the self-same Yuchi against whom they were now going to war. Everything had gone wrong with the capture of High Minko Makes War and the loss of the war medicine.

Now, so far away from those terrible days, he was still living in their shadow. He wondered, "If Father hadn't been the brutal and soul-sick man he'd been, would it have changed anything?"

"Your father is the finest war chief I have ever seen," Kosi Fighting Hawk had said. *"He has handed the Yuchi one stinging defeat after another. The warriors believe in him. And that is half the challenge of war."*

He carefully placed his feet, taking another step, wishing the wind wasn't whipping around. It was always stiffer so high on the stairway. The wooden steps were shifting. He needed to have a crew attend to them. His chest continued to sting with each movement he made.

Did I have to let Smoke Shield do this to me?

Did any of this have to happen?

He looked out at the night, wondering what had happened to the boy who had once been called Grape. How did he end up like this?

"It always comes down to brothers." He swallowed hard, blinking back tears.

––––––

Old White clapped his hands in satisfaction as he stood in the morning sunshine. Puffy clouds scudded off to the northeast, driven by mild winds from the gulf. For two days the group had huddled beneath the landing ramada until inquiry had brought Old White to a Skunk Clan man who was willing to Trade the use of an empty house for a copper nugget.

In between bouts of pouring rain they had moved the packs here, swept out the refuse, driven out a nest of mice and two wood rats, and taken up residence. Paunch spent most of his time inside, looking odd with a completely shaved head. He had the most peculiarly shaped skull, like an oversized crabapple with dents in it. Looking at him took some getting used to.

Funny what people would do to themselves to avoid being hung in a square.

"Are you going out?" Trader asked, appearing in the door behind Old White.

"I think it's time one of us looks around." He nodded at the neighbor woman who had come out to pound corn in her pestle. Her name was Squash Blossom, and she'd been most curious, fascinated to hear they were Traders and staying for a while. She had taken to bringing bowls of steaming corn, beans, squash breads, and anything else, just to shoot speculative glances at their packs where they rested on the benches.

She had also proved to be a literal fountain of information on who was doing what to whom. According to her gossip, one would have thought she'd been present in the tchkofa when the decision was made to go to war against the Yuchi.

"Do be careful," Trader told Old White in a low voice.

"Oh, always." He took in the crowded houses, the ramadas, and screened latrines. It had been some time since he'd been in such a warren of humanity. "I want to see what they've done to my city."

Two Petals ducked out the door wearing a knee-length dress and without a word matched his pace, as if she'd planned this all along.

I had just made up my mind myself. But then, one didn't question a Contrary.

Or did he?

"I notice it was cold last night," he offered as he took a winding path that led around the shops where mica—Traded down from the north—was fashioned into ornaments and jewelry. After two days of rain, the craftsmen were busily engaged, sitting cross-legged as they carved designs into the shiny stone.

"Cold indeed," she replied. "I see ice everywhere I look."

"Find any in Trader's bed?"

"Oh, yes."

He cast her a sidelong glance. "How is that?"

"Time only stops for an instant," she whispered softly, her hands flicking this way and that. "Time lives and breathes, full and empty when we need it most. Why can't we stop the river, Seeker?"

"Because it was Created to flow." He smiled sadly. "You like him, don't you?"

"Wouldn't have him in my bed, that's sure."

"Then why do you go to his?"

"I have to be distracting. Failure would bring disaster. This is a hive. Can't you hear all the buzzing?" She was staring around at the people, the packed houses. "Thoughts and souls...souls and thoughts."

"I have some of the Kala Hi'ki's tea if you need it."

"The only time a person gets stung is if they move too fast. Can't threaten the bees. It makes the flowers lose color. The petals fall like leaves, but then, it's winter. Can't have leaves in winter...they'll grow out brown."

Old White let it go, figuring she had enough trouble keeping her Contrary thoughts in check without him adding to her confusion. That she could walk through such a large city and not be over-whelmed was progress enough from that first night at Rainbow City. And her mood was lighter, more cheery than the silent, inward-looking person she'd been on the trip downriver.

Was that just part of being Contrary? Sad and introspective for a period, then bouncing and happy?

He rounded a charnel house, passed one of the burial mounds, and stepped out on the eastern edge of the plaza. Across the chunkey court, the tchkofa stood, ringed by its palisade, looking like a mother turtle and her two babies where the round roofs protruded. The roofs had been covered with earth, and grass was growing on the soil.

The old familiar guardian posts stood watch, and the colors on the Tree of Life gleamed red and white. On the north, the high minko's palace stood defiantly against the sky. He stopped, just staring at it.

"The funny thing about time," Two Petals said, "is that you can get lost in it. When you bend it around, it takes you right back to where you started."

"Yes, it does," he whispered, then forced himself to study the Raccoon Clan palace atop its mound. "I have forgotten how big Split Sky City is. Somehow, after the Azteca and Cahokia, this place had grown small in my memory."

"When a snake swallows his tail, does he ever go all the way through?"

"Oh, yes. That's the magic of it, Contrary. He passes from this world to the next. Turns himself inside out, from the flesh to the Spirit."

He continued walking, responding to greetings. They encountered people going about their business, baskets perched on shoulders, jars in their hands. No one seemed to think twice at his presence, and that in itself was eerie. He was used to being the Seeker, and here he had become nameless. The irony of it carried a certain amusement.

They passed groups of men, all talking about war, about Yuchi treachery. But here and there, he caught snatches of other conversation.

Most of it hinged on why.

"At least some are wondering," he noted.

"Seeds are such small things," Two Petals said. "Isn't it odd how with just a little water and dirt they can become such large things as trees?"

"It's the water and dirt, all right," he agreed. "The best plantings are those well tended."

She stopped suddenly, eyes aglow.

He followed her gaze to where she had fixed on an open spot in the trampled grass. She was listening intently, then laughed, crying, "That's funny!"

"What's funny?"

"I've never seen a bird whirl around like that. It's some kind of crane, isn't it? How can it spin like that? Gods, it's a golden blur."

Not for the first time did he wish he could see through her eyes. It might even have been worth the kind of pain the Kala Hi'ki had endured just for a glimpse. Though, truth be told, he had seen some wondrous things while under the influence of the Spirit Plants.

He continued his walk, bits and pieces of memory coming back to him. In the eye of his souls, he could see a stickball game in the southern half of the plaza; he himself had run there, his racquets swishing in the air as he searched for the ball.

"Never was much good at that," he mused.

He remembered childhood friends, the sights of the Busk, with the women Dancing and Singing along the margins of the great plaza.

"I am home." And he wondered at the curious interplay of emotions. "What sort of man would I have been if I'd stayed here?"

"There is darkness there," she said, eyes fixed on something he couldn't see. "Let's go a different way." And she struck off, headed due east across the wide plaza.

He had to hurry, forcing himself to keep step. He kept having images flash, sights of long-gone days.

Is that where the darkness lies?

He was puffing as she led him around the tchkofa and paralleled the chunkey court. They were almost even with the Tree of Life pole when she stopped, staring at the empty wooden squares. She walked forward, almost in a trance. A young woman dressed in a simple brown dress stood before one of the squares, seemingly lost in thought. Her long black hair was worn loose, gleaming in the sunlight. She carried a brownware jar propped under one slim arm.

Two Petals walked up beside her, paused, and reached out to finger the wood. The woman's eyes widened, a look of dismay on her face.

"Their relief tingles against my skin," Two Petals said. "The blood made you what you are. They know that." She looked at the woman, eyes losing focus. "He is coming for you."

"Who?" she asked, responding in Trade Tongue.

"The final knot."

"I'm sorry," Old White interrupted gently. "My friend here has mistaken you for someone else." He grabbed Two Petals' elbow, whispering in Oneota, "Come, let's go look at the river."

When he glanced back, the woman was still staring, her lips parted, a shining disbelief in her eyes. Then she turned and fled.

"Power is Dancing." Two Petals pointed up. "Look at the colored lights."

But when Old White followed her finger, all he could see was a pattern of puffy white clouds against the light blue sky.

Something just happened back there. It wasn't idle ramblings.

But what?

He glanced up, nervous at being this close to the great palace. But when he turned to go, Two Petals fixed her eyes on the high palace atop its mound. A frown lined her smooth brow.

"Are you all right?"

"He's the final obstacle before I join my husband," she said in a worried voice.

"What husband?"

Even as he asked, she turned, hurrying back toward their house.

———

Morning Dew rushed into the house, blinking in the gloomy interior. Heron Wing sat on one of the benches, the raccoon bowl resting lightly in her lap. She laid it carefully aside, standing. "What's wrong? You look like you just stared into the eyes of a snake."

Morning Dew lowered her jar, smoothing her dress to keep from shaking. "The oddest thing just..." She swallowed hard. "I was going to fetch water. Normally T avoid looking at the squares, but for some reason, I stopped before my...my..."

Heron Wing lowered her voice. "There was nothing you could have done."

Morning Dew nodded, her heart pounding in her breast. "A woman came up beside me. She might have just popped out of thin air. She reached out, touched the square, and then she looked at me. Her eyes, by Breath Giver, Heron Wing, it was like seeing into another world, dark and endless."

"Did you know her?"

"No. A complete stranger. And when she spoke, it was in Trade

Tongue, with a hard accent. "She talked about their blood. The captives', I think." She shook her head, as if to rid it of the echoing. "The woman told me someone was coming." She couldn't stop wringing her hands. "I asked her who. She said...she said, 'The final knot.' And then this kind-eyed old man told me the woman had mistaken me for someone else. He spoke to her, used some language I've never heard before, and led the woman away."

"Did you know them?"

"No. I've never seen them before, and believe me, you'd know that woman. I've never seen eyes like that. She wore an oddly cut dress."

"Foreigners? Traders perhaps?"

Morning Dew wrinkled her brow. "I don't know. Perhaps." She stilled her hammering heart. "I just hope I never have to see her again. Once in a lifetime is enough."

And those accursed squares have already cost me enough!

NINETEEN

TRADER SAT in the sunlight before their house. Dealing with the endless thoughts, memories, and worries was like a whirlwind in his breast. Swimmer, sensing his disquiet, kept insisting that they play stick.

Trader would pitch it out, Swimmer charging after it, an occasional bark of joy bursting from him. The dog then leapt on the prize, turning, tossing the stick about and chomping it. As he pranced back —tail whipping back and forth—a look of pure glee shone in his eyes. Spitting the stick out at Trader's feet, Swimmer would stare up with a hawkish intensity until Trader did the whole thing over again.

In the days after their arrival, Trader had spent most of his waking moments protecting his precious goods from the rain. During that time, he had little chance to consider the implications of where he was. Then they had moved, packing their load to the house. Now, for the first time, he had absolutely nothing to do but sit. Paunch was hiding inside, fearful that some passerby would stop, point, and scream at the top of his lungs, "There's the traitor!"

Swimmer flung the stick at Trader's feet. Or at least came as close as a dog could to flinging it. Now he crouched down, eyes fixed intently, his tufted ears pricked in anticipation. Even his whiskers were quivering.

"Don't you ever give up?"

Swimmer tensed, quivering, eyes agleam, anticipating the throw as Trader picked up the chewed, slobbery stick and drew his arm back. Then Trader tossed it, sending it end over end. The dog's feet hammered the ground like a running buffalo.

"So, here I am," he mused. "And it's entirely unlike I expected." Nevertheless, he could feel his heart thumping with anticipation. He needed only scent the smoke, cooking food, the tang of the latrines, and the pungent aroma of the forest drifting in over the palisade to know that he was back.

What a difference he felt from that night he'd fled in panic. While he couldn't remember the exact route he'd taken, it had been just over there, cutting past the corner of the Skunk Clan mound.

He looked up toward the high minko's palace. "There, but for my brother's plotting, I would be sitting today." Except there would be no preparations for war with the Yuchi.

My fault. Why in the name of Power had he asked Born-of-Sun to send that messenger?

"How could I have known?" He glanced down as Swimmer dropped the stick on his foot.

What had changed since those heady days among the Yuchi? Some part of his courage had evaporated as he drew ever closer to Split Sky City.

A test? Perhaps. Power loved to test people, to see what they'd choose.

The problem was that nothing was working out like he'd planned. The idea had been to learn what the people were thinking, who was in charge, and then reveal himself in a grand show. He had imagined addressing the tchkofa, handing out wealth like some magical sorcerer, and seeing forgiveness in the eyes of his people. Instead, he was sitting in the sun, scared half to death at the prospect of facing anyone.

No, that was only part of it. The other part was knowing that Heron Wing was here, somewhere.

It's been ten years. Why am I still terrified of seeing her? But he was. If she gave him the wrong look, it would be like driving an arrow straight through his breast.

I couldn't stand that.

He should have been obsessed with Two Petals. He had never known a woman like her. Each night, she slipped into his blankets as soon as Old White had gone to sleep. She seemed obsessed. He simply couldn't understand her desperation to please him. *Insatiable.* He made a face, amazed at the arts she had developed to coax his exhausted shaft into yet another frantic joining. In the moon since they had first lain together, she had developed techniques that brought him to a frenzy of release. Last night he'd almost bitten his tongue in two to keep from waking the others with his cries.

But for the life of him, he couldn't fathom why she did it. It had nothing to do with love. When he awakened in the morning, she acted as if nothing had happened. He was just Trader, somehow peripheral to her life. Then, that night, she would become something else, another person.

"He's a good dog."

Trader looked up to see Squash Blossom walking over with another dish in her hands.

"I pulled him out of the river. He was half-drowned, clinging desperately to a raft of driftwood." He reached down, managing a single pat on the shoulder before Swimmer wiggled away, taking another position to alternately watch him and the stick.

"I've made squash bread," she said, beaming proudly.

"I'm still stuffed from breakfast." He sniffed, catching the odor of it over that of the city. "But I'd share some."

Needing no other invitation, Squash Blossom seated herself in the Sky Hand fashion, knees together. She was a little heavy, probably because all she did was cook. Her husband, Trader had learned, was a stone carver who left early each morning and returned late. Maybe to keep from blowing up like an overinflated fish bladder? They had three children, two boys and a little girl who peeked shyly around the house at him.

Trader took a piece of the hot squash bread, ripping it from the loaf and juggling it to keep from burning his fingers. He blew on it for the space of several heartbeats, and managed to pop it into his mouth without frying his tongue.

"Excellent," he said between chewing. "I can't tell you the times on the river when I would have given anything for bread like this."

"I thought all you Traders lived well," she remarked, smiling with satisfaction.

"At times, yes. I've enjoyed some spectacular feasts. The ones among the Natchez are best. I think it's because the Great Sun rules completely. He orders something and his people comply. If he says to empty the granaries for a feast, they do it. Right down to the last corn kernel."

"You must have seen some remarkable things."

"And some miserable ones, too." He ripped off another piece of bread. "Days alone on the river, the weather foul, and at every camp-site the wood is wet. Sometimes a meal is whatever is in ajar. I've stooped to chewing raw cornmeal and washing it down with cold water."

"Is that why you've come here? For the food?"

"Well..." He took a bite of the bread, chewed, and tossed Swim-mer's stick. "That wasn't the original plan, but I could live with it."

"What was the original plan?"

"The Trade," he said, swallowing. "Split Sky City is away from, the Father Water. Old White and I thought we'd give it a try. You see, in Trade, we look for special items."

"What's special in Split Sky City?"

"Woodwork for one."

"And our stone carving?"

He could see her apparent interest. "Among the best. Especially paint palettes. The Sky Hand stonecutters have developed better saws for cutting the slabs."

"And our stone statues?"

"If you promise to keep bringing me bread like this, I'll let you know that as good as the Sky Hand work is, the Caddo are better." He winced. "But it's hard to beat the Ockmulgee. They do things with granite you'd have to see to believe."

She nodded. "My husband says the same thing. About the Ockmulgee, that is."

"I don't know, though. If all the men march off to war, it may close the northern routes. We were thinking of heading back up through the Tenasee."

She shrugged. "There's Trade in the south."

"We'd have to save some of our goods."

She glanced at the door, lowering her voice. "That bald-headed man, is he mute?"

"Because he never speaks?"

She nodded.

"No. He's my partner's slave. We may Trade him off here."

She whispered, "You could do better. Koasati make much better slaves."

"That's what he is," Trader said, feeling relief. Since Koasati spoke the same language as the Albaamaha, when she did hear Paunch speak, it wouldn't make her suspicious. "We got him downriver from some Pensacola."

She considered that. Voice still low, she added, "I hope you didn't give much for him."

"You'd be surprised," Trader said dryly. Then he asked, "What kind of slaves would be available here?"

"We have lots of different kinds. Our warriors are among the best. They can take captives from anywhere."

"So I heard. I even heard that you captured some Chahta ones recently."

"Someone killed the men. Walked up in the middle of a foggy night and stabbed them right in the squares." She shook her head. "There was a terrible squabble about that."

"I'm sure. What about the women?"

"They're around. One was killed when she ran. Another had her tendons cut."

"Was that Morning Dew?"

"Oh, no. You heard about her?"

"It was quite the topic of conversation among the Pensacola down at Bottle Town."

"That's a story, let me tell you. For a while she was Blood Skull's, then she was Smoke Shield's, and finally Heron Wing won her. Bet against her...What's the matter? Something in the bread?"

Trader managed to swallow the mouthful, rasping. "No, bread's fine."

To cover himself, he bent down, pitching the stick so the woman couldn't see his face. As carefully as possible, he asked, "So, some woman named Heron Wing has her?"

"Some woman?" Squash Blossom made a futile gesture. "She's a clan leader among the Panther Clan. Her aunt is chief, the only female one we have. And a dwarf. You've seen dwarves?"

"There are more around than you would think." He took a deep breath, trying to still his beating heart.

"Heron Wing is also married to the war chief. Though how any woman could put up with Smoke Shield is beyond me."

Married? Well, what did you expect, you simple idiot? That she'd wait, pining for you for the rest of her life?

"What's wrong with Smoke Shield?" he asked, hoping he didn't sound as hoarse as he was.

"Personally—and you didn't hear it from me—I think he's the meanest man alive."

Trader threw Swimmer's stick. Unthinking, he pitched it with such power it sailed over the adjacent house roof. Swimmer fortunately lost sight of it, whirling, ears pricked, wondering where it went.

A distant clatter sounded. An angry voice shouted something obscene.

———

As they followed a very nervous Paunch through the growing gloom, Old White glanced at Trader. For reasons of his own, the younger man had insisted on taking his war club. Now, as they stepped out through the south gate, Trader seemed to relax, breathing easier.

"Are you all right?" Old White asked in Natchez.

"I'm just glad it's a big city. Lots of people."

"I'd really like to know what's worrying you." Old White had switched back to Trade Tongue.

"His heart," Two Petals replied. "It's the very beating of his heart. Thump. Thump. Thump. Bless the Spirits that I don't fall in love. Makes a man lose his focus. Like watching the world through water."

Love? Old White glanced at Trader, seeing him well enough in the gloom to know disgusted irritation when he saw it. In Natchez, he asked, "Who is she?"

"No one."

"Ah, I see. So that's why you've been so peculiar since we've come home. Is there anything I need to know about her?"

"She currently owns Morning Dew. You're going to have to approach her if we're going to Trade for her."

"I am going to have to approach her?" Old White smiled and sighed. "For a single man, Trader, you seem to have the most interesting entanglements with women. Is there a reason this one is such a problem for you?"

"I was to marry her."

Love...and an unfulfilled marriage. He could see Trader's upset in the bunched muscles of his shoulders. The man was flicking the heavy war club as if it were a willow wand.

"All in time, Trader. That was the distant past."

"Turns out she's married to this Smoke Shield. The war chief everyone talks about."

Old White bit off a curse. He still hadn't found the right situation to tell Trader what he suspected. But certainly, he wouldn't do it now, not in advance of such an important meeting.

"If you would prefer, I will approach her."

"It would make my life easier."

"But someday, if you stay here ..."

"That's for another time, Seeker."

"What are you babbling about?" Paunch asked anxiously. "That turkey talk is driving me crazy! You're not going to do that in front of the mikko, are you? He's going to be suspicious enough as it is!"

"Our apologies, Paunch," Old White soothed. "It was personal business between Trader and me."

They were making their way past Albaamaha houses, most with dormant gardens. The way wound through the village. Occasional dogs barked at them, and now and then a person would look out, sometimes calling a name, as if expecting someone who was late.

"This way." Paunch led them to one side, stopping before a large house set off from the others.

"This is it?" Old White asked.

"Yes." Paunch stepped forward, scratching at the door. "Mikko?" he whispered. "Are you there?"

"Who comes?" The voice was strained, as if worried at the interruption.

"It is Paunch, Elder. I have news."

"Paunch?" the voice asked in surprise. "One moment."

Old White could hear shuffling sounds inside the house. A moment later, the wooden door was opened and an old man peered out. He stared for a moment at Paunch. "Is that you?"

"Of course!"

"What happened to your hair?" He looked past him, voice hardening. "And who are these people?"

"Just let us in!"

Old White stepped forward. "We need to talk, Elder."

"Come back later."

"No," Trader said forcefully, stepping forward. "We will speak now. In private. I think you would prefer that to having this discussion before the entire Council."

Old White nodded to himself. The timbre in Trader's voice brooked no refusal.

"Paunch," the old Albaamo growled, "so help me, when this is over ..."

"He is doing only what we ask him to," Old White said in Mos'kogee, glancing around. "But I would suspect that the longer we stand out here discussing it, the sooner someone is going to get suspicious."

The door opened, the old mikko reluctantly making way.

Old White followed Two Petals inside to find a doubled hanging of thick fabric. Just the sort of thing to let a man slip out without flashing the light from inside.

The room was neat, the matting clean. Benches lined every wall. The fire was burning brightly, illuminating wall paintings of the Albaamaha World Tree, the Long-Tailed Man, and other culture heroes.

On the floor, no less than six plates lay, food partially eaten. Cups, half-full of liquid, stood beside the plates.

Old White glanced at the doorway leading into the back room. So, were five or six hiding back there? And, more to the point, were they armed and waiting to spring out and kill the intruders?

"Paunch," the old man cried, "what are you doing here?"

"You must be Amber Bead, the Albaamaha representative to the Council." Old White stepped forward. "And if we hear correctly, the leader of the Albaamaha resistance against the Chikosi."

The man's ashen expression was answer enough. Old White saw the door hanging to the back room sway the slightest bit. He gestured. "The rest of you need not interrupt your suppers. If you are part of Amber Bead's conspiracy, we would speak with you also."

"In Abba Mikko's name," Amber Bead almost pleaded, "who are you?"

"Ah! Yes. Poor manners on my part." Old White pointed as he spoke. "This is Trader, and this is Two Petals, the Contrary. As for myself, I am known as Old White."

"The Seeker," Paunch added reverently.

Amber Bead's frown deepened. "I've heard something of a man called the Seeker."

"I am he."

"What are you doing here?"

"Power has sent us. But we need a little more information." Old White seated himself calmly on a bench, lacing his fingers around his left knee. "Specifically, we need to understand how relations have grown so bad between the Albaamaha and Chikosi that people are considering open revolt."

"I'll tell you," a sharp voice came from the back room. A woman burst through the doorway, her hair shorn in mourning. Behind her, four muscular men, each with a knotted wooden club in his hands, followed. Nothing in any of their expressions boded for a peaceful evening discussing politics.

Old White reached out, laying a restraining hand on Trader as he started forward. Paunch had crouched down, looking anything but happy.

With his other hand, Old White fished in his belt pouch, producing a small cloth sack. This he held out over the fire, saying, "Easy now. You don't want me to drop this."

"What is it?" the woman demanded.

"Poison ivy. It's nasty stuff when it burns. Within moments, everyone in this room will be hacking and coughing. In some people—as I'm sure you know—it makes the throat swell shut. It would be a shame, but Amber Bead's house would be uninhabitable for a time. People would wonder why he moved out after so many people ran gagging from here."

All eyes went to Old White's sack.

"Now," he said pleasantly, "we've just arrived here. The last we heard, poor Paunch and Whippoorwill were being hounded through the forest like driven deer. So why don't you introduce yourselves and fill us in on all the events that have transpired since?"

The woman glared, a boiling anger behind her eyes. This one, Old White decided, was going to be trouble.

Amber Bead threw up his hands. "Who *are* you people?"

"Traders," Trader said simply. "But very *important* Traders." He gestured. "Please, have a seat. We need to know all there is about Split Sky City politics. Then, as a gesture of good faith, we'll be happy to leave Paunch here with you."

"And what is his purpose?" the woman asked, hard eyes fixing on Paunch.

"Well, we needed to find you, it seems. So we Traded a gorget for him from Great Cougar," Old White explained. "You see, if he'd hung Paunch and Whippoorwill on his squares, we'd never have been led here to interrupt your suppers. So please, be seated. The food is getting cold."

"If you are just Traders then I am the high minko," Amber Bead muttered.

"Might as well lie down and go to sleep," Two Petals said, her eyes fixed on the woman. "This is going to be a most boring night."

———

Trader looked up at the faint light graying the eastern horizon. The air was cool as they stepped out of Amber Bead's house. He kept glancing behind him, anxious lest one of the distrusting young Albaamaha men sneak up and brain them from behind. Two Petals, however, seemed oblivious. With her foresight, she'd warn them, wouldn't she?

"Smoke Shield, Smoke Shield, Smoke Shield," Old White mused. "That's all you hear about. He must be a madman. And to think, he'd actually dress his warriors as Chahta? What a cunning war chief he is. Twisted, evil, but cunning."

"One thing's sure, he's got the Sky Hand fooled. How could he do it, Seeker? It seems like every lie and plot can be laid at his door. To hear the Albaamaha tell it, he's an evil Spirit in human form."

"I have potions, powders, poisons. We could send him food laced with a concoction of water hemlock, nightshade, sacred datura, and death camas. And then there are the mushrooms. I have some green fungus scrapings. The slightest inhalation will make a man vomit his guts out. You name it, I have it...concentrated." Old White patted his pack. "Of course, if he is guarded by some malignant Power, it might warn him."

"My heart aches for Lotus Root. She has suffered so much. Now she's running, unsure of which course to take." Trader frowned. "On top of everything else, she has to wonder who we really are, and how we found them."

"It must have been something of a shock," Old White agreed. "One minute, you're plotting a meeting with the mikkos, the next, three strangers walk in the door and want to know everything."

Trader glanced at Two Petals. "You know, Seeker, if you hadn't

Traded that gorget for Paunch, we would have known none of this. He's been like a thorn in a blanket on the river; but he led us to just the right people, at just the right time."

"Next time the Contrary suggests buying slaves, 'I won't haggle for so long." Old White made a sucking sound with his lips. "This is a prickly knot to pick. It makes me even more suspicious about that Yuchi messenger's death. There has to be someone ..."

"Yes?" Trader glanced at him.

"If the Albaamaha are organizing an uprising, they can't be the only ones."

"Then who else?"

"Surely you know enough of politics to realize that there's always an opposition. It's the nature of men, be they Sky Hand, Azteca, Zuni, or Kaskinampo."

"You're right. Someone must be against Smoke Shield."

"And don't forget, he could do none of this without Flying Hawk's approval."

Trader nodded. "Don't I know? He raised me. I'll never forget his rages and poor judgments. In my later years, I have come to believe that killing his brother changed something in him. You wouldn't believe the fits he'd fly into over the smallest things. We were jumpy as grasshoppers around him."

"It goes back to his youth." Old White glanced at him. "Did he ever speak of his boyhood?"

"Rarely. I think it was too painful. Everything led back to the fire. Something terrible happened that night. Both of us were smart enough to never ask. Even at the mention of it, his face would cloud; if the subject wasn't changed, there would be a storm."

"He had a very difficult childhood."

"You knew him?"

"Oh, yes. He and Acorn both. My memory is of frightened, dead-eyed boys. Bear Tooth used to beat them unmercifully. I think their souls were both broken during those days."

Trader frowned; then his eyes widened. "Breath Giver take me, you're Kosi Fighting Hawk!"

"Who? Oh, the boys' uncle. No. He was Raccoon Clan, the tishu minko married to Midnight Woman's sister, Rose Bloom. He was a good man, but never up to facing down Bear Tooth. After Makes War's capture and death, Midnight Woman married Bear Tooth because he was an able warrior. You must understand: The people were stunned. Their high minko had been captured and tortured to death—the war medicine had been lost. Bear Tooth brought a new Spirit to a wounded people. He restored the Power, but by the Horned Serpent, he was a brutal and abusive man."

"People didn't talk much," Trader added. "At least not when I was around. But I did hear enough to know that while they missed Bear Tooth as war chief, not many missed him as a man."

"And your mother?" Old White asked. "What happened to her?"

"Childbirth. After my brother and I were born, the bleeding didn't stop. The story is that we were both large, the birth difficult. I came first, my brother sometime later."

"Did you ever hear what the fight was about? The one where Flying Hawk killed his brother?"

"A buffalo." Trader looked up as they slowed before the gate. A yawning warrior stood there, almost weaving on his feet.

"A buffalo?"

"Buffalo are rare in this country. They were both hunting, so the story goes, and both shot it at the same time. By the time the animal died, they had shot their quivers empty. Somehow they got into it over who had actually killed the buffalo. It turned to blows, and as they were rolling around on the ground, Flying Hawk picked up a handy rock and brained his brother. He has punished himself ever since."

"The passions people can get themselves into." They nodded at the guard, reaching back to pull Two Petals after them. She was staring at empty space over the warrior's head, whispering about the fireflies.

Since it was too early in the year for fireflies, and since the guard —who didn't speak Trade Tongue— didn't know what she was saying, it was easier to simply pull her away than explain why she wasn't a witch.

"I'm starting to have a passion of my own: Smoke Shield. Who *is* he?" Trader racked his brain. "I have gone through all of the cousins I can think of. Obviously he took a man's name that I don't recognize. Is he someone from one of the outlying towns? A boy I never met, or only heard of and have forgotten after all these years?"

"Close," Two Petals whispered, turning her intense eyes on him. Her lips had parted in anticipation. "The truth Dances around like wind-whipped leaves."

Old White shot her an irritated look. "I've asked around...subtle questions." Then he said softly, "Trader, I think he's your brother."

Trader gave him a hard look. "If that's a joke, it's not funny."

"It wasn't meant to be."

Trader felt his heart skip. "Gods, you're serious?"

"Don't do anything rash. Think this through before you go pounding off to kill him again."

Trader blinked, refusing to believe. "I hit him hard, Seeker. Crushed the side of his face. He wasn't moving, not even breathing. His eyes were fixed."

"Or so you thought."

"What do you mean, *thought!* I was there!"

"You told me it was the middle of the night. How well could you see? The man known as Smoke Shield is Flying Hawk's nephew. He hovered near death for four days after his brother hit him with a war club and fled into the night." Old White pointed a hard finger. "You have been punishing yourself for years for something you didn't do."

Trader stared, his souls reeling. But when he glanced at Two Petals, he could see the truth of it in her eyes, in the eager expression on her face.

He stood, wavering on his feet. *Rattle isn't dead. I didn't kill my brother.*

The first hot trickle of a tear slipped down his face.

TWENTY

TWO PETALS WATCHED her feet as she walked down to the canoe landing. She was hardly aware of the few Traders who cooked over blue-smoking fires beneath the ramadas. They watched her with only mild interest, their attention on the fish, clams, and breads that they cooked.

She didn't return the stare. No, her eyes were fixed on her feet.

Steps were a marvel. Each time one of her feet touched the earth, it was contact, a distinct moment in time. Like the beating of her heart, it marked that one instant of existence. Looking back in the damp ground, she could see the smudges where her moccasins had marked the earth.

Carefully, she stepped backward, placing her foot just so, shifting her balance to the position she had once held.

Why does time not move backward with me? Why can't I retrieve that moment in the past?

It puzzled her, because in the Dream, she had seen all of this unfold. Lived it backward.

"The rules of the souls differ from those of the flesh," one of the voices told her.

She had ceased to look around for the sources of those disembodied speakers. Better to just accept them. She didn't need that confusion, not now that all of the threads were so closely woven. All that remained was for Power to pull the weave tight.

When her souls looked into a future that was her Dream past, she could see it all rushing toward her.

"Are you ready?" a musical voice asked.

This time, she knew exactly where it had come from. She raised her eyes to the river, stepping carefully as she walked to the water's edge.

"Trader knows now."

"Good," the voice told her. *"Are you being a great rock? Allowing the souls to wash past you? "*

"Yes. The Kala Hi'ki taught me well."

"He is a good man. He sees through my eyes."

"I think he misses you."

"His souls will return someday."

"I know."

"Are you frightened?"

"Yes."

"Don't be. All of your questions will be answered."

She blinked her eyes, seeing a swirl out in the current, a sucking curl of water that reflected the early-morning light. She stepped into the cold waves, feeling the chill waters of the river trickling through the threads in her moccasins.

"Not yet," the soothing voice told her. *"But soon."*

She nodded, her heart beating urgently in her chest.

"He comes."

"I know." She stood there, watching the current. The river seemed to flex like a living thing. When she closed her eyes, she could feel the power of it. Could sense the life it sheltered, like glowing Spirits. Her souls could almost touch the fish, the water plants, and turtles sleeping deep in the mud. The water insects burrowed, and crawfish, clams, and mussels glowed like a thousand stars. They were nothing compared to *his* presence.

"Soon," she whispered, half in dread.

"You have other concerns now."

"Yes."

She heard the man's feet as he approached along the beach. Where her steps had been light and careful, his pounded, as though hammering anger into the earth. Then she caught the easy sound of his breathing. She knew the moment he saw her, felt the hot curiosity in his eyes as he appraised her, and slowed to a stop. When he addressed her, she couldn't understand the words, but understood his intent.

She turned, but even though she had been forewarned, the impact of his eyes made her gasp. "I am always all right," she managed to say, her souls reeling. As a woman, she should have admired his muscular body, the broadness of his shoulders, and the way his perspiration gleamed in the morning light. It accented his corded muscles, and gave his skin a faint glow. But all of it drained away as she looked into his eyes.

She swallowed hard. Looking beneath his eyes, she could see his souls twisting, knotting themselves around a fire that she could barely comprehend. They matched the deep scar on the side of his head, misshapen and maimed.

He spoke again, the Mos'kogee words like so much gibberish. But she felt the irritation behind them, mixed with barely hidden lust.

"Power is twisting around you," she said in Trade Tongue. "It curls, reaching, only to pull back."

He threw his head back, laughing. "Now, that's a smart woman if I ever heard one." His switch to Trade Tongue was facile. "I haven't seen you before, and your accent is foreign. A Trader's wife, are you?"

"No. I am no man's wife. But I have come here to meet my husband." She indicated the river. "He waits for me. Just out there."

Smoke Shield shot a disbelieving look at the water. "He must be a fish."

"No, a fisher."

He cocked his head, amused, his eyes narrowing as he studied her dress, took in the rope belt at her slim waist. His gaze lingered on her round hips, and she could feel his interest pique as if he could see through the material to her warm sheath.

"So that is what it is like to see through your eyes," she said. "There is no tree, only bark. No river, only water."

"Is that so? And what do you see?"

"What I have never seen before." She shook her head. "Even stones have friends.

He stopped, uncertain. "Stones?"

"You are not even a rock. There is only you. All the world is you."

He laughed it off, oblivious. "I would love to continue this fasci-

nating talk, but I must meet with my warriors in the Men's House."
He paused, allowing his Dreams to feast on her body. "But if you
would care to, let's say, converse more, I may have time this evening."
He jerked his head toward the city. "At the high minko's palace. Ask
for me. I am called Smoke Shield, war chief of the Sky Hand." His
smile curled with desire. "The guards will pass you; and I promise, it
will be well worth your time."

"I shall see you forever," she told him, feeling the swelling of
Power as it stretched between them. "Nothing shall stop it now."

"Tonight then?"

"Your Dreams will wrap around me all night long," she promised.
"I will Dance, stepping lightly around your souls. You will take me,
over and over, that I promise."

His grin spread. "Smart woman. I shall Trade a great deal if you
are as talented as you think you are." Then he turned, muscles
bunching as he started up the canoe landing, resuming his run.

"Oh, what a Trade you will make, my lover."

We've got to *hurry!*" Stone pleaded. He stood in the doorway, his
stickball racquets in his hands. "Morning Dew"—his voice rose to a
pitch—"they'll be *waiting!*"

"Yes, yes, I'm coming." She reached down, using a stick to
rearrange the coals around the base of a pot. The body of a duck
floated in the water, along with bits of sassafras root, wild licorice, and
large chunks of lotus root. She looked up at Heron Wing. "Don't let
this boil over. You know how foamy lotus root gets."

"I won't." She waved her away. "Go on. You'll have more than one
frantic little boy if you're late." She chuckled to herself as Morning
Dew picked up her racquets and ducked out the doorway.

Heron Wing sighed. I *am going to miss her when she finally goes.*

She shot a measuring look at the duck in its pot. Not even
steaming yet. She turned, replacing Stone's things. Why did little
boys scatter so much in the simple act of preparing for a stickball
game?

"Lady?" a pleasant voice called from beyond the door. "Would you
have time for a word?"

"Clan politics? Marriage counseling? A property dispute? What is
it this time?"

"Trade," the man said.

Trade? That was a curious switch. "Enter. Unless you would

prefer I step out." Some men were hesitant about being seen in a married woman's house. Their wives tended to get the wrong idea.

He ducked inside, and she turned, seeing a tall, white-haired man, his hair pulled up in a tight bun and pinned with a copper arrow. His ears drew her immediate attention. The lobes had never been pierced and stretched for ear spools. His face sported no tattoos to designate clan or people. Despite his age, he was well muscled, fit looking. But for his weather-beaten face she'd have placed him in his midforties. The face made him look sixty. He wore a heavy fabric shirt, done in odd zigzag patterns she'd never seen before. It was belted at the waist, from which hung a large pouch.

He studied her with kindly eyes, as if taking her measure. She lifted a no-nonsense eyebrow.

Then he glanced around the room, his gaze stopping on the raccoon bowl. He stepped over to it, running a gentle finger along its smooth curve.

"Quite a bowl," he said.

"Supposedly it's from up north. Made by a tribe called the Illinois. It was then Traded to the Yuchi by a man named Green Snake. One of our northern Traders obtained it from them."

"Things do get around," the man noted dryly. Then he looked at her. "You are Heron Wing?"

"I am. And you are?"

"I am known as Old White."

"I see, Old White. And what did you want of me?"

"Trade," he said reasonably. Then he frowned at the bowl. "Green Snake? The Trader?"

"Yes," she snapped, stepping over and protectively tucking the bowl under her arm.

He gave her an amused look. "What would you take for that bowl?"

"It is not for Trade." She felt herself begin to bristle. "Did you want something? If not, I have a busy day to attend to."

He chuckled. "Oh, the ways of Power."

She hadn't expected that. "Power?"

"How do you know Green Snake?"

Was it just her, or was he teasing her? "From a long time ago."

Then the man sat down, almost sprawling, as if he owned the

place. His eyes settled on the duck. "That looks like it is going to be delicious."

"Perhaps you should take your Trade elsewhere." She arched her back, nodding toward the door.

"Were I to do that," he said softly, "you would learn nothing more about Green Snake, the ways of Power, or the curious twists of fate."

She felt her tension drain away to leave confusion. "Who are you?"

He glanced toward the door, saying, "Before I answer that, tell me, will Smoke Shield be back anytime soon?"

"No!" The anger was back. Old White seemed to read her souls like tracks in mud. She flushed. "I think you should go."

"Actually, I came to offer Trade for the woman known as Morning Dew." He paused, adding sincerely, "And I must confess to being slightly curious as well."

"Morning Dew?" She stared, confusion rising.

He reached into his pouch, producing a long white pointed thing. "This is something called a walrus tusk. Probably the only one in the south. It comes from a creature that lives in the ice-bound wastes of the far north. Well, in the ocean up there, actually."

She took it, feeling the weight, staring into the stark white color that seemed almost translucent. "You would offer this for Morning Dew? In whose name?"

"In the name of her grandmother, Old Woman Fox. She would like to have her granddaughter back. Is that sufficient in Trade?"

She hefted the heavy tooth, wondering if it was really as valuable as the old man said. She considered Green Snake's bowl. No, this was a first offering. Played correctly, she could drive the price up. If this was an opening to communications with the Chahta, it would have to be handled delicately.

"I don't know if this is enough, or not. I have my own plans for Morning Dew."

"And those are?"

"Is there a reason I should share them with a stranger?"

"Since I am here as an agent of the current matron of the White Arrow, it might be prudent. If your plans for Morning Dew coincide with mine, it might have a serious effect on the value of our Trade."

Heron Wing narrowed her eyes, studying the man. He seemed completely at ease, as if negotiating the fates of peoples was as ordinary as bartering for a used blanket. "Morning Dew is the matron of the White Arrow Moiety. Her son, if she ever has one, will become high minko. Eventually this madness with the Chahta must end. I think she will be an excellent and talented leader among her people. In the future I would rather see us dealing with her than any other."

He nodded slightly, considering the sincerity of her words.

She seated herself, handing the tusk back. "All right, you have offered Trade for Morning Dew. It's not enough when compared with the future of my people. Do you wish to offer anything in addition to some tooth I cannot judge the value of?"

"I'll think it over."

"Good. Now, where did you know Green Snake? A lot of men could be named that."

"And many are." He smiled. "Believe me, it's a common name all across the land. This one, however, lived here, once. Hickory Moiety, born of the Chief Clan. Then, oh, perhaps ten winters ago, he had an altercation with his brother. Fled into the night, horrified at what he'd done."

She realized she'd stopped breathing, that he was watching her, studying her reaction. "What do you want from me?" She tried to keep her voice normal, and failed.

"Nothing. At least not the way you think," he whispered softly. "I am called Old White, but to most I am known as the Seeker. Perhaps you have heard of me?"

She frowned. "Legends…stories…tales of a man who traveled to far-off lands. The Seeker was supposed to find the ends of the earth, or so the story goes. I know the Natchez and Pensacola believe the legend."

"Always a legend." His lips bent in a wistful smile. "But then, there are worse things: like traveling around thinking you'd killed your brother, only to find out ten winters later that you'd just knocked him half-silly." He paused. "Or half-insane."

She shook her head in slow disbelief. "You really know Green Snake? How is he?" She hesitated. "I have hoped that he married… that he's happy. I'd always thought that, well, maybe he settled among the Caddo, or perhaps the Natchez."

"Sometimes, yes, for a season or two. He took the name of Trader. Nothing else. People on the rivers know him only as that."

"But is he happy?"

Old White's bushy eyebrows arched. *"Happiness* can be a relative term. Are you happy, Heron Wing? Wait! Now, before you pry away at me for an answer, ask yourself that same question. But ask it deep down between your souls, where the life you're living rubs against the Dreams you once had for yourself."

She sat stunned. "Who *are* you?"

"It appears that I am a legend." He clapped his hands to his thighs.

"You speak our language as if born to it."

"A man has to come from somewhere. I've yet to meet one that hasn't—though some scoundrels would claim it so."

She watched him, mind racing. "Why hasn't Green Snake sent word that he was alive?"

"He did," Old White snapped angrily. "The Yuchi who carried the message was murdered. Now people are preparing to go to war over it."

She glanced down at the bowl. "Traded from the Yuchi." She felt her souls slip sideways, staggering. "That's why they killed him." She stood, pacing, mind racing. "Smoke Shield must be half-frantic!" She turned. "You wouldn't know this mysterious message the Yuchi was carrying, would you?"

"Oh, yes."

"And it is?"

"Let us Trade. Who heads the opposition to Smoke Shield and Flying Hawk in Split Sky City? There is one, I'm sure. Just as there is among the Albaamaha."

She stared at him, her heart thumping out a steady beat in her chest. What kind of brazen fool would dare ask a question like that? *What is your game here, stranger?* "As far as I know, our Council is united."

The corners of his lips quivered. "And my memory of Green Snake's message is slipping away ever so slowly."

What did she do? Her desperation struggled against years of innate caution. She sighed, her heart sinking. This man knew her weakness.

"The opposition doesn't really exist as such. Not organized like you would expect. The Albaamaha are already ahead of us on that front. We have held some meetings, trying to understand what is going on. Some of us have suspicions. That's all. There are problems — things that don't make sense. But there are only a few of us:

those who fully understand Smoke Shield's ability to plot and manipulate."

"From your words I take it that you and your husband are not close."

She gave him a hard glare in response.

He nodded. "I suppose you're wondering if the Chahta could have made this recent raid?"

"Who *are* you?"

He stood, stepping to the door, looking out. Then he went outside. Checking the rest of the house, she figured. When he returned, he said, "I am Old White, the Seeker. And I also know for a fact that Great Cougar was in Feathered Snake Town at the same time he was supposedly here killing Albaamaha. I know that because I saw him there." He pointed. "With these eyes. The other thing I know is that Lotus Root has twenty-three scalps that Smoke Shield's warriors buried outside the hut where they found the tortured Fast Legs."

She shot to her feet. "You can *prove* this?"

"Oh, yes."

"I can have my brother call the Council. How soon can you produce Lotus Root?"

He waved her down, smiling kindly. "I admire your enthusiasm, Heron Wing, but there are other considerations. The Albaamaha are only part of the puzzle. We also have to deal with the Chaktaw."

She smiled. "Chaktaw? You don't often hear that pronunciation here."

"Whatever you call them, Great Cougar is planning something daring for the first new moon past equinox. Old Woman Fox wants her granddaughter rescued before the attack. Then, too, we'll have to deal with Born-of-Sun. He acted in good faith, sending that poor runner." Old White pulled thoughtfully at his chin. "Breaking the peace when a white arrow is offered is most definitely unacceptable."

She laughed, finding his assurance ludicrous. "Is that all?"

"Well, the major parts. There are some other things: details like copper, medicine boxes, Trade, balancing the Power, and a few other minor concerns."

"Who else knows you are here?"

"The Albaamaha ringleaders."

"And they are...who?"

He shook his head. "No, Matron. That is mine."

"I am no matron."

"You should be. You would serve your clan and people well." He looked at her. "For the moment we will deal with you, and only you. You can trust anyone you wish, but I will only trust you."

"Why?" she asked. "How do you know I won't just turn you over to Smoke Shield? I'm married to him, after all."

Old White pointed at the bowl. "You would have broken my arm to get that away from me." He paused. "Why?"

"He Traded it."

"Trader did?" He made a wounded face. "It came out of *my* canoe!" At her expression, he shrugged. "Well, yes, it was his idea to give the things away among the Yuchi during solstice. He did hand out each and every one. Well, at least the ones the Contrary didn't."

"Contrary?" She frowned. "What Contrary?"

"It's a long story." He gave her a harried look. "You haven't lived until you travel in the same canoe with a Contrary."

"And Green Snake's message?" she asked, trying to keep the hope from her voice.

"The Yuchi messenger was supposed to announce to the Council that Green Snake would be returning to his people. That he offered compensation for the murder of his brother. That it was a matter of Power, of restoring the harmony."

She felt a sudden excitement. "That is why Flying Hawk looked so confused in the Council. That is why the old fire wasn't in his eyes when Pale Cat stitched him up. He knows."

"What would that knowledge be worth, Heron Wing? What would it change? Who would it threaten?"

"Smoke Shield," she said softly. "He hated his brother, envied him, and took everything he ever had." "How do you feel about Green Snake?" "I will never forgive him." "For what?" "Not taking me with him."

TWENTY-ONE

A LONG PEELING rolled up from under the sharp chert blade, exposing white and straight-grained wood. Trader studied the wooden shaft he worked on. It was good white ash and straight as a stretched cord. He would have preferred to find his own; but this one looked perfect, and he'd Traded for it with a single freshwater pearl.

He lifted the shaft, testing the balance. A great deal of work lay ahead of him.

Thank the Spirits for that. His troubled souls were going to need the time, and working wood was as good a way to think things through as any.

Smoke Shield is my brother. I gave up everything, for nothing. He slowly shook his head, heart mired by the sadness and injustice of it all. Another of the thin peelings rose from the chert blade.

It felt like being robbed—a great hollow had opened inside.

I was a fool.

For that, he would never forgive himself.

The anger drove him to snap the stone in half. He closed his eyes. *Stop. Take a moment, and think.*

He laid his shaft aside, and stood, looking up at the sun, now high in the sky. Around him the city teemed with activity, smoke blowing on the breeze, midday light casting shadows from the thatched roofs.

He could hear talk, the thumping of the pestles in mortars, and chopping as someone took an adze to wood.

He stepped into the house and walked to the back, to rummage through his packs for a chert blank. This was good tool stone from the lands south of Cahokia. He studied the piece in the dim light, searching the milky gray chert for flaws. Finding none, he walked to the door, stepped out, and froze.

She sat on the log, back bent, elbows resting on her knees as she squinted up at the sun. Her long hair was free, the wealth of it falling down her back. She wore a bright blue dress belted at the waist with a strip of alligator hide. Her wide cheeks were smooth in the light, a serenity reflected in the set of her lips.

His knees went weak, his heart hammering at the bottom of his throat. The endless longing came welling up within him, almost suffocating. The world seemed to stop, to stretch into this one endless moment. He had to blink to ensure this wasn't a trick, some phantom conjured by his endless longing.

"I would like you to sit," she said gently. "It would be easiest if you continued to work on your chunkey lance. Nothing must be said in a hurry. It is a good day to just enjoy the sun, and live for this moment alone."

He swallowed hard, and tried to still his frantically beating heart. Desperate joy—fit to burst his chest— wavered with a consuming and terrible fear.

What if she hates me? How could I stand that?

She shot him a single, pleading glance, as though she, too, were on the verge of fleeing.

In the confusion of hope and fear, it took all of his will to step over and lower himself to the log. He fought the desperate urge to reach out, touch her. From her delicate scent, he knew that she'd washed her hair in water scented with redbud flowers.

When he lifted his small antler tine to chip a sharp edge on the stone, his hands shook.

"How...How did you know I was here?" His voice came out choked.

"Old White came to Trade some sort of tooth thing for Morning Dew."

His mouth had gone dry. He just kept gripping the stone as if it alone in the world was real. "I—I don't know what to say. So...many things ..."

"Then say nothing." She shifted slightly, her face still to the sun. "Old White said that you had just learned about Smoke Shield."

He nodded.

"I wish you'd killed him that night. It would have made everything so much easier."

"He's your...husband."

"Clan marriage." Her hand flicked in a tormented gesture. "People...People do some very stupid things when their souls are wounded and bleeding. They let their grief carry them into terrible mistakes. When a person is young, she can't see past the confusion. I didn't. You didn't. We just act, Green Snake. Then, for the rest of our lives, there are the consequences." A fragile smile crossed her lips. "But then, here I sit, so perhaps I am no smarter now than I was then."

He tried to still the churning in his souls. "I have Dreamed of you...every night."

"Why didn't you ask me to go with you that night?"

"I thought...thought you'd hate me."

"Hate you?" she cried, blinking back tears. "I *loved* you with all my heart!"

Loved! A fact from the past. Not the present. He lowered his head.

Softly she added, "And I never stopped, Green Snake. Not for one moment."

The world seemed to swim, the stone forgotten in his hand. "All those years...wasted ..."

"Oh, no. Think of the things you've seen, the peoples you've met." She looked around, eyes moist. "This place would have chewed you up, digested, and deposited your souls in the latrine of its petty squabbles." She paused, struggling with herself. "If you had stayed, you would have had to kill him anyway. Or he would have killed you. That part was inevitable. He hates you too much."

"I didn't mean to hate him."

"To know Smoke Shield is to hate him. You have had ten precious years free of his poison." She gave him a look filled with longing. "He doesn't know that you're here. You could turn around, climb into your canoe, and paddle away. You have a life out there."

He took a deep breath, stilling the trembling inside. "I *don't* have you!"

A desperate hope lay behind her misty eyes. "Are you still the same man I once knew?"

He shook his head. "Something died in me the night I struck Rattle down. Now I travel from town to town, people to people. I serve the Power of Trade."

She smiled, on the verge of tears. "He takes. You serve. You are still the man I once knew."

"Am I?"

"Oh, yes," she whispered sadly. "Wiser now, gentler, but seasoned and tried. You can't hide that soul shining in your eyes, Green Snake." A pause. "Not from me."

Words deserted him.

"You have friends up and down the river?"

"Many."

"Wives?"

"No."

She steeled herself, fists knotting. In a strained voice, she said, "I need to collect my son, Morning Dew, and a couple of packs. We could be on the river with enough time to reach Great Corn Town before dark. Or there are camps along the shore where people often stay."

His gaze bored into hers. "Why?"

"You have filled my Dreams since I was a little girl. Can't we live them now? Morning Dew would get back to her people. You could teach my son things he would never learn here. If he chooses to return someday, he will do so with great knowledge and wisdom. I would see some of the same marvels that you have, and enjoy life with a man I love. Smoke Shield will never have the opportunity to finally destroy us."

"Living on the river comes with risks and miseries of its own: heat, cold, insects, bad food, bad water, and at times, some very dangerous people."

"Something must be given up for another thing gained."

He nodded, smiling. "If it were only that easy."

She arched her eyebrow in an old and achingly familiar way.

He threw his head back, a warmth spreading through his chest. The sunlight seemed brighter, warmer. His heart was beating regularly again, the richness of his blood coursing in his veins. I *am alive!* He laughed, feeling it bubble up from deep inside him.

"Then, we're leaving?" Hope leapt in her voice.

"Staying," he told her gently, and saw the worry grow in her eyes. "It is more than just you and I. Power has sent us to restore the balance."

"At what price?" Her voice turned hollow. "I won't lose you *twice!*"

He glanced up. "Here comes trouble."

Squash Blossom had rounded the corner of her house, a heaping plate in her hands. She hesitated at sight of Heron Wing; then she pasted a big smile on her face as she hurried forward.

"Clan Leader! Come to Trade with our new neighbors, I see?"

Heron Wing recovered immediately. "Indeed. And I wouldn't want to interrupt his meal." She stood, saying stiffly, "I will send Morning Dew here this afternoon. See if she meets your requirements. If so, we can discuss the value of the Trade you offer."

He got to his feet, trying to tell her so many things through his level gaze.

She smiled. "I have a duck roasting. Until later."

Trader watched her go, then resettled himself, struggling desperately to control his pounding heart. He shot a glance at Squash Blossom, wishing he could strangle her. He was surprised to see her looking wistfully after Heron Wing.

"Poor woman," she said obliviously. "She's so good, and the war chief, he treats her terribly. Whatever you Trade with her for, you treat her right, you hear me?"

"I *won't lose you* twice!" The words Sang in his souls. "I'll Trade her the sun and stars, Squash Blossom."

———

Old White pondered the ways of Power as he walked slowly home. He could feel it, crisp in the air around him. Since the *Katsina* had appeared to him in the Oraibi kiva, his life had been orchestrated. Nothing seemed left to chance, as if he and the people involved were gaming pieces, moved across a blanket by Power. He had been called to the Contrary, and she had led him to Trader and his copper. They had needed a box, and the Kaskinampo had brought the war medicine. Their trials among the Yuchi had been for a purpose. Green Snake had asked Born-of-Sun to send a messenger, only to have him murdered by Smoke Shield, who was Trader's not-so-dead brother.

The Chahta had played their role, providing Paunch to take them to Amber Bead—and Breath Giver alone knew what role Whippoorwill would finally play. Smoke Shield had taken Morning Dew, who now resided with Heron Wing. And Old Woman Fox had wanted her back desperately enough to betray Great Cougar's raid. All of the pieces had been prepared, moved into position. The very intricacy of it amazed him.

He glanced over his shoulder at the high minko's palace atop its mound. Somehow, it had all started there with death and fire, setting the waves of the future in motion. It had led to murder and attempted murder among brothers, to passions that even now burned so bitterly in human souls.

But who plays for which Power? That he could only wonder. And, finally, what were the stakes? And who would gain in the end?

He chuckled nervously to himself, sensing the coming climax. He could feel it—a tension in the very air around him. Was it his imagination, or did the city seem to wait, anticipating the final confrontation?

He shook himself free of the foreboding. When Power was involved, something had to be sacrificed as an offering. And, were that the case now, what was demanded? A life? Someone's happiness? Did the red Power of Raven Hunter demand additional chaos and strife, or was Wolf Dreamer's white Power the force that needed appeasement?

Let it be me, he pleaded. He was old, tired of the burden he'd carried over so many trails, from one end of his earth to the other. I *have done your bidding, waiting for my time to atone.*

He passed around the head of the sheer-walled ravine that separated the Skunk Clan palace from the high minko's. The walls were almost vertical, having been dug out, the earth carried to build the high mound and to create a defensive barrier too steep to be stormed by warriors attacking from the river. In that narrow defile, a literal rain of arrows could be directed down on any hostile forces.

That was the way of men: the needs of war constantly in balance with the desires for peace.

In contrast, he would remember the glow in Heron Wing's face when she had returned from Trader's. The effect had been as if she'd shed the weight of the ten hard winters since Trader's disappearance. The woman had literally beamed with joy and anticipation, her steps airy.

Could that be the trap awaiting us? Is that the fatal flaw Smoke Shield's Power has bet on? The ramifications of Trader and Heron Wing being exposed were too painful to think about. Smoke Shield would strike with rage and merciless efficiency.

"Gods," he whispered. "Love is our weakness here."

But it was too late to step back. Trader and Heron Wing had met, each assured that their passion burned just as brightly as it had those long winters ago.

"You could kill us all," he muttered unhappily.

He rounded the Skunk Clan mound and picked his way through the houses. If Smoke Shield hadn't hesitated to kill a messenger under the protection of a white arrow, would he even pause at the notion of murdering his brother?

He rounded the corner of their house to find Trader seated on his log. The partially formed chunkey lance lay across his lap, forgotten, as Trader stared blissfully up at the sun. He seemed to radiate joy.

For the moment Old White watched him, emotions torn. *What did I miss in life that I never loved like that?*

He considered the women he had known: the Forest Witch, Silver Loon, and all the others. Oh, his passion for them had burned brightly at first, a consuming fire that had roared into an inferno so hot it had scorched them both, only to fade into ashes as the fuel was spent.

Prodding himself forward, he walked up and settled wearily on the log. "So, she came."

"She came." Trader sounded Dreamy.

"I don't suppose I need to remind you that she's a married woman."

Trader shot him a sour look.

Old White nodded. "That's what I thought." He rubbed his bony shins. "Well, when the time comes, given your influence with the woman, she'll Trade us Morning Dew." He chuckled. "She's a sharp one. An excellent Trader. She's going to hold out for all the advantage she can get. I think, in the long run, she's going to be more concerned with long-term benefits to her people than all that Trade Old Woman Fox sent."

Trader grunted noncommittally.

Old White shot a glance at their doorway. "Given your lack of concern, Two Petals must have returned."

Trader's rapture finally cracked. "You didn't find her?"

"No." Old White felt the first premonition. "No one even mentioned her. I thought surely she'd be back by now."

Trader's smile faded. "Did you ask Heron Wing about her?"

Old White made a face. "For some reason her mind was on other things."

Trader shook his head. "It's not like her to be gone this long. Something's wrong. Let's go find her. You take the Old Camp side; I'll search the Hickory half."

Old White sighed. The day had already worn him out. The notion of searching up and down through half of Split Sky City was dismal. He hitched himself to his feet. "Meet back here just after dark. It shouldn't take that long. A Contrary usually generates a lot of attention. Just head toward the center of panic."

Trader nodded, slapping his thigh to call Swimmer before he started off.

Old White took a breath, planning to crisscross back and forth between the palisade and the plaza.

Gods, tell me that the price we have to pay isn't Two Petals!

A cold fear began to build deep between his souls.

Hair was such an amazing thing. Paunch ran a hand over his bald scalp after passing an old acquaintance. The man hadn't even given him a second glance. Of course, Paunch had applied a healthy amount of puccoon root to his face, hands, and neck to darken and redden the skin. Somehow it made him look older, different.

The changes in his fate still left him off-balance, unsure what to make of life, the world around him, or the Power that seemed to swirl through the very air. Farmer one moment, then fugitive, captive, slave, and now he was free again, and in the service of his people.

He hurried through the gate, nodding at the warrior who stood there, and traced his way to Amber Bead's house. There he scratched on the door, and was bid to enter.

He ducked past the hangings and into the dim room. Amber Bead sat by the smoking fire, a question on his face. "It is Paunch; you may come out."

Lotus Root and her guards stepped out from the back room. She shot him a hard look, as if trying to pry out his true loyalties.

"I did just as you ordered. I made my way to their house just in time to see the Seeker leave. By staying far behind, I was able to see that he went to Heron Wing's house. He was there for a time, and then she left. It was odd; he stayed there. The clan leader was gone for, oh, perhaps a hand of time, and then the Seeker went back to his house. I waited, but he and Trader just sat talking while Trader whittled on a stick. And I have no idea where the Contrary has gotten off to."

"She is of no consequence," Lotus Root said. "It's the men I worry about. What if they take what they know to the Chikosi? They could gain a great deal of wealth by exposing us."

Paunch laughed.

"What do you find so funny?" Lotus Root demanded.

"Wealth? I "traveled with them for nearly a moon on the river. Sometimes, when they weren't looking, I got a peek into their packs. Furs, gorgets, copper, carved boxes, medicine plants—the wealth is staggering. They could buy a town. You should have seen the piece they Traded for Whippoorwill and me: a copper gorget the size of my palm." He shook his head. "Whatever they seek, it is not more wealth."

"Are you sure they did no harm to Whippoorwill?" Amber Bead asked.

Paunch sighed, taking a seat beside the fire. "Very sure. She just took the first opportunity to run. I've been worried about her for days."

Amber Bead snorted. "She's the *last* person you need to worry about. She's so thick with Power my skin crawls when I'm around her."

Paunch narrowed his eyes. "She knows things, Elder. She knew when the Chahta were closing around us. She knew the Traders were coming. While I was shivering with fear, she was smiling, fully aware that we were going to be saved from the squares. She knew it all."

"Then what happened to her?" Lotus Root asked. "If she knew it all, she would have realized that she need only ride home in a canoe."

Paunch spread his hands. "I cannot tell you."

Lotus Root frowned at the fire. "The Traders said to wait for them to send for us." She kept knotting her fists, working her fingers as though kneading clay. "Why would they care for the fortunes of the Albaamaha?" Her hard eyes fixed on Paunch. "Did they ever tell you that?"

"They never beat me, kicked me, or worked me like a slave. They—"

"I didn't ask if they were nice!" Lotus Root barked. "I asked, what do they care about the needs of the Albaamaha?"

"They serve Power," Paunch replied irritably.

"And I serve *my people!*" she said fiercely. "Not some foreigners."

"Power serves us all," Paunch insisted.

"It serves the Chikosi, it seems to me." She was watching him as if he were a bug.

"Enough," Amber Bead said softly. "We need not squabble among ourselves. The mikkos are coming. They should be here within the week. We will have time to present all of this to them, thanks to the high minko's desperate need for labor."

Lotus Root pointed a finger. "Hear me, Elder. My advice is to sneak into the Traders' house in the night, and kill them both."

"The Contrary will see it," Paunch insisted.

"You believe that?"

"Oh, yes." He nodded.

"Then perhaps you should go back to them. You are a slave in more than body."

"Enough!" Amber Bead barked. "I know Paunch. He serves our people just as much as you do, Lotus Root."

"But he hasn't paid as much for the privilege as I have," she added fiercely.

TWENTY-TWO

LATE-AFTERNOON SUN CAST long shadows across Split Sky City. Golden light bathed the peaked thatch roofs, gleamed from the plastered walls, and gave the smoke-laden air an orange glow. Trader had pursued a roundabout path in his search for Two Petals. He had started at the south gate, winding around the Crawfish Clan grounds, awed at how the city had grown. For the most part the local dogs had allowed Swimmer to pass without too much growling and sniffing.

Trader stopped short as he walked out to the plaza. He had just finished searching the Panther Clan grounds. He took a moment, seeing his city again, as with new eyes. Every muscle in his body was charged, his souls practically flying inside him. Over and over, he replayed each moment of his meeting with Heron Wing, savoring each word they had spoken, hearing her voice as she said she had never stopped loving him.

The sunlight seemed brighter, the air—laden with the odors of the city as it was—smelled fresher in his nose. He marveled at the open plaza, seeing children running, playing at stickball. Two young men practiced chunkey on the nearest court. In the north, the great mound thrust up, the roof of the palace designed to add to the illusion of a wedge splitting the sky.

"Quite a place, isn't it?" he asked Swimmer. The dog was sniffing at something on the ground, his tail wagging.

Until now, Trader had avoided entering the Hickory Moiety's half of the city. The notion of coming here had been similar to the anticipation of peeling a scab from a wound. Heron Wing had changed that. Somehow she had healed something that had bled inside him for winters.

Now he took his bearings, turning, walking north along the rows of dwellings, workshops, and society houses that lined the eastern half of the plaza. He glanced this way and that, searching. Swimmer searched, too. But Trader wasn't sure it was for Two Petals.

He saw none of the signs that a lost Contrary was anywhere about. No crowds of curious people hovered at the house doors; none of the passersby chattered on about the odd woman who said things backward.

I should be worried sick! But, oddly, he wasn't. And that bothered him even more than the Contrary's sudden and complete absence.

It's not as if she's helpless. But the lingering memory of carrying her into Rainbow City remained. He could still feel how rigid her body had been. Like a piece of wood. The memory of it amazed him. Had he tried to hold himself stiff like that, the muscles would have trembled, lost their energy. But she'd been locked up tight the whole way. Frozen, but warm. By Breath Giver, the ways of Power were surprising.

Swimmer, it appeared, had found what he was looking for. He grabbed up a stick and dropped it at Trader's feet. They continued, Trader tossing the stick, and Swimmer charging after it with a happy yip.

A woman stepped out in front of him. He caught the barest glimpse of her face: young, attractive, with a frown marring her brow. She had her long hair pulled back in a bun held in place with a bone pin. The rest of her was obscured by an ungainly load of firewood.

That she could carry such, and move as easily as she did, left him with no doubt of her strength. He could see smooth muscles working in her calves as she plodded forward.

Nice, he thought. He'd never minded looking at beautiful women. Which led him to think about Two Petals, which in turn led him to think about Heron Wing.

The clatter startled him, almost made him jump. Swimmer dropped his stick, darting away.

Before him, the entire load of wood had crashed to the ground, the woman staggering to recover her balance.

"Blood and dung!" she hissed, holding up the carry strap. It had broken neatly in two. She glared down at the pile and then angrily kicked one of the pieces of wood.

"That's the wrong way," Trader told her. "You're headed north. Kick it that way."

She looked up with fiery eyes. "Easy for you to say. That's three trips without the thong."

"One trip," he insisted. "Provided I help you. I know a trick. Something I learned among the Cree."

"Who?"

"A people way up north of the Freshwater Seas." He bent down, pulling out the longest pieces of wood. "We'll build a litter. Make a square, if. you will. Hand me what's left of the strap."

She did, her eyes narrowing as she studied his face. "It's almost like I know you. It seems like it was something unpleasant."

"Like losing a load of firewood?" He fished a sharp chert flake from his pouch, cutting the remaining pieces of strap into equal lengths. Swimmer looked raptly at the pile of wood. It contained enough sticks to keep him happy for a moon.

"No. Are you a warrior? From the White Arrow raid?"

"Sorry." He grinned. "But it's curious the kind of a talent I have — being remembered for something unpleasant."

She looked confused as she met his eyes, then shook her head, frowning. "It's probably nothing."

He lashed the framework together, leaving the handles extending. "The trick is to pile the lengths of wood as closely as possible. Without another cord, they'll shift, try to roll off."

She flushed. "I should be thanking you instead of trying to figure out why I don't like you. You don't really have to do this. I have no desire to keep you from whatever you were doing."

"It's all right. I'm looking for a friend. She's missing. Probably got lost." He was quickly and efficiently laying the wood in parallel rows. The bent pieces he placed on the ends, trying to keep the next layer from rolling.

A slim brow arched. "How do you get lost in the city? She could see the high minko's palace, the plaza, everything's just…well, here."

"For most of us, yes." He clapped his hands as he placed the last of the wood in the pile. "Okay, let's see if this works."

She stepped to the front, bending, lifting. Trader admired the view as her fabric dress stretched over delightfully rounded buttocks. Straightening, they took a few tentative steps.

"Just don't bounce or the whole thing will fall apart.

"So, how could this woman friend get lost here?"

"She, um…sees the world differently than the rest of us. She doesn't speak our language, only Trade Tongue. The bothersome thing is that she often says things that make people uncomfortable. Unless you know her, she can be quite unsettling."

"A foreigner?"

"Yes."

"She speaks Trade Tongue, you say? With an accent? Traveling with an old white-haired man?"

"Very likely, but he's looking on the other side of the city at the moment."

A shiver racked her spine, shifting the wood on the litter. Her voice was different, cautious. "And you say you are a friend of hers?"

"I'd say, from the tone in your voice, you've seen her."

She exhaled. "No wonder I didn't think I liked you. That woman sent shivers up and down my souls."

"That firmly places you in the smart half of humanity."

"But you travel with her? Willingly?"

"I guess that says a lot about which half I fit in." He paused. "She's a Contrary. The real thing, not just someone who follows that path."

The woman cocked her head. "Is she your woman?"

"She is no one's woman. She sees this world through Spirit eyes."

"Why you?" she asked. "Why did you choose to care for her?"

"It's a long story, very long indeed. How far are we going?"

"Up past the Raccoon Clan palace. Almost to the foot of the Great Mound."

"That's Chief Clan territory."

"Well, she may be lost, but you seem to know where you're going. And you, warrior, speak with a fine Sky Hand accent."

"Like I said, I'm no warrior."

"What then?"

"Trader. That's my name: Trader."

"And you Traded for a Contrary somewhere?"

He made a face. "You don't Trade for a Contrary. It seems they find you."

"Seriously?"

"It was just below Cahokia."

"You mean, *the* Cahokia?"

"The very same. There's a creek there next to an abandoned town. The weather was crummy, and...Why am I telling you this?"

"Because I will listen. And you are probably trying to prove to me that no matter what I think about your Contrary friend, you're actually likeable."

"Why would I do that?"

"No, I'm not married. And from the look you gave me, neither are you."

He chuckled, "Sorry, my heart is given to another."

"The Contrary?"

"Gods, no!"

"Maybe you're in the smart half after all. But you were telling me about a creek below Cahokia. The weather was bad."

"She directed Old White right to my camp. Out of pitch-black night, she led him right to me and Swimmer."

"Who's Swimmer?"

"He's the dog who keeps dropping that stick at your feet. Hold it. We're about to lose some wood here." He used his hip to brace the load and restack the firewood.

"So, you have a dog, a Contrary, no wife, a companion named Old White, and travel to Cahokia? That sounds like quite a life."

"What do you do?"

"I'm a slave."

"They treat you all right?"

"You took that well. Not even a moment's hesitation."

"It was a distinct possibility."

"Oh?"

"A woman your age is normally married, especially one doing work like hauling loads of firewood."

"You're an odd man for a Sky Hand."

"As odd as they get."

"So tell me, Trader, do you have any news of the Chahta?"

"Some." They passed the Raccoon Clan palace atop its truncated mound, and the woman led the way to a large house just off the plaza.

In a controlled voice, she said, "I would hear it if you have time."

They wound their way past the ramada and the pestle and mortar.

"I should look for my friend. But yes, I would tell you what I know."

At that, a strikingly beautiful woman stepped out the door, glanced at Trader, and smiled. "Hello!"

"Hello yourself." Lowering the wood, he rubbed his hands to clean them of the bark. "I am called Trader. I helped your slave carry her wood home."

"She's not my slave. I am Violet Bead, second wife to Smoke Shield." She inclined her head to the house immediately south. "I live there."

At that moment, Heron Wing ducked out—and stopped short in shocked recognition as her eyes met Trader's.

"I should be going." He glanced at the slave. "Sorry to inconvenience you."

"Trader?" Violet Bead asked. "That's no kind of a name. What is your clan?"

"Violet Bead," Heron Wing said shortly, "the man is a river Trader. I am negotiating with him over Morning Dew's value. Now go away."

Trader tried to keep a straight face as Morning Dew turned her shocked gaze from Trader to Heron Wing, her lips parting in disbelief.

Violet Bead, however, was giving Trader a swift and thorough appraisal. "When you're done here, Trader, come see what I have available." Then she looked hard at his face. "Don't I know you?"

"Can't say that you do. It's been a long time since I've been to Split Sky City. Unless, well, did you spend any time with the Natchez?" He changed to that tongue. "You live dangerously for a woman of the Chikosi."

Violet Bead shook her head, "Sorry, what?"

"Nothing. A Natchez joke."

"Come see me," she reminded, before turning and striding toward her house.

Trader arched a brow as he watched the saucy sway of her hips. "Is she always like that?"

"Unfortunately," Heron Wing said in a dry voice.

"You're *Trading* me?" Morning Dew cried.

"Shhh!" Heron Wing snapped, glancing after Violet Bead. Then, to Trader, "What are you *doing* here?"

"Looking for the Contrary. That's when your slave's wood strap broke. Two Petals is missing."

"Gods!" Heron Wing cried, hands up. "This isn't funny! Violet Bead is a terrible gossip."

Trader considered that. The tall woman had paused, looking back from the ramada at her house. "So, what do we do?"

"Morning Dew," Heron Wing ordered. "Go with him. Just get away from here. I'll explain everything later. Help him find the Contrary. Go!"

Trader turned, amused at the burning glare that Morning Dew was giving him. If looks were sharp, this one was peeling his skin off. "So, you're Morning Dew?"

Her eyes went molten, jaw muscles bunched.

He led her back out onto the plaza. Once out of earshot, he said, "Do me a favor—try and look slightly subdued instead of like you're about to rip my testicles off."

"You *knew!* What were you doing? Spying, determining the value of your Trade? That's why you didn't react when I told you I was a slave?"

He led the way back past the Raccoon Clan mound. "It wouldn't have been a bad idea, but no."

As the anger drained, her expression fell. "Gods," she whispered, "I thought she was my friend."

Trader stopped, pulling her, almost unresisting, behind the curve of the Raccoon Clan charnel house. Swimmer was trying to figure out why this had nothing to do with playing fetch. "She is. Look at me. Old Woman Fox asked us to Trade for your release. We didn't know that Heron Wing had you until we arrived."

She couldn't suppress her amazement. "Old Woman Fox? My *grandmother!* She sent you here to *Trade* for me?"

"She did." He glanced around. "But I wouldn't shout that at the top of my lungs. Some here might not approve of the idea. Not with relations between the Chikosi and Chahta being what they are."

"Gods," Morning Dew whispered, a hand to her breast. "She's alive! Tell me everything."

Trader related their time in White Arrow Town, answering her questions as best he could. Beyond Old Woman Fox, he could supply little information about who was or was not alive.

"All right," she finally admitted. "I'm just excited, that's all." She grinned. "I'm finally going home." Then her expression fell. "How do I tell them what happened here?"

"You will find a way."

"How soon will this happen?"

He winced. "Well, that's a problem. Old White and I have some obligations here. It may take a while."

She nodded. "But you're Traders. You can go when and where you wish. You came all the way down from the upper rivers, through the Yuchi..." Morning Dew's eyes sharpened. "From upriver. Cahokia. The Yuchi bowl..."

"Yuchi bowl?" "You're Green Snake." "Are you always this quick?" She nodded to herself. "That's why Heron Wing panicked when she saw you. If Smoke Shield learns that you're seeing Heron Wing ..." She reached out. "Come on. Let's go look for your lost Contrary. We need to make this look good—something Violet Bead would believe. So, what do we do? The Trader explanation won't be good for more than a day or two. She's going to be eaten alive with curiosity." Morning Dew studied him with different eyes. "You do resemble your brother. But you're just enough different." "We were twins, but not identical." "No wonder I didn't like you." "That's all right. I don't like him, either." She took his hand, leading him out into plain view. "We're holding hands."

"Why? I thought we were looking for Two Petals." "Yes, we're looking for your spooky friend." "And we have to hold hands to do that?" "Of course. You're my new lover." "Do I have anything to say about this?" "Do you want to be close to Heron Wing? Any other way and rumors will fly straight to Smoke Shield's ears."

"Ah, I see. No one would care about a man sniffing around Heron Wing's slave." He grinned. "I'm only a little slow."

———

Old White sat on the log before their house, poking at the fire with a long branch. He had been everywhere, even peeking into society houses where he had no business. He had asked after Two Petals, describing her looks, how she was dressed. Nothing.

He growled to himself. He'd been too concerned with Trader that morning, aware the man was half-shocked by the revelations about Smoke Shield.

Why didn't I keep my eye on her?

Because she's the Contrary, guided by Power.

But was Power enough to keep her safe?

"Seeker?" Trader called from the darkness.

He glanced up, seeing Trader and Swimmer approaching with Two Petals in tow. "Thank the gods, you've found her. Two Petals, I've been worried half out of—"

The woman wasn't Two Petals, but almost matched her height and age. This woman was thinner, lithe and athletic. She considered Old White with clear and intelligent eyes.

"You didn't find her?" Trader asked, stepping into the firelight.

"No." He glanced at the woman. "And this is?"

"Morning Dew."

"Ah, of course." He arched an eyebrow. "When did you see Heron Wing to make the Trade?"

"Power got in the way. For the moment, Morning Dew is my new lover."

About to say something, Old White snapped his mouth shut. Then after a breath, he managed to rasp, "If I only had *half* the complications you have with women, I would die a happy man!"

"It's a show," Trader said, "a way of keeping suspicion away from Heron Wing."

"Are you really the Seeker?" Morning Dew asked, bending down to peer at Old White.

"Are you really Old Woman Fox's granddaughter?"

"I am."

"Then we have two for two." He smiled up at her.

"Come and sit. We're not sure how to get you back to White Arrow Town yet; but sometime soon we'll figure it out, even if it means slipping you to Great Cougar's warriors."

"No Trade yet," Trader said, pausing as Morning Dew seated herself. "Morning Dew will fill you in. I want to run down to the canoe landing. Maybe Two Petals went to the canoes for some reason. Come on, Swimmer." The dog followed happily as he slipped away into the darkness.

Morning Dew dropped her head into her hands. "Great Cougar is sending warriors?"

"Around the new moon."

"You haven't told the Chikosi?"

"Is there a reason we should?"

She lifted her head, studying his face in the firelight. "She knew."

"Pardon me?"

"The Contrary. That was her, before the squares that day. She talked to me, and you pulled her away."

Old White smiled. "Things are always confusing around the Contrary."

"The blood made me what I am. Those were her words." She glanced down at her hands. "She knew." Morning Dew paused. "Do you know what she meant by the final knot?"

"It may be that Trader is the final knot. A knot ties something together."

"Is he *anything* like his brother?"

"What do you think?" Old White asked softly.

"When I first met him I was confused, and then I began to like him." She paused. "Heron Wing still loves him. But she's trapped."

"For the moment."

She stared at the fire. "The Contrary came to me on purpose, didn't she?"

"Yes."

"The firewood cord broke for a reason. Everything that has happened to me has been for a reason. Power has been behind this all along. It brought me here, broke me down, and watched as I rebuilt myself." She looked down at her hands. "When Green Snake told me you'd been sent by my grandmother, I could barely keep from bursting."

Trader appeared from around the side of the house, Swimmer trotting behind. "She was there this morning. The old Albaamo who sells firewood saw her. She walked out, almost as if she was going to walk into the river. Then Smoke Shield showed up. They talked, and he left. Later, she walked back up the landing. No one has seen her since."

"Smoke Shield?" Old White frowned. "And they talked?"

"Do we go search the palace?" Trader's worry reflected in his face.

Old White leaned back. Did they? Was he ready for that confrontation? "No. She knows what she's doing, Trader. She has seen all of this in her vision. Whatever it is, leave it to Power."

"But my brother is a—"

"I said, *leave it to Power.*"

Trader seemed to wilt. "Gods, I just hope she knows what she's doing."

TWENTY-THREE

FIRELIGHT FLICKERED warm and yellow on the great room furnishings. Smoke Shield watched as it played on Flying Hawk's worn face. The high minko sat propped on his tripod, staring vacantly at the flames. His mind seemed to be floating, gone far away to something beyond Smoke Shield's comprehension.

I am going to have to kill him soon. His souls have turned to water.

Smoke Shield continued, "I think we have enough food to support five hundred warriors for no more than a week. The tishu minko has dispatched runners to every town. Warriors should begin arriving from the south within days. I have sent orders upriver that those warriors should join us en route to the north." He paused. "Are you hearing anything I say?"

Flying Hawk stirred, glancing at him. "You have a dilemma."

"Indeed."

"The Yuchi, or the Chahta?" Flying Hawk ran callused fingers over his stone mace. "So I am curious. What will you do? Turn, as you first planned, and strike the Chahta, or continue your march north? For once, you have tricked yourself, Nephew. Or Power has laid a trap for you."

"It is I who lay the traps."

"I wonder. The death of the Yuchi lies upon your shoulders. You broke the white arrow's Power. The pattern of it only comes clear at the end. When you sacked White Arrow Town, it was a sign, a portent that you would spurn the protection of the white arrow carried by the Yuchi. Power has woven this—a complex fabric upon which you now are to be judged."

"You only endured a cut to the chest, not a blow to the head. Why are you talking as if you are addled?"

"Because your brother is woven into this just as intricately as you are. Your actions and his are pulling the warp and weft. I can feel it as surely as I can feel the breeze on my face. Forces are moving beyond your control, events you could no more stop than the wind."

"Meaning what?"

"I am not sure. My best guess is that Green Snake will come at the head of a Yuchi army." He glanced at Smoke Shield. "Do you remember what the Yuchi said about Green Snake playing the high chief in chunkey? I sent my slave out to talk to the Traders down at the canoe landing today. A man came in from the north— a half-Yuchi Trader who shuttles back and forth over the divide. He told the whole thing. Green Snake and Born-of-Sun played to twenty, and for the tie-breaking point, Green Snake shattered his lance on the stone. In the process, they have made an alliance. By killing the Yuchi, I fear that you have made a critical mistake. Now, when Green Snake comes, it will be with force behind him."

"Then we will destroy him and his warriors." Smoke Shield chuckled at the absurdity of it. "As if the Yuchi could defeat us." His mind was racing. "Let him come. Green Snake, the traitor to his people, comes to reclaim his own. Nothing he could do would alienate our people as much as marching at the head of a Yuchi army."

Flying Hawk gave him a piercing gaze. "You never understood him "

"Oh, I understood just fine. The *wondrous* Green Snake! People thought that when the sun rose, it burned just for him. He never had the strength or the cunning to make a true high minko. What was given to him freely became mine by strength, audacity, or will."

"Answer a question for me. It is long past. The truth can't hurt now. The past cannot be changed. Did he really let the Yuchi prisoner loose from the square like you claim he did?"

Smoke Shield narrowed his eyes. "Why would you ask that?"

"Because I finally know you. Perhaps I see you clearly for the first time." He paused, waiting, weary eyes locked on Smoke Shield's, then said, "So, you did. One last lie to bury any goodwill Green Snake might have had left to him."

"The sword had nothing to do with it." Smoke Shield made a belittling motion; in his souls he remembered the shame and fire in Uncle's eyes as he handed over the long stone ceremonial sword that had been promised to Green Snake.

"It had everything to do with it. It was going to be my gift to Green Snake, his honor to finally kill the Yuchi war chief. And after he had driven it through the Yuchi's heart, he would have taken a man's name and followed me to the tchkofa. That is why you cling to it even to this day. It is your last symbol of victory over your brother."

"And I bear this!" He pointed to the scar that marred his face.

"In the beginning, I thought we were the same, you and I. I, too, fought with my brother. But what I did once, in a fit of momentary passion, you have done over and over again in your souls."

"Do not push me, Uncle."

"No." He leaned his head back. "You have won, Smoke Shield. I will not hinder your march toward whatever destiny Power has planned for you. Just tell me what you want me to do, and it shall be. So far as we are concerned, you are high minko. I will only hold this position until you ask me to address the Council on your behalf. On that, you have my word."

Smoke Shield studied him with wary eyes. "Why? Is your fear of me that great?"

Flying Hawk shook his head. "It was, once. I finally understand the legacy of Bear Tooth's blood. A blackness was let loose the night of the great fire. All that was good died with young Hickory. Perhaps he should have let Acorn and me burn with him. All I have left is a weary acceptance."

Smoke Shield smiled, a sense of Power swelling within him. "I need nothing else from you, Uncle. When the warriors are assembled, I will have you call the Council. We will openly declare my brother a traitor, and ensure that he never sets foot in Sky Hand territory again."

He rose to his feet, stretching, and padded toward the hallway. When he looked back, it was to see Flying Hawk, his eyes fixed on the fire, no expression on his lined face.

When Smoke Shield stepped into his room, he was surprised to find his fire burning brightly, a bowl of water resting before it along with several folded articles of clothing.

The woman from the river rose, watching him with glowing eyes. Her hair was freshly washed, worn loose to hang down her back. A white fabric dress covered with mica beads shimmered in the firelight like a thousand stars. In her hands she held the long chipped-stone ceremonial sword.

"Put that down."

"Can you hear them?"

"Hear who?"

"The voices in the blood. They speak so many languages."

He stepped over and took the sword from her hands, sheathed it in its leather scabbard.

"So you came?"

She nodded, smiling in anticipation. "Power sent me to you."

"Did it?" He raised a curious eyebrow.

"Oh, yes. I am here to lead you to your destiny."

"Just what would that destiny be?"

"If you remove your shirt, we will begin by bathing the sweat from your body."

He was grinning in anticipation as he pulled his sweat-stained shirt over his head.

———

Two Petals lay with her hand on the man's bare chest. She marveled at each beat of his heart. She could sense the life within him, feel it swell and jet under the bone and muscle of his breast. The rising and falling of his chest, drawing life-giving air into his lungs, was a miracle.

Such a tenuous thing, life.

"What are you thinking?" he asked, glancing at her in the dim light. The fire had burned down to coals.

"Words are reflections. Like images in water. Air is drawn in, and the souls re-form it into words, into the shapes that suit them. So many are wasted, all carrying patterns and designs drawn by the souls. Where do those wasted words go? What finally hears them?"

"Who sent you here? What is your name?"

"Power sent me. I am Two Petals."

"You speak with an atrocious accent."

"Those are the flavors of my souls."

"And do my souls have flavors?"

"Of course."

He grunted, reaching out to clasp her throat, squeezing ever so slightly. "Are you a spy?"

She swallowed through the restriction of his grip, fear tingling in her chest. "I already know your plans, Smoke Shield. I have Dreamed it all. The march to the north, the attack on the Chahta. It is all for naught."

His hard black eyes burned into hers; then his voice dropped to a deadly murmur. "How do you know about that?"

"Because Power has sent me to tell you the future."

"And you expect me to believe you know the future?" His laughter was filled with danger.

"What Power sends, you would spurn? Oh, no, great High Minko. You'll never win that way."

"All right, until I crush your throat, I'll play your little game. What way will I win?"

"Great Cougar outthinks you. He comes with the first equinox moon."

Smoke Shield shifted, his eyes sharpening. "And where did you hear that?"

"I have Dreamed it all. Wait, my lover, and you shall see. When the Council is called after the great wind, you must be there. The only way to achieve your destiny is by denouncing Green Snake. Then, the Council will know the kind of man your brother really is. On that day, you shall seize a wondrous wealth, take it into your hands, and hold it close to your heart."

His eyes had narrowed. "What great wind?"

"The one that will topple the palisade." She laughed as his grip on her throat relaxed.

"You expect me to believe the palisade will fall in a wind?"

"It will."

"And this wealth?"

"Copper. Gleaming, beautiful copper. A piece that will make you the richest man in the world."

"You, I think, are a mad fool!"

"You still do not believe I am sent by Power? That I have seen the future? Challenge Blood Skull to chunkey tomorrow. You will win by three points. In the afternoon, a house in the Deer Clan Grounds will catch fire. A great panic will ensue before they put it out."

She watched the disbelief growing in his eyes.

"Wait, High Minko. You will see. But in the meantime, let us coax this fallen tree of yours into life again. You won't need that much energy to beat Blood Skull by three."

She thrilled as her fingers slowly conjured one more response from his depleted loins. As he slid into her sheath, she felt the Power swelling, the past sliding away, the future flowing down around her.

"If you are wrong," he whispered into her ear, "I shall hang your pretty body in the square. That stone sword you polluted with your woman's touch will one day slide into your heart the way my shaft now fills your sheath."

In her future vision she saw it, just the way he said. Could almost feel the stinging pain as the cold stone sliced through the flesh below her breastbone. Oh yes, it would happen just like that if Power turned suddenly capricious.

For an instant, she thought of Trader and Old White, and a cry of sympathy echoed hollowly within.

I am sorry, old friends. But this is the way it must be.

———

Trader and Old White sat in the shade of Heron Wing's ramada. Another search of the city, begun at dawn, had produced no sign of Two Petals. Somehow, they had ended up here, as if Trader would have been drawn anywhere else.

Morning Dew sat beside him, her firm fingers working cattail-root flour into dough. Swimmer sat, ears cocked, taking in every movement of her hands, absolutely delighted when she tossed up small bits for him to snap out of the air.

Two men walked out to the chunkey court, each dressed in a breechcloth. Sunlight glinted from their lances, and both removed stones from leather bags.

"Think I could go play?" Trader asked.

"Not without drawing too much attention to yourself." Old White stared across the distance at the men. "I should have thought to bring my pipe."

Morning Dew squinted, face pinched. "Blood Skull and Smoke

Shield." She glanced at Trader as he straightened, his expression hardening.

"So, there he is."

"There he is," she agreed.

"Too bad you can't just play chunkey with him," Old White noted. "We could end this and live fat and sassy forever."

"The new moon is seven days away." Morning Dew watched as Blood Skull took his mark, sprinted forward, rolled the stone, and then cast.

"Blood Skull is one of the opposition?" Trader asked, seeing the man make a good cast.

"He has no love for Smoke Shield."

Trader struggled to keep his attention on her words. His bones itched at the chance of playing his brother. What a match *that* would be.

"What do you plan to do about Great Cougar?" Morning Dew asked. "How do we stop a Chahta raid once it is in Sky Hand territory?"

"We could send a white arrow," Old White noted. "Invite them to a feast. Offer gifts in retribution for the dead at White Arrow Town."

"Good idea. Who's going to wander in and explain it all to the Council?" Trader countered. "Not that I don't like the idea, but this city is swarming with angry Chikosi. They all firmly believe that the last raid was committed by Great Cougar."

"Both the Chahta and Chikosi need a reason to stop the fighting. Finding that reason"—Morning Dew shook her head—"that defies me."

"*Chikosi* is a derogatory term," Trader reminded. "As a Chikosi myself, I can't abide the word."

"Guests?" Heron Wing's voice interrupted as she walked around the corner of the house, stopping cold at sight of Trader. Neatly folded clothes were in her arms.

He smiled up at her. "Morning Dew told you the plan?"

She gave him a humorless smile. "You are lovers, yes. Somehow, the notion doesn't leave me excited. How far does this go?"

Old White sighed heavily. "I suppose it falls on me to ensure that they maintain the proper decorum. Especially since you refuse Trade for the woman."

"Is there a reason why your words do not reassure me?" she asked warily.

"What reason would both the Chikosi and Chahta have to cease fighting?" Trader ignored the barbed exchange. He was watching Smoke Shield, his eyes narrowed. His brother set himself, raced forward, and released his stone. "He's better than he once was."

Heron Wing looked out at the chunkey court. "I suppose you've given some thought about what you'll do if he comes over here?"

Trader nodded. "Morning Dew and I will stroll off, hand in hand. Seeker? Do you want to stay under some petty excuse? Take the measure of our enemy?"

"I do indeed."

"I hope you know what you're doing," Heron Wing said as she stepped inside. Moments later she reappeared, her hands braced on her hips. "What are you *doing* here?"

Old White said, "We couldn't find the Contrary, so we decided we'd come see if there was a way to turn Great Cougar's raid into a happy celebration of peace. We thought of inviting the Chahta to an exchange of gifts. You arrived in the middle of our discussion about just which one of us was going to call the Council and give them the happy news."

"I think it should be you," Trader said.

"The two of you being here is like coals on dry tinder," Heron Wing said worriedly.

Trader looked back. "I don't suppose you'd want to come sit next to me? Just to see if we could get Violet Bead to make an appearance?"

Heron Wing gave him a pleading look. "We could still be in your canoe in a hand's time, Green Snake. That offer stands."

He nodded, aware of both Morning Dew and Seeker's inquisitive stares. He almost started as Blood Skull made his cast. "Not good. He's gripping the shaft too tightly."

"Invite the Chahta warriors to a celebration?" Heron Wing asked. "An equinox feast?"

"Does anyone know when the new moon falls?"

"Seven days," Morning Dew reminded.

"A feast? Will that be enough?" Old White wondered. "Besides, if the dates coincide, wouldn't Great Cougar be afraid to time his attack then? Or is he the kind of man to worry about a little thing like Power?"

"He is, and he does." Morning Dew tossed a piece of dough to Swimmer. "Great Cougar pays close attention to the rituals. So much so that just hearing rumors about an attempted Yuchi assassination under the Power of a white arrow might make him reconsider who his enemy really is."

"But we know that was a ruse." Heron Wing had taken up a position, leaning against her door.

"Exposing Smoke Shield's fraud is going to change a lot of minds," Trader reminded. "According to the way Morning Dew explains it, when Great Cougar hears Smoke Shield killed the messenger, he'll be twice as anxious to hit the Chikosi."

"Do you have to call us that?" Heron Wing asked.

"What?"

"*Chikosi.* It means 'aunty's people.' It's humiliating."

Trader glanced at Old White, shared a shrug, and turned his attention to Smoke Shield as he cast again. His brother was having a good day. "I could take him."

"Forget it," Old White reminded.

Trader spread his hands. "The only place the Chikosi aren't called Chikosi is here. By us."

"Whatever happens," Morning Dew insisted, "we're going to have to come up with something special to give both sides a reason to cease fighting."

"So, how long do we have?" Old White asked.

"Until they call the next Council meeting," Trader said. He looked back at Heron Wing. "I heard that warriors are coming up from the south."

She nodded. "The first ones began arriving today."

Trader shook his head as Blood Skull's cast went wide. "The thing is, if Smoke Shield marches all of his warriors out of Split Sky City before we figure a way out of this, there will be no way to call them back." He glanced at Old White. "We have to be at that Council meeting."

He nodded. "I wish I knew where Two Petals went. I always imagined that she'd be here. With us. You know, explaining the future."

Trader waited until Smoke Shield cast. "Heron Wing? When the Council is called, can you do that? Get us in?"

Heron Wing pursed her lips. "Maybe. It will mean telling both Night Star and Blood Skull everything, but yes."

"We will have some packs," Old White said. "Things that must not be opened until we are inside, and then only when the time is right."

"You don't ask for much, do you?"

"We ask for everything," Trader said. "And if we don't get it, we're never going to be able to stop that man out there from unleashing a mess we can't put a stop to."

Smoke Shield charged forward, bowled his stone, and cast his lance. It caught the sunlight, glittering in the air. Then it arced to earth.

"Yes!" They heard Smoke Shield's cry, and the man made a twisting jerk with his arm.

"Gods, he hasn't changed. Used to drive me to a rage every time he did that." Trader shook his head.

Morning Dew slapped the finished dough. "Another thing to consider: Let's say you do get into the Council. You make your claims, prove your case. How do you expect Smoke Shield to take that? What's to keep him from walking over and braining the both of you?"

Trader took a deep breath. "Now there's a question. We're going to look pretty silly if we end up with him chasing us around the eternal fire, leaping over the chiefs, scrambling this way and that, knocking over the Eagle Pipe and the black drink cup."

"Three!" Smoke Shield cried in glee. "I win by *three!*"

"Just don't forget the Chahta," Morning Dew reminded. "We may be running out of time."

———

Smoke Shield charged up the stairs, recklessly taking them two at a time, each leap shooting him upward. The wooden steps of the Sun Stairs shivered under his impact.

Three points! Just as she said.

Gasping for breath, he trotted into the palace yard, patted the guardian posts, and cut across the great room. Entering the hallway, he pulled the door hanging aside and stared at the woman. She lay curled on his bed, her long black hair laid out in a swirl over the blankets. "Three points," she said, sensing his presence.

"I would like to know how you knew that."

"It was what I saw." She turned her head, fixing her odd, depthless eyes on his. "This is terribly difficult, you know. Speaking like this."

"How would you normally speak?"

"Backward."

"Well, you're not very good at Trade Tongue."

She lowered an eyelid skeptically. "Neither are you. Talk about an accent."

He entered the room, pulling back the blanket to expose her naked body. "Not dressed?"

"I can wait until we're finished."

He traced his fingers along the curve of her back, over the round moons of her buttocks, and down the slim thighs tucked against her calves. Her breasts were hidden by her arms.

"And you think I have time to linger with you?"

"I know you do."

"I keep forgetting, you have seen the future."

"Bide your time. The first warriors have arrived. Some from Red Reed Town will be late. They began to play around and capsized their canoe."

"You know this, do you?"

"As will you, when it is finally reported."

He kept staring at her body, remembering the things she had done the night before. He rubbed his chin. It wasn't like he really did have anything to do. Nothing that wouldn't wait, anyway.

TWENTY-FOUR

HERON WING HAD WAITED, ensuring that Stone and Morning Dew were deeply asleep before she'd risen, dressed, and slipped out into the night. The darkness was almost complete. Heron Wing conjured images of wading through soot. Thick and inky, an impenetrable cloud cover had come rolling down from the north and ensured that no starlight penetrated the gloom. Split Sky City might have been a Dream.

The scent of smoke hung richly in the air—not just that of the cook fires, but the more pungent aroma of burned thatch. A house had caught fire that afternoon: one of the Deer Clan weavers'. For a moment, it had looked as if it would spread from house to house, but a change in the wind had allowed several brave individuals to collapse one of the burning roofs and stop the spread.

Heron Wing practically had to feel with her feet, stepping carefully down the beaten path. The trail hugged the northern boundary of the plaza. This wasn't her way—not sneaking around in the middle of the night like this. What she was doing was more akin to Violet Bead's doing.

But she is not in love. She nearly tripped in the dark. *This is madness!*

Gods, she was acting like a silly girl. And hadn't she been the one who gave the lectures about the mistakes of passion?

She oriented herself, approaching the bulk of the Skunk Clan mound, and felt her way around its edge. Halfway into the maze of houses, she kicked a pot, hearing it clatter. Immediately a dog began barking. Someone shouted harshly to silence it.

Heart pounding, she stood, frozen until her breathing grew normal. The house had to be somewhere close. And she couldn't let Swimmer bark. That pesky Squash Blossom would immediately wonder who was at the Traders' at this time of night.

Why didn't I plan this better?

It was impulse. She'd been lying in her bed, thrashing around in her blankets. Her souls had remained locked on one thing: No matter how much sense it made, the knowledge that Morning Dew and Green Snake were playing lovers had been gnawing at her all day. With so much in the balance, that her souls had fixed on that defied her best ability to explain. Not only that, she wasn't an idiot. The speculative, veiled looks that Morning Dew was giving Green Snake were more than just sham interest.

And why not? He's a handsome man. Those broad shoulders, the ropy muscle, and the slim waist would catch any woman's eye. But it was more. Something about looking into his eyes; seeing the reflection of his souls was enough to trigger any woman's interest. Violet Bead, with just a glimpse, had responded immediately with an invitation.

And now I'm being every bit as foolish and careless as she is.

Violet Bead had always liked living on the dangerous side. The fact that she showed great discretion was proved by the fact Smoke Shield hadn't cut her nose or ears off. Generally that's how her people treated adultery.

So what am I doing?

She eased around the side of what she thought was Green Snake's house. Feeling with her toe, she found the log where she'd sat with him that day.

"Swimmer?" she whispered. "Swimmer?"

The dog was a black shape that slipped out from under the door hanging. She bent down, fluffing his ears. "Hello, Swimmer. Is your master home?"

She straightened, slipping the hanging back. "Green Snake?"

"Who comes?"

"Who were you expecting?" she whispered.

Fabric rustled. He peered at her in the darkness. "What are you doing here?"

Words died in her throat.

"Heron Wing?"

She sighed. "I came for you." Then, "Gods, I'm making a mess of this."

A hand found hers in the darkness. He led her into the interior, where she had to feel with her feet lest she step into the fire pit, or knock over something.

"Are you sure?" he asked as he pulled her into his arms.

"More sure than I've ever been in my life." She wound her arms around him, feeling the muscles in his back. For long moments, she just clung to him, wondering at the sensation of her body pressed against his.

"Where's your bed?"

"This way." He released her, and she pulled her dress over her head. Cool air bathed her skin. Then his hands were on her waist, pulling her down to his pole bed.

She fought the urge to gasp as he pressed the length of his body against hers. His skin was warm, the ripples of muscle sliding under her fingers. She rubbed herself against him, sliding her thighs and breasts along his body.

"I have Dreamed this," he whispered. "Night after night, I have lain with you."

His gentle hands found her breasts, his mouth drawing her nipple into its warmth.

Taking a deep breath, she did what she had never willingly done with a man. She reached down, grasping his shaft, tightening her grip.

This should have been mine.

Her first surprise was the anticipation in her loins, the building tingle that brewed deep in her pelvis. She tried to pull him to her, but he resisted, his hands smoothing her skin, tracing lightly over the narrow curve of her waist, around the swell of her hips. His hot breath purled along her centerline to her navel while his hands followed the length of her thighs.

She squirmed as his warm mouth pressed into the hollow above her pubic hair. Then his fingertips stroked up the insides of her thighs. A strangled groan filled her throat.

She was panting, heart racing, as his body slid up hers. She pulled her knees up, reaching down to open herself. A sigh slipped past her lips as he slid smoothly into her sheath.

For the moment they lay there, and she savored the sensation of him deep inside her. He began gently, the barest movement of his hips. She wrapped her arms around him, seeking to pull the whole of him inside her, to wrap her souls around him, and hold him there for all eternity.

I never knew... I never knew....

The final surprise began when the movement of his hard shaft inside her stoked an ever-growing tingle. It built, expanding, swelling around the slick sides of her sheath to burst through her hips and pulse up her spine. She fought the urge to cry out, gasping for air, her hips bucking and rolling under him.

In the pulsating afterglow, her sheath tightened around the hard length of him. She matched his desperate thrusts; then he tensed, his muscles bunched. Her loins exploded again, each tingling burst timed to the jetting of his seed. Even after, as she felt him soften, she continued to milk mewing sounds from both of them.

They lay panting, his hands cupped around her shoulders. She marveled under his weight, oddly touched that he didn't just slump heavily atop her like some somnolent log.

"I never knew," she whispered.

"We have to be quiet."

"Who would have-thought a woman would make noise like that?" she complained.

"You've never had the pleasure?"

"Not with a man."

He chuckled at some private joke.

"Do other women do this?"

"I may be wrong, but I think *all* women do."

She drew a breath. "Gods, until the day I die, I will remember this night. For that, I thank you."

"Well...wait."

"What?"

"Let's take a moment, and then we'll do it again."

She frowned, thinking of Smoke Shield. After the man jammed his spear into her, grunted, and collapsed, he rolled over and went straight to sleep.

Breath Giver? Please, let this night last forever!

The night's chill ate into Heron Wing's skin as she walked slowly up to her ramada and leaned against one of the poles. She drew the rich wet scent of the city into her lungs, her eyes on the graying sky to the east. Equinox was coming; Father Sun was rising nearly due east. She glanced to the south, knowing that Pale Cat was awake, standing on the east side of the Panther Clan palace, aligning his sticks and strings, measuring the sun's slow path to the north.

The Chahta are coming just after equinox. The thought was discordant compared to the honey-warm memories she had just spun in Green Snake's bed.

At just the thought of it, she felt her loins freshen. She crossed her legs and tilted her head against the polished wood. What if she threw herself at his feet and begged him to run away with her? They could hold each other forever, night after night, and without complications. She was a married woman—among a people who prided themselves on fidelity.

What have you just done?

How many times had she herself lectured her clans-women about indiscretion?

Divorce was Smoke Shield's option. It was the Sky Hand way. Not for the first time did she long for the freedom her sisters among the Chahta, Ockmulgee, and Yuchi had. There it was just a matter of sending notice to the husband. If the house belonged to the maternal clan, the man's possessions were simply set outside.

"But we are Sky Hand," she softly said to the glowing sky. "We have always prided ourselves on being different."

Things wouldn't change. It was ingrained in them, sucked up as surely as mother's milk. She had steadfastly hammered it into Stone's head, just as the teachings had been hammered into hers.

The last of the distant clouds began to glow with deep purple light.

"No matter how good that was, I can never do it again. Not while Smoke Shield is my husband."

She closed her eyes, a single hot tear breaking free to streak down her cheek.

So many warriors in town, and more to come. Morning Dew watched some of the young men pitching a ball back and forth with racquets. She turned back to the basket she was working on, slipping long thin splits of cane down over the willow twig steins that gave it form. She followed a pattern her mother had taught her. Two over, two under. With more time, she could have made something a bit more intricate, but she had never had the predisposition for such exacting work. Her grandmother's creations, however, had always amazed her. Old Woman Fox made baskets with such a tight weave they'd hold water.

"Watch this," Grandmother had said once when Morning Dew was a little girl. Then Grandmother had proceeded to pour water into the basket, and set it in the middle of the fire.

"Won't it burn through?"

"Not a good one," the old woman had said. "You put the right Power into the making of a basket, and it'll boil water."

Morning Dew had watched in awe as exactly that had happened.

"Can't do it too often, though. Fire, that close to water, the Powers conflict: It's the anger of both spirits that kills the basket. Makes it lose its resilience."

What of my resilience? She considered that. What had become of that girl of so long ago? Shaking her head, she remembered passing her first moon in the Women's House, listening to Grandmother's skepticism about Screaming Falcon's raid: *"How would you save our people?"*

She frowned at the partially completed basket, remembering how she'd arrogantly told her grandmother that a new day was coming. That Screaming Falcon would make sure of it.

"And if he didn't, I would."

"So you will accept responsibility for your people, no matter what?"

"On my blood."

When she looked out at the warriors running with swift surety as they feinted, dodged, and threw the ball back and forth, she wondered just how she could ever fulfill that promise.

"Morning Dew?" Stone emerged from the house.

"Here, Stone."

"Mother's still asleep."

She glanced at the door, then up at the sun, nearing midday.

"She was up late."

"Doing what?"

"Clan business. Your mother is a very important woman."

"She counsels people on marriages."

"That's right."

"Marriages are really important," he stated firmly.

"Yes, they are."

Stone reached down, picking up a clay figurine of a dog. "Can I have a dog someday?"

"Sure."

"Can I have Swimmer?"

"I think he already belongs to Trader." She smiled warmly at him.

"I like Trader. He plays with me."

Which was a wonder, given who the boy's father was. Morning Dew arched an eyebrow. The boy might be Panther Clan, but he'd still been sired from Smoke Shield's loins. She placed a hand to her own abdomen, forever thankful the man hadn't planted his seed in her.

"He could marry Mother."

"She's married. To the war chief."

"But he's never here."

"I know." Thankfully.

"Maybe Mother was helping to plan a wedding last night. That takes a lot of work."

"Yes, it does."

"Everyone has to be invited. There are feasts and presents," he insisted with a solemn nod.

"I remember. A lot of work."

"Everything stops. Lots of people come for the feast. Even people who don't like each other. For that one day, they all get along."

"So, when you're Panther Clan chief, are you going to make sure there are plenty of marriages?"

"I am."

She laughed. "You'll be a good chief."

Then she glanced at the doorway. *Up most of the night? Would Heron Wing marry Trader?* In a heartbeat, if she were free. The longing in Heron Wing's eyes when she looked at Green Snake was almost like a scream.

Something was nagging at Morning Dew's souls, more than just the unsettling notion that Heron Wing might have sneaked off to be with Green Snake. Gods, had she?

She glanced around. The Chikosi weren't Chahta. They had different beliefs about adultery. It was the woman who paid the price for spreading her legs.

Heron Wing, you're playing with disaster.

She slipped another piece of split cane down between the willow stems. Compared with Smoke Shield, Green Snake might well be worth it. She had caught herself looking into his eyes, listening raptly as he talked about the Copper Lands, the Caddo, and the Oneota. In his presence, she had found herself smiling, her souls at ease. By Breath Maker, she could listen to the man talk all day.

Stone was playing with his clay dog, trotting it across the ramada matting, making barking sounds as he tossed a little twig. "Get it, Swimmer."

So who will I marry if I ever get home?

She was a matron and, with her mother gone, head of the White Arrow Moiety. Young, strong, and healthy, there would be suitors aplenty. She frowned as she fitted another split. *Am I to be a second wife?* "Not hardly," she whispered.

"What?" Stone turned.

"I was thinking about marriage. About being a second wife."

The boy looked over at Violet Bead's house. The woman's two daughters were playing at making clay bowls, their laughter carrying. He made a face.

Morning Dew lifted an eyebrow. "Exactly."

She considered the likely candidates, boys she had known who were coming of age. The ones worthy of her rank had already been married. But there were other towns, other lineages and clans.

What if he turns out to be another Smoke Shield? That was the calculated risk of a political marriage. Fortunately for her, divorce would be an easy matter. Bless the Chahta for that.

Pale Cat appeared, stopped, said something to Violet Bead's girls, then came on.

"Uncle!" Stone cried in delight, charging out with his clay dog in hand. Pale Cat smiled. He nodded to Morning Dew before laughing and scooping Stone up. "How's my boy?"

"Good. Swimmer and I were playing."

"Swimmer? Is that your dog's name?" Pale Cat turned his attention to the clay dog.

"Yes. He's Trader's dog, too."

"Trader?"

"He was here a lot yesterday."

"Indeed?" Pale Cat said curiously.

Morning Dew stood. "He was here to see me."

Pale Cat gave her a knowing smile. "Smart man." He glanced at the house. "Anything to this?"

"Possibly. He has offered Trade to Heron Wing. I think for the moment, she would be one slave short."

He gave her a probing look. "When you go, she'll miss you."

"As I will miss her." A pause. "How do you stop a war, *Hopaye?*"

"By giving people a reason not to fight. Is my sister here?"

"A moment. I'll go get her."

She hurried toward the doorway, averting her face lest Pale Cat read her building concern. Inside, she knelt before Heron Wing's bed, gently shaking her shoulder. "The *Hopaye* is here. He needs to talk to you."

"Yes, what time is it?"

"Midday."

"Gods!" Heron Wing rolled out of bed, picked up her dress, stared at it, then tossed it aside. "How did I sleep this late?"

Morning Dew picked up the discarded dress, watching Heron Wing walk stiffly over to pull a dress from one of the under-bed boxes. She tugged it on, went to the water jar, and wet her hands, scrubbing at her face. Not bothering to comb her hair, she wrapped it in a thick knot and slipped a copper pin through it.

"Do I look like I slept half my life away?"

"You'll pass. But don't yawn...it's a dead giveaway."

"Of course." Heron Wing stretched one last time and walked out the door; but she seemed oddly stiff, as if tender.

Morning Dew lifted the dress to fold it, and caught the unforgettable musk of copulation. "Fire, Heron Wing. By the gods, don't get burned."

She fingered the fabric, frowning. Trader's scent clung to the garment like old smoke.

What does it take to stop a war?

TWENTY-FIVE

SMOKE SHIELD HAD revelations when he was in the sweat lodge. Something about the close, hot darkness and the biting steam that prickled on his skin. Here there were no distractions, just the darkness and the heat. Notions and ideas came upon him, usually to be brought to fruition later, as had happened with the White Arrow Town and the Chahta raids. Now he was considering the Prophet.

Nothing in Smoke Shield's life had prepared him for Two Petals. The woman filled his thoughts as he spooned water onto the hot stones. It exploded as it trickled over the hot rocks, bathing his slick skin in steam.

He gasped, drawing the heat into his nose and throat. It prickled along his arms, coaxing sweat to bead. He leaned his head back in the darkness, and whispered, "Thank you, Power."

That it had sent the woman to him was a gift, one that he still could not comprehend.

"Nephew?" his uncle's voice called.

Rot it all, why did the man always have to interrupt him here?

"Coming."

He reached out, muscles lax from the heat, and pulled back the hanging. He crawled out into the cool daylight to find Flying Hawk standing with his arms crossed, a dark look on his face. Smoke Shield climbed unsteadily to his feet, slicking the moisture from his wet skin.

"Blood Skull tells me that you have recalled the scouts from the Horned Serpent River Divide. Is this true?"

"It is."

"Why? By the gods, they're our eyes on the Chahta!"

"I did it to allow Great Cougar to send his warriors into my trap."

"Trap? What trap? This afternoon the Albaamaha mikkos are meeting to discuss moving our supplies north!"

Smoke Shield chuckled to himself. "Do you trust Power, Uncle?" He cast it away. "Of course you do. That's why you've been brooding over the murder of the Yuchi. Forget it. White Power is weak, draining away like the falling river after a flood. Soon it will be gone. Faded. The red Power is in ascendance."

"What are you talking about?"

"Let me ask you, what is the last thing you would expect Great Cougar to attempt?"

Flying Hawk frowned. "A massed strike at Split Sky City."

"Good answer—and the right one. I should have seen it myself." Smoke Shield looked down at his glistening body. He tightened the muscles in his belly, enjoying the way the light gleamed on the rounded knots outlined under his skin. He could almost feel Two Petals' fingers skipping lightly across them before dropping lower. *No, don't think about it. Not now.* He didn't want his shaft stiffening in front of Flying Hawk.

"Great Cougar is going to strike at Split Sky City?"

"That's just what he's going to do." He forced his gaze to meet the old man's. "Uncle, did you know that our scouts have grown bored? Did you know that some have even taken to gambling with the Chahta, sharing fires?"

Flying Hawk blinked, slowly shaking his head. "What?"

"They've been out in the forest for how long? Think about it. What's a lonely, bored man going to do? The Chahta speak our language. We have the same customs and rituals. And now that they're sharing food, gaming, swapping stories, what kind of easy prey would they be for the cunning Great Cougar?"

"I don't believe it."

"Of course not. We aren't meant to." He looked around at the city. "Not that I have any particular fondness for the fools, but I have called most of them back rather than allow them to be needlessly butchered." He waved it off. "Oh, I left just enough to be captured by

Great Cougar. He's probably on his way now, followed by a horde of warriors."

"How do you know all this?" Then Flying Hawk's face brightened. "You have a spy?"

"Oh, yes. One sent by Power. She has told me things."

"This woman you keep in your quarters?"

"The very same." Smoke Shield flexed his right arm, watching the muscles bulge.

"And how does she know these things?"

"She has seen the future and told me how it will all happen," Smoke Shield said, looking off to the south.

Flying Hawk clearly thought he was raving, but just enough doubt remained. To still it, Smoke Shield said, "Oh, it will occur just like she says it will, Uncle. And what if I had ordered our warriors north? When Great Cougar drove his forces through the hills to the west, there would be nothing to stop him. Split Sky City would be like a fresh ear of corn, ready for the shucking."

"But our plans ..."

"I have changed them." Smoke Shield crossed his muscular arms. "So when the Great Cougar's warriors arrive, we shall crush them like a nut between two stones."

"What of the outlying farmsteads? Even if the scouts are captured —as you insist they will be—we'll see smoke, and the Albaamaha will come fleeing before them!"

"Great Cougar's plan is to make haste. He'll leave the Albaamaha alone for the time being, figuring he can burn them out on the way back as a distraction to lure us into ambush after ambush. I don't intend on letting him do that. Just the opposite, actually. I want to drive his survivors east, into the hills. They'll be easier to hunt down that way."

"Your spy told you all this?"

"She sees the future. Power is my ally, Uncle." Smoke Shield's eyes narrowed. "And don't you forget it. Act against me, and I will know."

He had asked the Prophet, *"Should I kill Flying Hawk now and become high minko?"*

"No." She had stared into his eyes, a slight smile on her lips. *"He still has a role to play. Flying Hawk's moment of surprise must be complete. Only when sad tears well in his eyes will he fully understand."*

Smoke Shield narrowed his gaze as he studied his baffled uncle. Yes, he would enjoy the sight of the old man's tears. For that promised moment alone, he would bide his time.

Flying Hawk lifted his arms helplessly. "Blood Skull also tells me that you have ordered the warriors to make camp north and east of the city."

"That's right. I want any of Great Cougar's spies who might slip through to think we're unprepared. He will see an unsuspecting city, our defenses collapsed and laid flat. In that last moment, the discipline of his warriors will break. They will charge forward expecting an easy slaughter...revenge for White Arrow Town. And then I shall hit them from each side. The surprise will be complete."

"Your spy told you all this?"

"Some. The Prophet may know the future, but I know war."

Flying Hawk nodded, a strange light in his eyes. "But...what about the Yuchi?"

Smoke Shield laughed. "Power will warn me. The Prophet will tell me the way to smash the Yuchi. And after I demonstrate my leadership by breaking the Chahta, my warriors will follow me to the ends of the earth!"

———

As he sat before his house, Trader ran the shaft of his new chunkey lance through his hands, feeling irregularities in the wood. Then he reached down for the damp piece of hide. He'd dabbed it on a bowl of finely sifted sand. Wrapping the sand-impregnated hide around the shaft, he began laboriously running it up and down the wood, smoothing and shaping.

"We have more than enough to worry about as it is," Old White said mildly. "Do I need to remind you that the last person Two Petals was seen talking to was Smoke Shield? I don't need to tell you how the Chikosi feel about a married woman bedding any man she's hot supposed to."

"I said, leave it be."

Old White sighed before he looked down at Swimmer. "Your master could kill us all."

Swimmer thumped his tail in reply, then dove for his stick, figuring that any attention was an open invitation.

Trader growled under his breath, then added, "Last night was a miracle, a Dream. I would not Trade that for anything."

Old White tossed the stick. "Just don't forget who she's married to." He watched the dog charge off, catch the stick on a bounce, and come trotting back. "Hang it, where is Paunch?"

"Maybe the Albaamaha mikkos delayed the meeting?" Trader lifted the lance, staring down its length with a practiced eye. "One of them might be late getting here. Even if equinox is tomorrow."

"Paunch should have at least come and told us that it was postponed."

A female voice spoke in accented Mos'kogee. "They refused to let him come for you."

Trader glanced up and stared. *"Whippoorwill?"*

The slim woman rounded the corner of their house, her long hair shining. She wore a clean brown dress belted at her narrow waist. Her feet were clad in moccasins, and she carried a fabric pack over one shoulder. Slim brown fingers clutched the strap. Whatever the pack contained, it wasn't very heavy, but bulky, with irregular knobs and lumps sticking out here and there.

She walked up, cocking her head, and Trader almost shivered at the sight of those knowing dark eyes. "My sister sent me. Come."

"Your sister?" Old White asked.

"The Contrary. She's busy. If you still wish to address the mikkos, you must come with me."

"Why are you doing this?" Old White asked.

"Because Power is battling over the future. I am on the side of my people."

Trader reached for his war club while Old White grabbed up his pouch of herbs. After giving the reluctant Swimmer a stern order to stay, they hurried after the girl.

"They wouldn't let Paunch come?" Old White asked.

"Lotus Root and her people don't trust you."

Trader kept shooting glances at the woman. Whippoorwill seemed completely oblivious to the fact that she'd vanished in the night after coupling with him on a distant river.

"Where have you been?" Trader demanded.

She gave him an eerie glance. "Where I needed to be."

Shaking his head, Trader was aware of Old White's prying look. But the Seeker held his peace as they threaded their way through houses. They skirted around the plaza where people were congregating in expectation of a stickball game between Thunder and High Towns. Walking wide of the crowd, they exited the south gate. Whippoorwill, Trader noticed, walked with an airy grace. She almost seemed to float as she led them serenely through the Albaamaha village and down a slight rise to a large Council House.

There, two burly Albaamaha stepped forward to bar their progress. Trader recognized both men from the night at Amber Bead's. "No one may pass. This is Albaamaha business."

"Power calls them," Whippoorwill said, as if that were explanation enough.

"I said, *woman,* that no one will pass."

Old White stepped forward, withdrawing his hand from his large belt pouch. "We would speak with the mikkos."

"Go away, old man." The Albaamo grinned.

"And you." The other smacked his club into his hard left palm as he grinned at Trader. "You've got a club. Try and use it, please."

Old White sighed, raising his hand. "Have either of you ever seen chili?"

Both bent to stare at the fine red powder on the Seeker's hand. Old White blew.

"You old fool!" one cried. The other backpedaled, wiping at his face.

The second man barely hesitated, his club swinging in an arc, cracking loudly as Trader blocked it. But be-fore he could strike a counterblow, the man sneezed. Then both were sneezing and then pawing at their faces.

"Witched!" the first howled. "We're *witched!*"

The second man had dropped his club, hands to his face. He staggered back against the wall, sniffing and coughing.

Whippoorwill walked past them, unconcerned, through the doorway.

"I'm going to have to get some of that," Trader told Old White.

"I'm afraid the source is far, far from here."

Trader ducked through the doorway and stepped into the Albaamaha Council House. The place was rude in comparison to the fine buildings other peoples constructed for the purpose. The benches were uncovered, the floor just dirt without matting. High overhead the wall poles had been bent together and tied, saplings running between them and covered with thatch. A crackling fire burned in the center.

About the margins, a collection of twelve old men were seated along with assorted women of similar age.

Lotus Root held the floor, a warrior's bow in her hands, arrows scattered at her feet. She gaped in disbelief.

"Master!" Paunch cried from the side. "Trust me, I tried to... Whippoorwill?" He struggled to his feet, rushing across the floor to hug his granddaughter. "By the Ancestors, I was so worried about you! Where have you been?"

"Bringing the Traders," she said simply, and walked over to Lotus Root. "You will let them speak. Red Awl's ghost knows. Like me, he too has seen. He was right all along."

"You dare call up my husband's ghost?" Lotus Root's eyes widened.

Whippoorwill slung the pack from her back, handing it over. "This is what you seek. He is here, returned from where the Chikosi left him."

Trader watched Lotus Root take the pack, open it, and glance inside. She started, swallowed hard, and sank to the floor as if her legs had lost all strength.

Old White walked over to Lotus Root. The woman looked dazed. He reached down, pulled the fabric on the pack back with one finger to glance inside, and then let it fall closed again.

Straightening, he turned to the stunned mikkos, looks of consternation on their faces. "I am Old White, called the Seeker. As Amber Bead knows, Power has brought us here."

"I have heard of you," one of the old men said. "But this is Albaamaha business. Why are you here?"

"To bring Power back into balance," Old White said with authority. "Chaos is about to be let loose."

"I have seen," Whippoorwill said, walking to Old White's side. "Grandfather was my witness that day. He was there. Together we watched Screaming Falcon retreat from Alligator Town. If you will save our people, you will listen to what I saw in my vision."

One of the guards came stumbling in, his face wet with tears, eyes red and welling. Amber Bead waved him back. The man—his expression that of misery—blinked and sank to his knees.

Old White nodded, saying, "First, let us hear Whippoorwill's vision. And then, my friends, let us consider how to bring this trouble with the Chikosi to an end."

Whippoorwill began to speak.

———

Great Cougar stood on the high bluff overlooking the Horned Serpent River. He wondered if this was how a hawk felt, staring down at the world below. The last of his long line of warriors had made the Horned Serpent River crossing and were climbing out of canoes. The water near the bank had been churned muddy, like a bloom of brown rolling out into the current to be borne downriver. His warriors scrambled up the slope. From his high vantage they looked like miniatures, their roached hair pinned, shields, bows, and arrows clacking, war clubs hanging from their belted loincloths. Their moccasined feet added to the beaten stipple on the bank as they filed into the woods. The last of them pulled the canoes up, other willing hands dragging the dugouts into the trees, flipping them over to drain, and stacking them like cordwood.

The effort had been massive, the largest such undertaking he had ever directed. For most of the day he had stood, watching canoe load after canoe load of warriors with their weapons and supplies ferried from one bank to the other.

Earlier that day, he had also watched the shocked and chastened Chikosi scouts, their arms and legs bound, be ferried the other way. Under guard, they would be marched to Feathered Serpent Town and held until he and his warriors returned. Then, along with any additional captives that had been taken, they could spend their time in the squares.

Five! We only captured five along this entire stretch of river! So where had the others gone? His few scouts, the ones he had slipped back, deeper into the forest, had reported seeing Chikosi trotting happily back toward the Black Warrior Valley. They had looked carefree, relieved. Why would Smoke Shield pull off his scouts? It didn't make sense.

The five they had captured—the friendly ones who had taken to talking with his scouts—had seemed shocked, almost stunned. They had looked at their sheepish Chahta counterparts as if they'd been rudely betrayed.

"We know nothing!" they had cried. "The rest were told to return home! To prepare to head north to fight the Yuchi!"

The Yuchi? Great Cougar watched the mud slowly drifting along the bank, headed off toward the gulf.

Could the Chikosi really have been called away?

He glanced up at the sun. All of his warriors had made the crossing by midday. Now, even if they were spotted, it would be a race. Any Chikosi scout he might have missed could travel no faster than his fleetest of runners, and they were already on the trails.

Tomorrow was equinox. All he had to do was push his fast-moving force to Split Sky City. And who knew? Perhaps the rumors of war with the Yuchi were true?

"By Breath Giver's grace, let it be."

Split Sky City would be in flames before the Chikosi could even think of turning back from the north. He turned, heading into the trees at a dogtrot.

———

Flying Hawk panted as he reached the top of the Sun Stairs and braced one hand on the gate to look back at Split Sky City where it spread below him. The city was packed. Two towns played a game of stickball in the southern plaza beyond the tchkofa. From here, he could see the Men's House, where even now, Smoke Shield was enjoying the company of his picked band of warriors.

He shook his head, reaching down to massage his nagging knee. The long climb was becoming ever more difficult. But the pain in his knee was nothing compared to the worry chewing away at his souls.

Turning, Flying Hawk entered the palace grounds and touched the guardian posts reverently as he passed. He nodded to the guards, entered the great room, and walked to the hallway. There, he stopped in the dim light and called, "Prophet? Are you there?"

"Come, Great Chief," the woman said in Trade Tongue.

Flying Hawk pulled the hanging to the side and stepped into Smoke Shield's room. The woman wore a beautiful white dress decorated with chevron quill work. She sat on one of the benches, knees pulled up to the side. Her long black hair hung loosely about her shoulders, freshly washed and combed so that it caught glints in the firelight.

When her large dark eyes met his, his souls swam, as through drawn inexorably into the timeless depths. He swallowed, struggling to get a grip on himself.

"My nephew tells me—"

"I do not speak your language, Great Chief. You must talk in the Trade Tongue."

He frowned, trying to place her accent, but couldn't. In Trade Tongue, he said, "My nephew tells me that you predict the future."

"I predict nothing. I am the rock, letting time flow past, watching it part and head backward. It won't be long now. At the head of the stream I can look down the river…see the swirls and eddies I have traveled." She smiled. "My husband will encircle me. I can count the courses of the sun until that moment. Together, we will Dance as we exchange worlds."

Flying Hawk cocked his head, trying to make sense of it. Time? Her husband? Exchanging worlds? Gods, she was spouting nonsense!

He demanded, "Why are you here?"

"To live the Dream." She stared off to the side, saying, "He doesn't understand. Odd, isn't it, that the simplest things elude people?" She turned her eyes back to Flying Hawk. "You are a butterfly, fluttering about in the sunlight, but winter comes. Where will your colors be then? Your wings are already faded, Great Chief."

"Your souls are unhinged!"

"Oh, no. They are right here." She tapped her chest. "They Dance within me, circling around and around, awaiting the caress of my husband."

"Smoke Shield? Is that what you seek here? To marry him?" He chuckled. "You poor deluded fool. I don't know what stories they tell in your foreign land, but here, among the Sky Hand, you will only be a third wife. More like a paid woman, actually, since you have no clan or family." He shook his head. "You have tricked yourself, as well as Smoke Shield." He made a casual gesture. "Not that I mind so much. It's something of a delight to see him fall for your deceit after all the others he has misled."

She studied him as though he were some odd discovery, but refused to rise to his bait.

Flying Hawk sighed then, a sinking feeling in his breast. "What would I have to give you to entice you to leave? Copper? Pearls?

Perhaps some sacred object? Something that would make you a rich woman wherever it is that you came from?"

"I am only here for a moment, but much will happen before I join my husband." She smiled. "Your brother has come back from the dead. Even now, that fateful piece of stone hangs from his side. The blood of murder still lingers, hidden in the crevices."

"Stop that!" he cried, his chest tightening. Then his eyes narrowed. "Ah, so that is your game? You think my brother is back from the dead?" He thumped his breast. "Since the day I killed him, I have carried his memory here, struggled to be what he would want me to be. But I'll have you know this: I'll never fall for your lies."

"You only delude yourself, Great Chief. But Power wills it so. You can save yourself, but you won't. You could rally to Green Snake and—"

"Green Snake!" He burst out laughing. "I fear that slip of the tongue has revealed you, Prophet! Now I know you for what you are: a Yuchi spy."

Her eyes widened, and she smiled wistfully, as if at a silly child who amused her. "You know the truth about the Yuchi. Blood still stains the white arrow and haunts your Dreams. The wound in your chest heals poorly, your souls reluctant to renew flesh mutilated in deceit."

Flying Hawk slapped his hand angrily against the door frame. *This time, Smoke Shield, you have gone too far. Gods, how do I rid our people of your folly?*

"You cannot," she said, as if hearing his thoughts. "Your fear of Smoke Shield is greater than your fear for your people. You have lost so much of yourself, nothing will bring it back. Your brother will destroy you, and that you will not be able to bear."

"My *dead* brother?" He stared at her in sudden hatred. "I should kill you."

"But you won't," she said simply. "Smoke Shield hovers over you like a great black cloud. His lightning is flickering in the depths. In the end, he will belong to my husband. Power will have its due."

"Do not toy with me, woman!"

Her dark eyes seemed to expand, drawing him in. He braced a hand on the door frame as the room seemed to waver.

"When all is gone, High Minko, black raven wings will enfold you." Her voice sent an eerie chill through his souls. Images of the Spirit Being from his Dreams flickered in his memory.

Shaken, Flying Hawk turned, hastening from the room. His souls were churning, thoughts a jumble. The image of his brother sprawled beside a dead buffalo washed through him like a flood. He felt the stone in his trembling hand—saw again the bright red blood. It oozed from his brother's ruined face and broken skull.

Brilliant scarlet mixed with vibrant green grass beneath his brother's crushed head.

Oh, yes. If I could bring you back, I would. You were my strength, and I need you now in a way I never have before.

But the dead were dead. He might be able to call upon his dead brother's souls—to plead as he so often had for forgiveness—but in the end, it all fell to him.

Think! She has purposely tried to mislead you!

The woman was a Yuchi spy! And this whole nonsense about Great Cougar attacking the south side of the city? What lunacy! But his nephew had taken her bait like a hungry bass did a small frog. She had convinced him to hold his warriors to the south, awaiting an attack that any logical thought precluded. Why?

Green Snake! She mentioned Green Snake! And then it hit him. Green Snake was coming at the head of a Yuchi army. By now they would have heard of Bullfrog Pipe's murder under the protection of the white arrow. They would be enraged and—with Green Snake as a guide—would be slipping down from the highlands, avoiding the main trails, taking the back routes.

Gods, we're like ducks floating over a submerged alligator!

How did he counter this latest madness? How did he rid himself of the cottonmouth in their midst?

Flying Hawk stumbled out into the great room, his eyes on the smoldering fire pit. Faint wisps of smoke rose from the hearth. The palace was silent, most everyone at the stickball game. He shot a quick look back at the hallway and then at the war clubs hanging on the wall. He could walk back and smack the woman's brains out. She couldn't defend herself, even against his old muscles.

But how do I hide her body? The memory of his brother's blood, so vividly red in the sunlight, remained to haunt him.

No, even if he succeeded in removing the body, the matting would have to be replaced. Smoke Shield, cunning as he was, would search for sign of what had become of her. He'd see the new matting first thing and put it all together.

If the "Prophet" remained, however, and led Smoke Shield even further into her mad schemes, then perhaps there would be a way.

He pursed his lips, nodding, seeing how it might be done.

"Blood Skull," he murmured. "I need Blood Skull. He hates Smoke Shield enough as it is."

Was it his imagination, or did he hear wings rasping in the air as he hurried for the stairs?

TWENTY-SIX

OLD WHITE SIGHED, stretched his aching back muscles, and rolled his arms as he stepped out into the frosty night and away from the Albaamaha Council House. Low clouds scudded from the north, breaths of wind tugging at him. His entire body longed to do nothing more than lie down and sleep. He yawned as he looked back at the Council House. Yellow light glowed from the doorway, people standing around in knots, speaking in low voices.

Off to one side, Trader talked to Whippoorwill. Was it Old White's imagination, or did a large black wolf lurk in the inky shadows behind her? He blinked, craning his neck, but the thing had faded into the night.

I *must be tired. I'm seeing things.*

Lotus Root emerged, squinted in the darkness, and walked over to him, the bulky fabric sack cradled in her arms. She stopped an arm's length away, as if uncertain.

"It's all right," he said. "Whatever it is that you wish to say to me."

"I am still uncertain."

"So are we all," Old White agreed.

"Did you mean what you said in there?"

"I did."

She looked away, as if searching for something in the night. "If only I could believe Whippoorwill's vision is true."

"It will be."

"A great deal remains to be seen."

He smiled. "Do you understand what you must do? How difficult it will be?"

"I do." She looked up, arms clutching the fabric pack to her chest. "How do you think she found him?"

"She said he called to her…that she dove down to find him."

"How could she have known?"

"Because it is a thing of Power." Old White glanced at Whippoorwill's slim form. "I think your people would be well served to follow her counsel."

Lotus Root gave him a level stare. "You know, Chikosi, I will never forgive you."

"I know, and I understand." He smiled. "But I have learned many things in my travels: One is that nothing is forever. Not even Split Sky City, though the Chikosi and Albaamaha may go on for a long time yet."

"Then I shall see you when I am called." With that she turned, walking off into the darkness, her bundle clutched to her chest.

Amber Bead had waited discreetly. "Seeker?"

"Yes?"

"The runners have been dispatched. We shall know soon enough if what you say about Great Cougar is true."

"If Trader and I are wrong, it is an inconvenience. Assuming we are right, however, it will save everyone a great deal of grief."

Amber Bead scuffed at the dirt with his foot. "No matter. We still have a great deal to overcome. It does not pay to underestimate Smoke Shield." He looked back at Trader. "You are wagering that the Council will take the word of a stranger and a disgraced Chikosi… Chief Clan though he might be."

"That is true."

The old man sighed, looking back at the mikkos. "Come the morning, there will be doubts."

"There always are."

Amber Bead shook his head. "I have never placed much faith in Power. Too often its name has been invoked to the detriment of my people."

"And it will again, no doubt. But for the moment, Trader and I must ride this river, and trust to the forces that have brought all of us together."

"Bringing Smoke Shield and Flying Hawk down, let alone convincing the Council—this may kill us all."

"No man lives forever, Amber Bead."

"No. But then, I have no desire to end my days on a Chikosi square." And with that he walked away.

Old White took a tired breath, seeing that Trader was alone. He hadn't seen Whippoorwill leave, but Trader stood, head down, as if lost in thought.

Old White walked over, and said, "It's late, Trader. I'm so tired you may have to carry me home."

"Age has crept up on you?"

"That and a lack of sleep. If you find a woman in your bed tonight, would you mind moving your blankets outside?"

Trader stared back at the darkness where Whippoorwill had stood. "When she left, she called me husband."

"Lucky Trader."

They started for the dim trail that led up onto the terrace.

Trader asked, "What was in the pack Whippoorwill gave to Lotus Root?"

"Bones."

"Red Awl's?"

"So it would seem."

"Do you think we solved anything back there?"

"That, my young friend, is going to depend on the future." He sighed. "All we have to do is discredit Smoke Shield and Flying Hawk, manage to stay alive, and figure out a way to keep Great Cougar and his warriors from killing any Chikosi. Or the other way around."

"Right. Overthrow a high minko and his tricky war chief, and stop a war. Shouldn't be any trouble at all. If Heron Wing, Swimmer, my canoe, and I are missing in the morning, you carry on without us."

"And then there's Two Petals."

"She can carry on, too."

"Your confidence is so reassuring."

It was then that the first stiff gust of wind came howling down from the north.

The equinox celebration barely had a chance. The rituals, of course, were attended to, offerings made at sunrise to thank Mother Sun for her journey north and the promise of the planting season that would begin with the first new moon.

The games were poorly attended, stickball matches more battles against the blowing wind than the opposing teams. Most people spent the day struggling to keep the thatch from peeling off their roofs and their possessions from tumbling away. The celebratory feasts were held inside buildings that swayed and rocked as gusts savaged them, whistling and hissing around gaps in the eaves.

Anything that wasn't tied down went twirling away, including baskets, latrine screens, ramada roofs, and occasional bits of fabric. Little whirlwinds, spawned in the gaps between houses, sucked up bits of debris, charcoal, and ash, and batted them this way and that. Fine grit filtered down into stew pots and coated bedding, food, and matting.

People passed with their arms up, trying to shield their eyes and mouths from the grit, bits of thatch, and matting that pattered against them.

Trader and Old White had slept late, hardly bothered by the shuddering house around them. The poles creaked and groaned while the wind sang a rasping sound through the thatch. Particles of soot filtered down, shaken loose from above, only to scurry this way and that as they rode the draft. Trader had tied the door hanging by its corners to keep it from flapping, but it batted back and forth with crisp snaps.

The draft carried away the fire's heat, wicking it in all directions. Trader grumbled to himself, poking at the embers that boiled their smilax, lotus, and hominy corn stew.

"We could have done without this," Old White muttered, his buffalohide cape pulled tight around his shoulders.

"Thankfully, we're not out on the river." Trader studied Swimmer where he lay beside one of the pole beds. His normally black hair was tinged gray with fine soot and dust.

"Put a lid over that," Old White suggested as a beetle fell from the weakened thatch, just missing the stew pot.

"You worried about eating a beetle?"

"Food's food," Old White told him. "Among the Yamparika I ate crickets, grasshoppers, and other things. In dry years they make nets and drive the hoppers like we do deer. Then they smack them with flails. They grind them up on stones, make a kind of bread out of them, and bake it on flat rocks. But here, who knows? Some beetles can be poison. Among the Azteca I heard of people mashing them to make poison for their arrows."

Trader hurriedly placed a flat piece of bark over the rim. "Poison beetles?"

Old White shrugged. "My guess is that beetles don't like being eaten any more than any other creature."

Outside they could hear someone shouting. Voices— barely audible over the din—called back and forth, then faded. Then more people ran past, their words carried away with the wind.

"What do you suppose that's about?" Trader glanced at the door.

Old White looked up at the roof, then cocked his head to listen. He sniffed the angry air. "I don't see our house falling apart, can't hear anything collapsing, and I can't smell smoke, so nothing upwind is burning. Whatever it is, someone else can handle it."

Trader made a face. If fire broke out on a day like this, everything downwind would go up. "I saw a town like that. Over among the Caddo. They had a big wind, and one of the houses caught fire. Burned the whole place down. Killed ten, maybe twenty people."

Old White extended his hands to the coals. "Can't think of a better reason to build a roof from earth. Now, down in the southwest, you've got to work to burn one of the towns. All the walls are made of dried mud bricks or stone. They put dirt over the roof. To burn those towns you have to set a hot fire inside, something that will catch the inside poles on fire."

"I'll keep that in mind next time I have to burn a southwestern town."

Trader checked under the lid to see the stew boiling. "How do you think Great Cougar is doing? He and his warriors must be having a miserable time of it. If he's on the way, the trees are lashing, branches cracking and falling. Some of the old forest giants will be crashing to the ground."

"Better him than us." Old White stared thoughtfully at the coals. "Might slow him down some. If he's at the head of that big a war party, it'll give him fits."

Trader pulled out their bowls. "You really think Smoke Shield has Two Petals?"

Old White took his bowl, lifted the lid off the pot, and dipped out some of the boiling stew. "That would be my best guess. If she were anywhere else, we'd hear. A Contrary, as you well know, causes commotion. But if he had her hidden away in the palace he might be able to keep a lid on her just like we've done with that pot."

Trader sighed. "What if she's actually up there?"

"I don't know. I've been wondering." Old White blew across his steaming bowl. "The thing is, Trader, we can't just climb up there and start searching the place."

"Maybe we should go as soon as we eat?" He nodded his head toward the shaking walls. "This is about as good a distraction as we're going to get. Smoke Shield might be out trying to be useful, you know, tying down roofs and such."

Old White shot him a disbelieving glance.

"Well," Trader said in frustration, "we have to do something! She's *our* Contrary! The gods alone know what he's doing to her up there. Beatings? Rape?"

"May the ghosts of the long dead help him if he does."

"You sound pretty unconcerned given what you've learned about Smoke Shield."

"You didn't see her with Black Tooth at Cahokia."

"Could we be so lucky with Smoke Shield?"

"We can hope."

"I still think we should go up there."

"If she's up there, it's because she wants to be," Old White countered. "She's seen it all. Trust her."

"All right," Trader muttered. "I'll go. Alone."

Old White screwed his face into disgust. "Now, that's just —"

"Anyone there?" a woman's voice called at their door.

Swimmer barked happily, his tail wagging.

"A moment!" Trader called. He lowered his bowl and walked over to unlace the ties.

Heron Wing, followed by a slim man, ducked past the flap. Trader took long enough to glance out at the houses around him, seeing ripped thatch and naked ramadas. Then he retied the flap and turned.

"Dark in here," Heron Wing said wearily. Her hair was in disarray despite having been pinned back into a severe bun. Her cloak was speckled with bits of matting and other debris. She wore a plain brown dress, belted at the waist.

The man who accompanied her was a little older than she, with pleasant features. He was staring at Trader, a slight smile on his lips. He wore a white knee-length shirt. Pouches were tied to a rope belt. A large gorget and strings of white shell beads hung at his throat. The cougar-hide cape had been thrown back on his shoulders. Gleaming black hair was pulled in a bun held in place by a long copper pin. His face had been tattooed in dotted lines.

It took a moment, then Trader smiled. "Pale Cat?"

"Green Snake?"

They clasped each other, a warm joy in Trader's heart as he held the man at arm's length. "You look good, old friend."

"As do you."

"What are you doing here?"

Pale Cat gave him a sober look. "The southern palisade just blew over. People are swarming over it like ants. That is, when they're not dodging flying baskets and ramada roofs. My sister thought it was a perfect opportunity to meet with you."

"We have stew. Hot and bubbling," Old White said.

"Thank you, but I must fast on the equinox." The man reached down, taking Old White's hand. "I am Pale Cat, *Hopaye* to the Hickory Moiety of the Panther Clan."

"I am Old White, known as the Seeker." He made a sour face. "Well, *Hopaye*, I hope it wasn't your greeting ceremony this morning that set Mother Sun off." He gestured around at the creaking walls.

Pale Cat raised his arms, and let them fall. "I leave it to others to call the winds. If Power is annoyed, I'm sure Smoke Shield is at the bottom of it. But half of the southern palisade falling fiat? It may be an even stronger sign that Power is displeased."

"Oh, yes," Old White agreed.

"We need to talk," Heron Wing said, seating herself. She flashed a look at Trader—one that communicated more than just greeting. He caught himself before smiling back.

She said, "I have told Pale Cat some of the things you have told me."

"How do I know we can trust him?" Old White asked.

"You may trust him." Trader seated himself, trying not to edge too close to Heron Wing. Gods, if he could so much as hold her hand, it would be a gift. "If he is even half the man I knew, we are safe."

Pale Cat smiled wearily. "I would hope that I am. But we may not have much time. If the wind stops, well, I'm not sure I want to be seen leaving here."

Heron Wing shrugged. "Everyone will want to see the palisade. Some of the houses to the south may have been crushed. Who knows what the extent of the damage might be?" She got straight to the point. "Have you found the Contrary?"

"No." Trader gave Old White a narrow look. "And we've heard nothing. Have you?"

Heron Wing shook her head. "Neither of us have. And believe me, Pale Cat would be informed if anyone had a Contrary in their care."

"Then she's gone to Smoke Shield," Old White said softly. "I would just like to know if she did it willingly."

"A woman *has* been in the war chief's room in the palace," Pale Cat told them. "She arrived a couple of nights ago. The guards let her pass because she claimed to come at Smoke Shield's request."

Trader winced.

"We've had this conversation," Old White reminded. To the others he said, "Trader doesn't share my faith in the Contrary's abilities."

Trader took a deep breath to calm himself. "I just hope he doesn't hurt her."

Old White grunted. "Power protects its own."

"Smoke Shield has little respect for Power," Pale Cat told them darkly. "Unless it's red and filled with pain."

"He should learn humility," Old White muttered. "A failing that no doubt can be laid at his uncle's feet."

Heron Wing clasped her hands. "Wide Leaf stopped by this morning. Something happened among the Albaamaha last night. She didn't have many details, but the mikkos met."

Trader glanced at Old White before saying, "For the moment, the Albaamaha are the least of your worries. The mikkos heard the entire story from Lotus Root, but they also heard from us and one of their Prophets."

"They have a Prophet?" Pale Cat asked.

"A woman named Whippoorwill," Old White told him.

"Ah, yes." Pale Cat crossed his legs. "I have spoken with her in the past. What did she tell them?"

"That the Chikosi and Albaamaha cannot afford to fight." Trader shot the *Hopaye* a measuring look. "She had a vision; in it, the Albaamaha and the Chikosi split sometime in the future." He gestured around. "When this place is abandoned."

"Abandoned?" Heron Wing asked, frowning.

Old White sipped his stew and said, "Matron, cities are born, grow, live, and die. Only the rivers are forever."

Pale Cat nodded. "If that is the will of Power, so be it. What else was said?"

"If we can figure out a way to get them into the tchkofa"—Old White stared thoughtfully into his bowl—"they will present their evidence against Smoke Shield in the Council."

"In the Council?" Pale Cat and Heron Wing asked in unison.

Trader gave them a grim smile. "Assuming we can figure out a way to get ourselves into the Council, it should be a very interesting session." His expression fell. "But we have a more pressing problem. Great Cougar is on his way here with a Chahta war party. A big one."

"But the palisade just collapsed!" Pale Cat stiffened.

In a reasonable voice, Old White said, "That seems like as good a reason to broker a peace as any other I can come up with. Our problem is that we might not have a great deal of time."

Pale Cat frowned. "Smoke Shield recalled most of the scouts. They should be here within a couple of days. He only left a scattering of them to watch for the Chahta. I have to warn him."

"No," Trader said sharply, "you do not!"

Pale Cat and Heron Wing stared incredulously at him.

"We don't need a party of warriors rushing out to fight the Chaktaw," Old White insisted. "That will only compound our problems."

"But what about the farmsteads?" Heron Wing asked. "The Albaamaha will be defenseless."

"That has been seen to," Trader told her. "The mikkos sent runners out last night. The Albaamaha are being warned to withdraw, to take everything they need, and stay out of the way. By the time the Chahta charge down from the divide, they should find empty houses in their path."

"You have done all this?" Pale Cat asked incredulously. "By yourselves?"

"Well," Old White growled, "Smoke Shield sure wouldn't have been any help."

"But," Heron Wing asked, "how can you make a peace with the Chahta? Not even the Council knows what you've done!"

Pale Cat had stiffened. "By what authority do you meddle in *our* affairs. Seeker?"

Old White gave him a hard look. *"Hopaye*, Power has sent me from one end of the world to the other. It called me here from the western deserts. It took me to the Contrary, and to Green Snake. Oh, I promise, when the time comes, you'll get more explanation than you'll want."

"I give us the right," Trader said softly. He raised his eyes to Pale Cat. "I am Chief Clan, from the high minko's line. Smoke Shield must be stopped. Power has been abused. The Yuchi messenger, the murdered Albaamaha— that is only the beginning of it."

"I side with them, Brother." Heron Wing's voice left no doubt.

Pale Cat turned veiled eyes on Heron Wing. "Sister, I would hope that the love you so poorly disguise when you look at Green Snake hasn't tempered your wits." He glanced up, studying both Old White and Trader. "I, too, serve Power. I also serve my people, and would not see them led into disaster." He clapped his hands on his thighs. "So, if you have some plan to mollify Great Cougar, perhaps now is the time to convince me why I should trust you?"

Trader shrugged. "We have some ideas."

"Such as?" Pale Cat asked coldly.

"Old Woman Fox gave us the idea, actually." Old White took a moment to swallow the last of his stew. "According to her, you took the White Arrow Town war medicine. Is that correct?"

"It is," Pale Cat said softly, "but that's not something the warriors are going to let you just give back."

Trader turned his gaze on Old White. "He's got a point."

Old White ran his finger around the inside of his bowl before he licked it clean. "After all we've been through, you're worried about a bunch of possessive warriors?"

"I don't believe I'm hearing this!" Heron Wing looked stunned. "If you take the White Arrow war medicine, the warriors will be enraged. Smoke Shield will be livid!"

"See!" Old White grinned happily. "There's another benefit."

Trader enjoyed their shocked expressions. "Power won't let us down now."

Pale Cat's voice hardened. "Power, my friends, is leading you into a quick grave."

Old White spread his hands. "Trust us, *Hopaye*. We still have a few tricks in our bag."

"And you know Smoke Shield," Heron Wing shot back. "He is as cunning as a weasel, and twice as dangerous. If he can twist the truth out of your Contrary, you'll be dead before you can bring any of this to a satisfactory conclusion."

"Oh, yes," Trader agreed. "I'm sure that he's planning on paying me back for that blow I gave him."

Old White had fixed his gaze on Pale Cat. "Tell me, *Hopaye*, how many warriors sleep in the Men's House these days?"

TWENTY-SEVEN

SMOKE SHIELD WALKED WEARILY through the palace great room, stopping only long enough to step over and run his fingers over the captured Yuchi relief of the warrior holding a severed head. "Soon, I shall own your people. Within days, the Prophet tells me, the Chahta will arrive. After I break them once and for all, I shall move north. The story your people tell about the severed head shall become ours. And there is nothing you can do about it."

Then he turned, surprised that Flying Hawk was absent; but then, the old man knew his days were numbered. "And there is nothing you can do about it, either, Uncle." Since the Prophet had promised that he'd see the old man weep, he'd been delighted with anticipation.

He entered the hallway and ducked into his room. She was waiting, a warm pot of water and folded cloths resting beside the fire. He stared into her dark eyes and said, "The palisade fell, just like you said it would."

She nodded. "The vision is flowing so fast now. The Chahta are across the divide. Your warriors are moving. Power draws the weave tight."

He looked down at himself, seeing soot and bits of debris. "I spent most of the day at the palisade. It is good for the people to see the man who will be their high minko acting like he should. We salvaged some of the logs and began clearing debris. The four-times-cursed

Albaamaha were like geese, more interesting in squawking than working. You could see it in their eyes, as if they were heartened by the collapse of the palisade."

"They shall not act against you. Few understand how their lives are going to change. Split Sky City will be a different place after this. The falling of the walls is but the first sign of the changes to come."

He narrowed an eye. "I could have used more warriors, but that scheming Blood Skull was missing all through the day. I sent him to ensure that the warriors are where I want them, but he shouldn't have been gone so long."

"The Chahta will see no warriors when they arrive." She smiled at him. "It's a fascinating game, misdirection. You are good at it. Even the Underworld marvels."

"Is that how it will be? My name spoken among the worlds?"

"It already is."

He grinned, stripping off his dirty shirt and breech-cloth. "Wash me. And while you do, tell me what will come next. I am interested in Green Snake and his dealings among the Yuchi. You have already told me I will denounce him before the Council."

She wet one of the cloths and began sponging his body. "Your brother has made peace with Born-of-Sun, the Yuchi chief. They have discussed a lasting alliance."

"So, he really has betrayed us." He reached up to finger the scar. "Will I ever have the chance to repay him for this? He won't be killed before I can get to him, will he?"

"In the end, I promise you will see him stand before the Council. There, before your people, you will denounce him and expose his true nature so that all might see. And when that time comes, my lover, you shall take his wealth." She smiled. "Power cannot be stopped."

"After I destroy the Chahta, how will I defeat the Yuchi?"

"Look no further than your Dreams, High Minko."

"In my Dreams?"

"All great Visions are like Dreams. Ever so clear, and with a truth all their own."

"But I need to know how! What obstacles are in my way?"

She was washing his genitals now, her fingers adding to the effect of the warm cloth. He watched himself stiffening in her hands. She looked up, excitement in her eyes. "I have things to tell you…about treachery, a stunning theft that will rock your warriors, and betrayal that will enrage your very souls." She waved down his sudden dismay, and added, "All in due time, my lover. First, let me tend to this swollen member."

———————

Heron Wing tossed a handful of corn into the fire. It was little enough offering to the winds for ceasing that angry blow. She could hear cold rain pattering outside, and the drips falling from the eaves had a reassuring rhythm. Glancing up, she was so relieved that her roof had survived. Many had not, and now people were sheltering with family, or spending a miserable night listening to water plopping into pots placed under leaks.

She dropped her head into her hands, worry chewing at her insides like a voracious wood rat. The slow and eroding fear that had become her constant companion was new. Living like this, she decided, was like a slow death.

Even when Smoke Shield had been at his worst, the subtle knowledge that he might beat her, or perhaps even disfigure or maim her, had been tempered by the knowledge that clan justice would make him pay in the end. People liked and respected her—and perhaps Smoke Shield knew that deep down inside. It had held him back, supplied a restraint that not even he was willing to challenge.

Through all of those dark days, she had been buoyed by a deep-seated courage, some hard fiber woven into her souls that had kept her resolve from crumbling. But now, with so much at stake, she had to face the fact that deep down, she was terrified.

The sensation of complete impotence had left her adrift, helpless. Not even in the days following Green Snake's flight had she experienced this. Though her heart was broken and the future had grown uncertain, she still had possessed the core belief that she would manage. The birth of her son, and her people's constant reliance on her counsel, had given her direction.

Then Old White had walked into her house; and her world had fallen apart like the ramada roofs in the wind. No matter how she tried to picture it, the future was dark and menacing. Should even a whisper be passed that Green Snake was here in Split Sky City, Smoke Shield would act with immediate savagery.

Nor did the Traders' wild plots hold much hope of success. She glanced over at the fire where it flickered. She half expected to hear shouts on the night, the cry of triumph as Green Snake was apprehended. And once captured, even if Green Snake kept his mouth closed, Smoke Shield would be coming, eager to know if she'd seen Green Snake, and what they'd talked about.

He will destroy me.

She glanced at her son's bed. On this night he was at his aunt's, tucked in safe where he couldn't witness any odd comings or goings.

Pale Cat accompanies Green Snake. He'll ensure that nothing goes wrong.

But not even the protestations of a *Hopaye* could save them. This thing was too dangerous.

Trust in Power, Green Snake had said. But it was Power that had taken him from her in the first place.

Gods, why couldn't we have just climbed into your nice northern canoe and left this place?

"Are you still awake?" Morning Dew asked from her bed across the room. The woman lifted her head, black hair tumbling around her face.

"Go back to sleep. It's nothing."

Morning Dew dropped her head back to the bedding, but a moment later flipped the blanket off and stood. She walked over, awkward with sleep, to seat herself beside Heron Wing. Her knowing eyes studied Heron Wing's face.

"Do I want to know what is happening?"

"Not if you value your life." She glanced at the woman, seeing concern behind her dark eyes. "My whole world has become chaos."

"Green Snake?"

"Is it that obvious?"

Morning Dew smiled. "I thought I was in love once." She shook her head. "But if our roles had been reversed, I'm not sure. Had I had to spend ten years away from Screaming Falcon, I don't know that I'd be as committed as you are."

"Perhaps it was being married to Smoke Shield. I had time to dwell on a better man."

Morning Dew stared wistfully at the fire. "I am a worthless woman."

Heron Wing lifted her eyebrow. "Oh?"

"My husband meant everything to me. Hardly a moment passed without me thinking of him. When I married him, it was the most marvelous day of my life. We only had days, but they were miraculous. Then, after the raid, I don't know what happened. I lived with the horror of what was happening to him. Then, after that night..." She shrugged. "Can you love someone, and then, when it's all over, barely grieve for them? All I remember from those days was worrying about myself. Not him." She glanced at Heron Wing. "I cried when he died, but I think now that I was crying for myself."

Heron Wing smiled, laying her arm over Morning Dew's shoulders. "Don't you know what grief is? You always cry for yourself, for what you've lost."

"That seems selfish in some way."

"Survivors are always selfish." She glanced up at the dark roof. "That's what worries me about Green Snake and this insane scheme of his. I'd be happy to embrace selfishness right now. I want him to come and take me away. I want to be a survivor, Morning Dew. I want to have what you had, even for a couple of days." She closed her eyes. "One night wasn't enough."

"What are they doing tonight?"

"Risking their lives. The Seeker has a plan to appease the Chahta war party when it comes." She glanced at Morning Dew. "Nothing will make much difference if your people and mine start fighting. Like tossing a burning torch on a roof, there will be no way to stop it."

"What are they—?"

"Are you there?" a voice called from the darkness.

"We're here," Heron Wing answered. "But wait a moment. Let me put something over the fire."

She stood, shuffling through the pots to find a large round bowl. This she laid over the flames, dousing the room in darkness. "Come."

She felt the draft as he entered, heard the door hanging rasp on wood. Once sure the fabric was in place, she used a stick to pry the bowl out of the hearth. The light flickered, gained strength, and she turned to see Green Snake. Water beaded on his smooth skin, and his hair sparkled with droplets. He was dressed as a warrior, his hair back in a bun pinned with a little white arrow. The partially finished tattoos on his face had been painted in, and a war club hung from his belt. Heavy leather straps rested on his shoulders.

He swung the wooden box from his shoulders, and Morning Dew gasped, staring with disbelief.

"The White Arrow war medicine!" she cried, rising to stand an arm's length from the intricately carved wood. "How did you get it?"

"With a great deal of risk, danger, and harrowing escapes." Green Snake's grin grew wider. "Almost cost me my life. Such close calls I never hope to have again."

Morning Dew's expression remained stunned. Heron Wing, however, arched an eyebrow as she crossed her arms. "Who knows it's missing?"

"No one." Green Snake raised the box, letting firelight gleam on the pearls and shell inlaid into the wood. The Chahta image of a falcon shone from the box lid. "At least, not yet."

"How did you get this?" Morning Dew asked again, as if having trouble breathing.

"I told you, at risk of—"

Morning Dew stamped her foot, chin lowering as she gave him a disapproving stare.

"All right," Green Snake said easily. "The Seeker has made a study of plants. Not just ours, but from all over. He mixed up a concoction of datura, hemp, and bits of root of this and that. Pale Cat sprinkled it into one of the black drink cups and had them all drink out of it. When he stepped to the doorway and gave me the sign, I just walked in." His expression turned quizzical.

"And then what happened?" Heron Wing prompted.

"It was an odd sensation. That was the last place I was before Rattle—I mean, Smoke Shield—came to the door and I struck him down. It brought back curious memories." He shook it off. "No matter, being dressed as a warrior I just walked past the sleepers; the idea was that if any of them awakened, they'd just see another warrior walking through. With so many strangers in town, who'd know?"

"And why did you bring it here?" Heron Wing asked.

Green Snake cocked his head. "Does that bother you?"

"Yes," both women replied.

Heron Wing crossed her arms. "That's a very Powerful medicine. A *man's* medicine. What do you intend on doing with it in a *woman's* house?"

He gave her that familiar old smile, the one that barely curled the corners of his lips. "Can you think of the last place Smoke Shield would think to look for it?"

"*Here?*"

"Precisely." He gestured with the box toward her back room. "I could put it back there if you'd sleep better."

"Sleep? With that thing here? I doubt it." Heron Wing gestured her acceptance. "But I suppose that's the best we can do."

Green Snake stepped into the storage room. She heard boxes and ceramic jars being moved. Then he emerged, clapping his hands.

"Now," he said easily, "the next problem is how to let Great Cougar know we've got it."

Heron Wing crossed her arms. "What? No magic potion for that in the Seeker's bag?"

Morning Dew had a strange look on her face, one filled with disbelief and awe.

"Sorry," Green Snake said. "Somehow, getting word to Great Cougar isn't a matter of leaves and herbs. We're just going to have to hope that we have enough warning...that either I or Old White can slip away and offer it to him."

Heron Wing rubbed her tired face. "I suppose that you know the Council has been called for the day after tomorrow?"

"Pale Cat said as much."

"Why didn't he take it to the Panther Clan palace?" she demanded. "Smoke Shield certainly isn't going to search there!"

"No, but Panther Clan warriors would recognize that box." Green Snake pointed toward the hidden medicine. "If one of them sees it, we're undone."

"And your house?"

Green Snake shrugged. "We're running out of space under our floor."

"Under your floor?"

Green Snake grinned. "Trade that we didn't want itchy fingers to lift when we were out of the house."

Heron Wing took a deep breath, rubbing her hands over her arms. "It gives me the shakes, knowing such Power is there, behind that wall. I can feel it now. How am I supposed to sleep here?"

"You could come to my house," he said, the grin widening.

Heron Wing placed her fingers to her temples. "Don't—not even in jest. That's like a knife to my heart."

Morning Dew seemed to come to herself. "Go with him, Heron Wing."

"What?"

"There are no secrets here. You yourself said that one night wasn't enough." She placed her hands on Heron Wing's shoulders, looking into her eyes with steely resolve. "The medicine belongs to *my* people. It was carried by my husband. It won't bother my Dreams. And, as to anyone seeing you, this city was turned upside, down by the wind. Half the houses are hosting people who are dislocated until they can fix their roofs. Assuming you rise early—and aren't seen leaving Green Snake's—who will know?"

"Do you know what you're suggesting?"

Morning Dew's eyes filled with compassion. "I do. Now go. If anyone comes looking for you, I'll handle it. Trust me."

Heron Wing pursed her lips, her heart hammering. "I can't do this thing."

"A moment ago, you were desperate. Don't learn the lesson the way I did. Tonight may be all that you get."

———

Matron?" Old White's hand settled lightly on Heron Wing's shoulder. "It will be light soon. You should go."

"I keep telling you, I'm not a matron." Heron Wing sat up, Green Snake shifting beside her.

The Seeker crouched in the darkness. "It's one of the curses of old age. I sometimes awaken early."

"I hope we didn't disturb you last night."

She heard his hoarse laughter. "Nothing that memories...and a loathing envy for a lost youth can't cope with."

She pulled the blanket back, standing in the cold air. She found her dress and pulled it over her head, belting it at the waist.

"Is it morning?" Green Snake asked muzzily.

"You sleep. You had a busy night."

She could see his teeth in the darkness, smile beaming.

"Thank you, Seeker," she said as she stepped to the door hanging and looked out into the predawn gloom. Seeing no one, she slipped along the wall, rounded the corner of the house, and followed her way quickly through the maze of Skunk Clan houses. She forced herself to keep from breaking into a run as she hurried along the northern margins of the plaza, aware that others were already about. If she met someone, what did she say? Clan business? Not coming from the direction of Old Camp Moiety grounds. That wouldn't do.

She passed the empty squares and cut across to her house where it stood just east of the Great Mound. Passing the mortar and her tattered ramada, she ducked into her doorway and sighed with relief.

Gods, what would have happened if I had slept the morning away? "Bless you, Seeker."

She sighed, walked to the fire, and used a stick to fish for coals. After pushing them into a pile atop the ash, she went to the box of kindling by the door for tinder. Within moments a thin filament of smoke was replaced by a tiny dancing flame. One by one, she fed sticks until she had a fair blaze. Only then did she retreat to her sleeping bench and pull her dress over her head.

Her gaze was drawn to the back room: She could almost feel the presence of the White Arrow medicine box. The thing was going to weigh on her until Green Snake managed to send it to Great Cougar; but how on earth was he going to manage that? She shivered at the thought of the thing's Power.

"Gods, and you slept here?" she asked, turning to Morning Dew's bed. She blinked, rubbing her eyes. The blankets lay fiat.

Heron Wing stood, stepping around to see that the woman's bed was empty. "Morning Dew?"

Silence.

She stepped back, seating herself on her bed, staring across the room. Morning Dew had gone, too? Had the Power of the box driven her out?

Or, did she, too, have a man that she had gone sneaking off to? "No, she would have told me."

At that moment, a dark shape filled her door. An angry Smoke Shield burst into the room. He stopped short, seeing her sitting naked on her bed. His hands kept curling into fists, the muscles in his arms bulging and swelling.

"What are you doing here?" she asked, a sudden fear rising in her breast.

"So, it is not you."

She grabbed up her blanket, wrapping it around her body. "What are you talking about?"

"One of my wives is betraying me. The Prophet told me." Then he marched to the back room. As he did, her heart tripped in her breast.

"What are you…?" The words died in her throat. She felt faint. He would see the medicine box, know immediately what it was.

She should have run after him, sought to distract him. Instead she sat, frozen in horror. He was tossing things about. A ceramic jar shattered in a hollow pop, and then he came storming out, a thunderous darkness on his face. He stopped, bouncing on his toes. "Where is the box?"

"What…box?"

"The White Arrow war medicine. Where is it?"

"I don't—" His hard slap snapped her head back.

"The Prophet said it was brought here!"

Heart hammering, she glared up at him. "Do you really think I would have foreign war medicine in *my* house? It's *men's* Power, you fool!"

His next blow shot yellow light behind her eyes and knocked her sideways. She blinked, vision spinning. Her fingers clutched desperately at the blankets.

"Where is it?"

"I don't know what you're talking about. Tear the house apart if you wish. I have nothing of yours."

He stood, trembling with rage, his nostrils flaring. The twilight cast a black shadow down the deep scar on his head. "Violet Bead," he muttered. "It must be Violet Bead." In his violent haste to leave, his shoulder hit the door frame hard enough to shake her entire house.

Heron Wing lay panting, heart pounding. She wet her lips, tightening her fingers in the coarse weave of the blanket.

The Prophet told him.

Her gaze fastened on the doorway leading to the rear. She'd seen Green Snake walk through that door, heard him as he found a place for the medicine box.

She forced herself to climb to her unsteady feet. Pressing fingers to the stinging side of her face, she stepped to the doorway.

Smoke Shield had made a mess. But despite the wreckage, she could see where Green Snake had placed the box the night before. He'd moved her baskets to clear a space that now lay vacant along the back wall.

Gone! The box is gone!

Who…? Then it hit her with the force of Smoke Shield's fist.

"Gods," she whispered. "Morning Dew …"

A terrible scream rent the quiet air.

Heron Wing hurried to her door, leaning out to stare toward Violet Bead's, where a naked young man came crashing out into the dawn. Behind him, Smoke Shield leapt like a panther.

The naked man squealed in terror, struggled to rise, and then Smoke Shield was on him, howling and screaming like some enraged cat. She saw Smoke Shield's arm rise, could make out something in his hand. The meaty impact of breaking flesh and bone sent a tremor through her. Again and again, Smoke Shield hammered the man's head.

A naked Violet Bead appeared at her doorway, desperately trying to pull Smoke Shield back. He rose, turning, clamping a hand to her throat. Violet Bead was pushed back into the house, and moments later the shrieks began.

Each was like a needle in Heron Wing's souls.

TWENTY-EIGHT

OLD WHITE ENJOYED the midmorning sun. He sat on the log before their house with his head tilted back to the warm rays. Beside him, Trader's wet piece of hide made a soft rasping as he sanded his chunkey lance. People were busy picking up trash. Anything burnable went straight to the fire pits. Others walked past with baskets, seeking the owners. It wasn't anything like the bedlam down by the collapsed palisade. •

Old White had walked down just at dawn, surprised at how much of the tall wall had blown over. The downed portion was half the length of the plaza. Not only that, but the southern end of the city had collected most of the detritus: pieces of roof and loose belongings.

"How could Flying Hawk have let the palisade get that far out of repair?" he asked. "I tell you, fully half the logs were rotted off."

Trader continued his sanding. "Maybe the time for palisades is over."

"Indeed?"

"How often do large armies march grand distances cross-country? It made more sense when Cahokia could put a thousand warriors on the river. Marching that many down here — where the travel is over-land — an army has to carry its provisions."

"Would you mind trotting out and telling Great Cougar that he doesn't know what he's doing?"

"He's motivated."

"Someone will always be motivated, Trader."

The sanding continued.

Old White watched a warrior appear from between the close-packed houses. He stopped, talking to Squash Blossom where she carefully burned a torn section of someone's latrine matting that had ended up wrapped around her ramada pole. The woman smiled, gesturing toward her house. The warrior nodded and stepped inside, followed closely by Squash Blossom.

"Warrior just went into Squash Blossom's."

"Hmm. What do you think that means?" Trader continued his sanding.

"That someone has discovered the White Arrow war medicine is missing."

"Stolen? The audacity of some people!" Trader ran the wet sand down the white wood shaft again. "This thing with Heron Wing and me...Tell me, do you think it's an abuse of Power?"

"No."

"Why not? She's a married woman."

"She was supposed to be married to you. The two of you love each other. What was the story you told? That Smoke Shield lied to get her? Said he'd coupled with her? That she thought it was you?"

"That's right."

"He used despicable means to obtain his ends. Which might be all right, but he has abused her the same way he has Power. You and I both know she would have kicked his sorry moccasins right out the door but for this silly divorce code the Chikosi have."

"There's that word again."

"Something tells me they're going to have to get used to it." Old White reached down, picked up a pebble, and tossed it. Swimmer, who was supposed to have been asleep, immediately launched himself after the stone, unsure of which way it had gone. He bounced to a stop, ears pricked, looking this way and that.

"Here we go." Old White watched the warrior emerge. Squash Blossom was still talking. She listened to something the warrior said; then she pointed right at their house. "I do believe the kind Squash Blossom just pointed that warrior in our direction."

"You didn't say anything bad about her cooking, did you?"

Old White watched the warrior approach and smiled up at him. "Greetings. Come to Trade?"

The warrior was a young man, his tattoos those of the Skunk Clan. A large white shell gorget engraved with an image of Flying Serpent hung on his chest. He had his hair pulled up in a bun; a new war club hung from the thick belt of his breechcloth. He might have passed nineteen summers, spare of body, with a slightly offset jaw. Stickball player, if Old White was any judge.

"Something was taken from the Men's House last night. The woman back there said you are foreign Traders."

"That we are. Down from the north." Old White indicated the white shell gorget. "That's a nice piece. Excellent craftsmanship. Would you part with it?"

He reached up reflexively, hand cradling the shell. "My brother made this for me. It was his gift when I was initiated to the Men's House. It isn't for Trade."

"Come on inside," Old White invited. "Let me show you our goods. I'll bet you'd Trade that for a mica effigy. I have a nice falcon... comes straight from Cahokia."

The suddenly nervous warrior followed Old White into the interior and stared around at the packs and benches. "Do you have a wooden box?"

"Lots of them. But you're going to need more than just that gorget." Old White bent to his packs, seeing the warrior drop to his knees, eyes on the wooden pack Old White carried. "That one's mine. I've carried it across most of the country."

"Wrong decorations."

Old White slipped his fingers through the goods until he found the mica effigy of Falcon with its long, folded wings. The warrior took his time inspecting each of their wooden boxes. His gaze lingered on the Chaktaw box Old Woman Fox had given them to Trade for Morning Dew. He tilted it, finding no holes for shoulder straps.

I wonder what he'd say if he knew he was standing on top of the legendary Sky Hand war medicine box and a wealth of copper?

"Here." Old White handed the piece over. "As you can see, it's already drilled at the top, ready to be strung on whatever kind of cord you prefer."

The warrior took the piece, turning it in his hands. He held it up to the light coming through the door and watched it flash. "This really came from Cahokia?"

"On the Power of Trade, it did." Old White made a gesture. "A lot of pieces are being Traded around today that are supposed to have come from Cahokia, but that is the real thing. Here, let me show you this."

He fished around for one of the remaining weasel hides. "Ever seen a white weasel before? They only turn that color up in the far north. Makes it harder for the hawks and owls to see them against the snow."

"You would trade the mica for my gorget?"

"I would. That's an extraordinary piece. I could get a bale of these weasel hides for that one gorget up north. Since the Trade has slowed, they don't get as much shell up there."

The warrior fingered the Falcon effigy, and Old White clearly read the desire in his eyes. Finally, the man shook his head. "I'm sorry. I cannot. My brother made this. It was a special gift."

"I understand completely." Old White clapped his hands to his thighs and stood. "But, perhaps you might know where another gorget—just as large and well made—might be? I don't have to Trade you out of your brother's gift. But another, equally fine, would do."

The warrior smiled. "I may see you later."

"We'll be here. It is our hope to spend some time in Sky Hand City." Old White smiled. "It gives people time to bring us the best."

He followed the warrior out into the sunlight. "Now, about this missing box: If we see it, how do we recognize it?"

"Do you know Chahta designs?"

"We do. Like you saw inside."

"This one is a war medicine box, with straps. The engraving is very fine, with pearls and shell inlay. It has Falcon on it, and the triangles with lines that the Chahta like so much."

Old White nodded. "You know, it wouldn't be the first time someone tried to Trade a stolen object. If anyone brings such a thing to us, one of us will stall him while the other slips away to the Men's House with the news."

The warrior gave him a suspicious sidelong glance. "Why would you do that? The box would bring you a fortune among the Chahta."

Old White gave him a fatherly stare. "Warrior, you saw that staff in there?"

"The Trader's staff?"

"That's right. We are here under the Power of Trade. Do you know what would happen to us if we abused it?"

"No."

"Like as not, we'd get out on the river and Horned Serpent would capsize us. Traders don't abuse Power." He paused. "Not and get away with it."

The warrior nodded, and then he smiled. "I understand." He touched his gorget. "I do want that mica piece. I'll be back."

Old White sighed as the young man walked to the next house, calling out to the occupants. He seated himself, rearranged his legs, and found Swimmer waiting for him with a partially chewed slick in his mouth. Old White reached down and tossed it as Squash Blossom came over, a contrite look on her face.

"Isn't this a better day?" she said by way of greeting. "That wind was terrible."

"It was indeed." Trader smiled up as he continued to sand his lance.

She shifted from foot to foot. "I didn't mean to get you into any trouble."

"No trouble," Old White said amiably. "You did us a service. That nice young man is going to Trade us a fine shell gorget next time he comes."

She glanced off toward the east. "So, someone took the White Arrow war medicine." She shook her head. "So many things don't make sense anymore."

"How's that?" Trader asked.

"If it had to do with the White Arrow raid, something always goes wrong. That's what people are saying. First the captives were mysteriously killed, and now the war medicine just vanishes. You know what the rumor is?"

"No." Trader squinted up into the sun.

"That it flew out of the Men's House in the middle of the night. My cousin, he's a warrior; he was there last night. That room was full of men. Many of them maintained some sort of vigil all night. Warriors do that. It courts Power. No one saw that medicine box vanish."

"Maybe something really was wrong with that raid," Old White said evenly. "Maybe whoever led it had the Power wrong."

"That would be Smoke Shield." She shook her head. "If Power's wrong, he's at the bottom of it." Then a horrified look crossed her face, as if she'd said too much. "I've work to do," she called with forced joviality and headed quickly home.

Old White considered that as he reached for his pipe where it lay in his pouch. "That brother of yours seems to be..."

"Elder?" a cautious voice called.

Old White turned to see Stone peering around the corner of the house. "Stone? What are you doing over here?"

The little boy slipped around the corner of the house, eyes lighting when Swimmer trotted over with his stick. He bent down, running his fingers through Swimmer's furry mane. "Mother sent me. She wants the Seeker to come. By himself."

Old White glanced at Trader, who gave him a nod. "All right." He rose, then considered. "Maybe a wise man would take a Trade pack with him?"

"And you're always wise." Trader gave Stone a wink.

"Can Swimmer come?" the little boy asked.

"Maybe another time," Trader told him. "We're in the middle of a stick game."

Old White grabbed a sack of fine milky gray chert blanks that had come from the legendary quarries south of Cahokia and gestured to the little boy. "After you."

They had walked out to the plaza before Old White asked, "Did your mother say what this was about?"

"She's upset."

"Did she say why?"

"I think it's because of Violet Bead. My father beat her this morning. He cut her nose and ears off." Stone looked up, wide-eyed. "He almost *killed* a Crawfish Clan man who was at Violet Bead's house. He hit him in the head with a stone."

"I see." Old White hurried along.

Violet Bead's house had a forlorn look, and it took a moment for Old White to realize why. All the personal effects: the mortar, the bowls, jars, and other items that normally lay close at hand, were missing.

He followed Stone to Heron Wing's door, and the boy ran inside, calling, "Mother? I've brought the Seeker."

Heron Wing stepped to the door, and Old White raised a questioning white brow. "What happened to your face?"

She gave him a frightened look, glancing this way and that before stepping out. "Stone? Could you run down and ask Uncle Pale Cat if he needs help mixing the salves?"

Stone looked uncertainly up at his mother, worry evident in his face. "Father won't kill the Seeker, will he?"

"No," she chided. "It's not like that. Go on. The Seeker's just here to Trade."

They watched as a reluctant Stone turned and started off, but he paused often and long to cast anxious glances over his shoulder.

"Do you want to start at the beginning while I show you these chert blades?" He pulled some of the blanks from the sack.

"You saved my life this morning, and Green Snake's, too. I wasn't home for a finger's time before Smoke Shield burst in. He did this to me." She indicated the swelling bruise on her face. "He said the Prophet told him the medicine box was here, and that his wife was betraying him. He...gods, what he did to Violet Bead ..." She struggled for control.

Old White sighed. "So he's got the box?"

The look she gave him told him just how close her souls were to shattering. "No. The box was gone when I arrived." She swallowed hard. "And so is Morning Dew."

———

Gods! Is everything a mess? Flying Hawk sat on his tripod in the great room. The place was packed. Before him, an angry delegation of Crawfish Clan men, led by Chief Wooden Cougar, stood with hard expressions, their arms crossed. Blood Skull stood to the side, hands on his hips, a thunderous anger in his eyes. Amber Bead stood in the rear, waiting to deliver his report on the meeting with the Albaamaha mikkos. Decisions had to be made about the palisade. Then, moments ago, Two Poisons had stomped in, expression like crowded storm clouds.

"One thing at a time," Flying Hawk said, raising his hands.

"Smoke Shield nearly killed one of my clansmen!" Wooden Cougar said through clenched teeth. "The man's face is smashed! *Your* nephew knocked one of his eyes out of the socket!"

In the back, Two Poisons huffed his displeasure.

"Quiet!" Flying Hawk ordered, lifting his mace. If only he could wade into the middle of them, smacking this way and that. All of the frustrations of the last moon were boiling within. "Breath Giver help me. What's happening to us?"

"It's Smoke Shield," Blood Skull said from the side. "His souls are out of control! First he starts trouble with the Albaamaha; then he conjures some Chahta raid, disrupting all the plans. For all we know, *he* is behind the theft of the White Arrow medicine box. Perhaps this trouble with Violet Bead is his way of covering it."

"My clansman may not live!" Wooden Cougar roared. His kinsmen grunted in assent.

"I said, *one thing at a time*!" Flying Hawk struggled to control himself. The old familiar anger was brewing, replacing the sense of defeat that had so long dogged his souls. "First, the Crawfish man. What's his name?"

"Two Beavers."

"He was caught with Violet Bead. There is no disagreement about that."

Wooden Cougar ground his jaws, then reluctantly shook his head. "No. But Smoke Shield's reaction was uncalled-for. The woman has a well-known reputation for dallying with men."

"As if her husband doesn't?" Two Poisons called from the rear.

"Silence!" Flying Hawk pointed with his mace. "Deer Clan shall have its time to speak."

Two Poisons muttered something under his breath and exhaled furiously.

Flying Hawk struggled to calm himself. "This is a case of adultery. Plain and simple. Smoke Shield acted within his rights as a—" He pointed his mace, forestalling Wooden Cougar's outburst. "*Don't* interrupt me! This Two Beavers isn't dead. We're not talking about murder here."

"Yet," Wooden Cougar interjected. "The *Hopaye* is working on Two Beavers as we speak. The man hasn't regained consciousness."

"If he dies, we will revisit this," Flying Hawk amended. "But until that time, he was caught in Violet Bead's bed."

"That is the woman's fault!" Wooden Cougar cried. "She enticed him."

"And she's paid the price. Smoke Shield cut off her nose and ears."

Flying Hawk watched Two Poisons fume in the back. "That is our law! Smoke Shield was right; the woman and Two Beavers were wrong. I don't want to hear more of this. If I do, the warriors will be sent to restore peace between your two clans. That's the end of it." He glared at Wooden Cougar. "I mean it. You—and Two Poisons—are dismissed!"

He watched as the Crawfish and Deer Clan delegations pushed their way to the doorway and stepped out. He could hear angry words in the courtyard beyond.

He sighed. In a couple of days, after people stewed for a while, some sort of restitution would have to be made.

Blood Skull muttered, "That's what happens when a man doesn't take his domestic duties seriously."

Flying Hawk shot him a warning glare, then asked, "What of the White Arrow medicine box? Has it been found?"

"No, High Minko." Blood Skull took a hard breath that swelled his muscular chest. "Warriors are searching the city as we speak. But with the palisade down, the thief could have walked right over the top of it. It wasn't like when we had gates where warriors would have seen everyone passing."

Flying Hawk shook his head. "I don't understand. The Men's House was full of warriors, wasn't it?"

Blood Skull shrugged. "Many claim they were awake all night, seeking Power for the coming fight."

"Come closer. The rest of you, please stand back. I would speak to Blood Skull in private."

He watched the room rearrange itself, the others crowding into the back. Amber Bead did his best to maintain his distance from the Sky Hand around him.

Blood Skull leaned close. "Yes, High Minko?"

"Did you do as I asked?"

"Yes, High Minko." Blood Skull's voice dropped to a whisper. "In your name I ordered most of the warriors north, as you directed. When the Yuchi try to infiltrate, they'll find a screen of scouts watching every trail." He hesitated. "Also according to your order, I told them that this was at the war chief's command. You have told Smoke Shield, haven't you?"

Flying Hawk sighed; the sense of defeat was welling again. "There are complications."

Blood Skull's penetrating stare fixed on him. "High Minko, the war chief *will* find out."

"I am hoping he won't until the Council is called tomorrow morning. You have told the tishu minko?"

"Seven Dead knows, and understands. He will back you, as will I."

"The collapse of the palisade along with the theft of the medicine box may buy us some time. And, as you have just heard, the war chief has other problems." With any luck Smoke Shield would be pestered all day by Crawfish Clan men demanding satisfaction for the beating of Two Beavers.

"This once," Blood Skull said, "I hope you are right." He hesitated again. "I have another report."

"And that is?"

"The Albaamaha, High Minko, they are moving. It seems that the farmsteads have been abandoned to the west. Half the Albaamaha are heading north, the other half to the south. I've had the same report from several bands of warriors traveling here. Do you know anything about this?"

Flying Hawk straightened, calling, "Amber Bead? Could you approach?"

The old Albaamo mikko stepped forward, bowing and touching his forehead in respect. "Yes, High Minko?"

"Blood Skull tells me that Albaamaha families have been seen moving north and south, west of the river. Do you know anything about this?"

Amber Bead looked oddly nervous. "Yes, High Minko. Those moving north are preparing to carry the food you need for the new town. Others are headed south in anticipation of logging activities. The mikkos are fully aware of the number of logs that will need to be cut to repair the palisade."

Flying Hawk sighed with relief. "A single ray of sun-shine in a day filled with storm. For that, I bless you, Councilor." He shook his head. "Imagine that. I am surrounded by nothing but trouble and confusion among the Sky Hand, and it is the Albaamaha to whom I can offer thanks for a job well done."

Some masked irony gleamed behind the old Albaamo's eyes. "Perhaps it was my desire to go fishing in your pond, High Minko."

"Quite so. And we shall do that. I promise." Flying Hawk tapped his fingers on his stone mace. "I send my compliments to your wise mikkos. At least we have solved the Albaamaha problems."

"Oh, indeed we have," Amber Bead replied, his head lowered.

"Thank you, my friend. I shall see you tomorrow at the Council. You may go."

He watched the old man turn and walk softly from the room.

Blood Skull had a curious look on his face as he watched the man leave.

"Yes, Warrior?"

"Oh, nothing," the man mused.

From the corner of his eye, Flying Hawk thought he saw movement, as if a dark, winged shadow flitted across the wall. When he looked, only the masks hanging from their hooks stared back.

"Nothing, Blood Skull? Then why do I sense that we are balancing on the edge of catastrophe?"

TWENTY-NINE

TRUST ME. The words echoed between Morning Dew's souls as she picked her way along the forest trail. Around her the endless maze of trees seemed to brood and growl. The way was precarious, filled with sticks and branches the fierce wind had ripped from overhead. Here and there she had to circle massive deadfalls where the gale had toppled old and diseased trees.

She had seen worse when the mighty storms blew in from the gulf. Then high winds and tornadoes blew down vast swaths of trees, often creating impassable barriers to travel.

Trust me. She had spoken those words with such conviction to Heron Wing.

Turning, she glanced back in the direction of Split Sky City. By now her friend would be fully aware of her treachery. She would have discovered the missing war medicine and realized what Morning Dew had done in the night.

She resettled the bulky pack on her back. The hardest part had been slipping the Powerful box into several layers of blankets without touching the wood and polluting it. Then she had managed to stuff the entire thing into a large burden basket. Even so, her heart pounded, fully aware of the Power her people placed in such boxes. With it, her husband had taken Alligator Town.

And now I carry it. That notion awed and humbled her.

She could imagine Green Snake and the Seeker's dismay when Heron Wing told them what she'd done.

I *had no other choice,* she told herself. The feeling of betrayal wouldn't last. They would remember that she was a captive—that her husband and family had died on the squares. They would understand the ramifications of her need to return the war medicine to her people—how it would change the Power of Great Cougar's raid. And as they did their anxiety would rise with each passing moment.

In her souls, she could see Heron Wing's expression: disappointment and the sting of betrayal behind her eyes.

"How did I grow so close to her?" she wondered, thinking back to her mother's dead body, the rising smoke as White Arrow Town burned, and how people screamed as they died. Her husband's pleading eyes burned in her souls. She could almost feel his ghosts reaching out to her.

"You will all rest easier now," she told the restless dead. "Morning Dew has set her feet on the path that will save her people."

She trudged resolutely forward, imagining the look in Great Cougar's eyes as he unwrapped the war medicine. She could already hear the awe in his warriors' voices as they realized what she had brought them.

Assuming, of course, that she could find them. She glanced around at the endless maze of forest. This section was old, cavernous beneath a high canopy. The boles of the mighty black oaks and interspersed beeches were huge, the diameter of a dwelling.

Leaving Split Sky City hadn't been so difficult. She'd taken a small canoe at the landing, paddling as far west as the river would take her, and then headed west as the last of the rain moved south. Oriented by the first of the constellations, she'd made her way in the direction she expected to find Great Cougar. He would be coming in a direct line, seeking to do with speed what stealth could not.

But knowing he was here, somewhere, in the dense forest was one thing. Finding him would be another. His warriors would be filing along in a long line, not a wide front. And even with a screen of scouts, what were her chances of crossing their path?

She ground her teeth, staring about as she hurried along. He had to be out here somewhere.

Trust me. The words lay like stale cornmeal on her tongue.

"What if I miss them? What if I finally reach the divide?"

"You won't," a Chahta voice said.

She turned as a warrior stepped out from behind one of the huge trunks. The man smiled grimly. "My apologies, Chikosi, but it appears that you will be spending the rest of your life in a Chahta town."

She grinned. "That, warrior, is my greatest hope. Do not let my Chikosi dress fool you. I am Morning Dew, daughter of Sweet Smoke, and matron of the White Arrow Moiety. You must take me to Great Cougar immediately. There is no time to lose. I have much to tell him." Her smile hardened. "And it won't be pleasant for either of us."

I'm sorry, Heron Wing, but my final betrayal will wound you to the quick.

———

The last light of day had dimmed to a feeble glow in the west as Trader, Old White, and Swimmer climbed the wooden stairs to the *Hopaye's* palace atop the Panther Clan mound. At the palisade gate they were met by a young man in a white hunting shirt and allowed to proceed.

Inside they passed the panther guardian posts, and each touched his forehead as they walked toward the doorway.

"It is Old White and Green Snake," Trader called cautiously.

"Enter," Pale Cat called from within.

They stepped into an ornately furnished room with animal totems, boxes, and wall hangings. Trader took a moment, marveling at the carved wooden posts along the benches, each done in the form of a Spirit totem. A fire burned in the central hearth; the altar behind it had been decorated with hides, feathers, and wooden statuary.

Then he turned his attention to the people. Pale Cat sat just behind the fire, wearing a white smock. He had his hair pulled back, a copper panther rising above the bun behind his head. Copper ear spools gleamed in the light.

Beside him sat a diminutive old woman, her hair white and pulled back. She wore a blue dress decorated with pearls, mica beads, and quillwork embroidery of a panther on the breast. Beside her sat a muscular warrior, his face tattooed with forked-eye designs. The man wore a breechcloth, and a raccoon-hide cape hung from his shoulders. His eyes gleamed like obsidian in the firelight. At sight of Trader, his gaze sharpened.

Heron Wing rose, forgetting any decorum, and hurried over to Trader, shamelessly taking his hands.

He stared into her worried eyes, smiled, and reached up to barely stroke his fingertips over the ugly bruise on the side of her head. "He'll pay for that."

"Old White told you?"

"No," the Seeker muttered, "I thought I'd let it be a surprise."

Trader gave him a reprimanding stare. "Of course he told me."

"Come," she said. "Meet the rest."

Trader reluctantly let go of her hand and followed her over to the fire. He hesitated long enough to say, "Swimmer? Over here. We're in enough trouble. I don't need you lifting your leg on anything." The dog obeyed, sniffing the matting as he trotted over to lie down beside Trader.

Old White seated himself amidst a crackling of bones. Then he sighed and extended his hands to the fire. "It was a most difficult day for everyone involved." He glanced at the dwarf woman. "You must be Chief Night Star. I'm Old White, known as the Seeker."

"Are you truly the Seeker?" the warrior asked before the woman could speak. Skepticism lurked behind his eyes.

"That I am." Old White smiled at him. "And who are you, Raccoon Clan warrior?"

Trader clapped his hands, crying, "Blade! You are the one they now call Blood Skull." Trader smiled. "It's been a long time."

The warrior turned his eyes on Trader again, slowly shaking his head. "It is difficult to believe that you have come back. Why, after all these years?"

"To balance Power," Trader said. "Believe me, it wasn't my idea." He studied the man. "You've grown since I saw you last. What were you? Twelve summers? We had some good times on the stickball field."

"I used to look up to you." Blood Skull nodded. "I reconsidered that after you failed to kill Smoke Shield. Why did you run?"

"Because I would not be the same kind of man as my uncle."

For a long moment, Blood Skull studied him through those hard eyes, and then he nodded. "That I can accept...even if I don't like it much."

A voice called from the door, "It is Seven Dead."

"Come, Tishu Minko," Pale Cat called.

Seven Dead entered the room, crossed the floor, and seated himself. He glanced around, fixed on Trader, and froze.

"My greetings, old friend." Trader reached out, taking the man's hands.

"Green Snake?"

"Most know me as Trader now. But yes."

"But from what Blood Skull tells me, you're up with the Yuchi."

"Then I am in two places."

"Why? I mean, what are you doing here?"

"We'll get to that," Pale Cat said. "I needed you all to be here so that we might have a unified front at the Council meeting tomorrow. A great many decisions must be made."

"How is the man that Smoke Shield clubbed?" Old White asked.

"Clinging to life." Pale Cat steepled his fingers. "Black Tail and I attended to him. The eye is lost forever, and his face is destroyed. We have done all we can for him."

"Will he live?" Night Star asked.

Pale Cat shrugged. "That is up to his souls. When I left, they were still wandering."

"And Violet Bead?" Heron Wing asked.

"She'll heal."

"Any word of the White Arrow medicine box or Morning Dew?" Trader asked.

"Nothing," Pale Cat said.

"Morning Dew has the White Arrow war medicine?" Blood Skull asked angrily.

"Perhaps"—Old White spread his hands—"we should start at the beginning. It is a very long story. At the end of it, we must decide how to deal with the Council tomorrow." He glanced from face to face. "The future of our people hangs on what will happen in the tchkofa. And there are surprises yet to come." Then the old man began to speak. Once again, Trader marveled at his eloquence.

When Old White finished his narration, the room was silent.

Blood Skull spoke first. "So we don't know if the Contrary serves you or not?"

Old White gave him a level stare. "She serves Power, Warrior. She always has."

It was Seven Dead who said, "And the Chahta are truly coming?"

"They are," Trader replied. "As Old White told you, taking the war medicine was going to be our way to blunt his wrath. That, and the return of Morning Dew."

Blood Skull dropped his head into his hands. "Gods, he was right all along?"

"Who?" Night Star asked.

"Smoke Shield. He had placed the warriors in position to ambush Great Cougar when he arrived. The plan was to lure the Chahta into the fields south of the city; then warriors would close from two sides, crushing him in the middle." He glanced up. "Flying Hawk thought he'd lost his wits, and asked me to move as many warriors as possible to the north to meet Green Snake's Yuchi warriors."

"There are no Yuchi warriors," Trader growled. "What would lead him to think I could command a Yuchi war party?"

"He wasn't smart enough to hear the Yuchi messenger out," Old White mused.

Seven Dead asked, "What do we do about Great Cougar's raid? If Morning Dew has taken him the war medicine, it will be a sign to him, proof that we're ripe for slaughter."

"It is not too late," Old White said. "Great Cougar is no fool. If we can talk to him before anyone looses an arrow, peace could still be negotiated."

"Smoke Shield will hear none of it," Blood Skull said through gritted teeth.

"There are higher authorities than Smoke Shield," Old White replied.

"Don't count on Flying Hawk," Seven Dead told him. "He's scared to death of Smoke Shield." He glanced at his brother. "I'm surprised that the old man had the courage to act behind the war chief's back and send warriors north."

"No matter how this works out, Smoke Shield will kill him when he finds out." Blood Skull rested his chin on his hands, lost in thought. "Why would the Contrary tell him we had the war medicine? Why would she warn him?"

"For reasons of her own," Trader told them. "The Seeker is right. She serves Power."

"That doesn't make sense," Heron Wing added. "Smoke Shield murdered a man under the protection of a white arrow. That alone should make Power turn its back on him."

"Patience," Old White added gently. "Power didn't bring us here just to abandon us."

"You place such faith in Power?" Night Star asked, her oversized jaw thrust out.

Old White smiled. "After all that I have seen, good chief, I do. Somehow, this is meant to serve us."

Trader sighed. "Even after all this, yes, I put my faith in Power."

"And you'd better be right," Seven Dead told him darkly. "From here, tonight, it doesn't look like it favors you at all."

"Ah," Old White said with a smile. "That's why we need your help. It's a small thing, really. We just need you to sneak us into the tchokfa tomorrow. Well, us and a few others. Oh, and a couple of other items as well."

Trader swallowed hard. Tomorrow, it would all come to an end. One way, or another.

———

The water lapped at Two Petals' toes. She stared out at the river, seeing the swirling surface, watching the ripples move as though churned by a great serpent's back somewhere in the deep. To her right, the sun remained but a glow beneath the eastern horizon. The surface had taken on a silver gleam, the same color as the nugget Trader had given the Kaskinampo chief.

Her husband's musical Song was like a soothing tonic. It washed around her souls with a warm gentleness that lulled her. She need not be excited; it was only a matter of time. And she had grown accustomed to time. After having watched it flow past her for so long, what was another short observance? She had almost reached the headwaters of her journey. Were she to turn inside herself, she could see her long-awaited goal.

She tilted her head back, sniffing the wet scents of mud and water. Through it, she thought she could detect a subtle musk.

She said wistfully, "I'll be coming soon."

"Yes, I know."

"So little, and so much is left."

"What will be, will be."

"Will the Dreams end?"

"Only the confusion."

She smiled at that. A sense of relief washed through her.

"He comes."

"Of course."

She heard the first faint slaps of his hard feet on the damp sand, seeing him through the eye of her soul. That vision had greater clarity than anything her eyes observed.

She knew the moment that he saw her, could feel his curiosity as he pounded toward her. She could sense the rhythm of his heart, knew the swelling of his lungs and the heat of his muscles. Her tongue tasted the sweat that glistened on his skin.

He slowed, panting. "You're here again?"

"I wished to speak with my husband."

"You don't have a husband yet," he chided.

"Yes, I know. But soon." Before he could say more, she told him, "You have a trial coming in the tchkofa today."

"What kind of trial?"

"Those who oppose you have gathered forces. Green Snake has laid his plans."

"Green Snake?" Smoke Shield's voice was laced with acid. "He has been in contact? With whom? Blood Skull?"

"Among others. They know what you've done. They have evidence."

"Evidence!" He spat the word. "They have nothing but accusations. I've heard them all before."

"You will hear them again."

"Nothing I can't handle, I assure you. But I thank you for your warning." He paused. "I assume he has an agent here, someone working on his behalf?"

"He does. Your uncle."

"Flying Hawk?"

"No." She kept her eyes on the river.

"He's my uncle, Prophet."

"Yes, he is."

"Sometimes the things you say are so confusing."

She lifted her arms helplessly. "It is so hard to speak this way, especially when the one I speak to will not listen."

"So, Flying Hawk is working with Green Snake. He should have known better. This time, he's gone too far." She heard the decision in his voice.

"You have bound yourself to the future, Smoke Shield."

"Just how does Green Snake think he can bend the Council to his wishes?"

"Through truth...and copper."

He lifted a mocking eyebrow. "Wasn't it you who told me last night that truth is an ever-flitting bird, flying here and there?"

"Its wings catch the light. Only the feathers, lost one by one, fall to the ground."

Smoke Shield squinted out at the river. "Why does he think a gift of copper will sway the Council?"

"Wait until you see it."

"Very well. You say it will be mine anyway."

She asked, "How much is your future worth?"

"I don't understand."

"You seek Power."

He clasped a fist before her face, the muscles in his arm swelling and corded. "I *have* Power."

"Does that mean that you have no desire to bind yourself to Power forever? In a way that can never be taken from you?"

His eyes narrowed. "You could do this?"

She shook her head. "No, but you could...if you will make the offering."

"What do I offer?"

"The copper is the only gift Power will accept. If you carry it out there"—she pointed at the swirling water—"Power will swell around you, and the people will stand in awe. At that moment, all of your Dreams of greatness will be fulfilled. You will become what no high minko ever has before. You shall experience what even the lords of Cahokia could not. That is the offering you must make. Otherwise, you shall wander homeless, and in shame."

"What you say, this is all true?"

"For the first time, High Minko, you have a choice." She smiled. "It is your future."

He chuckled. "Then I shall have to have this copper. And I shall do what even the lords of Cahokia did not."

"It doesn't come freely. It will cost you the copper." "Nothing comes free. As to the copper, I can always take more."

Mother? Are you all right?" Stone asked, looking up from the matting where he played with his little clay dog.

Heron Wing stopped short, staring down at the open box with its neatly folded dresses. Through the door she could see the long shadow of her house cast by the morning sun. The pointed tip almost touched the base of the Great Mound. "I'm all right."

"You don't sound all right. Are you sad about Morning Dew running away?"

"Yes, I am."

"I miss her."

"Me, too."

"She should have stayed."

"I know." She turned. "You must understand: People want to go where they think they're safe. For her, that was among her own Chahta."

"I know." He looked up. "But I've been practicing with my racquets. She'd want to see how good I am now."

"I'm sure she would."

She turned back to the dresses, sorting through them until she found a bright red one with round oyster shell beads sewn on the front. This she removed and shook out. Seeing no holes or stains, she removed her brown work dress and pulled the red one over her head. Then she closed the box and shoved it back under the sleeping bench. She combed her hair, wishing that her hands wouldn't tremble so.

Nothing would be the same after today. The gods alone knew what the future would bring. And somewhere out to the west, Great Cougar was approaching at the head of his warriors.

"Stone?"

"Yes?"

"I want you to listen very carefully. Sometime soon there may be fighting."

"Fighting?" He looked up wide-eyed.

"The Chahta might attack. No one knows when. If they do, and I'm not here, I want you to run and hide. You run straight east to the ravine, do you understand?"

He nodded, suddenly worried.

"When you reach the ravine, take the steep trail down and hide under the brush at the bottom. You be very quiet. When it is all over, I will come for you. If for some reason I do not, you wait for two days. Then you come out after dark and peek over the top. If there are no warriors, you go and find your kin among the Panther Clan."

He just stared at her in disbelief.

She settled beside him, placing her hands on his shoulders. "You know that the palisade is down?"

He nodded.

"That's why you have to go hide in the brush. Warriors could swarm all over the city. No house would be safe. That brush in the bottom is so green it won't burn. You can wait two days if you have to, can't you?"

He nodded.

She smiled. "It won't come to that, but what did I always tell you about being prepared?"

"I know."

"Good." She stood, trying to exhale the tension in her chest. Then she reached for the box that held her necklaces. She picked four of the thick white shell strands and hung them over her neck. Looking down at herself, she pressed her dress flat along her hips, and finally decided on a white sash made from the finest hemp. This she doubled around her slim waist and left the fringed tails to hang at her side.

"How do I look?"

"Stunning," Green Snake said from the doorway.

She turned, and her hand rose to her throat. "I wish you didn't sound so much like your brother."

"So do I, but there's not much I can do about it until he stops talking."

He wore a buffalo-calf cape edged with copper beads and a wide breechcloth with a long-tailed white apron. On the front of it an eagle had been embroidered in black thread. His hair was washed and pulled back in a bun that was pinned with a stunning copper pin that flared into a turkey-tail design.

"That's a Chief Clan symbol," she noted.

"If I was Panther Clan, you'd be like a sister to me. I wouldn't like that."

"Gods, how can you act so calm?"

"Part of the Power of Trade, I suppose." He grinned. "I'm hoping to Trade my brother's future for my own." He glanced down. "Stone? I need you to do me a favor."

Her son nodded, still cowed by the notion of having to go hide.

"Swimmer?" Trader called.

The dog trotted in, ears up, tail swishing.

"Stone? Will you take care of Swimmer while your mother and I are at the Council? Now, don't overfeed him! Only a few treats. But you can play stick all you want."

Stone's face beamed as he dropped his clay dog and went to run his fingers through Swimmer's thick fur. "You and me can play stick all day."

Heron Wing found a smile somewhere; then she noticed the square fabric pack Green Snake carried. It seemed to pull down on his shoulders, as though extremely heavy. "What's that?"

"A miracle," he told her. "Are you ready?"

"Breath Giver help me. No, I'm not. I'd give anything to be sitting in your canoe right now, headed downstream."

"Who knows? If this goes wrong, and I can get away, grab Stone and the dog, we'll be gone." He smiled courageously. "But let's try it Power's way first."

She nodded, willing herself to move. "Stone, you remember what I told you?"

He nodded, and she took one last moment to pat her son's head before walking purposefully for the door.

———

The familiar feel of the wooden pack on his back, and the heavy fabric bag over his shoulder, had a calming effect on Old White. Across countless mountains, deserts, forests, and swamps these familiar weights had been his companions. Now they accompanied him on their final journey across the beaten grass of the plaza.

Seven Dead waited right where he had said he would: beside the first guardian post. Blood Skull, dressed in finery, stood at his side, a battered war club hanging from his belt. Both men had pulled their warriors' locks through polished white shell beads, their faces were painted, and raccoon-hide capes hung from their shoulders.

"Looks like a fine morning, Tishu Minko," Old White greeted. "And good day to you, warrior."

"Seeker," Seven Dead greeted, tension in the set of his mouth.

"And the scouts we discussed last night?" Old White asked.

Blood Skull said, "I have sent twenty trusted men, all with precise instructions. They're spaced so that not even a deer could emerge from the forest without one knowing. All are fleet of foot, and should be able to outrace any of the Chahta scouts getting back here."

"Let us hope that Great Cougar comes later rather than sooner," Seven Dead said.

"On that, I most assuredly agree," Old White told him. He glanced up at the tchkofa stairs. "Shall we see what happens?"

"The guards at the top are Raccoon Clan." Seven Dead smiled grimly. "Appointing the guards is the tishu minko's responsibility."

"And the Albaamaha?"

Blood Skull jerked his head toward the side of the mound. "Just out of sight. Amber Bead brought them just as you said he would." He made a face. "I don't like the idea of Albaamaha leveling charges against Sky Hand in our own tchkofa."

Old White gave him a disarming smile. "You'd like a revolt even less, warrior. But think about it: In the eyes of Power, isn't justice, justice?"

"Are you always this persuasive?" Blood Skull asked suspiciously.

"After all my years, I would hope that some sort of wisdom has stuck to these bones."

"Let us go," Seven Dead said. "I can see Smoke Shield descending the Sun Stairs."

Old White nodded, following the man up the wooden stairway to the palisade. "And Green Snake?"

"He's already inside with Heron Wing and Pale Cat."

"No questions about his pack?"

"No. Should there be?"

"I'd hope not."

Blood Skull shook himself as if dispelling some presentiment, and then they nodded to the guards. "I just hope you can be as persuasive here as you were last night."

"More so, warrior. Wait and see."

Seven Dead gestured his respect as they passed the guardian posts, then hesitated at the doorway. "Elder, have you given any thought to afterward?"

"How's that?"

"No matter what happens today, it has crossed my mind that you might need protection."

Old White considered that. "I thank you for your offer, but somehow, I think not even Smoke Shield will dare to threaten me."

Blood Skull said darkly, "That tells me you know nothing of your enemy. A man who will kill someone under the protection of the white arrow won't hesitate at cracking your skull."

Old White raised an eyebrow. "I came home to die. If that's what it takes to bring Smoke Shield down, so be it."

———

Flying Hawk tried to keep his legs from trembling as he descended the Sun Stairs. It wasn't enough that he hadn't ordered the repairs—men were too busy trying to clean up after the windstorm. This morning his thoughts were on anything but the increasingly treacherous steps. Smoke Shield had caught him just as he stepped out into the great room. His nephew had clamped a hard hand to Flying Hawk's throat. Jutting his face close, he'd said, "I know what you've done, old man. I know the depths of your treachery! If you weren't on the way to the Council, I'd deal with you right now."

And he had thrust Flying Hawk away, leaving him to stumble against the wall, coughing and massaging his throat while his heart hammered.

"Gods," he whispered to himself. "He's going to kill me for sending those warriors north."

And Blood Skull? He'd have to be warned. Who knew the extent of Smoke Shield's rage?

"I've been a fool...such a fool." He reached the bottom of the staircase, for once heedless of the pain in his knee. The ache in his heart drowned any other discomfort.

He bowed to the Tree of Life and then reached out to run his fingers along the curling white stripe on its side. "I have always been tied to the red Power, but today, I can only wish you would smile favorably upon me." Then he remembered the dead Yuchi, and blood on the white arrow. No, white Power would never forgive that. He switched to the red, rapping it with his knuckles, binding himself to its Power, and continued on his way.

A small collection of people waited around the guardian posts.

Today's Council wouldn't generate much in the way of excitement. The discussion of the palisade was the most important consideration, though Smoke Shield's attack on Two Beavers might rear its ugly head.

He touched his forehead in respect as he passed the guardians, and climbed the steps to nod at the hard-eyed guards. What lay behind their worried stares? Some presentiment that boded him ill?

He touched his forehead as he passed the lines of clan totems and sighed, stopping just short of the doorway. Were there a way, he'd be rid of this whole business. He was tired of being high minko, tired of Smoke Shield and his schemes, tired of his entire life.

At the rasping sound of wings, he looked up, but found no great bird hovering above him in the sky.

Willing himself forward, he entered the hallway and stepped into the tchkofa. The fire, as always, was burning brightly. Since the storm, the boys who tended it had found no shortage of snapped wood to replenish the fuel stocks.

The chiefs sat in their respective places, though a crowd had gathered behind the Panther Clan. He walked to his stool behind the altar, aware of Smoke Shield's cunning glint. The man was smoldering, his anger apparent. But never had Flying Hawk seen his own murder behind those eyes.

Instinctively, he cast a glance at Wooden Cougar, who sat with Cleft Skull, the dent in the latter's head catching the light. Flying Hawk nodded, feeling curious sympathy for the clan chief and his worry about Two Beavers. There had been truth to the claim that if Smoke Shield had spent more time seeing to his domestic duties, none of this would have occurred. Two Poisons and Smells-His-Death stood at their places, looking slit-eyed at Smoke Shield.

For his part, the war chief stood stiffly, his muscular arms crossed; his unbending expression was for Flying Hawk alone.

Well, let the gaming pieces be cast. What I did, I did for the safety of the people. If that led Smoke Shield to kill him, so be it. Knowing his people, they would prepare his body with great ceremony and give his souls a proper start to the west. There, if he had the fortitude of Spirit, he would pass through the Seeing Hand as the great constellation set in the west. After that, he only had his murdered brother's souls to contend with.

He chuckled. After Smoke Shield, it would be a relief.

Flying Hawk clapped his hands, and Seven Dead stepped forward with a cup of black drink. Then, as was proper, the man tipped tobacco into the Eagle Pipe, careful not to touch the leaf. He tamped it with a wooden rod and lit the bowl from the fire.

Flying Hawk stepped forward, taking a drink of the hot, bitter tea, then puffing on the pipe. He exhaled the blue smoke and looked up at the morning light angling through the smoke hole. Then he considered his words. He could sense Power in the room, some brooding presence that demanded satisfaction.

"We send our earnest prayers to you, Breath Giver, and pray that you will bless us with sunshine and rain. We ask you to send us the order and harmony of the white Power. Let it fill our hearts with peace in these trying times. From the red Power we beg courage, strength, and the creativity to solve the terrible problems we face. Today, here, I ask you to grant us wisdom and health."

Grunts of assent came from the chiefs. Smoke Shield, he couldn't help but notice, remained silent.

Flying Hawk took a moment, wondering if this would be the last time he addressed the Council as high minko. One by one, he looked at the chiefs, even nodding to Amber Bead where he stood in the back. The old man behind Seven Dead was unfamiliar. And to his surprise, Heron Wing stood behind Pale Cat and Night Star. Another stranger stood obscured by the shadows in the rear.

Seven Dead and Blood Skull were watching him with a curious intensity. He glanced back at Smoke Shield, could see his barely contained rage. Was this more than just the problem of the palisade?

"Today," Flying Hawk began, "we must address the situation of the palisade. Our good councilor, Amber Bead—"

"I think there is something more pressing," Smoke Shield interrupted, stepping forward.

Flying Hawk sighed, turning his weary gaze to his nephew. "Yes, War Chief? What is it?"

Smoke Shield ground his teeth. "May I have the floor?"

"You may."

Smoke Shield stepped forward, lifted the large shell cup, and drank of the black drink. Then he bent, taking a pull from the pipe and blowing smoke toward the opening. He raised his head to the sunlight. "Breath Giver, hear my words and know they are true. I have come to address this Council, my heart weeping."

He turned, staring at each chief in turn. "I have come to speak of treachery!"

Flying Hawk shook his head. "There is no treachery. I ordered the warriors to move in your name. I could not—"

"What?" Smoke Shield cried in amazement. "You did *what!*"

Flying Hawk spread his arms. "It is not treachery to order our warriors north to intercept the Yuchi."

Smoke Shield gave him a look of utter disbelief. "Great Cougar comes from the *west* Our palisade is down, and you have ordered the warriors to the *north?*"

Flying Hawk explained, "The war chief has been under some distress. His—"

Smoke Shield stomped up to glare into his face. *"You* are Green Snake's agent! You are the one setting us up for betrayal! And now you have ordered the warriors away! Great Cougar could be here at any moment!"

"This is a fantasy, War Chief. Told to you by your witch. Only you believe that Great Cougar is making some impossible strike at Split Sky City."

Smoke Shield's muscles were knotted, his mouth working. "Old man, you may have killed us all!"

Flying Hawk heard the gasp from the chiefs.

"You see," Wooden Cougar said just loud enough to be heard, "he has lost his wits."

"Enough!" Smoke Shield thundered, his finger lancing out at Wooden Cougar. "Power has sent me a Prophet. Here we sit, blaming each other, and all the while, Green Snake is working his evil to undermine us. I tell you, Great Cougar is coming, and I have no doubts that Green Snake is plotting with the Chahta, as well as the Yuchi. The coward seeks to destroy us so that *he* is declared high minko!"

Pale Cat stepped forward. "How do you know this, War Chief? Tell us what you have heard." He paused. "You do refer to your brother, don't you?"

"My brother is a Yuchi traitor!" Smoke Shield turned, narrowing his eyes. "As to the rest, I have my own sources of information."

Pale Cat nodded patiently. "Is that what the Yuchi messenger was coming to tell you under the white arrow? That Green Snake was returning to his people? Is that how you know?"

Smoke Shield's hard lips curled. "I said, I have my sources. And they come straight from Power."

Blood Skull then stepped forward. "If you knew Great Cougar was headed this way, why did you withdraw most of the scouts from the Horned Serpent River Divide?"

"They were becoming too fond of the Chahta. I told you that. You know that I was setting a trap for Great Cougar, and then you let this old...the high minko order them away? Are you plotting with Green Snake, too?"

It was Night Star who asked, "How do you know that Green Snake is plotting against us? From the rumors I've heard, all he did was Trade and play chunkey with the Yuchi."

"Trade and play chunkey?" Smoke Shield laughed, clapping a hand on his thigh. "He sent an assassin to murder our high minko! That must have been some Trade."

"Next you will be telling us that he murdered the White Arrow captives, and stole their war medicine out of the Men's House," Pale Cat said in an even voice.

"I wouldn't put it past him."

Seven Dead asked, "So, how did he do all this?"

Smoke Shield turned to Flying Hawk. "From right under our eyes. No one would notice the high minko in the Men's House. He could have walked right out the door, the White Arrow war medicine in his hands." His smile was a frightening thing. "Is that it, Uncle? Did you fear me so much that you had to call my cowardly brother back? Don't you remember how he left?

He didn't even have the courage to kill that Yuchi captive, and now he marches with them."

Flying Hawk raised his hands in despair. "You think I took the Chahta war medicine? I did no such thing. I know nothing more about Green Snake than what the Yuchi told us."

Smoke Shield's expression changed from rage to amazement that Flying Hawk would bring up the Yuchi messenger. "You go too far, Uncle! Do not change the facts. Next you will blame the Yuchi's murder on me, when all I did was save you from Green Snake's assassin!"

A strident voice called out, "There was no assassin! You have *lied* all of your life, and it stops now."

Flying Hawk turned to see the man behind Heron Wing emerge

from the shadows. He blinked as the stranger stepped past Pale Cat and into the circle before the fire. Smoke Shield gaped, as if in disbelief.

"Breath Giver take me," Flying Hawk whispered as recognition dawned. The man—so different, so much older than the boy he had known—could be no other than Green Snake himself!

Green Snake met Flying Hawk's incredulous gaze, asking, "Might your nephew address this Council, High Minko?"

Flying Hawk hesitated, confused. He took a breath to deny Green Snake's request.

"You may not!" Smoke Shield bellowed. "Warriors! Seize this traitor!"

As Smoke Shield started forward, Flying Hawk placed a hand on his shoulder. *By the gods, I am in charge here!* "He will speak, War Chief." And in a louder voice, "Or are you declaring yourself high minko without the Council's confirmation?"

Flying Hawk felt the building anger, the boiling hatred seething in Smoke Shield's body. *Yes, do it. Attack him here, and finish my problems once and for all.*

But Smoke Shield, sensing the danger, stepped back.

Through it all, Green Snake had stood, hands on his hips. His hard eyes had burned into Smoke Shield's, daring him to attack. He hadn't flinched; not even the slightest flicker of fear had betrayed itself.

Flying Hawk took a good look at him, seeing the corded muscle in his shoulders and arms. He wore a Chief Clan copper headpiece, and though the tattoos remained unfinished, this was a man to be reckoned with.

"You may take the drink, Green Snake." He indicated the pipe and cup.

With great dignity, Green Snake lifted the black drink, offered it to the sky, and drank. Then he bent, taking a long draw from the Eagle Pipe. When he stood and blew the smoke upward, he called out in a clear voice, "Breath Giver, Power has sent me here. It called me from the north, and I have followed its call. I have come to speak the truth, and make restitution to my clan for the attack on my brother. I have come to bring Power back into balance."

He turned, meeting the chiefs' eyes one by one. Finally, he nodded to Flying Hawk. "Many of you don't know me. I am Green Snake

Mankiller, son of Clear Crow, who was daughter of Midnight Woman. I am of the Chief Clan of the Hickory Moiety. It has been more than ten winters now since I lost my temper and struck down my brother."

He turned, pacing, talking to each of the chiefs in order. "I was in a rage, not even having finished my initiation into the Men's House. I struck my brother down. Gave him that scar you see on the side of his face." He paused. "And I hated myself for that. In shame, I left. For more than ten winters, I have traveled the rivers under the Power of Trade. All that time I lived with the terrible knowledge that I had killed my brother. But when Power thought I had been punished enough, it called me to return. Now, I find him alive."

"You should have stayed far away, coward," Smoke Shield hissed.

Green Snake ignored it. "So, now I have returned." He glanced at Smoke Shield. "But apparently not at the head of a Yuchi army. And, I assure you, I have not come back to step in and have myself declared high minko should my uncle pass."

"Then why are you here?" Smoke Shield demanded.

"To make restitution. As I have said. And to balance Power."

"You?" Smoke Shield cried in amazement. "You who couldn't even kill a Yuchi prisoner?"

Green Snake's eyes narrowed. "Why don't you tell them the truth, Brother? Or do you want me to tell the Kala Hi'ki's story? Do you want to explain how you came to the Men's House that night? How you told me you had coupled with the woman I wished to marry? How you said that she had been lying with other men down by the river? Do you want to tell the chiefs all the things you did to drive me into such a rage that I gave you that scar?"

"If you are so brave, why didn't *you* stay and tell them, then?"

The corner of Green Snake's lip twitched. "Because the most terrible part of that night was that I had acted just like you, Rattle."

Smoke Shield rocked on his toes. Flying Hawk recognized that stance: Smoke Shield struggled to keep himself from lunging at Green Snake.

"Now, I wonder," Smoke Shield said, finding his control. "Who really did kill the White Arrow prisoners?"

"I thought you said it was the Albaamaha?" Green Snake countered. "That's why you went after Red Awl."

Smoke Shield threw his head back, and laughter rolled from his throat. "So, you've heard those lies, too?"

Green Snake turned. "High Minko, on behalf of Panther and Raccoon Clans, we ask that the woman known as Lotus Root be allowed to address this Council. She was witness to the actions of the war chief in that hut above Clay Bank Crossing. She escaped, carrying off the war chiefs bow and arrows. Later, the Albaamaha discovered a warrior named Fast Legs stalking her. She was witness when Sky Hand warriors—dressed as Chahta— murdered twenty-three Albaamaha men, women, and children."

Flying Hawk gaped. "How do *you* know this?"

"She was hidden in the forest when the supposed Chahta chopped the bodies apart. She watched the war chief's men bury the scalps beside the hut where they were holding Fast Legs. She is just outside. She possesses the war chief's bow, the bag of scalps, and the bones of her murdered husband. Hear her story, High Minko."

Grunts of assent came from Raccoon and Panther Clans.

"I will *not!*" Flying Hawk snapped.

Green Snake nodded. "If that is the high minko's wish." He looked around at the stunned chiefs, at Amber Bead in the back, who now, for the first time, smiled and nodded.

"That was Smoke Shield's plan," Green Snake said. "His way of covering both his crimes, and his—"

"*Enough!*" Flying Hawk growled, stepping forward. "You are dismissed."

Green Snake inclined his head. "As my high minko wishes. But it is too late. The truth is set free. Lotus Root waits outside, ready to show anyone the evidence. However, before I leave, I have restitution to make." He turned. "*Hopaye?*"

Fuming, desperately aware of how close he had just come to disaster, Flying Hawk couldn't help but feel a rising curiosity as the *Hopaye* struggled forward, bearing a heavy fabric-wrapped pack. This, Green Snake helped him place before the fire.

All eyes were on the oblong shape.

"Uncle," Green Snake said. "Power sent me here. I only begin to know the ways and means of it, but I offer this to my people in restitution for my actions the night I struck down my brother."

He bent, lifting one side and slipping the fabric from a carved wooden box. When he stood clear, the thing lay bathed in the firelight. As if on cue, the shaft of sunlight caught the edge of the wood, shooting its rays across the Sky Hand design with its inlaid pearls, shell, and copper.

"What is that?" Smoke Shield asked sourly. He'd been watching Green Snake like a hunting cougar. Death lay behind his eyes, curled and prepared to spring. Flying Hawk chuckled to himself. No matter what, Green Snake was now a walking corpse.

"The Sky Hand war medicine," Green Snake said. "The medicine High Minko Makes War carried when he was captured by the Yuchi. Power has seen fit to return it to our people."

"And you would consider this restitution?" Flying Hawk asked. "Leave it. And be gone from this place by nightfall."

"What?" Green Snake stared, disbelieving.

Flying Hawk looked around. "This should be clan business, but all may hear. You have been gone, Green Snake, fled because of cowardice. Perhaps it was fitting. You have just said that you meant to kill your brother. But for Power, he would have died. No, I think there was a reason you were made to leave us. As clan leader, I order you to leave our lands. Go back to your Yuchi friends. Work your poison elsewhere."

"After bringing you the Sky Hand war medicine, you would order me away?" Green Snake asked.

"By my authority as clan elder, I order you banished, Nephew. If you do not go, warriors will take you to the borders. And this time make sure you never return."

A sad smile hovered at the corners of Green Snake's lips. "That is your final word?"

"As leader of the Chief Clan, it is." He turned. "War Chief, escort this man to the canoe landing."

"You will *not* touch him!" a vibrant voice called.

———

Old White stepped forward, fixing Smoke Shield with hard eyes. "You are an abomination." He turned his attention to Flying Hawk. "And you, High Minko, are a disappointment."

"Beware, old man." Smoke Shield smiled in anticipation as Old White stopped before him.

"Wipe that smirk off your face." He glared at him.

Flying Hawk said, "You, whoever you are, have no right to speak here. War Chief, remove this irritation from my Council."

Old White grinned as Smoke Shield stepped forward. "I wouldn't do that, Grape. You are already Dancing on the thin edge of Power. There are grave consequences when you ignore your debt to the man who once saved your life. But then, you are already complicit in killing a man under protection of the white arrow. What would you care about a blood debt, when you agreed to the murder of innocent Albaamaha?"

Flying Hawk raised a hand, stopping Smoke Shield. "I don't know you. And, trust me, I'd remember any man who saved my life."

Old White turned, pacing out toward the black drink and the Eagle Pipe. He looked back. "I will drink and smoke, as is my right."

Smoke Shield started forward, only to have Green Snake step in his way. The two men locked gazes, violence literally crackling between them. Then Flying Hawk pulled his nephew back. The room was as quiet as a log tomb. Better to let this madness play out, then pick apart the lies.

Old White lifted the cup and took a deep swig of the bitter tea. Then he bent, pulling on the Eagle Pipe. He straightened, blowing smoke into the shaft of sunlight that now gleamed full on the medicine box.

"Breath Giver, I have heard your call. From the *Katsina's* message, until now, I have followed the path you laid out for me. I will now tell the tale I have had locked in my souls for fifty hard summers and winters."

He turned, facing the Council. *"Makatok!* It all began when Makes War, high minko of the Sky Hand, went north to war with the Yuchi. I was but a little boy when he marched out at the head of a line of warriors." He pointed. "That war medicine was carried on his back. Days passed, but no word of the war party was heard. And then several of our bloody and wounded warriors returned telling of a terrible Yuchi ambush. Our high minko, and the war medicine, were lost."

He shot a glance at Flying Hawk. "Midnight Woman blamed herself for the disaster. You see, she had teased her husband, goaded him to war with the Yuchi when there was nothing to be gained from it. When news came that he had died hanging in a Yuchi square… something changed inside her. She became different, as if her souls had withdrawn and hidden deep inside her. Not even her young son could coax a smile from her.

"As one of the leaders of the Chief Clan, it was mandatory that she remarry. In seeking a husband to replace the man she loved, she chose Bear Tooth. Not because she loved him, but because he was a cunning warrior. And in those next few years, Bear Tooth made a new war medicine. His raids drove the Yuchi back from the central Tenasee Valley. By him, Midnight Woman had two sons, twins. Grape here, and Acorn."

"We know all this," Flying Hawk complained.

"And you know about the night of the fire, too, don't you?" Old White turned. "Do you remember how Bear Tooth used to fly into fits of rage?"

"Of course. He terrified us. Why Mother ever put up with it is beyond my understanding."

"She did it because every time he beat her, she was punishing herself for her role in Makes War's death. Don't you understand? She *loved* that man, and blamed herself for his death."

"Death is part of war."

"Oh, to be sure." Old White nodded. "But love has a Power all its own. Midnight Woman accepted Bear Tooth's abuse because she believed deep down in her souls that she deserved it."

"This is an old, old story. Who are you?"

"I am Old White, the man they call the Seeker. I have traveled from one end of our world to the other. Some say I'm a legend." He could see a sharpening of interest among the chiefs. "But that distracts me from my story. The night of the great fire, a terrible wind was blowing—one even more fierce than the one that savaged this city at equinox. But in the palace, a greater storm was brewing. That night, Bear Tooth was enraged. Midnight Woman had told him that even she had finally had enough. She was moving her belongings to her sister's. That would be Rose Bloom, wife of Tishu Minko Fighting Hawk, of the Raccoon Clan."

He grinned at Flying Hawk's growing skepticism. "Bear Tooth couldn't stand the thought of it. The humiliation was too much for him. He'd known from the beginning that she was in love with a dead man—that every time he lay with her, she made love to Makes War's ghost. That night the full wrath of his anger broke free."

Old White looked down at the medicine box. "He beat her something fierce. Then he ripped the clothes from her body and took her on the matting. He slapped her, struck her, and finally choked the very air out of her lungs. That's when Hickory stepped into the room. He could no longer stand seeing his mother treated that way." He glanced at Flying Hawk. "Just after that he went to send you and Acorn away."

"How do you know all this?" Flying Hawk asked. "Did you piece this all together from bits and pieces? Is this something you learned among the Traders?"

Smoke Shield pointed with a finger. "I've heard enough. The high minko has *ordered* you and this coward to leave Sky Hand country."

"He can't," Old White said reasonably. "He has no authority over me."

"You are sadly mistaken, Seeker," Flying Hawk declared, a slow anger brewing behind the twitching muscles in his face. "If—of course —you're really the man of legend."

"Oh, I am indeed." Old White paused, staring into Flying Hawk's eyes. "But before that, I was known as Hickory, son of Midnight Woman of the Chief Clan. I was the one who went to your room that night, Grape. Don't you remember when I pulled back the hanging and told you to run to Kosi Fighting Hawk's?"

"Hickory is dead!" Flying Hawk gritted in a strangled voice.

"Did you find his body?" Old White asked calmly.

"There were bones everywhere! War trophies. Who could tell whose bones were whose?"

"You have no proof of any of this!" Smoke Shield bellowed as he paced belligerently back and forth.

Old White shook his head. "Such a sorry state of affairs you've led our people to." His hand slipped into the heavy fabric sack hanging at his side. "You don't even honor the return of your Ancestors' war medicine. For that alone Power will condemn you." From the sack, he withdrew a beautifully polished stone war club. It was a ceremonial piece, carved from solid rock; the handle was engraved with winged serpents; the Seeing Hand had been rendered on both sides of the monolith's blade. "Wasn't this missing from the burned wreckage, Grape?"

Flying Hawk's face took on a look of awe. "Bear Tooth's war ax! Gods, how did you get it?"

"I picked it up from where it stood propped on its special tripod beside the hearth." Old White tightened his grip on its stone handle. "And I walked back, stepped into their room, and *drove this blade into the back of Bear Tooth's accursed head!*"

Old White took a breath. The heavy ax shook in his grip. Slowly, he lowered it. "That is why you cannot order Green Snake from Sky Hand lands. You are not clan elder, Grape. *I am!*"

THIRTY

TRADER STOOD DUMBFOUNDED. Gods, even he had trouble believing it.

He saw Flying Hawk's awe turn to disbelief. The man staggered backward, propping himself on the tripod. His eyes fixed on the polished black stone ax. "He would have killed you for touching that."

"He would have killed us all," Old White said softly. "Once I made sure you and Acorn were safely out of the building, I went back. I pulled his body off of Mother's. He'd bled all over her. I started to drag her, trying to move her to somewhere where I could sponge the blood from her dead face. Then she coughed. She blinked, and I propped her up against one of the beds."

Old White sadly shook his head. "The blood was everywhere, and she touched it, looking first at the red smears on her fingers and then at Bear Tooth. She stared at me as if I were some incomprehensible being, like something out of her Dreams. I was told to go and find warm water, fetch some cloths."

Old White stared thoughtfully at the ax. "When I came back, she'd poured hickory oil all over herself. Then she reached down, picked up another of the jars, and..."

"What did she do, Seeker?" Green Snake prompted in the silence.

The old man looked at him. "She smashed it in the fire, Trader.

And the flames...The flames ..." He closed his eyes, the weight of the stone ax pulling at his slumping shoulders.

"We are to believe this?" Smoke Shield asked.

"That's when the Power began to change," Green Snake said, realization dawning. "That's why we were called back. So that the Seeker...Hickory, could tell the tale. It's time to heal the wounds, to call ourselves back into harmony with Power."

"And how will you do that?" Smoke Shield kicked out at the war medicine shining in the sunlight. "With an old box?"

"It's too late, Rattle," Green Snake told his brother. "The truth is free...no matter what you do to us. You are exposed, destroyed. You will never be high minko now."

Smoke Shield laughed. "How wrong you are! The Prophet has told me—"

Smoke Shield never finished. At that moment, a man hastened through the entry, calling, "My chief!" He was young, wearing a brown hunting shirt. He raced along the back wall, whispering to Wooden Cougar. The Crawfish Clan chief listened, shock expressed on his face. Then he stood. In a hoarse voice, he stated, "Two Beavers is dead."

A rustle of fabric was accompanied by the dark looks shot between the clan chiefs.

"Murder," Two Poisons said, turning eyes on Smoke Shield.

Wooden Cougar pointed at Smoke Shield. "Either restitution must be made, or the same punishment must be meted. Those are the laws of our people. To do otherwise is to invoke blood feud between our clans!"

"The man was with my wife!" Smoke Shield bellowed. "He was *in her bed!*"

"Smoke Shield is right! There are extenuating circumstances," Flying Hawk snapped, but his heart didn't seem to be in it as he kept staring wide-eyed at the Seeker.

Green Snake shook his head, seeing the way it would go. If something wasn't done, the Council was going to tear itself apart. Even now, Flying Hawk still insisted on defending Smoke Shield? It was lunacy!

Then Green Snake heard it: clear, as though disconnected from the growing din in the tchkofa. The Song was so sweet—just as it had been when he was a child. He glanced down at the medicine box, hearing what Two Petals must have that night in the Kaskinampo camp.

"I will offer restitution for my brother!" Green Snake shouted over the din. He reached down, unfastening the straps. "But it will come with conditions."

"What conditions?" the fuming Wooden Cougar asked.

Green Snake ran his fingers along the wood, feeling the Power. It began to swell, running from the box through his fingers, hands, and arms. "The war medicine is returned to our people. That part of the Power is restored. But it deserves the care of those who would respect it. Not some war chief who calls it an old box and kicks at it with his toe. Not a war chief who kills an Albaamo councilor, rapes his wife, and then murders innocent people while dressed as a Chaktaw. The war medicine is for a people who do not murder messengers bearing the white arrow!"

Wooden Cougar raised a fist. "Then what do you offer, Green Snake?"

"This!" He flipped the lid back, lifting the edge of the box. He was watching Smoke Shield's eyes as the heavy copper thumped onto the floor.

Gasps came from around the room. The sunlight shot brilliant beams of copper-colored light that filled the tchkofa. It shone on the faces of the chiefs as they moved closer.

Wonder grew in Smoke Shield's eyes. His mouth dropped open, arms spreading, as if to take in the copper's reflected brilliance.

Green Snake cried, "I offer copper in restitution for my brother's murder of the man Two Beavers. I do this with the condition that he leaves this land, that he divorces the Panther Clan woman known as Heron Wing." He turned hard eyes on Smoke Shield. "And when you leave, you will *never* come back."

"By Breath Maker, it's beautiful!" Smoke Shield whispered as he bent down, running his fingers over the copper. "It's just as she said."

"Where is the Contrary?" Green Snake asked.

"By the river, waiting." Smoke Shield gestured off toward the canoe landing, only vaguely aware of the chiefs who had come to crowd around. "...For this."

"That is your life, Brother. What's it worth? Heron Wing?"

"Take her!"

"The murder of the Yuchi messenger?"

"What does it matter? He was just a Yuchi."

"He was under the protection of the white arrow!"

"My Power is *red*, you fool! And with this, it's complete!" Smoke Shield bent, lifting the heavy piece. "You said it's mine to give?"

Green Snake nodded, his heart beginning to pound. "I offered it for your life."

"With this, I shall become *greater* than the lords of Cahokia!" Smoke Shield turned and bolted for the door. Lowering his shoulders, he knocked Blood Skull and Seven Dead out of the way. In a flash, he was outside.

"Smoke Shield, wait!" Flying Hawk called hoarsely. Tears had filled the old man's eyes, streaking down his cheeks. "Take that, *and you condemn both of us!*"

"That was offered to us!" Wooden Cougar stepped forward, his fist shaking in threat.

Old White leaned close. "Trader, we'd best follow. If the Contrary's in the middle of this, she may need us."

————

The surface of the river looked glassy and smooth in the morning light. It reflected a golden sheen as sunlight sent fingers down into the water. Two Petals sat in the bow of the small dugout she'd chosen. Dragging it down to the shore had been a trial, but she'd managed. Now she waited, her back cupped in the concave hollow where the bow had been scooped out. She ignored the curious stares of the Traders where they sat by their ramadas. The women who walked down to dip ceramic and gourd jars into the water shot curious glances her way. Two fishermen were carefully stowing their trotline, ensuring that the bone hooks, rope, and wooden floats didn't tangle.

She closed her eyes, drawing in the scents of the landing. Time was slowing around her. As it did, her heart beat with relief.

Then—ever so faintly—she heard the first faint strains of Singing. It rose from the water around her. She smiled at the growing strength of the Song. "My husband comes."

A voice near her said, *"He will make you a good match."*

She opened her eyes to see Deer Man. He stood with his hoofed feet merged in the wood of a nearby canoe. Sunlight glistened on the antlers growing out of his head. A smile lit his face, and he had thrown back his deer-hide cape. "I want to thank you for your help coming to this place," she said.

"*I shall visit you,*" Deer Man promised.

"My husband and I will welcome you. Together, we shall Sing and Dance."

Some of the nearer women backed away, staring at the empty canoe where Deer Man stood on his thin legs.

The Song was growing louder now, rising and falling. Deer Man began Dancing, his body weaving with the melody. Two Petals sighed, a thrill shooting through her body. She could feel time beginning to drift away, slowing. It was as if she could see the self of her past merging with that of her coming present: two shadowy images slowly slipping into one.

Overhead, a marvelous crow spiraled out of the sun's light. Brilliant colors of red, blue, yellow, green, and violet reflected from his iridescent feathers. She watched the bird soar in ever-decreasing circles. "Have you come to watch as well?"

"*It isn't every day that a marriage such as this takes place,*" Many Colored Crow cried with a laugh.

The women, she noticed, hurried away with their water jars, casting worried glances over their shoulders. The fishermen had stopped, staring wide-eyed. They tossed the rest of their trotline and bait into the canoe and pushed off. Paddles flashed in the sunlight as they left. Within moments, the shoreline was empty.

"They don't understand," she told Many Colored Crow.

Whippoorwill walked down the slope past the Traders. They didn't see the great black Spirit wolf that walked by her side, his yellow eyes gleaming. Two Petals smiled as Whippoorwill came to a stop behind the canoe. The Albaamo woman wore a plain white dress, her dark eyes meeting Two Petals'. Her fingers traced patterns over the wolf's back. "Once again, we cross in time, Sister."

Two Petals said, "My friends will need your counsel in the coming years."

"*I will Dance for you...always,*" Whippoorwill said through the Dream.

Two Petals lowered her gaze to Whippoorwill's belly. "He will grow up to be a great mikko for your people."

"*He will lead them into the future.*" She glanced up the slope. "*They come.*"

Two Petals followed her gaze. Smoke Shield appeared, the muscles of his legs flexing as he came trotting down the beaten trail. The heavy copper plate shot beams of light this way and that. The Traders above the landing stopped short, gaping. Many rose to their feet as Smoke Shield passed.

Two Petals heard the calls of dismay and let the words pass through her. Time continued to slow, her two selves drifting ever closer.

"Are you prepared, my husband?"

"*Yes.*" His Song grew, echoed by the river, picked up by the shore and the trees. Deer Man stamped his feet, heedless of the wooden canoe he Danced through.

Two Petals closed her eyes, her souls following Smoke Shield's approach. At the top of the landing, Trader and Old White hurried into view at the head of a group of chiefs. And behind them, she knew, came a growing crowd.

"*They come to witness,*" her husband Sang in his melodious voice.

"The offering is almost here."

"I *know.*"

Eyes closed, she watched Smoke Shield pant his way toward her. The man's chest was rising and falling, his eyes agleam with excitement. Oblivious, he stopped at the canoe's stern, stating, "I brought the copper!"

"Then your choice is made. Come, push us out into the river."

"To make the offering?"

"I have told you the price."

He carefully lowered the heavy copper into the canoe before pushing them out into the current. The small craft lurched as he jumped into the stern. Onshore, Deer Man was leaping, bending, his antlers flashing this way and that. Many Colored Crow circled close, his feathers rasping in the air. Her husband's Song permeated water, wood, and rang from the copper.

"Can you hear it?" she asked.

"Hear what?" Smoke Shield asked.

"The Song. It's so beautiful."

"I hear nothing."

"Oh, you will. In just a moment. I am coming into myself. Time is coming together."

"What are you talking about?" he asked irritably.

"The future. I will finally know it."

She opened her eyes, hearing Trader's voice from shore. He was calling for her, desperate for her safety. Poor Trader. She thought back, remembering his panic the night she had led Old White to his hidden camp. She smiled at the recollection of his interest as he watched her body, and then shared the Dream of their coupling. He had prepared her, taught her the arts she needed to bind Smoke Shield to her.

She smiled across the water at Old White, seeing the desperation in his eyes. She cupped her hands around her mouth. "When you are ready, Seeker, we shall come!"

"What? Two Petals! Stop this nonsense!" He was gesturing frantically for her to return.

Thank you, for all that you have done. She touched her breast as if to imprint the memory of him on her souls.

The Song was almost deafening now, her souls swaying as it filled the air around her.

"It is time." She laughed in reply to Smoke Shield's anxious questions. She stood carefully, balancing in the canoe.

"What are you doing?" he cried, hands gripping the gunwales in an effort to stabilize them.

In that one wondrous moment, the world stopped. She felt her past and future become now. Her souls merged. *I am whole! I am the One!*

She raised her arms, letting the warm sun bathe her. Laughter came bubbling up from within. Around her the world began to swell and recede, pulsing with the Song. She became it.

Her gaze fixed on Old White's. "Seeker? Time has stopped!"

And then, looking down past the canoe, she could see *him*. Sunlight shot down into the water, outlining his membranous wings. The colors of the rainbow reflected from his body as it rose beneath the canoe. She hadn't expected him to be so huge. And there, in the reflection of the sun, she could see his great crystalline eye, glinting up at her from beneath the surface.

"I am ready, my husband."

Smoke Shield was saying something, his words lost, drowned by the Song.

"Come," her husband said.

———

Old White gasped his way to the shore and placed his hand on Trader's shoulder. Behind them, the chiefs stopped short, staring. Diminutive Night Star rode in Blood Skull's muscular arms. The warrior lowered her to the ground as they all lined out on the bank. Each was panting from the run, staring in disbelief at Smoke Shield and Two Petals where they floated in the calm waters.

"What are they doing?" Pale Cat asked. "Who is that woman?"

"The Contrary, Two Petals," Trader said grimly. Then he cupped his hands. "Two Petals? Are you all right?"

Her words carried across the water. "When you are ready, Seeker, we shall come!"

Old White shouted, "What? Two Petals! Stop this nonsense!"

"That copper is ours!" Wooden Cougar bellowed. "Ours, Smoke Shield. Bring it back!"

Old White shook his head. "I think it belongs to Power."

"I'm taking a canoe," Trader said. "This has to stop."

"No." Old White laid a hand on his arm. "Trust to Power."

"Seeker you can't—" Trader stopped short, eyes on the bobbing canoe.

Two Petals rose to her feet, balancing on the slender canoe gunwales. She raised her head to the sunlight, lifting her arms. Then she looked down at the water, seeming to ignore Smoke Shield's barked questions.

"Two Petals," Trader cried. "Sit down! You'll tip over!"

She met his eyes across the water, calling, "Seeker? Time has stopped!"

He drew a breath to call to her, and blinked in disbelief.

In an instant the canoe's stern sank like a rock, spilling Smoke Shield into the river. The bow rose to point straight up into the sky. Two Petals dove, her hands spearing as her slim body arrowed neatly into the water.

Sunlight flashed on copper, the beam of it almost blinding. Then the boat was sucked down in a swirl.

Smoke Shield screamed, splashing about in the chop, staring this way and that. He bellowed, "No! No! Power is mine!" Then, as he turned toward shore, a terrible shriek tore from his throat. His body lifted on a fountain of foaming water, hung for an instant, and as

Smoke Shield uttered one last scream, he was dragged under.

Old White stared in disbelief.

Something sleek rose in a giant ring, water slipping smoothly from its curved surface. Rainbow colors reflected briefly, and then it was gone, waves splashing as they rose and fell.

"Two Petals!" Trader screamed, charging forward and diving into the river.

"Come back!" Old White shouted.

He stood helplessly, heart hammering, aware that the growing crowd behind him was deathly silent. Time had indeed stopped. The only movement was Trader as he stroked furiously toward the still-swirling water. Then he dove.

"Gods, no!" Heron Wing reached for Old White's hand, her grip crushing his bones.

"What just happened here?" Pale Cat asked.

"I don't know," Old White told him. "But the Kala Hi'ki told us a Horned Serpent lives beneath Split Sky City."

"Horned Serpent!" Blood Skull repeated in awe. Whispers of "Horned Serpent" went from lip to lip as the people stared.

The canoe shot out of the water like a leaping fish, the bow rising high. It seemed to freeze for a moment, hanging. Slowly tilting, it gained speed, and crashed down on its keel. White spray accompanied the loud slap of wood on water. The canoe bobbed there, swamped.

"Gods," Old White whispered.

He stood transfixed, waiting. Was it an eternity or a matter of heartbeats before Trader's head popped up, and he flipped water from his face? Trader gasped for breath, searching this way and that. Then he stroked over to the canoe, grasping its gunwale.

"Someone"—Blood Skull turned—"come with me while I paddle out there and bring Green Snake and the canoe back."

Old White released Heron Wing's hand as she hurried to find a place in the canoe Seven Dead and Blood Skull launched.

His feet rooted to the shore, Old White shivered, his souls in turmoil. Two Petals could not have held her breath this long. *Gods, she is gone!*

He turned, grief tugging at the bottom of his heart. As he pushed through the crowd, images of the Contrary filled his souls. He remembered that first moment she'd been carried out like a deer, bound to a pole, her mouth gagged. Again he saw her naked that day in Cahokia, watched her lean forward to blow the souls from Black Tooth's body. She laughed inside him, enchanting his memory.

"She now Sings with her husband," a soft Albaamo voice said from the side. "She has found peace and joy."

He turned to see Whippoorwill, her dark eyes shining. She placed a slim hand on his shoulder, saying, "The Kala Hi'ki saw it all. It is finished—justice is done. He will tell Born-of-Sun."

"What was that? Horned Serpent?"

She gave him a wistful smile. "What did *you* see, Seeker?" And then she turned, walking up the slope. Was it his imagination, or did the shadow of a huge wolf accompany her?

Old White sighed. Gods, he was tired.

Glancing back, he saw that Trader had been pulled into Blood Skull's canoe. They were towing the swamped craft back to shore. Old White watched them land, saw Trader step out to drag Two Petals' boat onto the sand and tip it so the water ran out. Then Trader froze, frowning. Finally, he reached down into the hull. When he straightened, it was to hold two large crystals up to the sun. The light played through them, shooting beams in every direction.

Old White placed a hand over his heart. He'd seen the like before...in the Kala Hi'ki's empty eye sockets.

THIRTY-ONE

AS FLYING HAWK walked aimlessly toward his palace, a sense of loss and stunned dismay overwhelmed him. He rounded the head of the ravine that separated the high minko's grounds from Skunk Clan's. People rushed past—everyone headed toward the canoe landing, desperate to learn more about the startling events that had occurred there.

I *don't understand!*

He had followed anxiously behind the chiefs as they stormed after Smoke Shield. In their wake, he had heard their amazement, listened to Wooden Cougar's shouts demanding that Smoke Shield return the copper.

Flying Hawk had stopped at the crest of the slope, watched Smoke Shield paddle out with the witch, and seen the canoe pulled down by something large and shining in the depths. He had seen the flash of copper and watched Smoke Shield's body partially rise, heard that last hideous scream as he was dragged beneath the waves.

Horned Serpent! The witch must have called the creature up from the depths.

Why? The question consumed Flying Hawk as he stopped, looking back at the people flocking toward the landing. He blinked, shook his head, and resumed his weary pace. He walked like a man in a Dream —as if the events he had just witnessed were fantasies.

Could he really have seen Green Snake and Hickory in the tchkofa, or was that illusion? Had he watched a real piece of copper tipped out of the old war medicine box? Or a Dream creation: something resurrected from a restless nightmare and replayed among his reeling souls?

Smoke Shield! Gods, what happened to you?

Flying Hawk remembered his nephew's gleaming eyes, the awe on his face as the copper thumped onto the tchkofa floor and literally blazed in the sunlight. The instant his nephew had laid his hands on the copper, a pain stabbed deep through Flying Hawk's chest. Even now he could feel it aching like a splinter between his souls.

He was confused, overwhelmed by the bits of conversations, images of Green Snake, and, finally, Hickory—returned from the dead to brandish Bear Tooth's ceremonial war ax. He could still see it, sleek in the shaft of light shining through the tchkofa smoke hole.

Gods, how he remembered that ax!

Hickory lives!

After all those long hard winters, why had the man picked this moment to return? And how had he found Green Snake, let alone the long-vanished war medicine?

This is the work of Power, come to punish Smoke Shield for his abuses!

"And me. It has come to punish me." He stopped again, looking back, a sense of futility draining his energy. He walked on—a man bereft. His life had been looted clean of accomplishments, struggles, and sacrifices.

It was for nothing!

In that instant, he saw his brother's face. Acorn lay on that long-ago clearing, his bleeding head on the grass. But instead of the blood-smeared, sightless eyes, Acorn was staring at him. The slack mouth no longer gaped in a death rictus, but curled with a profound satisfaction. Laughter burst from Acorn's lungs, a fine spray of blood misting the air.

Flying Hawk clapped hands to his ears as he rounded the base of the great mound, walked to the high Sun Stairs, and began the long climb to the top. His knee burned and grated with each step.

Under his breath, he muttered, "One thing they cannot take from me: I am still the *high minko!*"

He winced at the pain in his knee, climbing resolutely. His breath began to labor, and he stopped, halfway up. Looking south, he could see the whole of Split Sky City. The plaza grass was greening, verdant in the sunlight. Smoke still rose from the tchkofa fire to trail away on the lazy air. The multitude of houses peppered the grounds, and beyond the southern chief mounds, he could see the long section of flattened palisade.

"Should have seen to that," he muttered to himself, remembering that somewhere out to the west—if the reports could be believed—a Chahta war party was closing on Split Sky City, a determined Great Cougar at its head.

He clamped his eyes shut, imagining his own war parties. He could visualize them, spread out, searching the forest trails to the north for a Yuchi war party that would never come.

How did I make such a mess of things?

Resuming his climb, he advanced a step at a time.

The stairs were uneven. Somehow, he'd forgotten to order the slaves to replace and reset them. So many things had occupied his thoughts—most of them grim premonitions of disaster at Smoke Shield's hands.

As he neared the top, he looked back at his city one last time. People still threaded their way toward the huge crowd at the landing. He couldn't see that from here; the bulk of the mound and palace blocked the view. It was better that way.

When he looked up, Flying Hawk started. A man was standing on the top step. He looked young and muscular, with shining black hair and dark glinting eyes. As their gazes met, Flying Hawk staggered; Power flashed between them.

The man smiled, flipping back a sleek cloak of midnight feathers. Sunlight seemed to beam from his flesh. Flying Hawk had to squint against it.

The man took one step down, his feet clad in snow-white moccasins, and his long hunting shirt might have been made of the finest tanned leather. A scarlet belt snugged his waist, and a war club hung there.

"Who...Who are you?" Flying Hawk rasped. But he knew: the Spirit Being from the night he'd seen the great Seeing Hand weep.

"I have gone by many names, High Minko. Once I was known as Raven Hunter, but that world is long lost. Among your people, I am the Blood Twin, the boy born of First Woman's menstrual blood as she bathed in the Sacred River just after the Creation. The red Power runs in my veins and is shed from my wings."

He lifted the arms beneath the raven cloak, only to spread large wings that seemed to suck the very light from the air.

"Gods!" Flying Hawk cried, raising an arm in defense.

"One of them, perhaps," Raven Hunter replied with amusement. "But do not be afraid. I have come to grant you your greatest wish."

While every bit of remaining sense told him to run, some odd attraction compelled him to climb those final steps. He stopped just below Raven Hunter. The pain in his knee had faded, and his breath returned, as fresh in his lungs as it had been in his youth.

"What do you want from me?"

"Nothing. Everything." Raven Hunter lowered his inky wings. "For most of your life you have served me.

But Power ebbs and flows." He looked out over the city, a faint smile on his lips. "I encouraged the growth of red Power among the Sky Hand. It began when Makes War went off to fight the Yuchi, and, well, you know the story." He chuckled. "But the white Power, too, will pass, and finally, Split Sky City will fade as Cahokia before it."

Flying Hawk lowered his eyes to the wooden steps. The next one had turned, shifting in the soil. He could see where rot had softened the wood. "Then, nothing is left for me."

"Nothing here," Raven Hunter agreed. "But I am curious: If I could grant you one wish, what would it be? What one thing would you change?"

Flying Hawk swallowed hard as he was flooded with memories. He saw again the great fire; the flight in the night to Kosi Fighting Hawk's; his youth; the murder of his brother; the first man he killed in war; his wife's death; confirmation as high minko; Smoke Shield's wound; the struggle for authority; and those final moments when Horned Serpent dragged his nephew below the waves.

Of all the mistakes, which one would he undo?

And then he knew. He stared down at his hand, seeing the angular rock, could feel its rough surface, gripped so tightly. The sunlight changed, grass beneath him, a dead buffalo hunched to his right, its sides bristling with deeply embedded arrows. His brother was staring up at him, horror reflected in his eyes.

Flying Hawk released the rock, letting it fall from his fingers.

The world seemed to swim, shimmering and wavering like heat waves above a great fire.

When the world came back into focus he was perched on the high step. Raven Hunter watched him with knowing eyes that sparked of midnight.

Flying Hawk blinked at the hot tears welling in his eyes. "I would see Acorn again. I would have him laugh, and place his arm over my shoulder as he did when we were young."

"I, too, know what it is to fight with a brother." Raven Hunter's voice was warm with understanding. He opened his great black wings in invitation. "Come. Acorn awaits you."

Flying Hawk placed his foot on the' rotted step, shifted, and felt it roll under his weight. Then Raven Hunter's wings closed around him, cloaking him in darkness. He felt himself falling....

I am free! The thought filled Heron Wing as she walked down the path at the head of the Sky Hand delegation. Beneath her feet, new grass was springing up. Green shoots rose in the Albaamaha fields, weeds mostly, but the fields lived under late-afternoon sun. A warm breeze was blowing up from the gulf, white puffy clouds marching before it. In the distance, the trees had softened where flowers and the first buds tipped the branches. The living forest contrasted with the forlorn farmsteads. She could only hope that one day soon, they would be full of men, women, and children—that life would return to normal.

She glanced to either side, seeing Seven Dead, Blood Skull, Green Snake, and Old White—or did she call him Hickory now? Just behind, Night Star was borne on a litter, and Vinegaroon—his alligator-hide cape gleaming on his shoulders—followed in his rolling gait.

Of those requested, only Flying Hawk was absent. His twisted body had been found at the foot of the Sun Stairs. From the looks of his broken bones and splotches

of blood here and there on the steps, he'd fallen the entire distance from a dislodged and rotten wooden step just below the summit. When they had lifted his battered corpse, a single, midnight-black raven feather had been found beneath him.

Everything is changed.

Flying Hawk was dead. Her souls stumbled over it all: the Council session; Green Snake and Old White; shouted accusations; the revelation of the medicine box; and then the wondrous copper.

And what, in the name of Breath Maker, happened at the canoe landing?

She shook her head, remembering the swirling of rainbow colors in the water, the canoe rising bow first into the sky, and the Contrary's graceful dive into the depths. Once she would have felt relief at Smoke Shield's death. Now, his last scream would haunt her.

One does not abuse Power.

Shifting the long leather sheath she carried, she glanced at her hand, rubbing the tips of her fingers where they'd traced the deep grooves in the canoe's stern. It was as if giant teeth had gouged out the hull. The gashes had been deep, exposing fresh wood. How did one explain that?

Heron Wing glanced at Green Snake. He'd remained oddly reticent about what he'd seen down there in the depths. When she asked, he'd smiled, a faint shake of the head his only answer.

As people began to slowly disperse, someone had run down calling that the high minko was dead. So they had gone, determined the cause of the accident, and watched Pale Cat supervise the removal of the body. She had found Stone in the company of Wide Leaf, and Swimmer had appeared to follow in Green Snake's footsteps.

In the confused aftermath, one of the scouts had charged into the city, crying, "The Chahta come! It's

Great Cougar at the head of a huge body of warriors! He sends a white arrow, asking that only certain people meet with him!"

The Chahta? Asking for her? On impulse, Heron Wing had made a quick trip up the bloodstained stairway to Smoke Shield's room. She now carried the thing she had taken, and could sense an eerie presence within the leather.

Gods, how brave you were.

Now she traveled to meet the enemy—herself, the requested chiefs, Green Snake, and Old White. Across the field she could see where Great Cougar and a few others waited less than a bow shot beyond a huge body of warriors.

Heron Wing glanced back. The river was still between them and Split Sky City. The few warriors left were scrambling to organize some sort of defense. They'd be no match for the force arrayed at the edge of the trees.

"Do we have any chance, War Chief?" she asked Blood Skull.

"Not against so many," he answered bitterly.

His promotion sat him well, she thought. But now, glancing at the massed Chahta ranks, she wondered how long he'd have to enjoy it. The other chiefs, so animated after the morning's events, now walked in cowed understanding of their desperate plight.

Beside her, Old White was smiling, one of his Trader's packs on his back. He carried his Trader's staff, the white feathers fluttering. The Seeker, at least, seemed completely at ease. To her right, Green Snake had a pensive look, as if his souls were still lost in the swirling waters of the Black Warrior River. Periodically, she could hear the click of the two crystals he carried in his hand. Ignored at his side, Swimmer coursed back and forth, nose to the ground, tail swishing.

Gods, will Stone be all right? If worse came to worst, Wide Leaf would ensure her son's safety—even if she had to disguise him as an Albaamo boy. Heron Wing glanced again at Green Snake.

I can marry you now. But the Chahta might have other ideas about that. To herself, she murmured, "I might like being Morning Dew's slave."

"She would treat you well," Old White said mildly. "But, let us see."

"You have another trick up your sleeve, Seeker?"

He grinned. "Always."

Great Cougar stood in front of four warriors, all with arrows nocked in their bows. A wicked-looking war club with copper blades filled his hands. He wore a gleaming copper gorget on his breast in addition to a breechcloth with a white apron, its point falling between his knees. The Chahta war chief had painted his face half in red, half in white. That, Heron Wing thought, might be prophetic: War or peace, the man could go either way. It would depend on his demands.

To her surprise, it was Old White who took a couple of quick steps to gain the lead, calling, "War Chief! Look at the sun shining on that gorget! It fits you proud."

"Hello, Seeker." Great Cougar smiled. "Imagine finding you here. Were the Albaamaha worth the Trade?"

"Oh, you'd be surprised!" Old White brazenly walked up to the man, smiling as if at an old friend. "Perhaps, when we bring this all to a conclusion, you would join me for a meal? I've been thinking about that shell cup you showed me. Obsessed by it, actually."

Great Cougar couldn't stifle his laughter. "Seeker, you amaze even me. We're here to talk war, not Trade."

"Ah, but they're the same, aren't they? Each is but a method of obtaining something. In Trade it is Power, or an object. In war there is honor, land, revenge. One is white, the other red."

Blood Skull glanced anxiously at Seven Dead. "Does he speak for us now?"

Old White waved him back. "Later, War Chief."

"Where is Smoke Shield?" Great Cougar asked.

"Dead." Old White made a dismissive gesture. "It seems that Power finally caught up with his scheming. It's a tale for later, and one that tops all of my feeble attempts."

"You asked for us, War Chief," Blood Skull interrupted. He stepped forward. "I am Blood Skull Mankiller, war chief of the Sky Hand. This is my brother, Seven Dead, our tishu minko. What do you wish to discuss?"

"Where is High Minko Flying Hawk?" Great Cougar asked.

Before Blood Skull could speak, Old White interjected. "It seems that he took a bad fall this morning and bounced down the length of the Sun Stairs. The man never did seem to keep his mind on repairs."

Blood Skull shot Old White an irritated look, saying, "The high minko's body is being prepared for burial. A runner has been sent requesting that Sun Falcon Mankiller, of the Chief Clan, travel to Split Sky City as soon as possible. The Council would like to discuss the possibility of him assuming the high minko's chair."

Great Cougar shot a measuring glance at Green Snake. "I have been told that you are Smoke Shield's brother. Wouldn't you be the new high minko?"

Green Snake stepped forward, his preoccupation with the morning fading. "Greetings, War Chief. I am a Trader. Not a high minko. But it will be my honor to offer advice to whomever the Council confirms." Then he smiled as if at an old friend. "It is good to see you again. I would compliment you: The charade at Feathered Serpent Town was brilliantly done. It would have worked, but Old Woman Fox was desperate to Trade for the return of her granddaughter."

Great Cougar narrowed an eye. "I shall have words with the woman."

"She did no harm, and served Power in her own way." Trader

waved in dismissal. "But I would take it as a personal favor if you would let her know that we shall be returning her Trade. We did not get the opportunity to use it as she requested."

"You would return it?" Great Cougar asked. "Even given who you really are?"

Green Snake nodded politely. "I am bound by the Power of Trade. You received the White Arrow war medicine?"

"Gods!" Blood Skull spat, face darkening. He looked murder at Green Snake.

Great Cougar couldn't mask a satisfied smile. "Trader, your actions on our behalf are worthy and appreciated. That is why we are talking now...instead of burning Split Sky City. Had Matron Morning Dew not insisted with such fierce determination—and threatened to walk off with half of my warriors—we would have charged across your flattened palisade at first light this morning."

Blood Skull and the others gasped.

"Then the great Morning Dew serves all of us well," Old White added. "But enough of blood and burning. Trader and I would like to offer restitution for the dead at White Arrow Town. As I understand it, Smoke Shield started this by acting like an arrogant fool last summer. If you will offer something to appease the dead at Alligator Town, we can make a satisfactory conclusion to the trouble between our people."

Heron Wing saw Seven Dead place a restraining hand on Blood Skull's arm when he started forward to protest. Behind her, the chiefs were whispering apprehensively.

"My warriors are hungry," Great Cougar stated bluntly. "We expected to find food in Split Sky City."

"That might be arranged," Seven Dead said, stepping forward. "But, perhaps we would feed you here...a bit farther from the walls?"

"What's left of them." Great Cougar seemed to steel himself. "Before we go any further, there is something else. The other reason I have decided to talk before destroying you."

Blood Skull continued to bristle.

"Easy, War Chief," Heron Wing whispered.

"And that is?" Seven Dead asked politely.

Great Cougar raised his arm, and the warriors parted behind him. Morning Dew stepped through their ranks. Heron Wing recognized the beautiful dress she wore. It was one of her favorites.

Morning Dew's hair was washed, combed, and gleaming in the sunlight. The dress emphasized her full breasts, narrow waist, and round hips as she strode up to stop beside Great Cougar. She looked Heron Wing straight in the eye, nodded, and said, "Good day, Matron."

"I am not a matron."

"That is the Chikosi's great loss."

"I shall miss you, Morning Dew."

The woman smiled, then looked down at the long object in Heron Wing's hands. Her eyes widened, one hand rising to the decorated quill work at her breast as if to still a suddenly pounding heart.

Heron Wing stepped to her, offering the long stone sword she'd taken from under Smoke Shield's bed. "The man who owned this is dead. I have brought it to you. It is my gift, along with the freedom that I promised." She smiled ironically. "Though it seems that you obtained it in a different manner than I had planned."

"I can't take that." Morning Dew stepped back a pace.

"It became yours the night you killed the Chahta captives."

Whispers broke out. Blood Skull began cursing under his breath.

Morning Dew swallowed hard, looking down at her hands. "How...How did you know?"

"For a long time I didn't. Then I remembered the blood on your hands the day Thin Branch brought you to me...and how frantically you scrubbed to remove it. It was more than a bloody nose would merit. You didn't mourn for your husband and brother—though I know you loved them with all of your heart. Then I understood: You made your peace with them the night you set their souls free, didn't you?" Heron Wing dropped to her knees, extending the stone sword. "Only the bravest woman alive could have done what you did. You have earned this through your sacrifice and raw courage. As the winters pass, take it and hold it, and remember the strength and daring you demonstrated that terrible foggy night."

Morning Dew reached out with trembling hands, taking the long ritual sword, pulling the handle back to see the blood-encrusted stone. As if the sight steadied her, she straightened, head high, saying, "Thank you, Heron Wing. I shall always honor you."

"Can we make an end of this?" Blood Skull fumed.

Morning Dew ignored him, calling, "I would address the man known as Green Snake, of the Chief Clan, of the Hickory Moiety."

"Me?" Green Snake asked, obviously surprised.

Heron Wing studied Morning Dew's stiff posture: It was a mixture of excitement tempered with uneasy resolve.

Morning Dew stared straight ahead as she firmly said, "I am Morning Dew of the Chief Clan, matron of the White Arrow Moiety of the Chahta People. You are Green Snake of the Chief Clan, of the Hickory Moiety. We are both descended from the line of high minkos. As a means of ending hostilities between our peoples, I am here to propose marriage between us."

Marriage?

Heron Wing gaped, her heart hammering. "Morning Dew?"

In a low voice, Morning Dew said, "I am a matron. We need a symbol, a reason to make peace....And, it seems I must have a husband." She turned back to Green Snake. "Are you in agreement?"

Heron Wing turned to stare at Green Snake, reading the confusion on his face. He glanced at her, helpless, eyes frantic.

Heron Wing felt herself crumbling. *Gods, yes, it makes perfect sense.* "In Breath Giver's name, Green Snake, tell her yes."

"Yes," he replied weakly.

How could I have just said that? Her souls were wilting. Assuming he still married her, she, Heron Wing, would be a second wife. Worse, she would have to share this man. Somehow, in her Dreams, she had thought she could have him to herself—at least for a while.

Everything comes at a price, Heron Wing.

Morning Dew stepped forward, taking Green Snake's hand. She turned, looking back at her warriors. "My husband and I thank you for the hard run you have made through storm and rain, up steep hills, over fallen trees, and across swollen streams. Because you have worked so hard—have run with such diligence—it appears that you have managed to arrive just in time for my marriage! I congratulate you all!"

A cheer went up from the warriors. They clacked their bows against shields and war clubs. Great Cougar, looking somewhat disappointed, added his voice to the rest.

Her world reeling, Heron Wing watched as Morning Dew turned to the Sky Hand. "This is a most auspicious marriage! Can the Sky Hand provide a feast worthy of this occasion? We will need games! I propose a grand stickball match in the plaza. The best of your Sky Hand shall play my Chahta! I will wager our restitution for Alligator

Town against what you would offer White Arrow Town. Let Power decide!"

Heron Wing blinked. It was masterfully done. A complete defusing of tensions. She stared helplessly at Morning Dew. *Are you the same woman I once washed?*

Old White glanced at the shocked chiefs and stated, "Hickory Moiety, and the Chief Clan, can feed them if no one else will." He clapped his hands. "Besides, there is enough wood in that fallen palisade to make a spectacular bonfire!" Old White laid a familiar hand on Great Cougar's shoulder. "Now, about this tooth." He pulled the walrus tusk from his pack. "It's more than fair Trade for that spectacular cup of yours. This comes from the far north, from a beast."

Heron Wing didn't hear the rest as Morning Dew reached down and helped her to her feet. "Forgive me, my friend," she whispered into Heron Wing's ear. "It was the only way."

EPILOGUE

TEN WINTERS HAD PASSED since Horned Serpent swallowed Smoke Shield and took the copper. Green Snake sat under one of the Trading ramadas above the canoe landing and watched sunset burn yellow and red in the western clouds. The warm light shot burning beams across the sky to merge with bluish purple in the darkening east. Columns of insects rose and whirled on transparent wings. Behind Green Snake the familiar sounds of the city intruded. He could hear the thump, thump of the pestles where women pounded corn. Children laughed, and a dog barked.

Before him the river glowed a molten copper color, as if the great plate had floated to the surface and become the river itself. The smooth waters swirled, flowing silently on their endless journey to the gulf. He fixed his eyes on the center of the current, remembering the day the Contrary's canoe was upended.

He reached down, running a hand through old Swimmer's thick fur. The dog huffed a satisfied sigh, his attention fixed on the river. The hair around his muzzle and head had gone white, half the teeth had fallen from his jaws, and he hobbled on stiff joints.

But he seemed to see well enough despite his now-blind eyes—oh, yes, he did.

Trader smiled down. "I still think it's a miracle."

Swimmer's tail thumped in companionship as it had through all the long years.

"We've seen some things, you and I." He'd been devastated as Swimmer's eyesight began to fade.

The suggestion had come from Born-of-Sun: *"You have Horned Serpent's scales. Use them, as the Kala Hi'ki did when he was still alive."*

So Trader had fixed the crystals on a piece of cloth that he tied over Swimmer's eyes. Now they caught the sunset light as Swimmer turned his head, fixing on a fisherman's canoe out in the river.

Just after each spring equinox, he came here with Swimmer to relive the great journey down the rivers. Here, for an afternoon, he could be with Old White and Two Petals. Their voices would echo in his souls, and he shared their companionship again.

"Nothing is forever," he whispered, thoughts going to the wooden pack that rested on the altar in his house. It was only after Old White's last adventure that Green Snake had dared to open the curious wooden box. There, inside, he had found drawings made on thin sections of hide. Each had been perfectly rendered. Some he knew: dolphins, whales, cougars, and so forth. The Great Palace at Cahokia was familiar; a mountain shooting smoke and fire was not. Others were strange: the image of a bearded white man with blue eyes; a bloodred stone temple with bodies strewn down its steps; a masked Dancer with a round face; animals with flippers, a white snow house with a short man in furs by the door.

"Still here?" Heron Wing asked as she walked down and joined him under the ramada. "You stay longer every spring." She glanced at him. "Not thinking of following Two Petals and Old White, are you?"

He gestured toward the water. "I was watching the light. Look, the copper has come to the surface."

"Well, no one's ever found it down there, and Breath Giver knows, enough have dived for it." She seated herself beside him, taking his hand. "Old White knew what he was doing. So did the Contrary. Whippoorwill has told you often enough. Why don't you believe her?"

"Oh, I do. Remember, I *saw* it that day when I dove down. It wasn't just the light in the water, Heron Wing. His sides glowed like a rainbow, and Two Petals, she was riding on his back. She looked back, smiling, as Horned Serpent dove down."

"Then you know Old White found what he was looking for."

To change the subject, he said, "A Trader arrived. Stone won the

White Arrow Town stickball match for the Sky Hand. He scored an incredible six points. Morning Dew hosted a feast in his honor. I thought you'd want to know."

"Serves her right. She taught him." Heron Wing pulled her long hair back, streaked now with gray. If anything her face had grown more beautiful with age. She had developed a serenity of soul that no woman he had ever known possessed.

She laid her hand on his. "Then you know Morning Dew sent for you. There's some sort of squabble between the Chikosi and Chahta over the new farmsteads up on the divide. She would like your help settling it. And she may want another child now that she's weaned the last one."

"You'd think she was founding her own clan."

"A clan? You keep giving her sons. I think your first wife would like a daughter to continue her line."

"You'll always be my first wife, no matter when I married you."

"I know." She smiled into his eyes. "And you keep giving me daughters. But it might be wise to spend a couple of moons at White Arrow Town. She loves you, too."

"Anything else?" he asked.

"Councilor Lotus Root would like to see you when you get a chance. She wishes you to take a proposal to the tchkofa. And High Minko Sun Falcon would like to know when you're going to travel up to see Born-of-Sun again."

"I'd rather stay and play with your children. Stone may live and breathe stickball, but he needs a little work on his chunkey game."

"My son will be fine." She glanced at him. "Come, let's go home, and you can decide which of your obligations you wish to attend to."

With Swimmer hobbling along behind, they walked up from the canoe landing. He still hadn't grown used to the changes in Split Sky City. The palisade was long gone, and people had been moving away. Most now lived around the river towns, where the soils were better. Only a few of the old houses were left, but the entire valley still flocked here for the celebrations, and to bring their dead for burial in the clan mounds.

At the top of the slope he turned to look back at the river, and the old familiar ache deadened his heart.

Heron Wing read his longing. "The Seeker was dying. He knew it, Pale Cat knew it, and you knew it. What did you expect?"

"Do you think he found Horned Serpent and the Contrary down there?"

"You were there."

"Then why do I still miss him so?"

"Because he's not really dead." She searched his eyes. "You can feel that in your souls, can't you? Eight winters have passed since he left. By now he's walked halfway across the Underworld; who knows what sights he's seen?"

Old White's words echoed in Trader's souls. *"Don't be a silly fool! Of course I'm going. I'm the Seeker, and I'm not ready to be a corpse. Worse, I can't stand the way you fuss over me!"* He'd looked down at his shrunken body. *"Down there, my souls can see things no one else has."* He'd lifted his sack of copper, accumulated through intricately conceived Trading. *"It's not that wondrous plate that Smoke Shield took, but it ought to be enough,"* He'd grinned. *"Besides, Two Petals owes me. She said she'd come when I was ready."*

He and Old White had paddled a canoe out to the middle of the river—one last shared journey. Old White had dressed in his best: a white, beaded shirt, belted at the waist; his pouch of herbs, his pipe, and some tobacco at his side. He'd pulled what remained of his stringy white hair tightly behind his head and pinned it with a copper turkey-tail pin. A wealth of shell bead necklaces had hung around his spindly neck. The old fabric pack slung over his shoulder was once again weighted with the stone war ax.

The old man had been failing, frail, little more than a walking skeleton. Food either wouldn't stay down or passed straight through. He could barely hold the paddle.

"Do not do this thing!" Green Snake had pleaded.

"I am the Seeker," Old White had said with a knowing but tooth-less smile-.

Trader had watched, tears in his eyes, as Old White had laid his paddle to the side. Then he had risen, clutched the sack of copper, and emptied it into the river. Copper gleamed as it floated down into the sunlit depths. "Fair Trade for passage to the Underworld."

The old man had struggled to lift the large round stone he had chosen for the purpose. He had glanced back, meeting Trader's eyes—that one long look more expressive than any words. Then Old White had said, "Power keep you, Trader."

With that he had grinned happily...and stepped over the side.

In that instant, Trader would have sworn he heard a musical Song, the melody rising and falling as the waters closed over Old White's body. The canoe seemed to rise, water sloughing around a huge sinuous body. Was it a trick of the sun, or had the river suffused with rainbow colors?

And then the musical Song faded, and there was only silence, and Trader's empty canoe bobbing on the water.

AUTHORS' AFTERWORD

Readers who are interested in the actual archaeological sites mentioned in *People of the Weeping Eye* and *People of the Thunder* should know that Split Sky City is, of course, the Moundville Archaeological Park outside Moundville, Alabama. It can be reached by traveling fifteen miles south from Tuscaloosa on Highway 69. The Red Wing mounds lie just south of Minneapolis, Minnesota. Cahokia—the crown jewel of North American prehistory—rises just east of St. Louis, in Illinois. Signs on I-70/55 west of Collinsville will direct the traveler. We chose the Shiloh Mounds, located in the Shiloh National Battlefield, Tennessee, for the Yuchi's Rainbow City. White Arrow Town is based on the Lubbub archaeological site near Aliceville, Alabama. The site lies on private property, and is accessible only through John Blitz's excellent monograph, *Ancient Chiefdoms of the Tombigbee*. All of the towns referred to along the Black Warrior River are real, and are on private land. You must read the archaeological literature to learn more about them. Feathered Serpent Town represents the Kellogg and Yarborough sites northwest of Columbus, Mississippi. These sites, too, are on private property. The Forest Witch lived atop the great Mound A at the Poverty Point site in northeastern Louisiana. Readers of our *People of the Owl* should be more than passingly familiar with the place. The Mississippian compo-

nent we refer to just south of Poverty Point did exist, but was bull-
dozed by the landowner.

BIBLIOGRAPHY

Adair, James
2005 *The History of the American Indians*. Reprint of the 1775 edition published by Edward and Charles Dilly. The University of Alabama Press, Tuscaloosa, Alabama.

Anderson, David G.
1997 The Role of Cahokia in the Evolution of Southeastern Mississippian Society. In *Cahokia: Domination and Ideology in the Mississippian World*, edited by Timothy R. Pauketat and Thomas E. Emerson, pp. 248-268. Bison Books, University of Nebraska Press, Lincoln, Nebraska.
1994 *The Savannah River Chiefdoms*. The University of Alabama Press, Tuscaloosa, Alabama.

Atkinson, James R.
2004 *Splendid Land, Splendid People: The Chickasaw Indians to Removal*. The University of Alabama Press, Tuscaloosa, Alabama.

Beck, Robin A., Jr.
2003 Consolidation and Hierarchy: Chiefdom Variability in the Mississippian Southeast. *American Antiquity* 68:641-664.

Bense, Judith A.
1994 *Archaeology of the Southeastern United States: Paleolndian to World War I*. Academic Press, San Diego, California, New York, and London.

Blitz, John H.
1993 *Ancient Chiefdoms of the Tombigbee*. The University of Alabama Press, Tuscaloosa, Alabama.

Blitz, John H., and Patrick Livingood
2004 Sociopolitical Implications of Mississippian Mound Volume. *American Antiquity* 69:291-303.

Brain, Jeffrey P., and Philip Phillips
1996 *Shell Gorgets: Styles of the Late Prehistoric and Protohistoric Southeast*. Peabody Museum Press, Cambridge, Massachusetts.

Brown, Calvin S.
1992 *Archaeology of Mississippi*. Reprint of the 1926 edition. University Press of Mississippi, Jackson, Mississippi.

Brown, Ian W. (editor)
2003 *Bottle Creek: A Pensacola Culture Site in South Alabama*. The University of Alabama Press, Tuscaloosa, Alabama.

Brown, James A.
1996 *The Spiro Ceremonial Center*. Memoirs of the University of Michigan Museum of Anthropology No. 29, Ann Arbor, Michigan.

Carstens, Kenneth C, and Patty Jo Watson (editors) 1996 *Of Caves and Shell Mounds*. The University of Alabama Press, Tuscaloosa, Alabama.

Cobb, Charles R.

2000 *From Quarry to Cornfield: The Political Economy of Mississippian Hoe Production.* The University of Alabama Press, Tuscaloosa, Alabama.

Culin, Stewart

1975 *Games of the North American Indians.* Reprint of the *Twenty-fourth Annual Report of the Bureau of American Ethnology, 1902-1903.* Dover Publications, New York.

Davison, Gerald, John M. Neale, and Ann M. Kring

2004*Abnormal Psychology.* John Wiley & Sons, Hoboken, New Jersey.

DeJarnette, David L.

1975 *Archaeological Salvage in the Walter F. George Basin of the Chattahoochee River in Alabama.* The University of Alabama Press, Tuscaloosa, Alabama.

Diaz-Granados, Carol, and James R. Duncan

2004 *The Rock Art of Eastern North America: Capturing Images and Insight.* The University of Alabama Press, Tuscaloosa, Alabama.

Dickens, Roy S. Jr., and Trawick Ward (editors)

1985 *Structure and Process in Southeastern Archaeology.* The University of Alabama Press, Tuscaloosa, Alabama.

Dye, David H., and Cheryl Anne Cox

1990*Towns and Temples along the Mississippi.* The University of Alabama Press, Tuscaloosa, Alabama.

Emerson, Thomas E., Randall E. Hughes, Mary R. Hynes, and Sarah U. Wisseman 2003 The Sourcing and Interpretation of Cahokia-style Figurines in the Trans-Mississippi South and Southeast. *American Antiquity* 68:287-313.

Emerson, Thomas E., and R. Barry Lewis (editors)

1991 *Cahokia and the Hinterlands: Middle Mississippian Cultures of the Midwest.* University of Illinois Press, Urbana and Chicago.

Fairbanks, Charles H.

2003 *Archaeology of the Funeral Mound.* The University of Alabama Press, Tuscaloosa, Alabama.

Finger, Michael

2004 Shiloh: Emergency Archaeology. *American Archaeology* 8(2):30-38.

Fisher-Carroll, Rita

2001 *Mortuary Behavior at Upper Nodena.* Arkansas Archaeological Survey Research Series 59, Fayetteville, Arkansas.

Fundabrook, Emma L., and Mary Douglass Foreman 1957 *Sun Circles and Human Hands.* Southern Publications, Fairhope, Alabama.

Gibbons, Whit, Robert R. Haynes, and Joab L. Thomas 1990 *Poisonous Plants and Venomous Animals of Alabama.* The University of Alabama Press, Tuscaloosa, Alabama.

Gibson, Arrell M. .1971 *The Chickasaws.* University of Oklahoma Press, Norman, Oklahoma.

Gibson, Jon L., and Philip J. Carr

2004 *Signs of Power: The Rise of Cultural Complexity in the Southeast.* The University of Alabama Press, Tuscaloosa, Alabama.

Granberry, Julian

2005 *The Americas That Might Have Been: Native American Social Systems through Time.* The University of Alabama Press, Tuscaloosa, Alabama.1993 *A Grammar and Dictionary of the Timuca Language*, 3rd ed. The University of Alabama Press, Tuscaloosa, Alabama.

Grantham, Bill

2002 *Creation Myths and Legends of the Creek Indians*. University Press of Florida, Tallahassee, Florida.

Green, Michael Foster

2001 *Schizophrenia Revealed*. W. W. Norton, New
York. Hawkins, Benjamin

2003 *The Collected Works of Benjamin Hawkins, 1796-1810*. Edited by H. Thomas Foster II.
The University of Alabama Press, Tuscaloosa, Alabama.

Howard, James H.

1968 *The Southeastern Ceremonial Complex and*
Its Interpretation. Memoir Missouri Archaeological
Society No. 6. Springfield, Missouri. Hudson, Charles M.

2003 *Conversations with the High Priest of Coosa*.
The University of North Carolina Press, Chapel Hill,
North Carolina, and London.

1979 *Black Drink: A Native American Tea*. The University of Georgia Press, Athens, Georgia.
1976 *The Southeastern Indians*. The University of Tennessee Press, Knoxville, Tennessee.

Jackson, H. Edwin, and Susan L. Scott

2004 Patterns of Elite Faunal Utilization at Moundville, Alabama. *American Antiquity*
68:552-572.

Jackson, Jason Baird

2003 *Yuchi Ceremonial Life*. University of Nebraska Press, Lincoln, Nebraska.

Jenkins, Ned J., and Richard A. Krause

1986 *The Tombigbee Watershed in Southeastern Prehistory*. The University of Alabama
Press, Tuscaloosa, Alabama.

Jones, Charles C.

1998 *Antiquities of the Southern Indians, Particularly the Georgia Tribes*. Reprint of the 1873
edition. The University of Alabama Press, Tuscaloosa, Alabama.

Keesing, Roger M.

1975 *Kin Groups and Social Structure*. Holt, Rinehart and Winston, New York.

Kidder, Tristram R.

2004 Plazas as Architecture: An Example from the Raffman Site, Northeastern
Louisiana. *American Antiquity* 69:514-532.

King, Adam

2003 *Etowah: The Political History of a Chiefdom Capital*. The University of Alabama Press,
Tuscaloosa, Alabama.

Knight, Vernon James Jr.

2005 Characterizing Elite Midden Deposits at Moundville. *American Antiquity*
69:304-321.

1997 Some Developmental Parallels between Cahokia and Moundville. In *Cahokia:*
Domination and Ideology in the Mississippian World, edited by Timothy R. Pauketat and
Thomas E. Emerson, pp. 229-247. Bison
Books, University of Nebraska Press, Lincoln, Nebraska.

1990 Social Organization and the Evolution of Hierarchy in Southeastern Chiefdoms.
Journal of Anthropological Research 46(1):1—23.

1986The Institutional Organization of Mississippian Religion. *American Antiquity* 51:675-687.

Knight, Vernon J., and Vincas Steponaitis

1998 *Archaeology and the Moundville Chiefdom.* Smithsonian Institution Press, Washington, D.C., and London.

Lacefield, Jim

2000 *Lost Worlds in Alabama Rocks: A Guide to the State's Ancient Life and Landscapes.* The Alabama Geological Society, Birmingham, Alabama.

Lambert, Patricia M.

1999 *Bioarchaeological Studies of Life in the Age of Agriculture.* The University of Alabama Press, Tuscaloosa, Alabama.

Lankford, George E.

2004 World on a String: Some Cosmological Components of the Southeast Ceremonial Complex. In *Hero, Hawk, and Open Hand: American Indian Art in the Midwest and South,* edited by Richard F. Townsend and Robert V. Sharpe, The Art Institute of Chicago and Yale University Press, New Haven and London.

1987 *Native American Legends. Southeastern Legends: Tales from the Natchez, Caddo Biloxi, Chickasaw, and Other Nations.* August House, Little Rock, Arkansas.

Larson, Lewis H.

1980 *Aboriginal Subsistence Technology on the Southeastern Coastal Plain During the Late Prehistoric Period.* University Press of Florida, Gainesville, Florida.

Lehman, Melissa, and Gerald Smith

1997 *Chucalissa: Excavations in Units 2 and 6, 1959-1967.* Occasional Papers No. 15. Memphis State University Anthropological Research Center.

Lewis, R. Barry, and Charles Stout (editors)

1998 *Mississippian Towns and Sacred Spaces.* The University of Alabama Press, Tuscaloosa, Alabama.

Lewis, Thomas M. N., and Madeline D. Kneburg Lewis 1995 *The Prehistory of the Chickamauga Basin, Tennessee.* Vols. I and II. Edited by Lynne P. Sullivan. The University of Tennessee Press, Knoxville, Tennessee.

Martin, Joel W.

1991 *Sacred Revolt.* Beacon Press, Boston.

Martin, Susan R.

2000 *Wonderful Power: The Story of Ancient Copper Working in the Lake Superior Basin.* Wayne State University Press, Detroit.

Mason, Carol I.

2005 *The Archaeology of Ocmulgee Old Fields, Macon, Georgia.* The University of Alabama Press, Tuscaloosa, Alabama.

McEwan, Bonnie G.

2001 *Indians of the Greater Southeast.* University Press of Florida, Gainesville, Florida.

Meyer, William Edward

1928 *Indian Trails of the Southeast.* United States Bureau of American Ethnography Report No. 42. Smithsonian Institution, Washington, D.C.

Millspaugh, Charles F.

1974 *American Medicinal Plants.* Reprint of the 1892 edition. Dover Publications, New York.

Mirarchi, Robert E.

2004 *Alabama Wildlife.* Vol. I. The University of Alabama Press, Tuscaloosa, Alabama.

Mistovich, Tim S.

1994 Toward an Explanation of Variation in Moundville Phase Households in the Black Warrior Valley,

Alabama. In *Mississippian Communities and Households*, edited by J. Daniel Rogers and Bruce D. Smith, pp. 156-180. Smithsonian Institution Press, Washington, D.C. Moore, Clarence Bloomfield

1996 *The Moundville Expeditions of Clarence Bloomfield Moore*, edited by Vernon James Knight Jr. Reprint of 1905 *Journal of the Academy of Natural Sciences in Philadelphia*. The University of Alabama Press, Tuscaloosa, Alabama.

Moore, David G.

2002 *Catawba Valley Mississippian: Ceramics, Chronology, and Catawba Indians*. The University of Alabama Press, Tuscaloosa, Alabama.

Moorehead, Warren K.

2002 *The Cahokia Mounds*, edited by John E. Kelly. The University of Alabama Press, Tuscaloosa, Alabama.

Morgan, William N.

1999 *Precolumbian Architecture in Eastern North America*. University Press of Florida, Gainesville, Florida.

Morse, Dan F., and Phyllis A. Morse (editors)

1998 *The Lower Mississippi Valley Expeditions of Clarence Bloomfield Moore*. The University of Alabama Press, Tuscaloosa, Alabama. 1983 *Archaeology of the Central Mississippi Valley*. Academic Press, New York.

Mould, Tom

2003 *Choctaw Prophecy: A Legacy of the Future*. The University of Alabama Press, Tuscaloosa, Alabama.

Mount, Robert H.

1975 *The Reptiles and Amphibians of Alabama*. The University of Alabama Press, Tuscaloosa, Alabama.

Muller, Jon

1997 *Mississippian Political Economy*. Plenum Press, New York and London.

Nairne, Thomas

1988 *Nairne's Muskogean Journals: The 1708 Expedition to the Mississippi River*, edited by Alexander Moore. University of Mississippi Press, Jackson, Mississippi.

O'Brien, Michael J.

2003 *Mississippian Community Organization: The Powers Phase in Southeastern Missouri*. Kluwer Academic/Plenum Publishers, New York, Boston, and London.

O'Brien, Michael J., and Robert C. Dunnell (editors)

1998 *Changing Perspectives on the Archaeology of the Central Mississippi Valley*. The University of Alabama Press, Tuscaloosa, Alabama.

Pauketat, Timothy R.

2007 *Chiefdoms and Other Archaeological Delusions*. AltaMira Press, Lanham, Maryland.

2004 Resettled Farmers and the Making of a Mississippian Polity. *American Antiquity* 68:39-66.

1994 *The Ascent of Chiefs: Cahokia and Mississippian Politics in Native North America*. The University of Alabama Press, Tuscaloosa, Alabama. 1993 *Temples for Cahokia Lords: Preston Holder's 1955-1956 Excavations of Kunnemann Mound*. Memoirs of the University of Michigan Museum of Anthropology No. 26, Ann Arbor, Michigan. Pauketat, Timothy R., and Thomas E. Emerson (editors)

1999 *Cahokia: Domination and Ideology in the Mississippian World.* Bison Books, University of
Nebraska Press, Lincoln, Nebraska.

Pauketat, Timothy R., Lucretia S. Kelly, Gayle J. Fritz, Neal H. Lopinot, Scott Elias, and Eve Hargrave

2005 The Residues of Feasting and Public Ritual at Early Cahokia. *American Antiquity* 67:257-280.

Pearson, James L.

2002 *Shamanism and the Ancient Mind: A Cognitive Approach to Archaeology.* AltaMira Press, Walnut Creek, Lanham, Maryland, New York, and Oxford.

Petersen, James B.

1996 *A Most Indispensable Art: Native Fiber Industries from Eastern North America.* The University of Tennessee Press, Knoxville, Tennessee.

Phillips, Philip, and James A. Brown

1984 *Pre-Columbian Shell Engravings from the Craig Mound at Spiro, Oklahoma.* Part Two. Pea-body Museum of Archaeology and Ethnology. Pea-body Museum Press, Cambridge, Massachusetts. 1977 *Pre-Columbian Shell Engravings from the Craig Mound at Spiro, Oklahoma.* Part One. Peabody Museum of Archaeology and Ethnology. Peabody Museum Press, Cambridge, Massachusetts.

Powell, Mary Lucas

1989 *Status and Health in Prehistory.* The University of Alabama Press, Tuscaloosa, Alabama.

Powell, Mary Lucas, Patricia S. Bridges, and Ann Marie Wagner Mires (editors)

1991 *What Mean These Bones?* The University of Alabama Press, Tuscaloosa, Alabama.

Power, Susan C.

2004 *Early Art of the Southeastern Indians: Feathered Serpents and Winged Beings.* The University of Georgia Press, Athens, Georgia.

Redmond, Elsa M.

1998 *Chiefdoms and Chieftaincy in the Americas.* University Press of Florida, Gainesville, Florida.

Rolingson, Martha Ann

2000 *Toltec Mounds and Plum Bayou Culture: Mound D Excavations.* Arkansas Archaeological Survey Research Series 54, Fayetteville, Arkansas.

Scarry, John F. (editor)

1995 *Political Structure and Change in the Prehistoric Southeastern United States.* University Press of Florida, Gainesville, Florida.

Scarry, Margaret, and Vincas P. Steponaitis

1996 Between Farmstead and Center: The Natural and Social Landscape of Moundville. In *People, Plants, and Landscapes: Studies in Paleobotany,* edited by Kristen J. Gremillion, pp. 107-122. The University of Alabama Press, Tuscaloosa, Alabama.

Schusky, Ernest L.

1983 *Manual for Kinship Analysis,* 2nd ed. University Press of America, New York.

Sheldon, Craig T. (editor)

2006 *The Southern and Central Alabama Expeditions of Clarence Bloomfield Moore.* The University of Alabama Press, Tuscaloosa, Alabama.

Shetrone, Henry Clyde 2004 *The Mound Builders.* Reprint of the 1930 edition published by D. Appleton & Co. The University of Alabama Press, Tuscaloosa, Alabama.

Smith, Marvin T.

1990 *Archaeology of Aboriginal Change in the Interior Southeast.* Florida Museum of Natural History. University Press of Florida, Gainesville, Florida.

Speck, Frank G.

1909 *Ethnology of the Yuchi Indians.* Anthropological Publications of the University Museum. Vol.1, No. 1. The University of Pennsylvania, Philadelphia.

Squire, E. G., and E. H. Davis

1973 *Ancient Monuments of the Mississippi Valley Comprising the Results of Extensive Original Surveys and Explorations.* Reprint of the 1848 Vol.1 of the Smithsonian Institution. AMS Press, New York.

Steponaitis, Vincas

1991 Contrasting Patterns of Mississippian Development. In *Chiefdoms, Power, Economy and Ideology,* edited by Timothy Earle. Cambridge University Press, Cambridge and New York.

1991 Excavations at 1Tu50, an Early Mississippian

Center near Moundville. *Southeastern Archaeology* 11:1-13.

1983 *Ceramics, Chronology, and Community Patterns: An Archaeological Study at Moundville.* Academic Press, New York. Stone, Linda

2000*Kinship and Gender: An Introduction.* Westview Press, Boulder, Colorado.

Swanton, John R.

2001*Source Material for the Social and Ceremonial Life of the Choctaw Indians.* Reprint of the 1931 Bureau of American Ethnography Bulletin No.103. The University of Alabama Press, Tuscaloosa, Alabama.

2000 *Creek Religion and Medicine.* Reprint of the

1928Bureau of American Ethnography Report No. 42. Bison Books, University of Nebraska Press, Lincoln, Nebraska.

1998a *Indian Tribes of the Lower Mississippi Valley and Adjacent Coast of the Gulf of Mexico.* Reprint of the 1911 Bureau of Ethnography Bulletin 43. Dover Publications, Mineola, New York. 1998b *Early History of the Creek Indians and Their Neighbors.* Reprint of the 1922 Bureau of American Ethnography Bulletin 73. University Press of Florida, Gainesville, Florida.

1929 *Myths and Tales of the Southeastern Indians.* Bureau of American Ethnology Bulletin 88. Smithsonian Institution, Washington, D.C.

1928 Social Organization and Social Usages of the Indians of the Creek Confederacy. United States Bureau of American Ethnography No. 42. Smithsonian Institution, Washington, D.C. 1928b Religious Beliefs and Medicinal Practices of the Creek Indians. United States Bureau of American Ethnography Report No. 42. Smithsonian Institution, Washington, D.C.

1928c Aboriginal Culture of the Southeast. United States Bureau of American Ethnography Report No. 42. Smithsonian Institution, Washington, D.C. Sylestine, Cora, Heather K. Hardy, and Timothy Montler

1993 *The Dictionary of the Alabama Language.* The University of Texas Press, Austin, Texas.

Thomas, Cyrus

1985 *Report on the Mound Explorations of the Bureau of Ethnology.* Reprint of the 1894 12th Annual Report of the Bureau of American Ethnography. USGPO. Smithsonian Institution Press, Washington, D.C.

Townsend, Richard R, and Robert V. Sharpe (editors) 2004 *Hero, Hawk, and Open Hand:*

American Indian Art of the Ancient Midwest and South. The Art Institute of Chicago and Yale University Press, New Haven and London.

Urban, Greg

1994 Social Organization in the Southeast. In *North American Indian Anthropology,* edited by Raymond J. Demallie and Alfonso Ortiz. University of Oklahoma Press, Norman, Oklahoma.

Walthall, John A.

1994 *Moundville: An Introduction to the Archaeology of a Mississippian Chiefdom.* Special Publication No. 1. Alabama Museum of Natural History. The University of Alabama, Tuscaloosa, Alabama. 1980 *Prehistoric Indians of the Southeast: Archaeology of Alabama and the Middle South.* The University of Alabama Press, Tuscaloosa, Alabama.

Welch, Paul D.

2006 *Archaeology at the Shiloh Indian Mounds.* The University of Alabama Press, Tuscaloosa, Alabama.

2001 Political Economy in Late Prehistoric Southern Appalachia. In *Archaeology of the Appalachian Highlands,* edited by Lynne P. Sullivan and Susan

C: Prezzano. The University of Tennessee Press, Knoxville, Tennessee.

1997 Control over Goods and the Political Stability of the Moundville Chiefdom. In *Political Structure and Change in the Prehistoric Southeastern United States,* edited by John F. Scarry, pp. 69-91. University Press of Florida, Gainesville, Florida. 1991 *Moundville's Economy.* The University of Alabama Press, Tuscaloosa, Alabama.

Williams, Mark, and Gary Shapiro (editors)

1991 *Lamar Archaeology: Chiefdoms in the Deep South.* The University of Alabama Press, Tuscaloosa, Alabama.

Winter, Joseph C.

2000 *Tobacco Use by Native Americans: Sacred Smoke and Silent Killer.* University of Oklahoma Press, Norman, Oklahoma.

Yerkes, Richard W.

1986 *Prehistoric Life on the Mississippi Floodplain.* The University of Chicago Press, Chicago.

A LOOK AT: BLACK FALCON NATION SERIES

BOOK ONE: IT SLEEPS IN ME

From *New York Times* Best Selling author Kathleen O'Neal Gear comes the first book in a captivating, otherworldly tale of prehistoric romance and intrigue.

Sora is the wise but young High Chieftess of the Black Falcon Nation. For many winters her heart belonged to her husband, Flint, a great warrior. They shared a true bond, and together they explored the world of passion and love. But Flint was murderously jealous, on more than one occasion beating men to death for merely casting a longing glance at Sora. Unable to live with his rage, Flint divorced Sora, leaving her—and the clan—forever.

Remarried, Sora tries to bury her memories of Flint. But she is forcibly reminded of her lost love when, on the eve of war with a neighboring nation, she is visited by Skinner, an old friend of Flint's, who brings word of Flint's death. Sora notices something strange about Skinner; it is as if he carries a part of Flint's soul inside him. When he starts revealing secrets only Flint would know, Sora must discern whether it is the clever witchcraft of enemies who want to seize her power and destroy her nation, or the spirit of her one and only true love.

———

BOOK TWO: IT WAKES IN ME

From New York Times Best Selling author Kathleen O'Neal Gear comes the second book in a captivating, otherworldly tale of prehistoric romance and intrigue.

According to the tradition of the Black Falcon People, each person has three souls: the eye soul, which stays with the body forever, the shadow-soul, where all evil is leached and shed at death, and the reflection-soul, which lives on among the Blessed in the Land of the Dead, pure and clean. But on rare occasions, a shadow-soul can sneak into a living person's body to commit hideous crimes.

Sora, the High Chieftess of the Black Falcon Nation, has been plagued with blackouts and fits since her seventh winter. As her world went dark, two gleaming eyes burned to life inside her. She named these occurrences the Midnight Fox, and remembered nothing after them. Now accusations are being made against her by rival clans. She has been accused of seven murders, including the murder of her friend and Loon People War Chief, Skinner. With villages rallying against her, and plagued with this terrible spirit illness, she looks for healing of her soul and mind, the strength to lead her people, and the courage to save her own life.

AVAILABLE NOW

ABOUT THE AUTHORS

W. Michael Gear and Kathleen O'Neal Gear are New York Times bestselling authors and nationally award-winning archaeologists. They have published 75 novels and over 200 non-fiction articles in the fields of archaeology, history, and bison conservation. In 2021, they received the Owen Wister Award for lifetime contributions to western literature and were inducted into the Western Writers Hall of Fame. They live in beautiful Cody, Wyoming.